HAPPY TO HAVE NOTHING

STUART HOBROW

Published by Pigeon Tree Publishing in 2020

ISBN: 978-1-8383159-0-0

For Nadia, Yasmin, Amelia and my mom

If only doing the right thing meant that all the mess caused by the wrongdoing was forgotten…

1

The snow settling on the Hampshire countryside had the pupils at King Alfred's Comprehensive School excitedly peering out of classroom windows rather than making progress in their learning. Children were not used to seeing snowfall on this scale in these parts, so its impact was immediately captivating, particularly amongst the younger ones at the school. Consequently, behaviour management became a challenge for even the most respected academic staff. It was a blessing for all concerned when the bell rang for morning break time, so that the students could expend their energies in snowball revelry. While some teachers were able to gain respite in the staff room with a caffeine fix, some less fortunate ones on playground duty inevitably dodged the white missiles thrown by teenagers who had temporarily lost their respect for authority. By the afternoon, the smell throughout the school was mustier than usual. The drying out of wet garments on sweaty kids, combined with the heat being thrown out by piping hot radiators, resulted in a less than aromatic odour and steamy windows.

Ali had decided not to venture outside into the cold and wet conditions earlier on, preferring instead to admire the white blanket that snuggled the surrounding hills in the distance from the warmth of the sixth form common room. She turned her nose up at the clammy smell in the corridor as she set off to her sociology class. There was the usual chaos of students scattering in different directions on the way to their lessons. Noisy chatter echoed off the walls, causing a pulsating din that was further intensified by the fact that this changeover was the last one before the Christmas holidays commenced. Festive excitement reigned.

She dodged some of her peers who were loitering, and

carefully cradled her folders and the package on top of them as she swayed to avoid any collisions. She navigated her way to an intersection where she was at less risk of being barged into and rested against a barrier near a staircase. This was a fabulously strategic location, Ali thought. She would be able to spot Mel scrambling her way through the masses and onto the staircase leading to her business class on the upper floor. Ali placed her files carefully on the floor behind her feet and held the present close to her chest.

Under normal circumstances, it would be such a pleasure to give a gift to a special mate. For Ali, though, this time it was out of necessity rather than generosity. Since returning to school after half term she felt like she had been drifting her way through countless lessons on her school timetable. Having to set foot into the same classrooms as Robert had been awkward enough. Having to watch him sit next to the git that hijacked her long-term pursuit for his affections grew increasingly painful. Having to confront the reality that one of her closest friends *was* the git felt just like a punishment.

She desperately wanted to reach the winter break so that she could literally hide away from public life. She needed time to deal with the emotional imbalance this had caused her. For now, though, Ali felt that giving a Christmas present was the right thing to do. Mel had already endured a year of spiteful experiences herself, and the gift might help to rescue what remained of their friendship. She hoped it would also be the beginning of her own healing and recovery. Ali drew her inspiration from Mel's mum, who said that her wisdom was not down to her age. Poppy proposed that it was firstly passed on through family genes, and then came from her own experiences and from watching people.

'Doing the right thing is sometimes the hardest thing to do,' she had once said, 'but watch a problem unravel if you are able to do it. It separates the brave from the weak, the wise from the

2

weary.'

Ali had every reason to believe that her late friend understood what it was like to be in a dilemma, and to trust her advice. And so, she stood, waiting for her antagonist to appear on the crowded staircase, and for that to be the closure to the autumn term, 1996.

At last, the figure she was waiting so tensely for darted into view.

'Mel!' screeched Ali over the humming of corridor chatter.

Mel looked across and saw Ali with her hand in the air. It was the way she looked when she was about to answer a question in class – up straight with five fingers pointing at the ceiling for a fleeting moment, and then gradually rescinding in slow motion and bending at the elbow almost apologetically. Mel was briefly rooted to the spot watching Ali gesture for her to go across, and thus she became an obstacle difficult to avoid for the wave of other students. Her arm was knocked, and the file she was carrying fell to the floor with a thud. A terms worth of notes scattered onto the floor of the hectic corridor rather like the snow showers that had covered the ground outside. It was fortunate that she was only carrying one file at the time, as her academic work was being trampled on by hordes of children's feet. Ali raced across to the staircase. They both bent down and hurriedly picked up the pages strewn across the floor, many of which were now tattooed with the dirty footprints from teenagers that had earlier been partying in the snow outside. This did little to alleviate the awkwardness that had existed between the two girls since October.

They nervously glimpsed each other out of the corner of their eyes, but both girls initially refrained from making full contact. It was Ali who broke the silence, but not before she had taken a deep breath in an attempt to control herself. It didn't work very well, as she proceeded to gabble.

'It was stupid of me to yell to you across the corridor like that Mel. Do you think you'll be able to get these dried? I'll help you if you like. Let's lay them out on the radiators in the common room. When I dropped some of my psychology notes once, I…'

Ali stopped abruptly in mid-sentence. Mel hadn't looked up from her pile of stained sheets, and an edgy atmosphere had engulfed the area where the girls were frantically grabbing papers.

'Look Mel,' Ali continued, with a calmness that she was previously devoid of. She paused for a moment and exhaled. 'Whatever happened at half term is going to be 'last year' in a couple of weeks. It'd be great if we could have a go at sorting things out before the New Year. I'm dealing with the fact that *you're with* Robert. Do you think you could deal with the fact that I'm *not* with him?'

2

Azalea Robertson lifted her head from the position she held while listening intently to her daughter. She looked into Poppy's eyes, and that motherly gaze was as reassuring as a warm embrace.

'I like this boy, mamma. But I worry I will offend you if I see a white boy. It would shatter my heart to think of you and papa listening to people sneering about me.'

Poppy only ever wanted to please her family but knew one day she would be judged on her preferences for a partner. Though tolerance of the African-Caribbean communities by 1973 had long been established in large cities, the recent bouts of unemployment in the West Midlands did bring about pockets of tension for black people who had retained their jobs where white people had not. Derek was from Glasgow, and while a mixed-race relationship was not unique, neither was it commonplace in the Birmingham suburbs. There had never been a time when Poppy needed her mother's sagacity more.

'Child, no person can say what the colour of true love must look like. Love can only be judged on what it feels like in your own heart.'

Her words of wisdom were spoken softly, and in her unmistakable broad Antiguan tones. Azalea's straight talking was exactly what Poppy had been seeking, after all she trusted and respected her mamma more than anyone in the world. It had been her strength and courage that was so evident after their arrival from Antigua in 1968. Then fifteen years old, Poppy remembered how her dad's application for employment at London Transport had been rebuffed. And then there was the setback of finding severe housing shortages in many African-Caribbean communities including Brixton. But Azalea refused to let their plans collapse in the face of this adversity.

'We not come all this way across the big ocean to fail our hopes and promises to each other,' she proclaimed at Joel's increasingly desperate efforts to look after his wife and children. Resolutely, she declared, 'We not gonna sow our seeds in a furrow that renders no harvest, so we go scatter them in a different field to grow our crop.'

Finding alternative places to grow their aspirational seeds is exactly what they did. The brave decision to move to Birmingham paid off. Joel gained employment in the paint shop at the British Leyland plant in Longbridge. He managed to secure a position for his son too, though Malcolm would be on the production line. Derek Burchell worked alongside Malcolm at the car factory and lived two doors down in the same terraced housing block as the Robertson's. He had moved down to the Midlands from Scotland with his family, where his father sought work as a miner. Derek and Malcolm had become social buddies, and he was immediately attracted to Poppy on his calls to their house. Joel liked Derek – he held respect for the fact that he was known throughout the shop floor areas at British Leyland for his work ethic. There had been talk of promoting him to a position of shop steward. He'd once joked with Joel in his distinctive Glaswegian ascent,

'We've got loads in common, you and me. I'm an immigrant too you know.'

He was enthralled with Poppy's stories about growing up in Antigua. While the family's life story was hardly glamourous, the descriptions of hot sunny days, white sandy beaches and crystal-clear seas were of a vibrant land that could only exist in his imagination. Though Derek was fond of his own roots, it just seemed so incongruous to the high rise, concrete jungle in which he had been raised. His obvious and genuine affection also fanned the flames of fondness that Poppy was developing for this lad in return.

Back in the cramped kitchen of their terraced house Azalea offered some prudence in her conversation with Poppy.

'Just one thing honey– how you know this boy gonna love and care for you?'

The question seemed simple enough, and surely warranted an obvious, straightforward answer. Azalea knew she was setting her daughter a conundrum, and for Poppy it turned into an unexpected body shot. In her eagerness to please her mamma, Poppy's mind went blank. She stumbled with her words, so that what she was thinking was nothing like what came out of her mouth.

'I don't know mamma. I just…want him in my life. How does anyone ever know? How did you know with papa?'

When Azalea was a younger woman, she had been in this quandary herself. Her reply completely dumbfounded Poppy.

'It is a riddle that could have many answers, precious one. Me? I would ask him to paint you a picture.'

Poppy heard the answer, but it made absolutely no sense. It seemed to have no correlation to the question she had asked. While she remained stunned, her mother continued to explain. When her husband Joel initiated his interest in this young maiden in the back streets of St Pauls in Antigua, she rebuffed all his attempts of romance.

'The more the boy come back, the harsher he be feeling the sharpness of my tongue. Why he think I ever like him more than the next boy?' She wasn't going to be duped into a relationship by any old scrap that came along. It was Azalea's challenge to truly discover the depth of Joel's feelings towards her.

'So, one day he give me this gift, a picture no less.'

She nodded in the direction of a small, framed canvas, no more than ten inches square, which hung in the hallway. She revealed that Joel used to love sketching and would have gone to Art College if the need to earn money for his family were not so imperative. He painted Poppy a moonlit scene of her favourite part of the island. The moon shone on the waters over Darkwood Beach, with the outline of Boggy Peak as a gorgeous backdrop.

'"Why you not paint me a sunset?", I asked him. He say, "Before I go to sleep, I look up at the stars and moon. The moon smile at me, and the stars wink. They know the next thing I see after them is you in my dreams."' It captured Azalea's heart. 'He paint me a memory, not just a picture.'

A bewildered Derek took on the same challenge laid down by Poppy. He sourced paint from within the workshop where Joel worked, and cut out a square from a used hessian sack as a make-shift canvas. He stretched this out over a wooden frame that he put together from remnants he found at work too. In truth, art was never a talent he felt blessed with. His idea merely came from a conversation he and Poppy had about when the family first arrived in England. She had explained how they left the heat of the December sunshine in Antigua for the cold, wet, gloomy winter skies of London. As exciting as emigrating seemed, overcoming the miserable British weather had been a challenge for Poppy ever since. She simply missed the vividness of the colours in Caribbean. Even when the sun shone at its brightest in her new homeland, Poppy always felt that the outlook was slightly smudged and smeared.

What Derek produced was an abstract swathe of different colours which he had imagined from Poppy's portrayal of her homeland. Turquoises for the crystal-clear ocean, blues for the sky, greens for the surrounding hillside, yellows and oranges for the sun. Poppy's eyes lit up when she first saw it, and then her vision quickly became distorted as tears began to form.

'I didn't know where to start painting you a picture Pops; I just tried to think about what you must have seen when you looked out on Antigua,' he told her.

As amateur as his exploits seemed on the surface, Derek had

struck Poppy's inner emotions deeper than he could have imagined with his sweeping colour scheme. He really had listened to her. He had understood her. He did love her.

'You not paint me a picture Derek, you paint me a memory,' she told him, and their own journey together began. Within a year the pair got married. Baby Lewis arrived in 1977, followed by Melanie two years later.

3

Mel stared out at a robin singing his heart out at the top of a willow tree in their back garden. He was confidently puffing his red breast out and perusing his territory, before the brick cutter started and birds that had been partially hidden in the branches of leafless trees scattered in all directions. Not the robin. He wasn't fazed by the noise and would happily compete with the aggressive noise of the blade until he decided it was time to venture elsewhere in his realm. The only thing that made it easier for Mel to cope with school and homework on dank, dark winter days was the thought of her birthday in February. It was an opportunity to have fun and quality time with her family, a genuine excuse to put her pen down from studying – even if only for a short time.

It soon came around. Silently Poppy craved for it to be the following year so that she would feel blessed to be able to see her daughter reach adulthood, and yet paradoxically she was constantly fighting time and the changing skies of the different seasons. Her weakening well-being made any celebration more acutely precious. How she craved to be able to turn back the clock – or at least tug on the hands to slow it down. Cruelly for her, it was the time of the year where it seemed that someone had started spinning the earth more quickly, as lighter evenings and longer days embraced the arrival of spring. At least the extension at the back of the house had all but been completed by then.

The numbers on the calendar in Mel's form room at school seemed to merge into each other, and despite the consistency of the earth's orbit the days began to race by as if competing to get themselves into the lull of the past as quickly as possible. In quick succession arrived the final hours of the summer term, the last day as lower sixth scholars. For some it offered a chance to recharge batteries, and for others to throw themselves into part time jobs to start generating funds for the expenses of university life. Mel had succumbed to the lack of exciting prospects for her break.

'Ali, please come round to my house for a bit. All I've got to look forward to is looking after my mum and pushing her around in a wheelchair. At least I'll keep fit.'

Poppy was becoming more tired more often. The wheelchair that she loathed and so often banished from sight became an accessory she couldn't do without. The logistics for getting her round became more complicated, but no one minded the palaver. They were delighted that she didn't let it get in the way of trying to lead a proactive life. It was just that it was symbolic of a cruel situation, a reminder of a diminishing existence, and an acknowledgement of a disease that couldn't be overcome.

'Fair enough. My parents are away in London watching a show tonight anyway. Are you sure your mum won't mind?'

Mel shook her head. 'What about you Rob - do fancy a sarnie at mine?'

'Nah, you're alright. Thanks anyway, I just wanna get back to mine and slob out.'

'Lazy git. Me and Ali will have to tackle the dragon by ourselves then!'

Mel would often give the impression of being at loggerheads with her mum. But the reality was very different, no better demonstrated by the fact that Poppy was always the one she wanted to run to if there was any good news. Mel knew her mum would be over-the-top proud with her latest report and would make a fuss when she got home.

The trio reached the driveway to Mel's house where, out of sight, she felt Ali and Rob hanging back. Mel didn't get flustered and realised they wanted a quiet chat without her. She didn't look over her shoulder at either of them but gestured a friendly wave that they would see as she carried on walking to her front door.

'Take your time Ali, I'll get the kettle on. Laters Rob.'

Ali and Rob stopped looking so coy and sniggered as their friend turned the key and disappeared. Mel couldn't close the door quickly enough, and although resigned to the idea that her friends were flirting because they fancied each other, it still felt a bit too weird for her to handle comfortably.

She stood with her back to the door, the palms of her hands attempting to lie flat on the cold metal flap of the letter box. She felt the morning post lodged there and turned around to yank the letters out from the tightly sprung flap. Mel jerked to a halt as she looked down the corridor. Poppy would normally have scrutinised the post by now and flooded the house with aromatic smells of Caribbean cuisine. Mel couldn't recall her mum saying that she was going out, and then felt guilty for not paying attention to the plans that her mum would have explained to her that morning, probably while Mel was trying to watch TV or listen to her music. As she listened to the silence, she felt inclined to call out anyway.

'Mum?'

There was no answer, and the quiet that remained confirmed her mum's absence. As she kicked off her shoes Mel was thinking about how Poppy would no doubt be reminding her of the very minute when she had relayed the agenda for the day, and she started worrying about whether she was meant to have gone somewhere to meet her. She shuffled round to the kitchen to put the letters on the worktop for her parents and turned to grab the kettle. The shrieking and wailing that began instantly were those of a girl deranged. The abomination that tortured her eyesight lay still on the floor, bent double. Mel had flashbacks from the time her mum had collapsed at the cathedral green, because once again she wasn't moving.

Mel howled 'MUM!' and sank to her knees bedsides the woman that was her universe. Mel could see the tablets still gripped in her hand. She laid her hand on her head; it was cold and there was no response. She scrambled up onto her feet, staggering as she ran back to the front door. She twisted the catch and screeched for Ali. The desperation in Mel's voice was horrifying to bear witness to, but Ali raced after her friend and into the hallway.

'Mel! Mel, where are you?'

Ali didn't wait for an answer and instinctively raced to the back of the house and into the new extension. There she found an image so repugnant that she took a sharp intake of breath and involuntarily shuddered. For a second, she watched a daughter cradling the limp and lifeless body of her mother. It bore no kind of resemblance to normality or reality, and the lady crumpled next to Mel was unrecognisable to the one that Ali had spent time caring for on Wednesday afternoons. Mel looked up at Ali, her face was bright red.

'Ali she's not breathing. She's dead. Mum's *dead*,' she raged.

Ali's instincts were reminiscent of those at the cathedral green. She screamed at Mel to call an ambulance and dropped to the floor to begin feeling for a pulse. The arrival of the medics within minutes inflamed the panic in Mel's eyes. Their initial attempts to revive Poppy were futile, and the equipment strewn across the newly laid concrete floor looked like carnage to Mel. Although disturbed and struggling to think straight, Ali managed to channel some attention onto her friend freaking out.

'Mel you've got to phone your dad. Quickly!'

'I can't, I can't, I....'

'Where's your phone?'

Mel's gaze was fixed on the intensity of the paramedic's efforts and pointed to the lounge. The old beige telephone had a circular dialling disc, and Ali instantly recognised it as the one which Mel joked about her mum putting a lock on so that her kids didn't run up a large phone bill. Ali went to pick up the handset and noticed the silver barrelled accessory attached to where the finger hole would be for the number '2'. Poppy hadn't unlocked the phone that morning. Ali scurried back to the kitchen.

'Mel, the phone's locked. How can I call your dad?'

'Upstairs, there's a new one.'

Racing up to the landing, Ali found a push button phone. This one would ordinarily be unplugged and hidden from Mel and Lewis when no parents were around to vet the landline usage. Ali picked up the handset ready to punch in the numbers and froze. She had called Derek at work a couple of times when she had been helping on her enrichment. In this tense situation she found herself in, her mind went blank. The harder she tried to remember the sequence of digits the more agitated she became. Ali knew she needed to go back downstairs to ask Mel if she knew the number. She stood there gripping the handset, looking out of the small window onto Wood Street. Grey clouds were rolling across on the horizon and it made her remember how Poppy would call that an attempt to muddy the sky.

Ali snapped out of it when she saw a figure out of the corner of her eye at the bottom of the stairs. She replaced the handset onto the unit. The wire had become twisted and the telephone had shifted on the small corner table on which it sat. Ali was struggling to retain control in this crisis, and inexplicably felt a compulsion to straighten the wire and sit the unit square before going back downstairs. Mel was nowhere to be seen when she eventually ventured back downstairs.

The sight of a body lying on a stretcher in the kitchen was the most sobering antidote to Ali's loss of focus. A white sheet covered the face. There would be no successful rescue this time, no remedy for a satisfactory outcome. Poppy had been convulsing for some time, unable to reach her panic button to alert the emergency care team. Her death was gut-wrenchingly shocking. As poorly as Poppy was becoming there had been no sign of rattling at death's door.

Robert had watched anxiously as the flashing blue lights of the ambulance raced down the street. He paced from foot to foot as he waited for news but didn't dare enter the residence. He automatically assumed that it was Poppy who was in some distress and didn't believe for a second that the situation inside would be out of the control of the medics. When the door burst open, he expected to see a calm situation, either of a bullish Poppy being wheeled through to the ambulance or Ali coming out to explain that everything was normal and well. Instead Mel thundered out and looked straight through Robert as if he were invisible. An elbow hit his midriff as she forced her way out of the driveway and started sprinting away from the house, down the street and out of view. Robert shouted after her, but his attempts to get her attention were futile. Ali appeared at his side and found him staring at fresh air.

'Where did Mel go?'

'Down there,' he shrugged and pointed to the far end of Wood Street. 'What's going on Ali?'

Without flinching, the words tumbled from her lips. 'Poppy's dead.'

Robert threw both of his arms up onto his head as if in pain, blocking his eyes and smothering his ears. This unexpected declaration stung him.

'Will you help me?' begged Ali. 'I don't know what to do.'

Robert reluctantly released his arms. 'We've got to get hold of Derek and Lewis.'

'I tried but couldn't remember Derek's number. The medics said the hospital will work out how to phone him. He's going to be in pieces.'

'I'll go and phone my mum; she'll have the number written down somewhere.'

'What about Mel?'

'I don't know, Ali. Shall we go and find her?'

'Yeah, I reckon so. She shouldn't be by herself. This wasn't meant to happen, it's just madness.'

4

Mel clambered up the familiar banks of Aethelred Hill overlooking the city and nestled against the boulder that had been witness to countless secrets and life experiences of others. She had butterflies in her stomach and just kept playing the words 'my mum's dead' repeatedly in her head. She needed to convince herself that this was real.

She slipped down off the stony companion and paced around. She caught sight of a small child walking alongside her mother, holding hands and giggling. Mel threw herself to the floor onto her knees and buried her face into the palms of her hands. The thought that she would never hold her own mum's hand again was unimaginable. Sobbing uncontrollably, it didn't go unnoticed by the woman and her child, who both made a beeline for Mel.

'Are you ok love?'

Without withdrawing her hands Mel nodded, 'I'm fine…just need a few moments to work things out by myself.'

The woman felt guilty for interrupting her peace.

'Oh, I'm sorry.' She walked a couple more paces, then turned back round. 'Hope everything turns out ok love.'

Mel hoped so too, but she couldn't begin to understand how it was going to be ok after witnessing such torment. When she was sure the woman had walked away, she took her trembling hands off her wet, and now snotty face, and looked up at the sky. Grey clouds were ganging up on the pureness of the blue fragments that still shone through where there were gaps. 'Muddy sky,' Mel whispered to herself, the first thing to enter head. She was already echoing the memory of the pillar in her life.

The looming clouds did not bring any rain, and they began to drift away. In their place the sun was doing its best to announce itself to the late afternoon sky around the scattering of fluffy formations. Mel looked out over at the cathedral, and directly above it sat one remaining, over-sized cumulus plume. It sat low in the sky, blocking the glare of the sun. It caused the rays to burst around the edges, and as it did so the rays gave the effect of a halo. Mel sat upright. Rather than being amazed at the phenomenon, it filled her with hurt. She wagged her finger and vented her anger.

'Don't you do that, mum. Don't show me you're there. Why? Why now?'

She sat back down deflated, resting her elbows on knees and her chin on knuckles. The thought of growing up without her mum being able to see her achievements hurt, but the hardest thing of all was simply not being able to ask her anything again.

She had cried herself out of tears, and a toxic mix of misery and irritation began fermenting inside. It was eerily quiet on the hill, and that was exactly what Mel liked about going up there. As she collected her thoughts, she could usually block out the chorus of the pigeons in the trees that formed a screen on the brow. Today the pigeons were pissing her off something chronic. She got up and ran towards the group strutting at the base of one of the tree trunks, causing them to scatter. She watched as they circled in the air above before coming to rest on one of the trees at the other side of the bank. Mel picked up a stick and went over to the tree, where she launched the missile in the direction of the birds she was stalking. The attempted strike failed miserably, but the harassed targets had been sufficiently alarmed to flee the hilltop for the time being. Mel turned to take her place once more on her favourite rock, at which point she heard someone call out to her.

'Thanks very much for that!'

It startled Mel, as she had assumed that she was alone.

'Thanks for what?' she replied.

A lad appeared from beyond the tree line carrying what looked remarkably like Mel's choice of weaponry for the pigeon attack. The boy smiled at her as he tossed the stick in a safe direction away from themselves and any wildlife.

'Oh God, I'm sorry mate.'

'Don't worry about it. It didn't quite get me – or the pigeons. What've you got against the birds?'

This was a good question, for which Mel had no legitimate reasons.

'I hate them. They strut around looking hard, bobbing their heads as they stare at you, looking you up and down. And pretending to be something that they're not. But it doesn't take much to scare the big, ugly things off. And they crap everywhere, they're dirty vermin.'

'Putting on an act? Isn't that something we all do? Getting found out for your weaknesses doesn't always have negative consequences you know. After all the pigeons manage to survive, don't they?'

Mel hadn't asked for this unusual lesson in ornithology, but there she was on top of a hill embroiled in a disagreement about pigeons while trying to get her head round the fact that she would be going home that evening to begin a life without her mum. It was surreal and yet what the lad had to say was quite profound.

'Blimey, if I'd known you were a pigeon whisperer, I'd have made sure the stick bloody well hit you.'

He laughed and was enjoying the banter. 'You know what, they're actually really clean. Some people pay good money to eat them as a delicacy. And they're dead smart – think about homing pigeons, and they used to take messages back from war.'

'No offence, but I really don't give a shit.'

She didn't, but at the same time it made her think. She was taken back at the knowledge of this bloke who seemed to have arrived out of thin air, and even more amazed that he was prepared to strike up a conversation over a topic that he obviously thought was interesting. Mel didn't even have a clue who he was.

'Fair enough. They've all scattered now anyway. But they always come back again don't they?'

'That's because they're stupid!'

'Or because they're strong willed? They're fiercely loyal you know, finding a mate for life and sharing the raising of their young. Can't say that about all humans.'

He was right. 'Why the hell do you know so much about the ruddy things, dude?'

The lad didn't have time to answer before some voices called out, making both of them jolt.

'Bit crazy seeing you up here Oli. How're you doing?'

'Hiya Greeny. I'm alright thanks fella. How are you? Hi Ali.'

'Yeah, all's fine.' With good reason Robert did not sound convincing. 'I see you've met our friend Mel. She joined the sixth form this year.'

'Ah, her name's Mel. Well I don't think she's enjoying sixth form by the looks of things; she seems a bit feisty and stressed.'

Mel looked at him. 'Would that make me a good pigeon?' she asked sarcastically.

Oli nudged Robert's chest with his elbow. 'See what I mean?'

Robert tugged Oli's arm and indicated with a sideways nod of his head to join him away from the two girls. The lads move back towards the pigeon trees, as Robert gave an insight into the present difficulties with Mel.

'Oli, I promise you this isn't bullshit – she found her mum dead on the floor this afternoon, and just ran away up here. She's been gone hours.' Oli glanced back across his left shoulder and watched as the two girls hugged. 'Her dad is going out of his mind at home; we said we'd bring her back.'

'How old was her mum?'

'Does it matter? Forty-three, middle aged.'

'Middle aged? Are you mad? That's no age to be leaving your

kids behind. No wonder she's lost her mind. You and I both know what it feels like to have a hole that big dug into your heart, Greeny.'

The sunlight had softened and was lowering with each passing minute as it became early evening. Ali watched it as it danced through the leaves and branches. The dew drops that were beginning to form reflected slithers of light. They sparkled occasionally like stars that had floated from the sky the previous night, to rest on the leaves and branches until the next dusk, where they would once again have to make their way above to light the night sky. A hazy amber glow streamed from where the sun was retreating behind the trees and the hillside. It was different watching a sunset from up high. The beautiful array of colours made Ali feel serene; she couldn't put her finger on why, but it was almost as if the glow was whispering as it melted away. In contrast, her friend was a bundle of emotional mayhem. It felt very intense trying to speak with her.

'How long are you gonna be on this hillside looking at the town, eh?' she asked in a soft tone.

'Look, if you don't want to be here you can fuck off and leave me be.'

Ali said nothing at first; she didn't know what to say or how to respond. Mel was like a geyser about to gush and she didn't want to be the one to set her off.

'I do want to be with you, but I think your dad needs to be with you more. He's freaking out Mel.'

Mel pictured her dad heartbroken at home and felt her eyes well up.

'I don't want to go back there; I just can't do it.'

Mel walked across to the edge of the bank to be by herself and sat down. By this time, the lads had sauntered back across to the rock. Ali and Robert formed a huddle, and the council of war talked through their strategy in hushed tones. Mel had zoned out, and Ali's appearance at her side some minutes later made her jump. Ali crouched down and grabbed hold of her friend's hand.

'Mel, we're going to go now but I promise it'll only be for a short while. Will you try to get your head together just a little bit by the time we get back?'

A forlorn looking Mel quietly acknowledged this with a couple of nods. Robert rubbed his hand gently on her back and called across to Oli.

'Look out for Mel until we get back, would you?'

With that, the pair started disappearing down the windy track of the hillside. At first, Mel wasn't sure she was comfortable with being looked after by a guy infatuated by wildlife; she'd only just met him. But on the other hand, she *knew* quite a lot about him already once it clicked in her mind who he was. She paired together the fact that his love of pigeons was probably more about knowing how to cook them at catering school, rather than being a twitcher. As Oli tentatively placed himself down next to Mel, he was completely unaware that she knew about his own previous personal challenges. Mel didn't object or turn to look at him as she spoke.

'So, what you the hell are you doing up here by yourself anyway Oli?'

'I come up here a lot; I like that it's quiet. I like being in my own space – it gives me time to think. Helps me to tone down the negative things buzzing round in my head. I'm a much better person when I realise what I have got, not what I haven't.'

Mel was struck at what a friendly and confident lad he was – nice even. She felt glad that Robert and Ali had taken time to help sort his mess out.

'I like coming up here too – but not so much today.'

'I hope it's ok for me to say, but Greeny told me about your mum; I'm ever so sorry.' Mel would have said something, but she had a lump in her throat from his kind comment, and Oli didn't want to add anything else to stir up any more emotions. 'I know you want space of your own Mel, but I'll just be right here to keep you company before the others get back. I promise I won't hassle you anymore.'

'I registered what you said to me earlier, about weaknesses; well here's me showing you mine. I feel like nothing without my mum. You're wrong, 'cos nothing positive's gonna come from this.'

Oli took the risk and responded. 'How can I sit here and tell you you're wrong Mel? And I wouldn't even if that were so. I bet your dad's a good guy though – I'm sure your mum would want you to look after each other?'

'Yeah? Well where the hell is he now then? And anyway, there are things that nobody other than my mum would truly understand, so how's that gonna work with him?'

Mel's thoughts had bounced between grief and her own fears of the potential for the condition to be hereditary. That hung heavy in the minds of her and Lewis. It was not something she was going to share with a near-as-damn-it stranger.

'At least give your old man a chance to come good, Mel.'

It was getting close to dusk, but where there had been clouds in the afternoon was now a clear sky that maintained the faintest embers of daylight. It was enough to be able to watch as a group of pigeons returned to the trees behind them. Mel squinted and puffed out her cheeks as she watched one of them but was taken with how amazing it looked in flight. It flapped heavily, then soared and stooped. She could hear voices approaching and turned in the direction to where three shadowy figures appeared through the dimness on the pathway. Derek had been reluctant to leave the house and the turmoil surrounding it, but after talking to Ali and Robert he was distraught at the thought of his daughter crumbling alone on a hilltop. Without a word being spoken he walked up to within a yard of Mel and held out his hand in a gesture for her to grab hold of it. She sprung up and threw her arms tightly round his neck causing him to almost lose his footing. Derek gently cradled his sobbing girl. Oli was right – he had come good.

It took longer than usual to walk home from Aethelred Hill because of the darkness. Mel and Derek joined Lewis in collective grief in the sitting room where the curtains had been drawn since the mid-afternoon. Not many words were spoken as there was an abundance of shock and disbelief at what had happened. It was difficult to be anything but numb. The phone rang numerous times during the evening, each time Derek conveyed the dismal news to Poppy's nearest and dearest. Her network of friendships was vast, and he would be reliant on the kindness of others to disseminate the sorrow and ease the burden of carrying out that task. The despair in the room was unbearable, so Mel retreated to the kitchen.

She stood in the corner of the newly built extension. Although there was total silence, the freshly plastered walls echoed of the bickering about colour schemes. However pathetic that seemed at the time, these were the characteristics that made the house feel like their home. Once again Lewis had excelled in his ability for protracting the process. The lengthy and vivid descriptions about what was to be done in the new space had failed to translate into action. This always amused Poppy. She knew her son meant well, and that it would eventually get done following much needed nagging. That's the way it always tended to roll with the Burchells. But for now, the dullness of the walls was a match for her emotions. The unfinished details summed up the void and incompleteness in the hearts of the family. And yet, less than a year earlier it had all been so different.

5

Long term prospects in the car industry began to dwindle, coercing Derek to invest time and energy in retraining for a career in quality assurance. It was a timely decision. He lost his job at British Leyland in 1981 and began searching for employment opportunities with his newly acquired skill set. The family moved to Thatcham, where Derek was in easy commuting distance to his new job at Simonds Brewery in Reading.

They were welcomed into the community, and Poppy immersed herself into volunteering at the parish church. The Caribbean cuisine she served at local fates was renowned, though this wasn't how she cemented herself into local folklore legend. That accolade was the result of her equally well received rum punch.

At one stiflingly hot May fate the interest in Poppy's concoction was higher than usual. Since there was an urgent need to address an area of rising damp in the bell tower, Reverend Florey relaxed his attitude towards the sale of alcohol as it meant that much needed funds were acquired. The punch was delicious in taste, and thirst quenching. The overriding pineapple hints disguised its alcoholic content, fooling many a church fate attendee of its strength. Given that Poppy was a most trusted member of his congregation, there was no reason to doubt her integrity that the man of God would find a small drop heavenly. It was the miscounting of little top ups that followed that did the damage. Reverend Florey continued to sip from his paper cup completely oblivious to the potency of the liquor. How it always tickled the congregation on many a sad occasion or gloomy day to remember Reverend Florey drunk, and then cutting short his sermon the morning after innocently consuming more than was good enough for even the most tolerant drinker of alcoholic beverages.

Their gut-wrenching decision to leave Thatcham was out of necessity rather than choice. Poppy's worsening condition came as little surprise to her or Derek, as was the prediction of the gloomy prognosis in February 1981. She couldn't have predicted the headful of gloom the GP handed out on a visit to the surgery for a routine check-up.

'Your blood shows signs of a genetic disorder,' she was told, 'a mutation of genes in the DNA. This causes changes in the muscle fibers that make it difficult for the muscles to work properly. Nothing is conclusive until we carry out further tests, but it's possible that you have Steinert Disease.'

At first, it was difficult to be overwhelmed because neither Poppy nor Derek fully understood what they were being told. Doctor Fowler clarified it for them.

'It is more commonly called Myotonic Dystrophy and affects around one in eight thousand people in the UK.'

'Dystrophy?' exclaimed Derek. He knew the word, and while the context was not immediately understood, it initiated panic that there might be the onset of diminishing health. For once Poppy was speechless.

'Progressive muscle-wasting and weakness,' the doctor continued.

'Well, what does it do – I mean what are the symptoms?'

'It gradually causes muscles to debilitate, possibly leading to disabilities. It could eventually affect the heart, or the muscles used for breathing.' The doctor paused. 'At which point the condition becomes life-threatening. The condition is usually hereditary.'

That caused confusion: there had never been mention of this with her parents. Perhaps they didn't even know? That was when Poppy became frightened.

'What about our kids?' she asked.

Looking directly at Poppy, Doctor Fowler remained calm, focused, and professional.

'Well, that's an important question. They will have to undergo tests too – and on a regular basis.'

The realisation that her life was going to alter at an increasingly rapid pace was a difficult situation to manage. Her myotonic dystrophy would not only require professional care, but also specific medication. While she had been happy to put her trust in the staff at the Royal Berkshire Hospital in Reading, budget cuts and workforce reorganisation would see a reduction in the help available to Poppy going forward. Thus, the postcode lottery meant that by staying in Thatcham she would no longer be eligible to receive the medication she desperately required, and her condition would deteriorate more quickly.

In typically stoic manner, Poppy wouldn't follow through with the relocation until Mel had completed her GCSE exams. To anyone who knew the lady in their neighbourhood they were delighted that their friend didn't leave as suddenly as expected. Publicly there seemed to be little change in her health and well-being, and Poppy was as charismatic and positive as ever.

'You only get rid of me when I decide I have had enough of you,' she would jest.

She disguised her breathlessness well enough, but privately her family could see the toll that her condition was beginning to take through bouts of extreme tiredness. Despite this, Poppy was endlessly encouraging of Mel to perform well in her finals.

'Dig deep and remember you're amazing,' she would tell her daughter before each and every exam.

There was more than a touch of guilt in the household over Lewis' exams two years previously, when he had been preoccupied with a double dose of worry. Firstly, his mum had reacted adversely to a change in her medication dosage resulting in her being bed bound for a month. Lewis was supposed to be on exam leave, using the time to swot up on his subjects to give himself the best chance of half decent grades. Instead he cared for Poppy during the daytime while his dad was at work and Mel was at school. Secondly, he and Mel had been awaiting the results of their most recent blood test results to find out if there was any evidence that they had inherited their mother's condition. Unsurprisingly, Lewis was scared and anxious. Revision plans suffered immeasurably, and consequently he didn't perform to his expected levels. Nobody questioned or ridiculed him, for everyone knew he had been on the receiving end of incredibly unfortunate circumstances and timing.

It was with much optimism that the Burchells arrived in Winchester in July 1995, where it was hoped Poppy would receive the specialist care she needed from the Royal Hampshire County Hospital. The removal truck was already waiting outside their new home by the time the Burchells arrived.

'That's it there, number sixty-four,' pointed Lewis, thinking he was being helpful to his dad.

'We can see that professor. The removal blokes are standing outside,' mocked Mel sarcastically.

It was a beautiful sunny Thursday morning. The air was already warm at nine o'clock, with just the slightest breeze. It was one of those glorious days where everything just seemed to move in slow motion. There was bird chatter and singing from the tree lined road, making sixty-four Wood Street all the more inviting to be moving into.

Derek parked directly outside the house. 'I wonder if it's always this easy to park right outside,' he pondered. 'Maybe we could ask the council to designate a space by painting a lined area.'

Poppy frowned at the suggestion. It was the last thing she wanted to happen and dismissed it immediately.

'I don't want no road tattoo promoting me being ill, mister.'

Mel and Lewis helped their mum out of the car. They each held one of her arms as they walked up the path. The semi-detached property looked pretty enough in the sunshine, just as it did when they viewed it four months previously. The entrance to the house was through a small porch area at the front, and then on through a main door. There was vehicle access for a single car in front of the porch, currently occupied by the removal truck, which looked rather bloated in the confined space. There was a decorative patch of no more than six foot square next to the small drive, which had been laid with what must have previously been decorative hard-core. The stones were now a tired looking grey colour, long overdue for replacement. The patch was ridiculously overgrown with weeds.

'I can't wait to start tidying up that grubby patch,' said Poppy, glancing down at the messy exterior.

Nobody had the heart to tell her that she would find it physically challenging to even do that. Poppy certainly didn't want to admit it to herself.

'I can help you with that mum,' replied Lewis sensitively.

'Thank you, son. That will be nice.'

Derek unlocked the doors and went over to speak with the removal men. At that point, a boy's voice shouted out from the direction of the semi-detached property next to the Burchell's.

'You're moving in then?'

The owner of the questioning could barely be seen past the removal truck. The architecturally different semi-detached building next door sat further forward than theirs. Out of sight of the unidentified voice, Mel rolled her eyes at the person for stating the obvious. She peered round the side of their house, and there he was.

'How's it goin'? I'm Robert.'

'This is my brother Lewis, you'll have a lot in common with him,' mocked Mel, referring to her brother's previous state-the-obvious comment. 'I'm Mel. Whatever made you think we were moving in?'

Rather than answer the question, Robert grinned at her dry humour. He liked her instantly.

'Alright Lewis?' he asked. Lewis nodded an acknowledgement. 'That your mum and dad?' he continued inquisitively. Mel watched her brother leading Poppy into the main hallway of the house. 'Sorry, didn't mean to hold you up. Just thought I'd say 'Hi' while I had the chance. I live here at number sixty-six.'

Mel smiled. 'Nice. Well, best go in and get sorted. See ya later.' And with that she went inside to start helping with lifting and unpacking.

No sooner had Mel gone inside to find out her mum's instructions than the first boxes were being brought in by the removal men. The very first thing that Poppy did was to unpack the contents of a portable, plastic storage box that Lewis carried in for her. The items inside were bubble wrapped and bulged far greater than their actual size and shape. Poppy carefully took the packaging away to reveal some photo frames containing a few of her favourite memories. She stroked the sides of each one and wore a proud smile. Taking temporary pride of place on the windowsill in the living room were a black and white wedding portrait, and a family snap. The latter was somewhat dated, guaranteed to draw huffs and puffs from both of her children as they recoiled at the outfits they adorned as toddlers. Poppy adored her photos.

Three hours later, the latches on the back doors to the truck were being bolted and the crew of sweaty men were on their way. Within a couple of minutes, there was a knock on the front door. Mel went to answer thinking that the removal team had discovered a rogue box rattling around in the cavernous rear storage area. Standing inside the porch was Robert, with a pen and a piece of paper.

'Hi, it's me.'

Mel was beginning to wonder whether Robert always stated the obvious, or if he was just a nutcase.

'Yep, I can definitely see that. Wasn't long ago that it was you as well. What can I do for you?'

'We – well my mum – thought you guys might not have your kettle unpacked yet, so I – we – wondered if you'd like a brew?'

'Er, that's really kind of you but I think we're alright.'

Mel was interrupted by Poppy walking down the corridor before she could finish. 'That's a top-notch idea young Robert. My name's Poppy, Mrs Burchell to you mind. And I like my tea strong with one sugar.'

'Right. That's no problem Mrs B,' he responded with a cheeky grin. 'I thought it might perk you up. Must have been a long day seeing how tired you look.'

Poppy was indeed physically and mentally shattered, more through her condition than the move. Robert wasn't to know that. He happily took the family's tea order and returned promptly with the much-needed refreshments for the family and knew to not overstay his welcome.

'I can see you're busy, so I'll get going. But give us a knock if you need anything else, or if you need my help,' he said, and left them to it.

'He's a lovely boy,' Poppy reflected.

It wasn't meant to be a loaded assessment, but Mel couldn't help agreeing with her mum.

The next morning, Mel went round to number sixty-six to return the cups they had borrowed from their neighbours. A woman answered the door and pleasantries were exchanged.

'Hi, I'm from next door. I've brought your cups back.'

'That's good of you. I was going to send Robert round to get them later. What's your name love?'

'Didn't Robert tell you?'

Mary screwed her eyes up and shook her head.

'I'm Mel. Mel Burchell My mum said to say thanks ever so much for the drinks, Mrs…?'

'It's Miss to be exact. Ainscow. But drop the formal darling. I'm Mary. And I believe you met master Spitley yesterday?'

'Spitley?'

Mel was puzzled. She inadvertently looked at Mary's wedding finger which confirmed she was not married. 'Oh, okay then,' she replied.

'Robert carries his dad's surname – to clear up the confusion.'

'Crappy name ain't it, Mel?' he said as he came to the door. Mel deduced that Robert must've also been on school holidays, otherwise why else would he have been hanging around at home on a Friday.

'I'd like to see your Grandad hear you saying that, he'll clip you round the ear and give you a mouthful about how he fought in the war for you,' interjected Mary defensively. Robert said no more about names.

'Are you nearly straight next door?'

'God, no. We're slowly getting there though.'

Peering from around his mum's shoulder Robert posed a question.

'Mel, what are you and the others up to today? You got any plans?'

'Don't be so nosey Robert!' Mary interrupted.

'Erm, unpacking probably Robert,' scoffed Mel, not quite believing he seemed to overlook how blatantly obvious she had made it that they were still swamped by boxes next door. 'Other than getting tidy I'm not sure what else to be honest.'

'Well look, you're going to need a break at some point, right? Well why don't I show you around town a little bit, so you can get your bearings. It'll be too bustling in town to do it tomorrow.'

He meant well, but Mel wasn't sure whether her mum and dad would prefer to explore Winchester by themselves. He could sense her reluctance.

'If none of you want to that's no problem. I just thought it might help you. I'll show you the school too if you want – you are still at school, right?'

Mel hoped she had concealed her blushing at the unintentional insult. Did he really suspect that she might be a little younger than she was?

'No actually, I start sixth form in September.' She knew she sounded defensive, and quickly set about changing her tone. 'What about you?'

'I'm staying on in shit-form too hopefully.' He chuckled at his comically crude reference to the post-sixteen opportunities at the local school.

'Er, thank you Robert!' bellowed Mary's voice of authority in response to Robert's colourful language.

He smirked like a naughty schoolboy being reprimanded for a childish prank. Robert looked older than he was. He had clearly been shaving for a while and possessed a shadow that morning. The give-away sign of his youth were one or two spots dotted around his chin and cheeks. He had dark hair that flopped on his brow as a centre parting, and it twitched like curtains when the breeze caught it.

'Tell you what, if you're sure it won't put you out, I must admit it'd be a good idea to get to know the best way to walk to town and the school. Let me go and ask my mum and I'll let you know.'

6

'We only live next door and still you manage to get lost on the way home?'

That was the first comment Mel was confronted with when she got back home. She didn't think it warranted her mum's sarcasm. 'I don't think so, I'm not Lewis.'

'I heard that sis. Go and do one.'

'Hey, you two! That's enough of that.' Poppy was wagging her fingers between the two siblings. 'We not want the neighbourhood getting the wrong impression of us.'

It didn't stop Mel sticking her tongue out at her brother when Poppy's back was turned, at which Lewis shook his head back at her.

'I've not been gone that long. Anyway, I couldn't just throw the cups on the floor. I got chatting to Robert's mum, she seems really nice.' Mel knew her mum would be intrigued to find out more.

'What's her name then?'

'Mary. Ainscow.'

'You see the dad of the house anywhere?'

'No. Actually I think she's on her own, cos I didn't see a wedding ring on her finger. And Robert's surname is different. He's Spitley.'

Poppy tutted and shook her head in a disapproving manner.

'Mind, we should not judge the dear lady. We not know what she been through.'

With mere scraps of detail Poppy had incredibly managed to dismiss Mary's misfortune, and then defended the woman all within the same sentence.

'Robert's offered to show us around the town,' Mel continued. 'Like, where the school is and the dole office, Lewis,' she shouted up the staircase in her brother's direction.

'I need to call the hospital at ten o'clock, then I be ready to go,' said Poppy.

'Mum, we don't know how far everything is, I don't think you should be coming without dad knowing.'

'No, no, no. Don't be so silly girl. I'm not an invalid you know!' protested Poppy.

In truth, Poppy was physically devoid of the ability to be able to meander around town for long. While it was futile attempting to win the argument, Mel was anxious about her mum losing her ability to walk independently. Taking Poppy out galivanting needed thought and planning, not a decision on the spur of the moment. It wasn't a great idea, and she knew her dad would be irate about it when he got home from his induction day at the Hovis factory in Eastleigh.

Lewis didn't join in the walk, much to the annoyance of Mel. She had banked on there being an extra pair of hands in case the outing became too much for her mum. Instead, her brother had insisted on pleasing Poppy by weeding at the front of the house, at least that way he would feel useful. The route into the town centre took in the avenue which led up to King Alfred's Comprehensive School, which was locked and deserted in the summer holidays. The sixth form annexe was at the rear, so it was difficult to get a good view of it from the road.

The three adventurers meandered at a gentle pace towards the high street. On the opposite pavement, a lad of similar age bellowed across to Robert.

'Oi Greeny! You tosser.'

The source of the abusive tirade proceeded to cross the street, seemingly oblivious to the company alongside him.

'What're you up to muppet?' came the equally unnecessary follow-up.

There was the customary 'shump' – something between a

handshake and fist bump. Grinning, despite the less than friendly banter, Robert greeted the lad with a volley of his own.

'How's it goin' Chinny, you loser?'

It wasn't difficult for Mel to work out the lad's nickname. His chin was undeniably chiselled, and more obvious for the fact that he was both pale and gaunt. The lads had a customary handshake as their greeting. When Robert remembered who was with him, he became self-conscious and remembered his manners. The heat rushed to his face and neck, making it impossible to disguise the reddish glow it created.

'This is Mel. Her family have just moved into the area. We've just been down to take a look at the school cos she's starting at Alf's sixth form in September.'

'Is that right? Nice to meet ya, Mel. I'm Dave Jewkes.' He snorted before continuing, 'Yeah, the school's great – other than the teachers. They're all pretty much a bunch of...'

'And this is Poppy, Mel's mum.'

Robert was timely with his interjection, and along with his wide-eyed gesture and head nodding succeeded in diverting any continuation of the obscenities that would have undoubtedly tumbled out of Chinny's foul mouth.

'Oh,' Chinny began cautiously, and now a little awkwardly. 'Well Winchester's a lovely place missus. Has Greeny showed you the cathedral yet?' Jewkes had suddenly morphed into a silver tongued, connoisseur of culture.

Poppy had no chance to answer, as Robert was keen to remove the party away from the current conversation.

'We're just going that way now actually mate, so catch you later yeah?'

'Yeah, nice one. Hey, I've just seen Croftsy down that way actually.'

His statement was accompanied with an over exaggerated wink that was unavoidable for everyone to notice. Though Mel looked at Robert for some clarity or explanation he chose not to dwell on the comment and didn't respond. With that, the character that was Dave 'Chinny' Jewkes was gone. It was a confused looking Poppy who attempted to seek some clarity.

'Who is Greeny?' she enquired.

'That's me, Mrs B. Cos my name's Spit-ley, it's a joke about phlegm.' Once more, Robert looked embarrassed. 'Aargh, I really hate my surname.'

Although she initially looked aghast at such a comment, once the explanation had been processed the nickname tickled Poppy and she burst out in laughter as if she had been one of the pupils to have instigated the labelling of it. Mel and Robert looked at each other and sniggered too, not so much at the name but at the mother figure finding it so amusing. The giggling, though, was making Poppy breathless and wheezy. Mel cut short her chortling.

'Mum, I think we should take a break on that bench we passed round the corner.'

She was astonished when her mum agreed to her recommendation. Poppy had conceded so limply and without putting up her usual feisty resistance to being told what to do. From the moment they left home Mel had been concerned about how her mum would find the energy to walk into town and back. She had barely paused throughout the forty-five-minute whistle stop tour of Winchester's highlights.

'There's a much nicer seating area closer than that, Mel,' Robert was gesturing in the direction of an alleyway across the road.

They crossed over and walked the fifty yards through a jitty that led out onto the cathedral green. The buildings either side of the jitty had blocked out the bright sunshine temporarily like a tunnel, but once they reached the end and turned towards the direction of the benches the glare found them again instantly, causing them to squint. Artificially and fleetingly blinded, Robert collided with another passer-by.

'Woah, sorry!' exclaimed Robert, and looked up to see who had been barged into. 'Ali!' he blurted out.

Alison Crofts didn't even have the time to respond, and it wasn't Robert that she was staring at. At that very same moment she had been bumped into by her peer, Mel let out a shriek as Poppy collapsed. Mel clung on to her mum to stop her from falling onto the gravel pathway. Ali was the first to react and reached across to grab Poppy's other arm. Together with Mel, they managed to gently place her onto the grassy verge next to them. Poppy was not responding to being placed down to rest, not even to protest at being man-handled. With amazing calmness Ali took control of the situation.

'She's not breathing. Call for an ambulance Robert. Go!' was the order she barked out to him.

Mel was rooted to the spot. What she was witnessing was so illogical. There was the vision of horror as her mum lay motionless on the ground, against the vista of the huge cathedral and the bright blue sky. What seemed like an eternity was happening in just a split second. She was snapped out of her inert and mute state by Ali calling for assistance.

'Please, can you keep her head tilted backwards? Use your face next to hers to feel for any breathing. Tell me if you feel anything.'

Ali didn't even know who Mel was, or her relationship to the women. Sub-consciously though she had assumed there was a family link. Ali was familiar with cardiopulmonary resuscitation from her Health and Social Care course at school, and from her training in the Army Cadets. She had only ever practised on a dummy, but she instinctively remembered that the chest compressions she was now performing on Poppy would help to keep the blood pumping around her body, and hopefully oxygen to her brain. She had hated practising mouth to mouth, but after thirty compressions her training had told her to top up the oxygen by breathing into her mouth. She accidently nudged Mel out of the way, held Poppy's nose, and breathed. There was no reaction, so she started the compressions again.

Mel was beginning to freak out silently, and her hands had started to shake. Inside her head Ali was screaming for Robert to hurry up. Up to that point she had just about remained composed but was mightily thankful when she was joined by a qualified first aider from the nearby shopping precinct. Then an off-duty GP appeared as well.

Robert was an athletic boy who had always enjoyed playing sport. He sprinted back along the jitty, but in his desperation to get to a phone box quickly he stopped thinking clearly and couldn't remember where the nearest one was. A familiar face suddenly took his eye.

'Chinny!' he yelled at Dave Jewkes, who had appeared from the newsagent opposite. Robert raced towards him. 'Mate, have you got your new mobile thingy with you?'

Chinny liked to think of himself as a bit of a trendsetter often to be seen wearing designer gear. The recent revolution in mobile phones had captured his imagination too, and after endlessly pleading with his parents he landed himself with a Nokia 232 as a birthday present, much to the jealousy of many a King Alfred's pupil. It was little wonder that Chinny was so precious about his new gadget.

'Get stuffed Greeny…'

'No time to piss around Dave – I've got to call an ambulance.'

Chinny knew his mate was being serious. It was unusual for Robert to call him 'Dave' as this was usually reserved for when he was being chastised for sloppy play on the football field. Bedsides, his normally jovial friend looked completely freaked out. Without consent Robert yanked the phone from the pocket of Chinny's track top and thrust it in front of his face.

'Dial 999 for me Dave.'

He unlocked the device, did as he was asked, and passed it back to Robert.

'Hello, I need an ambulance urgently.'

The shrill of the sirens cutting through the warm summer air, and racing through the winding historic backstreets, were completely out of context with the peace and tranquillity across a vast portion of the cathedral green. People meandered along the gravel pathways running parallel to the nave, while others were dotted on the carpet of grass stretched out in front of the grand west front, all blissfully unaware of the unfolding drama at one of the entrances to the open expanse of the tourist trap. In that top corner of the grounds a woman struggled for breath and grappled with her own existence. Each breath was a struggle, but Poppy had at least regained some consciousness. Within minutes of Robert making the call, an ambulance crew had arrived, and an oxygen mask was swiftly introduced to stabilise Poppy's breathing. One of the paramedics was briefed on her status by the doctor who had been assisting.

'You need to speak with that young lady too. She's the one who ensured the woman was able to regain consciousness.' The doctor nodded in Ali's direction which grabbed her attention. 'I wonder if you realise that you've saved this woman from terrible medical consequences. Her vital organs were at risk of closing down you know. She might have died if it weren't for your intervention in fact. That's a pretty impressive achievement for someone as young as you,' he added.

Ali was looking at the GP talking to her but was instead listening to an entirely different conversation between the other paramedic and the girl who had helped her with the ill woman.

'She's got myotonic dystrophy. There's a medical identification card with her meds listed on it. We've been walking nearly an hour round town. I, I just think she's shattered,' stuttered Mel, holding her hand on her forehead, as if comforting herself to think logically.

'Ok – Mel, is it?'

'Yeah, Mel Burchell.'

'Try to stay calm. As you're a close family member it would be best if you accompanied us in the ambulance so that you're there when the hospital staff start carrying out further tests, ok? They'll want to talk to you and find out who is the next of kin.'

And with that, the patient and her daughter were in the ambulance, blue lights flashing and siren blaring on the way up to the hospital just a short ride away. There was no time for Mel to thank Robert, or the girl with him called Ali.

7

The whole episode seemed quite surreal to Ali, and as the Cathedral green returned to the normality of being a tourist magnet, she confided with Robert about how petrified she had been. Robert put his arm round Ali to reassure her, and she found this as comforting as it was intended to be. She wanted to know more about his association with the pairing that had disappeared in the ambulance.

'So, you know them because they moved in next door to you yesterday?' she quizzed.

'Yeah. I just wanted to make them feel... like... like Winchester was their new favourite place. It's a horrible thing to happen to anyone, but even more so in a strange place.'

Ali smiled at the fact that Robert had been so thoughtful in trying to help the family settle in.

'It's a good job they were with you then Robert, they must have felt comfortable letting you show them around. You probably made them feel at home. Did you know that the lady had a medical problem?'

'Poppy? Nah, didn't have a clue. Nobody said a word when I asked if they'd like me to show them around. I only realised that something wasn't right because she held onto Mel quite a lot while they were walking.'

'Well I guess they're unlikely to have wanted to hang out their dirty laundry in a neighbourhood they've only just moved into,' concluded Ali diplomatically.

'I feel really bad for bringing them out now.'

'Don't think like that, Robert. You were trying to do them a favour. They won't blame you.'

As they tried to take stock of the events of that afternoon, Robert broke the stony silence that enveloped the two of them briefly. He decided to look forward positively.

'Mel's going to be chuffed that you'll be in sixth form with her after all of that.'

Ali would have to take Robert's word for that. Though she had made a significant impact on the lives of the Burchell family, she knew next to nothing about them to signify the start of any such friendship. Ali said nothing but thought how becoming friends at school would be scant consolation to Mel if her mum didn't make it through at the hospital.

On arrival at accident and emergency barely a mile away, Mel was shown to a waiting area while Poppy was examined thoroughly. She needed to get in touch with Lewis and her dad and found enough change in her purse to phone her brother from one of the payphones. Fortunately, he heard the ringing and stirred from his slumber to answer it. Upon hearing the news about his mum, Lewis was beside himself for not going on the walk with them. Through sheer panic, he was suddenly full of questions about what had happened. Mel watched the call credit ticking down on the digital screen, struggling to deal with the interrogation. She became agitated at there being too much to say and not enough time to get it in, and so she had to be firm and quite abrupt.

'Lewis stop whimpering and listen carefully, I've only got a few pence left on this phone. You've got to get hold of dad straight away to tell him what's gone on. He needs to be at the hospital with mum. She's been moved up to the intensive care unit.'

She explained the situation as best as she knew it to be and told her brother that he had to be the one to call the Hovis factory in Eastleigh to inform his dad. It was the kind of responsibility he would ordinarily shy away from, but this time there was no choice in the matter. Before that he had to pick the phone lock with a paperclip; fortunately, it wasn't the first time he'd done it.

His fingers trembled as he placed his tips into the numbered circular holes of the dial. He breathed heavily, pondering what words he was going to use when he spoke to his dad. With his senses heightened, the ring tone seemed so much louder, and then he flinched as the call was answered at the other end. Despite breaking down, Lewis managed to splutter out enough words of explanation to the patient receptionist. Derek's meeting with the human resources manager was interrupted by a clerk.

'Mr Burchell, I'm ever so sorry to interrupt like this. I have your son on the phone, he did say it was quite urgent. I think it's a call you need to take?'

Derek was so embarrassed. He surmised that 'urgent' to Lewis would obviously be the equivalent of not being able to find the 'on' switch to the kettle, or something trivial like that. But as he raced from his induction in Eastleigh, he was burdened with guilt at thinking so spitefully about his son and for his absence so soon after moving to their new home. It made his journey more torrid, exacerbated further by acidic stomach cramps until he arrived at the hospital.

At the reception to intensive care he could already see Mel through the glazing of the fire doors, pacing up and down and looking forlorn. Derek gestured with his hand while he acquired information from the administrative staff. It was through relief rather than anger that Mel's fists were clenched inside her pockets when the doors swung open. She kept telling herself to 'get a grip, get a grip' hoping that her dad wouldn't notice how distressing the previous two hours had been. Mel stood frozen and with heavy eyes looking at him, as her dad lay his hand on her shoulder and gave it a gentle squeeze.

'How ye daein sprog? I'm so proud of ye.'

It was always a sign of his own apprehension when Derek slipped into his Scottish dialect – either that, or if he was telling his kids off. After doing his best to comfort his daughter, Derek sought reassurance of his own that the love of his life was stable.

It was disturbing to see Poppy lying so helpless. The lump in his throat painfully stretched his windpipe, but he would refrain from allowing the tears to sting as well. What he really wanted to know was whether she was going to improve.

'I'm Doctor Mannan, the neurologist overseeing your wife's recovery, alongside my colleague Doctor Pallister. We want to carry out a series of tests on her heart and her lungs. It's likely that will take at least a few days.'

'What then?' Derek asked apprehensively.

'To be honest, Mr Burchell, considering what happened today she is doing remarkably well to be able to breathe independently.'

'That's not the answer to the question I asked you. C'mon Doctor, give me an idea here.'

'Until we know the results of further tests, we'd be speculating about the quality of her life going forward.'

'You know what I'm getting at. Why are you being so reluctant to tell me what I need to know?'

The doctor coerced Derek to a private meeting room at the side of the ward where her words would be more audible.

'It's not in our nature to cause anguish and panic, Mr Burchell.'

'Well that's kinda ironic. You choosing to be evasive is causing me more harm than good. Tell me honestly, if it were your partner wouldn't you be asking what their life expectancy might be?'

The doctor sighed at the rather despondent looking Derek, whose head had dropped and his body language quite defeatist.

'From what we know at this stage, worst case scenario could be six months, but I am doubtful that is the case.'

'Six months?' he responded with shock. Derek probed one more time. 'And...best case?'

The consultant had already offered more than she had intended to and gave no response. Her cautious approach to

Derek's blunt enquiry was as good as telling him that time wasn't the family's best friend.

'I realise there's a lot going on for you all right now.'

'Aye, we're used to putting up a fight in this family, Doctor.'

'Poppy will benefit immensely from that strength, I'm sure.' There was a slight and uncomfortable pause. 'Sorry to bombard you, Mr Burchell. We've requested the medical records from Berkshire for your children, and wondered if you could you confirm when your son and daughter last had their blood tests taken for genetic screening?'

'Blimey, that would be when Lewis was about to finish secondary school. Two, maybe three, years ago I think.'

'Yes, that does tie up with the dates they've told us.' Doctor Mannan scribbled some illegible writing on a notepad in her hand. 'Have you and your wife ever had to visit your GP with any concerns about either of them at any point?'

'No. Why?'

'Have they ever showed signs of any of the symptoms of your wife's condition?'

'Such as?'

'Any problems with lifting, sports, walking?'

'No. None; what is this?'

Derek knew exactly what Doctor Mannan was angling towards, and despite this, a bubble of calmness remained around him.

'Look, we know from our consultations that there's a fifty percent chance that the kids might inherit the condition, but so far there's been absolutely nothing to concern them or us. Believe you me, if there was, we would've moved heaven and earth before now to get them seen by the best consultants.'

'Well, obviously that's great. From what you are saying all seems well. And I mean no offense by my next suggestion...' She paused and looked up from her notes.

'Go on,' said Derek.

'I would be keen to advise another round of screening as they enter adulthood, just as a precaution. In light of Poppy's condition, I'd like to see them have an ECG as heart problems can sometimes affect those who are otherwise without any symptoms.'

At that point Derek started to feel tense. This was just too much to deal with alongside Poppy's sudden decline.

'I don't want my wife to get the slightest whiff of this conversation, Doctor. I realise it's well intended, but right now our focus is to get that woman back home as quickly as possible and without further worry for her or my wee ones. This is something we're going to have to shelve for now. Ok?'

And with that, the ad-hoc meeting with the medical professional ended abruptly as Derek swiftly removed himself from the room. It wouldn't be a subject matter that could be avoided indefinitely, but the mere mention of further tests for the kids would make them fall apart. He wasn't about to let that happen to them.

The rest of the day was spent at Poppy's bedside, sometimes joined by Mel and Lewis. They breached the visiting rules for an extra hour while the nursing team were preoccupied with dispensing medication to patients throughout the ward. Shortly before having to vacate the premises, Poppy stirred. Looking at the visiting party by her bedside, her robust words defied the state she was in.

'Lewis, you finish working on my front yard now eh?' she asked.

He looked at her, then did a double take as it felt like he was suddenly being cross examined. A wry smile spread over her face like the sun appearing from behind a gloomy cloud. Lewis chuckled, and then he could hold it back no more. He sobbed like an infant while giving his mum a gentle embrace.

'She got you with an upper cut there, wee laddie,' observed Derek, as he ruffled the verbally bruised and battered youth's hair.

Derek thought he was mentally prepared for Poppy's inevitable deterioration, but as he drove home exhausted that evening the tears that he had held back now filled his eyes, blurring his vision to the extent that he had to pull over. It was the realisation of how lonely it would feel to be without her. Mel had never seen her dad cry before. She was literally numb and couldn't think what to say as he sat sniffling next to her. Once he was able to drive safely again, he wasted no time getting home and hugged his two children like never before. None of them said anything, but that show of unity was a much-needed remedy for them all given the circumstances they found themselves in.

Poppy wanted to be as well informed as possible, even if that meant having to accept the inevitable – even if it meant she would have to be selective with conveying the truth to those closest to her. She hated that thought, of withholding information of such magnitude, but naturally wanted to protect them from any negativity as far as she possibly could. She did her own digging with the consultants too. Through persistence and insistence, it became apparent how unlikely it was that she would be able to shower Mel with love and affection when her youngest celebrated the milestone eighteenth birthday. As always, she was determined to fight against the wisdom of professional opinion, and she wouldn't let it cast a shadow on any upcoming celebrations such as Mel getting her exam results. She would have to continually wrestle with the thought of not being at her little girl's big birthday. But secretly, at least, it helped her to focus more acutely than ever on enjoying the time she had with the people that mattered most to her.

8

'Dad I told you we needed to turn left onto Romsey Road. That sign we've just passed says the town centre is this way, and we need to be heading away from the centre.'

'Yer bum's oot the windae!'

The frustrated lad smacked the palm of his hand against his forehead.

'For crying out loud, why don't you ever listen to me?'

'Oi, Lewis!' snapped Derek. 'I'm doing the driving sunshine, right?'

Derek glanced quickly to his left. He smirked and nodded in the direction of the prison as they passed it on the left-hand side.

'Any more of that from your gob and you'll be visiting me in that place once they've sent me down for my actions.'

Lewis sulked. He turned himself towards the door, trying to create a barrier between him and his dad. He placed his mouth on his fist and muttered under his breath.

'They can lose the bloody keys for all I care.'

Derek didn't like confrontation. One thing he had learnt from living in the high rises of Toryglen as a lad was that being a strong, together family unit was vital to get by. It was something no one could take away from you, a positive strength in being able to face up to the impoverished conditions that some of the families faced in the same block as him. A breakdown in the family unit only exacerbated all the other problems and challenges.

Mel piped up with her contribution. She didn't always have much in common with Lewis, but she would stick up for him if someone else tried to take advantage.

'Come on dad, he was right though, wasn't he?'

'Ay, the gobshite got *something* right for once, he did,' Derek quipped, and winked at his son. The friction in the car dissolved instantly.

After a pit-stop at the County Arms to seek clarity from the locals that they were finally going the right way, the car eventually turned into Bryon Avenue. The quiet cul-de-sac was scattered with large, detached properties, including the one whose drive they pulled onto at number thirty-six. The sound of their car engine prompted some activity inside, and Mel saw someone stand up from where they were sitting and glance out of the window. The woman that opened the front door did so tentatively, unsure of whom the three unexpected guests were.

Derek introduced himself and set about explaining to Mrs Crofts the circumstances for which resulted in them being on her doorstep. Throughout his revelation Mel and Lewis watched their dad talking, with admiration at how calm he remained so that Mrs Crofts understood the gravity of the events on the cathedral green without being panicked by them. Nonetheless, Mrs Crofts was flabbergasted. Such was the modesty of Ali's nature that she had completely played it down to her mum and dad in her own version. Delicately, Derek asked whether the family could take the opportunity to thank Ali for her selfless act.

'I realise that we may have burdened you with some fright Mrs Crofts, but you would be doing us a huge favour if we were able to pass on our gratitude to your wonderful wee girl.'

'Goodness, how rude of me. Yes, yes of course you can Mr Burchell. Please come inside all of you.'

'Oh please, call me Derek. This is my lass Mel, and my laddie here is Lewis.'

The three Burchell family members stepped inside the large, open entrance. The floor was beautifully furnished with ceramic tiles, and the decor was immaculate just like a show home. It was light and welcoming, and Mrs Crofts was doing her best to emulate it as a host now that she had collected herself once again after listening to the details of Poppy's collapse.

'It's nice to meet you, and you're all very welcome. Excuse me for one moment.'

She broke off to alert her daughter to the arrival of the family, planting her foot on the bottom step of the staircase and stretching herself vertically as if to give her voice every opportunity of being heard to the rooms upstairs. 'Alison! Could you come down into the hallway please love? There are some people here to see you.'

Maybe it was a build-up of feelings over the course of the previous twenty-four hours, or perhaps just raw emotion for the person that had been so willing to help their own mum, but no sooner had Ali appeared on the corridor than Mel raced towards her and practically leapt on the girl. She wrapped her arms around Ali and preceded to bear hug the startled peer.

'Thank you so much for everything you did yesterday. Without you I just don't know what we'd have done.'

Ali was completely overwhelmed, clueless about how to respond to the affection gushing from the girl attached to her. Once Mel had loosened her grip, the pale-faced heroine looked up to a row of faces smiling at her. She was, ordinarily, a girl who was unruffled. The perfectly straight bobbed hair she usually wore had been tousled by Mel's outpouring. Feeling completely self-conscious she ran her hand through it and tried to compose herself. It was feeling rather over-crowded in the hallway.

'Alison, you never told me half of what happened yesterday. I'm told you did something quite incredible,' a stunned Mrs Crofts declared. 'The Burchells have called round with news about the lady you helped.'

'Hi Alison, I'm Derek – Poppy's husband.'

Derek was nudged by Mel who less than discretely corrected her dad.

'It's Ali.'

'Oh, I'm ever so sorry. That's not a good start now is it?'

'No that's fine. Really. My parents usually call me by my full name. I only get called 'Ali' by friends at school.'

'Yeah my parents call me Melanie when I'm in trouble!' joked Mel.

'Which is a lot of the time,' muttered Lewis.

'Anyway, these are for you.'

Derek presented a bouquet to Ali. Mel had chosen them at the florist inside the hospital visiting area. There didn't seem to be an abundance of choice, but she thought that the combination of yellow, white and red flowers was poignant as it included colours on the flag of Antigua. Poppy would have approved, just as Mrs Crofts did.

'Oh, they're beautiful, Mr Burchell!' Mrs Crofts announced.

'Yes, they are,' Ali agreed. 'Thank you so much, you shouldn't have, there was no need. I just happened to be there, and I couldn't ignore someone in trouble.'

'Well, Poppy would tell you that's an understatement. Truly, these blooms don't go anywhere near far enough to say how grateful we are that you helped to...' Derek paused. He looked at Mrs Croft. What a dilemma to be in. He didn't want to devalue the significance of Ali's actions, which helped to save her life. But neither did he want to alarm her mum of the predicament that her own daughter had found herself in. 'Let's just say that we visited her this morning, and thanks to your instinctive reactions she's recovering very well.'

Helen Crofts alleviated any further awkwardness in the confines of the hallway by inviting everyone through to the lounge for a drink, but Ali had other ideas.

'Mum, is it ok if me and Mel go up to my bedroom please?' she asked, and they needed no second invitation following the nod of approval given to them by Mrs Crofts to skip quickly out of the corridor and thunder up the stairs.

Once the girls arrived in the bedroom and closed the door, Mel turned to Ali and felt the need to explain her show of affection from earlier.

'I'm really sorry if I embarrassed you earlier. I'm a very touchy-feely person.'

'Honestly, it's not a problem Mel. I'm sorry if I seemed a bit cold. I'm not really used to touchy feely.'

'The thing is, what you did… I think you're amazing Ali. I can't believe that we're the same age. I wouldn't have had a clue what to do if you hadn't been there.'

'Have you never done any first aid training at school or a club then?' Mel shook her head. 'Anyone who's done the training has an idea of what to do, and all I did was remember what I've been shown to do. You should thank the teachers at our school if you're looking for people to praise.'

Typically of Ali, she tried to deflect the attention and compliments away from herself, and the conversation shifted.

'Shit, can I just say, you've got a mad room? It's massive!'

'Thanks. Do you want some music on?'

'You've got a stereo stack? Argh, that's so nice. I've asked for one for Christmas. I've not even got a CD player at the moment, just a crappy cassette player. Can I look through your CDs?'

'Yeah, in that box over there.'

Ali watched Mel's dazzling green eyes light up as she flicked through each CD case. She was very expressive with her body language. Occasionally she screwed her nose up at something she didn't like and held the case up while looking over in comical horror at Ali who giggled.

'Really? Pink Floyd? My own dad loves that stuff!'

'So does mine! I went with him to see them last year in London. I didn't expect to like it, but they were amazing!' Ali further attempted to counter the mickey taking. 'I mean, 'Dark Side' - that's a classic.'

Mel's mouthed dropped open, unconvinced by the argument being put forward.

'You've got no taste,' protested Ali.

'*I've* got no taste? Well, what's this – Enya!?' Mel shrieked, as the banter around musical differences continued.

Ali certainly did have an eclectic mix of tastes, and there was nothing particularly evident in the CD storage box that would characterise what type of person she was. Mel finally laid her hand on something she deemed acceptable.

'Ooh, my bro went to Glasto in June and saw these.'

Mel thrust an Oasis CD in the air and nodded towards the CD player to seek Ali's blessing to put in on.

'Sure, be my guest,' she answered.

Ali had already registered that Mel was mixed race, and as she perused the music collection Ali found herself noticing other aspects of the girl's appearance. Mel was slim, and her sweater drooped off her frame. She had beautifully toned, olive skin that reflected the light pouring through the window. Her dark hair was thick and wavy rather than the tight curls of an afro. She was quite tall, or at least it seemed that way to Ali who was definitely shorter having stood next to her in the hallway. While Ali was by no means large, she was less slender than Mel, and in contrast she had pale skin, which did little to disguise the colour of her blushing whenever she was embarrassed. Ali waited for Mel to fumble around with the CD player before instigating another topic to chat about.

'I can't imagine how hard it must be to deal with your mum's condition Mel?'

'It's been getting worse quite slowly, so we hadn't really seen a change, but recently it's been more noticeable. She tries to live her life like there's nothing wrong. That's how we ended up in town. She shouldn't be walking any kind of distances.'

Mel felt comfortable speaking to Ali because she seemed genuinely interested in what was being said.

'She's not changed as a person. She's still my mum. She still nags me endlessly!' The girls chuckled empathetically.

'Yeah, I know exactly what you mean about getting grief from parents.'

Ali was an only child, and she felt that the expectation levels of her parents were set very high for her. It wasn't something she wanted to expand on with Mel at this point. It might have given a poor impression of herself or allow Mel to think she was a geek. Conversely, though the two girls barely knew each other, Mel was at ease in using the opportunity to completely open up.

'Can I tell you something though, Ali?'

It was noticeable that the tone of Mel's voice had changed. It was softer, less excitable. Ali didn't know how to respond but felt obliged to do so.

'Sure, you can – should I be worried?' she asked hesitantly.

'Ha. No, you shouldn't be, but I am.'

Mel's reply was hardly reassuring, and Ali could now feel her own heartbeat. She *was* worried. Mel continued.

'It's just…I've never told anyone this before.' And then she paused.

'Are you sure I'm the person you want to speak to about it, Mel? I mean, what about your family? You're obviously all close.'

Mel was looking down at her hands and gently shook her head. She didn't want to share the fears she had with them, she felt it would worry them unnecessarily.

'Whatever happens Ali, you will be someone I will have in my heart forever for what you did for my mum. I'm thinking we might be mates for a very long time, right?'

'I hope so, yeah.'

Ali was touched. She was not exactly a loner but was not overabundant in the friendship department. It felt nice to be wanted as much as this.

'Well, there's something you need to know then. It's about

my mum's condition. The thing is...' she took an in-take of breath before continuing and lowered the tone. 'The thing is it could be passed onto her children.'

Ali stared at Mel. Her mouth was agape, and her raised eyebrows forced her eyes to bulge.

'So, have you got it too, Mel?' asked Ali in disbelief.

Mel shrugged her shoulders.

'How would you know then?' Ali tried to enquire sensitively.

'Me and Lewis have had our bloods tested as kids, genetic screening I think they call it. We were both fine at the time. And we're told to look out for any symptoms, like if we develop difficulties with our muscles.'

Ali wondered if Mel was going to hit her with a bigger bombshell.

'And have you? I mean, been feeling any difficulties?'

'No. Well, not that I've been aware of. But they reckon there's a fifty percent chance that we could end up with the symptoms at some point. So, I keep worrying about the day when they suggest we get tested again. And then the horrible wait for the results. It just kills me thinking about it, and what if....?' Mel broke off, and a friend's arm folded itself around her shoulders. 'Thank you ever so much for listening to me Ali, and I'm sorry for landing that on you.'

'We're mates now, right? So, part of the deal is we'll support each other through the bad times and laugh together in the good times.'

This simple translation of their new bond was greeted with receptive smiles. Ali was by nature a rescuer, someone who wanted to help another, even if they didn't ask for it. Added to that, she was not used to this newfound close friendship that was being formed, and so the situation unfolding in her room was quite alien to her. Her thought process was that if she could demonstrate her own insecurities too it might somehow help Mel feel better.

'I think we've got to an age where we understand things a bit better, and so we worry more about it,' was Ali's preamble to telling Mel about something that was bothering her. 'Can I tell you something that I've not been able to speak to anyone else about either, Mel?'

As completely unexpected as this was for Mel, it was a perfectly timed distraction from her preoccupation. Mel was not being expected to abandon her own distress, rather it was an acknowledgement of how she might be feeling. It would be fickle of her not to return the favour for Ali.

'Well I'm not going to say 'no' am I?'

'Ok, here goes. When we go back to school in September, I'm going to be head girl for the year.'

'Really? That's amazing!' exclaimed Mel excitedly. However, the sour look on Ali's face painted an altogether different picture of reality.

'I know I should be over the moon. But you don't understand. I'm so nervous. I'm feeling physically sick at the thought of representing the school at events or speaking in assemblies. It's probably my worst nightmare.'

Mel was confused, so sought some clarity before offering any words of wisdom.

'How come you went for head girl if you knew you would find it difficult to deal with, Ali?'

'I didn't. It'd be the last thing I would have put myself forward for. I was chosen by the teachers. They get to vote for who they think should be the sixth form head boy and head girl. I don't think I really had a choice once they'd offered it to me.'

'Yeah, but you must have done something really worthy of earning their votes, otherwise someone else would have been chosen?'

There was no time to explain. A look of despair flooded both of their faces when they heard Mrs Crofts shouting upstairs that Derek and Lewis were ready to leave. It was mid-afternoon by this point, and Derek wanted to get home. He was beginning to feel fatigued by relentless worry, coupled with a lack of sleep and insufficient nourishment.

'Oh bugger! That's crap timing.'

Mel's expletive was as much an explosion of frustration at not getting the full range of gossip as it was an attempt to express an apology for the hasty exit. 'I'm really sorry Ali. If things were not so difficult at the moment, I'd ask my old man to come back later to collect me, so you could finish off telling me more about it.'

Ali was consoled by the fact that she'd been able to open up to someone who appeared genuinely interested in her feelings.

'Don't worry about it. We can meet up again soon if you like. Besides, you've got far more important things playing on your mind Mel. I'll give you my phone number if you ever want to call me.'

Ali scribbled the digits on the back of a discarded envelope, folded it as if there was some kind of secret code, and handed it to Mel.

9

With Robert only living a few metres away, Mel spent much of the next week in his company. He quickly became a rock of support, listening to her concerns regarding Poppy's condition. She was able to pour her heart out to him without fear of a negative reaction being inflicted onto her already confused state of mind. A little bit of dependency began creeping in. In Robert she had found someone who didn't patronise her by flippantly claiming that everything would be fine, or that she was too young to fully understand.

Robert always had a sensible perspective on the issues that concerned Mel, and he brought her up when she was feeling most down. But then, he refused to ponder on negatives for too long anyway. He had learnt from his own experience that over analysing a situation could only lead to a head full of hurt. Robert's dad walked out on his mum when he was just a small boy.

'Do you mind me asking why he left, Rob?' asked Mel gingerly.

Robert puffed his cheeks. He was stalling, trying to think of a valid explanation, but one that he could use to avert from having to tell the truth. He looked up at Mel. Her pretty green eyes were so full of expectancy that he knew he had to be genuine with her.

'He went off with someone else – another woman.' He surprised himself with how bluntly he responded.

Mel hadn't expected that. 'Bloody hell Rob, that's horrible – for you and your mum. Do you miss him?'

It was an obvious but most sincere follow up.

'Yeah, but it's difficult to miss a hazy memory. I can't really remember him too well.'

Robert shrugged convincingly, just like the previous matter of fact answer he had given. But this time he was bluffing and withholding his true feelings. Other than his mum, it wasn't something he had ever elaborated on with another person, preferring to feel as though the emotional bunker he had built for himself gave him the support to get on with his life. He feared that to displace that emotional protection and open up about the hurt would send him into a turmoil where he thought he would lose control.

He remembered only too well how heartache and heartbreak had rained heavy in the house for him and his mum when the man vanished. Mary reminded Robert from time to time about the distressing story of how she found him curled up asleep on the mat by the front door like a pet on more than one occasion after his father had left. As a young boy Robert had convinced himself that his best friend would be walking back through the door at any moment, and he wanted to be there to greet the returning loved one. In the darkness of night, half asleep and with his head spinning with hope, he would creep downstairs quite trance-like and collapse where his dad would be able to find him. In his innocence as a small child it just felt right for him to do that. It did nothing to curb the confusion, and it only added to the painful realisation that his dad wasn't coming back. Over time, he and his mum developed the bond and togetherness that only the best of friends can relate to. But it was warmer and deeper than that too. The love they had for each other gave them both the strength to move past this huge setback. Or so it seemed.

Robert resolved to always remain positive and upbeat, and this was what made Mel feel comfortable in his company. It was also the reason why she fell short of ever explaining to him that myotonic dystrophy was hereditary. She considered that even Robert might try to dismiss the potential severity of the medical condition with an optimistic overlay. This wasn't something that could be rescued with positivity, so instead Mel would withhold those conversations until she met up with Ali.

'Anyway, he's an arsehole.'

'How do you know that Rob? You were only six.'

'He left my mum, didn't he? She's an unbelievable person. That's all the evidence I need.'

True to his personality, Robert didn't allow negativity to dwell within the conversation for too long and was interested in finding out how the visit to Ali Crofts' house had gone at the weekend.

'She seems like a nice girl, a really sound person,' commented Mel.

She was coy about their conversations, other than alluding to the depth of gratification that was shown to Ali for her actions.

'Don't worry Rob, my mum has stored up a great big hug for you when she gets out as well,' she teased.

'Nah, I still feel really bad for suggesting the walk up into town. What Ali did? Wow, now that's definitely something that she ought to be praised for. Completely amazing!' advocated Robert. 'And she's such a lovely, modest girl. Hates being in the limelight.'

It was hard not to be struck by how well Robert seemed to know Ali's personality. Without elaborating on the conversation that the girls had shared, she concurred with Robert that Ali preferred living under the popularity radar.

'Do you know her well then, Rob? I mean, do you knock around with her at school?'

Robert was less comfortable in the conversation now that it was focussing on his association with Ali. Nonetheless, he believed Mel was someone he felt he could confide in.

'To be honest Mel, I wish I knew her better than I do. The thing is, I'm rubbish at chatting girls up. I don't know how to tell Ali how much I like her.'

Mel was thrown by the revelation and felt the blood rushing to her head. Firstly, she had not expected such a heartfelt response from Robert. Secondly, the tingle she experienced going down her spine confused her. Was it a bolt of jealousy on hearing that Robert liked someone else? Mel had a flashback to their infamous walk in the town. Something had obviously gone on between the two of them that she was not privy to, and maybe that explained Chinny Jewkes winking overdramatically at Robert when he mentioned seeing 'Croftsy' on his travels. She was embarrassed at how ridiculous it was of her to think that something had gone on behind her back, when Rob and Ali knew each other before Mel had arrived in town. It just didn't seem right that it wasn't already out in the open, and no doubt created smoke and mirrors for people to speculate on whether Robert's fondness for Ali went any deeper.

Both Mel and Robert began to feel awkward, and while they both sensed it, they didn't want the other to know it. There was a brief, stony silence while Robert pondered how careless he had been for revealing his thoughts about Ali. He dared not repeat it, and hoped that Mel misheard him, or perhaps just misunderstood. It was wishful thinking on his part.

'Do you think she likes you, Rob? Like, has she given you any indication that she's into you? Or said anything to make you think she is?'

Robert screwed his face up. His poker face gave Mel no indication as to whether he knew if Ali liked him or not. In truth, he wasn't completely sure. Robert got the feeling of being hot round the back of his neck, and for some reason his hearing felt muffled as if he were submerged in water. It was his turn to feel weird. He didn't know whether it was because of Ali, or because of Mel's edgy reaction. He was genuinely unsettled. Sensing she had outstayed her welcome, and not wanting to be part of another frosty moment, Mel made her excuses to leave.

'I've gotta get going mate. My mum should be coming out this weekend, so I'd better make sure the house is as tidy as possible. It's been so weird being in a new house and her not being here.'

The sofa in Mary Ainscow's living room had seen better days. As Robert and Mel moved to get up, they had to press the palms of both hands onto the saggy cushions and push up. As they did so in unison, the cushions sank, and her hand squeezed on top of his causing them both to stop in their tracks. They turned to look at each other. This was not a laugh-it-off moment as friends might do ordinarily, and the way they looked into one another's eyes suggested there was a mutual feeling beyond friendship. Robert blushed uncontrollably – again. Mel stood up, and in doing so the cushion she had sat on fell onto the floor. She bent down to put it back in its place, plumping it beforehand like she had seen her own mum do countless times. Her heart was racing, and she dared not look at Robert directly.

Instead she spent an inordinate amount of time arranging all of the scatter cushions. Out of the corner of her eye she noticed that Robert had moved away, giving her licence to make her move for the door that led to the hallway and front door. Although she didn't glance back, Robert followed her like a shadow and placed his hand on the catch to open the door for her.

The coolness of the air outside rushing through the doorway contributed to her regaining her senses. Turning to look at Robert standing close by her side, she smiled, then reached over to whisper in his ear.

'This past week feels like I've known you forever, Rob. Thanks for spending time with me.'

She pecked her stunned neighbour softly on the cheek as she squeezed past him and hurriedly made her way home.

Neither of them knew what that kiss meant. Robert stood in the doorway for an age, his mind all fuzzy. He went between smiling and shaking his head, swaying between convincing himself it was nothing to dwell on, and then to being embarrassed that it meant something. 'What the bloody hell are you doing Robbie boy?' he asked himself out loud but was not able to answer his own question.

He had started a conversation indicating that he liked Ali, and ended the evening mixed up about a girl that wasn't even in the equation until then. He wanted to regain control of this unusual situation, contemplating what would happen the next time he saw Mel, which was likely to be sooner rather than later given the proximity of their homes. He determined to play it cool and casual as though he was unaffected, acting as far removed from confused as was possible.

Mel tossed and turned in bed for what seemed like half the night, replaying the final few minutes of the previous evening with Robert in her mind. It was so surreal, it seemed like it never happened, and she had a job to convince herself that it really did. She fell into a slumber when her mind had been trashed by over-analysis, and it was mid-morning when her dad woke her up with a cup of tea.

10

The journey to the urban estate at the bottom end of town was a short ride from the hospital, and yet it was enough for Poppy to begin nodding off. A combination of medicinal overload and lack of sleep in a strange bed and environment was taking its toll. As she was wheeled in from the car, Poppy glanced over to the front of the house. She shook her head in a disapproving manner and started tutting.

'He had but one job to do, and he not even finish that properly.'

Yes, Poppy Burchell might have had a scrape with her own mortality, but she had come back home seemingly fighting fit, and already expressing her discontentment at Lewis' inability to weed. All seemed perfectly normal when she was dishing out the grief, and for once Lewis and Mel were more than happy to be on the receiving end of it. Echocardiograms concluded that her condition was worsening. To ensure her heart rhythm was stabilised, the cocktail of pills in her prescription would now also include mexiletine. The move over the county boundaries had reaped its rewards for being able to access that. After nine days apart, the Burchells could now take time to become habituated to family life in a new house, in a new street, in a new town.

The following weekend, Mel was able to meet up with Ali again. It felt like there was much to catch up on, matters to be resolved, and issues to be concluded. Before the gossip could commence, the teenagers had to hurdle the inevitable fuss of Ali's parents, understandably keen to hear news about Poppy's wellbeing. Standing once again in the hallway of the Crofts' house, Mel had to wrestle with a fit of childish giggles that was threatening to pour out. Ali was perched on the top step in her sightline mimicking puppets talking with her hands while Mel attempted to hold a sensible conversation with the adults. The more she tried to hold back the giggling in her throat, the more they tried to force their way out. She held it together with a demented grin and by talking through clenched teeth, as if imitating a ventriloquist.

'Thank you for asking, Mr and Mrs Crofts. She's been quite tired most days meaning she's had to have plenty of rest. That's quite unusual for my mum. She's usually the busy bee.'

Though she had been perfectly polite, the look on Mrs Crofts face spoke volumes of what she was thinking about Mel's unorthodox behaviour. Nonetheless, Ali's parents reiterated their kind offer to help in any way, before the girls disappeared upstairs like archetypal teenagers.

'How have you been then Mel? Bet it's so good having your mum home?'

'Can't begin to tell you how relieved I am. But it's really weird, 'cos we're all still getting used to the new house as well. She's so pleased to be in her own surroundings. Oh, and I've got something important to ask you.'

On hearing that, Ali was doubly alert.

'What? Come on, tell me!' she insisted, only for Mel to tease her by turning her head away with a wry smile.

'It might not seem the most exciting thing for you. But for my mum it means more than you can know. She wants to hold a small tea party to be able to thank you for your part in rescuing her the other week. Ali, I know just by looking at the expression on your face that you're gonna hate being in the limelight like you told me the other week. But it's also a party for getting our exam results, so my mum wondered whether there was a way to invite some school friends too if they can make it.'

That perplexed Ali. She was hardly the girl to ask to coordinate a posse of students, though Mel wasn't to know that yet.

'Your parents are invited too. Look, you don't have to say anything, just smile at the people who'll probably embarrass you by clapping. It'd honestly mean the world to my mum. You'd be helping me a bit too by inviting other people who might be going into sixth form, so I'll feel less of a newbie on the first day.'

Ali felt chuffed that Mel considered her to be a girl of such popular prominence. If only that were the reality. Ali tried to hide how bewildered she was at the task of getting a group of friends together. Besides, she already knew someone who could be relied on to muster up the requirements better than she could.

'Ok, ok I'm sold. I'll be there. It's unbelievably sweet of your folks, I'm really touched. I just don't want her to feel that I'm that special.'

Mel chuckled, 'I can't promise you that she'll ever stop thinking that about you, Ali.'

'When's it going to be?'

'Erm, last weekend before going back to school I think, on the Saturday. Don't tell me you're on holiday?'

'That would be too convenient, wouldn't it?'

'I promise I'll call you when I've told my mum the good news, and she's had time to think the arrangements through properly. Anyway, enough of this Alison Crofts, I wanna know about your thing.'

'Eh? What thing?'

Ali's attempts to sound oblivious were a poor performance. She knew exactly what Mel was getting at. Mel tutted at her attempted ignorance.

'Oh, that? Yeah, we got interrupted, didn't we? What did I even tell you?'

'You were going to tell me how you were chosen for head girl 'cos it wasn't something you exactly wanted? Ooh, before you do though, I've been thinking. There must be a head boy that you'll be working with together as a team, so couldn't he help you out if there were things that you didn't like doing?'

Ali's face beamed. She was picturing the person Mel spoke of as she digested the helpful suggestion.

'You're right Mel, he would help me. Fortunately for me, it just so happens that he's damn good at hogging the limelight and speaking in assemblies. He's got way too much confidence, but he's a really good guy,' she sniggered.

Mel was utterly intrigued.

'Who the heck is it? Not Chinny Jewkes?'

'No way. Confident, not arrogant.'

'Who then?'

'It's Robert.'

Mel tried desperately hard to conceal how stupid she felt.

'Oh, I can't say he's mentioned anything to me about that. I wonder why he didn't say anything when we talked about sixth form.'

She had grown close to Robert for sure, but the way her stomach dropped at this information was absurd. Just like the other evening when the mercury levels were rising with him, Mel couldn't understand the tinge of jealousy that shot across her. The only rational explanation was the sense that the feelings Robert held for Ali were mutual. Mel felt gutted, but she dared not let on that she and Robert shared an intimate moment together. For a start she hadn't figured that one out herself yet. Neither was she was going to tell Ali that Robert liked her. After all, that was a private conversation that took place between the two of them. The conversation needed steering away from herself quickly in case she dropped a clanger.

'So, go on then Ali, fill me in on how that all came about.'

Back in February at school, Ali had been asked to organise some war poems on a display board in preparation for a parents' evening. These were the products of the third-year history pupils who had been studying what life was like in the trenches during World War I. The display board was in a corridor that linked the main reception at one end to the canteen at the other end. Sandwiched in between was the school hall where whole school assemblies took place. It was along this corridor where parents would filter when they attended an event at the school, and as always, the senior staff were keen to ensure the fruits of their pupils' efforts were highlighted and on show for all to see.

As she was pinning the arrangement together, Ali noticed another pupil hanging around in the canteen area. Oliver 'Gammy' Gemmill was a scrawny looking kid. He was a loner, who bore the brunt of a significant amount of abuse from other pupils. His appearance was mostly unkempt, and personal hygiene was something that didn't seem to be a priority for him. He was therefore an easy target for playground hooligans. Nonetheless, he never reacted in a way to aggravate the teasing he endured. In class at least, he worked hard, and the teachers liked him. When he spoke, he seemed a nice, polite lad.

Ali couldn't help but notice him because the end-of-lunchtime bell had sounded a while beforehand, and he wasn't in his lesson. He was acting suspiciously, looking around twitchily to make sure no one else was in the vicinity. The reflection on the glass doors of the corridor must have camouflaged Ali because he seemed not to notice she was there. Had he seen her, it was unlikely that Ali would have witnessed what happened next. Oli started stooping into the waste bins that were used by pupils to throw away their rubbish – usually the remains of food. He began pulling things out of the bin intermittently. Ali thought he may have lost something, or maybe someone had cruelly thrown his books and stationery in there. However, when he then began to eat one of the items, she quickly realised that he was actually scavenging. She saw him put at least two of his finds into his bag before disappearing, presumably to lessons.

Ali found it difficult to assimilate what she had seen. Throughout the next week she found herself spying on Oli so much it became an obsession, but he was difficult to track. She wondered whether the main reason why he was a loner was so that he could be invisible, and less likely to draw attention to himself. In that way people wouldn't notice him scavenging. Ali thought she glimpsed him looking through bins before morning registration and at break time, but she needed to find a way to be able to see for sure whether he regularly checked them at the end of every lunchtime too.

Over the next couple of weeks, detective Ali managed to excuse herself from the start of different lessons that were immediately after lunch. She would politely ask to be excused to go to the toilet. Most staff would have blatantly refused to allow a kid to leave the lesson, arguing that there was plenty of time for personal relief during the lunch break. But Ali was a reliable and trustworthy pupil, top of the academic list in most classes. So, although it smacked of a lack of consistency or even favouritism, her teachers were none the wiser and sanctioned the request.

Ali crept around the vicinity of the canteen to watch Oli rummage through the garbage. It was difficult to know who was more surreptitious; Ali for conning her teachers to get out of lesson or Oli for wanting to forage through the waste bins. During one of her missions, Ali nearly jumped out of her skin when she heard someone whisper next to her.

'What the bloody hell are you doing Croftsy?'

It was Robert Spitley on an errand from another class. Robert was popular with staff and his peers, mostly because he represented the school in a range of activities, including sport. As Ali didn't follow the same interests as him, she didn't mix with the same people as Robert. She only knew him from some of the classes they shared. Before she even had time to think of a reasonable fable, he looked in the direction where Ali had been peering.

'Why are you spying on Gammy? Flipping 'eck, do you fancy him?'

Ali tried to hush Robert as he snorted, but Oli had heard the disturbance and disappeared instantly, glancing back as he left.

'I saw you blagging to be excused by Mr Williams before you went into his class. You must have it *really* bad for Oli. Don't worry Croftsy, I'll put a good word in for you,' Robert teased.

'No! Don't be stupid Robert,' pleaded Ali, but the jester in front of her continued with his comical rhetoric. Until, that is, she did something completely out of character. She hit her tormentor on the arm and proceeded to castigate him.

'If you stop being a prat for one minute you might be shocked to know what I saw him doing. Mind you, you're stuck so far up your own back side that I doubt you'd have the maturity to deal with it.'

Robert had never been on the receiving end of a verbal assault like that from a girl. It not only grabbed his attention and respect, but right there in that moment he liked Alison Crofts in a way he could never imagine he would. He felt his stomach churning weirdly as he looked at her. Ali never spoke out rudely like that ordinarily, but she didn't want Robert Spitley to think that he could overwhelm her. Despite this, the fact of the matter was that she respected Robert for his ability to deal with the limelight he got at school. Being popular and regularly being paraded in assemblies was not something that Ali could ever feel comfortable with in the way that he did.

'Ok Ali, wind your neck in,' said Robert cautiously. 'I was only taking the piss, but I'm sorry. You have honestly got my full attention if you want me to help you,' he continued, ever so sincerely. Ali's gut feeling was that his offer was genuine.

'You won't believe what I've seen, Robert, but you have to believe what I tell you. I just don't know what to do next.'

'Alright, but not here and not now. I've gotta get back to class.'

Robert had been absent for longer than was necessary to deliver a note to reception. Miss Woodley in maths would be sure to quiz him if he delayed for much longer. 'How about I walk back with you after school, and you can speak with me then?'

Ali nodded, and they agreed to meet opposite the main gates after their last lesson.

The sight of the two classmates walking together brought some inevitable sniggering and mocking from other pupils. Unsurprisingly, the key instigator was Chinny Jewkes who couldn't resist trying to wind Robert up. Fortunately, it did not last for too long as Ali and Robert walked a different way to her house than most of the other King Alfred's pupils. It finally gave them the privacy they needed to talk about Gammy Gemmill. It was a long, slow walk back to Ali's place. Robert listened with astonishment and kept stopping in his tracks to take in the information that Ali was giving him.

'You're shitting me. Gammy, a bin-dipper? Just can't believe it!'

'One thing, Robert – can you stop calling him 'Gammy'? Doesn't what I've told you make you feel even slightly guilty that the lad probably can't help what he looks like if he doesn't even eat?'

Robert puffed his cheeks out.

'I hadn't stopped to think. I feel really bad now.'

They lingered on the street corner near to Ali's house for an eternity while they devised a plan of action, perched against the street sign. Both agreed that they would need to involve someone senior at the school.

'Not Atkinson. He's a knobhead and probably wouldn't give a toss. It's got to be Mrs Simmons, she's sound.'

Ali might not have described the head and deputy head in quite the same way, but Robert was right in his assessment of Mrs Simmons. They were also clear that before doing this, they wanted to speak to Oli himself. Although they had no idea how he would react, Ali suggested that if someone was going to approach the deputy head about him, he would appreciate it more if he knew in advance. And that is what they did.

One lunch time as Oli was ghosting around the school out of sight of the other pupils, Ali and Robert had hidden in an area at the side of an annexe to the main building. This is where the bins from the canteen were emptied. Oli knew it, and from her snooping Ali was well aware that he did. When he heard Robert calling his name, Oli turned to bolt. But when he realised that Alison Crofts was with him it made him stall. She wasn't a pupil who would take it upon herself to taunt him. Very delicately and in a hushed tone, Ali broached the matter with Oli. His head slowly tilted towards the floor in apparent shame.

'I'm not a friggin' charity case. You don't need to get involved.'

Robert intervened and threw his arm around him.

'Listen Oli, whatever it is we're gonna help because we want to. Please, you don't need to worry.'

One of the most popular kids in the school stood reassuring perhaps the least popular, himself guilty of throwing cutting remarks at the disadvantaged peer.

'Now, c'mon Oli mate. What the hell is going on?'

And with that, the lad fell into Robert and sobbed like a baby in disbelief, overwhelmed that someone cared and wanted to understand. This generosity of feeling towards him was an anomaly in his life. Ali watched the tenderness being shown by Robert. It was yet another facet to his character that she hadn't seen before, and she was truly touched by the kindness he was showing to another pupil. Comforting Oli was empowering, giving him the confidence to open up about the adversity in which Ali had discovered him.

'My mum is mentally ill. She has phases where she finds it very difficult to cope and forgets things. Or sometimes she finds the simplest task difficult to deal with as if it's the most complicated thing in the world, and she falls to pieces. I've got a younger brother and sister at primary school too. So, I have to look after them and my mum when she's having a bad day – cooking, washing, cleaning and all that. She has to take lots of tablets, so I put them out for her in the morning to make it easy for her. The thing is, she doesn't have many good days.'

'Hang on, why can't your dad help?' asked Ali.

'He's not around anymore, he left us. That's when the problems started. She lost her job and claims benefits now. That's the only money we get.'

Robert froze rigid. He knew exactly what being a one parent family could be like. His own mum had the strength to pull through and hold down her job, and that was one huge difference between his and Oli's upbringing. The other difference was the additional, younger children. Oli was, essentially, a young carer with an incomprehensible amount of responsibility. The troubled lad was reluctant to bring it to the attention of the school, concerned about social workers interfering at home, and the adverse effect it might have on his mum. He was also afraid that the information would become public and lead to an increase in the teasing and bullying he already suffered. But at the same time, he understood the concern of his new friends, and that the situation for him couldn't go on as it was. Robert rallied around him once more.

'It doesn't have to be like this Oli, and it won't be from now on – either at home or at school. It's going to get better, and there'll be no more muck throwing aimed at you buddy.'

Oli was already finding it a challenge to overcome his inhibitions, particularly as the suggestion to speak with Mrs Simmons was intended for the very same afternoon at the end of their last lessons. Nervous though he was, Oli agreed to take the issues affecting him and his family by the scruff of the neck. It was during the afternoon that Oli remembered he had to race to pick up his brother and sister from primary school nearby and take them home. By then it was too late to let Ali and Robert know because they were in entirely different classes to him, and neither located in the same block nor corridor. It wasn't as if he could even ask another pupil to pass on a message; being isolated from any social groups had a whole manner of unfortunate drawbacks.

With no communication between them possible, Ali and Robert became anxious when Oli didn't show up in reception. Naturally, they suspected that he was frightened and had bolted, perhaps feeling he had been backed into a corner. It left the other two youngsters with a dilemma about what to do, but unanimously they decided to approach the deputy head regardless.

Mrs Simmons was visibly horrified at the unfolding story of Oli's ordeal being recited by Ali. She was experienced in child protection issues and showed the compassion that Ali and Robert hoped she would. She carefully explained to them that it was her 'professional responsibility to help Oliver' and by informing the necessary authorities, social services would be able to help the family more widely. So serious was the nature of what she had been told that phone calls were conducted that very afternoon to initiate emergency intervention.

There would be no attempts to split the family apart, just a concerted effort to ensure they were getting everything they were entitled to. Mrs Gemmill needed access to appropriate medication to stabilise the symptoms of depression, and in addition she received advice and guidance regarding benefit claims and initiating maintenance demands from the father of her children. Thereafter, regular coordinated meetings were arranged through the school and social services to hold different agencies to account regarding the welfare of the children holistically. Free school meals were immediately arranged, including breakfast. An emergency clothing allowance was passed to the family too. As a result, Oli had far less pressure on his young shoulders to accommodate the well-being of his mum and siblings. The local youth centre provided an outlet for him a couple of afternoons after school so that he could have his own space to enjoy his own interests – boxing became a must.

In the immediate aftermath of these life changing developments there remained two burning issues for the school. Firstly, they needed to find a way to curb the gossip of other pupils as it was immediately obvious that something had happened. When Oli returned to school the following week, he was well-groomed indeed – new uniform, new shoes, and a smart haircut. That only served to heighten the speculation. Secondly, they pondered the idea that if Oli had slipped through the net, then there almost certainly were others in their school that were facing similar pressures of being a young carer. Oli, Robert, and Ali came up with an idea and a plan of their own to help with this. Mrs Simmons agreed for the trio to highlight Oli's plight in an assembly, aimed at educating people to be more understanding and supportive of others that might be in a similar position to him. There was also support for a campaign to encourage young people to be confident about disclosing their problems without fear of being judged or penalised.

Oli's status in school was completely transformed. Kindness and tolerance prevailed where prejudice had existed on a scale which meant someone became an outcast. It was Ali and Robert's willingness to help others, coupled with their support for Oli, that won them unanimous recognition amongst the school staff when it came to vote for lower sixth form head boy and head girl. The awarding of the titles was undeniably well deserved, but unbeknown to those making the decision it wasn't well received by one half of the pairing.

Upon hearing the narrative, Mel was in awe of the efforts of her two friends. She was struck by their solicitude, and the maturity they showed in their pursuit of a positive outcome for a lad who had previously been rejected by all social groups.

'I am totally gobsmacked, Ali. That's a very sad story that's difficult to believe, and I think you're both amazing,' commended Mel. 'Whatever happens this coming year, me and Robert will be there to support you, ok? If you can accomplish something like that, I don't think you've got anything to worry about in that role. From what I just heard you completely deserve to have been voted as head girl.'

Ali smiled, and went to say something else but held back. She exhaled the breath she had taken in to respond to Mel's gushing compliment. That didn't go unnoticed by Mel.

'What?'

'I don't know. I mean…nothing. Thanks for believing in me.'

Mel suspected that wasn't quite what Ali was going to say. She was guarded about something else. In the brief time they had known each other, the girls' friendship had blossomed. They had both chosen to expose fragile aspects of their nature to one another, and in that sense, it had ensured some parity existed between them. They were genuinely content and comfortable at being able to talk together, sharing trivialities, gossip, and girl-crush secrets. Except, that is, when it came to Robert.

They chose to conceal their true feelings about him without either of them properly knowing it. There seemed no logical reason why neither of them wanted to share this with the other, but perhaps they feared a negative reaction, and a backlash that would result in their friendship collapsing. Both girls suspected that the other liked him more than just a friend, and so grew an undeclared suspicion of each other's intentions. There developed an inevitable subconscious rivalry for Robert's attention, and with it a slow, silent, and poisonous growth of jealousy.

11

By the end of August, Poppy had begun using a wheelchair more regularly. Amongst the specialist support available for her to access, an occupational therapist visited regularly. She gave Poppy guidance and confidence to be able to accomplish day-to-day tasks and was also on hand to make suggestions regarding how their proposed extension on the back of the house might best suit her needs. The decisions about design had to incorporate the reality that eventually Poppy could be permanently wheelchair dependent. The building work was scheduled to begin at the end of September.

The autumn term was now imminent for school children, creating last minute panic purchases for essential items and uniform that complied with school policy: new shoes, stationery, bags, and coats. Mel had been mostly preoccupied over the summer months with the new house, new friendships, and supporting her mum with her recovery. Having spent the last week sorting out her equipment, she had started to give thought to her first day. Though Mel was confident that she would be able to adapt to her new surroundings, it was inevitable that there would be a tinge of apprehension. After all, not only was she contending with a different environment, but this academic year would be the start of A Level courses that would define her future plans. The advantage she had of course was that she would be walking through the gates with two people she had got to know well in a short amount of time.

The summer holidays would not end before Poppy and Derek hosted the promised party, primarily to thank Ali for her heroism just a few weeks previously, but also to acknowledge the exam success of all the teenagers too. On the day of the party the clouds loomed ominously during the morning, but by the time the guests arrived, the sun had broken through the murkiness so that people had the option to mingle inside or out.

Ali's stomach had been churning the whole day, knowing that she was going to be the centre of attention at some point during the party, exactly the scenario she despised the most. However rudimentary she continued to believe her involvement to be, she was the one to react instantly to the emergency that presented itself. It was inevitable that the Burchells would forever correlate Poppy's survival with Ali's actions. Poppy's recovery had avoided an emotional catastrophe within a close family unit.

Poppy was in her element being able to socialise. She had invited the neighbours from either side, and immediately hit it off with Mary, much to the amusement of Mel and Robert. Remarkably, the teenagers hadn't seen one another since they had dabbled in their feelings for one another – or at least, not to talk to anyway. One morning in the week, Mel had watched Robert leaving home from her bedroom window, when he practically tip-toed his way to the end of the drive. All the time he was peering over at the Burchell residence to make sure no one was watching him. As soon as he reached the end of his drive, he sprinted off down Wood Street in a bid to stay undetected. That told Mel everything she needed to know. If Robert was embarrassed, then seeing each other for the first time following their moment of confusion would be awkward. The mothers' burgeoning friendship and accompanying frivolity proved to be an effective diversion from them having to hang out together, and the pair managed to avoid eye contact initially.

There was disparity between Robert's prophecy that he would be calm and collected, and the flummoxed state in which he found himself now. He couldn't comprehend if the churning in his stomach was because of his feelings for Ali coupled with guilt for what had happened with Mel. The same thought kept repeating itself inside his head.

'Shit, I've been an idiot to her, and she doesn't even know I like her yet.'

In complete contrast, Mel was poised, almost deliberate in choosing when to begin a chat with her friend.

'Alright Rob? Fancy grabbing a coke from the kitchen?'

Her composure was a pleasant surprise for Robert, immediately removing the possibility of it feeling cringeworthy by speaking to her again. They were on good terms by the time Ali's dad parked up on the road outside.

There was no need for Ali to have had any jitters either. Upon the family's arrival, Poppy and Derek's display of affection for them was genuinely heartfelt. By the time the proclaimed heroine had been able to remove herself from Poppy's clutches, most guests were beginning to salivate at the sight of the jerk chicken being barbequed by Lewis and Mel. Robert joined her in the queue.

'I didn't fancy my chances of being able to rescue you from Mrs B's embrace. She's strong as an ox!'

'Yeah, I know, I've got the marks and bruises as souvenirs.'

Knowing that Robert was going to be at the gathering, it had crossed Ali's mind how she might feel with Mel being around at the same time. She couldn't help feeling that Robert seemed to be quite subdued, and she put it down to the interest in his appetite. On the other hand, Mel was positively exuberant when she got to speak to her friend at the front of the food queue.

'So good to see you!' she squealed.

Ali wondered why on earth she had doubted Mel. There was nothing to concern Ali that being with Robert was going to cause an uneasy feeling between them.

The teenagers camped in one corner of the back garden, while the adults largely congregated in the living room and patio area. The girls turned their attention to starting school after the weekend and were making plans to meet at a convenient crossing point.

'Rob, can you do me a favour please?' It subtly irked Ali that

Mel abbreviated Robert's name. 'Can you take a picture of me and Ali please?'

He put down his plate and glass on the lawn next to him and put the strap of the camera around his neck. To the amusement of the adults watching, he started directing the girls where and how to stand. He was in his element zooming in and out with the lens, as if he had transformed into a professional snapper.

'You'd better take a couple, Robert; you're bound to mess up at least one of the shots!' mocked Ali.

He was lining up the last shot when he stepped backwards, onto the glass he had been drinking out of. The momentum turned his ankle so that he lost his balance and fell backwards. He broke his fall by putting his two hands behind him, and this prevented his backside from hitting the ground and an inevitable grass stain. He stayed static in that position momentarily, with his hips thrust upwards. Mel didn't offer any words of sympathy.

'Bloody hell clumsy, my mum's gonna love you for breaking a new glass. Good job my camera's ok. You look like you're playing twister in that position, Rob. In fact, the way you're posing, you look like a table!'

'Or a crab,' Lewis contributed from the other side of the garden.

Mel took a quick snap to keep as a memory.

'Yeah thanks for helping me girls, don't mind me stuck on the floor,' replied an embarrassed Robert.

With the adults beginning to offer similarly unamusing comments, he attempted to push himself back up, and in doing so he cut his little finger on a shard of the broken glass.

'Bollocks!' he yelped.

Ali could see exactly what he did and bent down to help him up.

'Shh, don't let Mrs Burchell hear that language. Come with me, I'll get you sorted out.'

They left Mel and Derek picking up the debris, and discretely made a beeline through the adults in the living room, so that they did not suspect anything was wrong. In the kitchen Ali held Robert's hand under a running cold tap, and perhaps spent more time holding it than was genuinely necessary. There was not much talking while Ali attended to him. Robert was happy to be a spectator, watching Ali taking control of the situation. He loved that about her, how she just instinctively knew what to do. He certainly didn't feel any pain. She found some kitchen roll and dabbed at the cut.

'Hold this on the cut. I'll be back in a minute.'

Ali borrowed her dad's car keys to get the first aid kit that he kept in the boot. Inside the small pouch there were some antiseptic wipes that were used to clean the cut of any dirt.

'Ouch! That stings,' Robert protested without much conviction.

Ali looked at him with a raised eyebrow as if to suggest he was being ridiculous. After smearing some cream on, she gently stuck a protective plaster over the affected area. Unbeknown to them, Mel had seen the two friends slope off into the house. After helping her dad to clear what remained of the broken glass from the lawn, she went inside to find out where they had disappeared to. When she realised that neither of them had noticed her approach, she stopped and hung back out of view, hovering outside the kitchen to listen to their conversation. She had not purposely intended to do so, but neither did she give up the opportunity to eaves drop.

'Does that feel too tight, Robert?'

'Nope, that feels alright to me. You're good at this, Croftsy. You'd be fantastic at looking after people.'

'This was nothing really. You should always clean a cut properly, but you seemed like a hopeless case so how could I resist helping you?' Ali mocked, and finally released Robert's hand.

Through the kitchen entrance Mel screwed her nose up in snarling fashion, anticipating that Ali was flirting.

'Seriously though Ali, you are just so good in situations where people have stuffed up. Look at what you did for Mrs B, and how you rescued Oli Gemmill. Is it something you've thought about doing when you're older?'

'Hmm, yeah. Maybe. Other lovely people helped me with Poppy and Oli though, didn't they Robert? It always feels easier with someone else to rely on.'

Robert felt himself beginning to blush, and Ali knew it.

'Maybe it's you who rescued me, Greeny – twice!' she taunted.

This was a moment Robert had hoped for, a vacuum when the sound of everything else going on around seems to be blocked out. He was sure that if he told Ali how much he liked her she would respond by saying she fancied him too. Feeling rushed, he panicked and couldn't think of the words to say, and the short lull in their conversation ended. The hubbub from the rest of the house faded back in, and the opportunity seemed to have gone. Mel had continued to listen intensely and didn't recall the chain flushing in the downstairs cloakroom. She felt someone tap her on the shoulder and was startled by the sight of Chinny's smirking face over her right shoulder. His right hand was placed on the top of his head in the shape of a fin.

'Are you sharking, Mel?' he enquired.

It was not a term she was familiar with and frowned in puzzlement.

'What the hell are you on about?'

Chinny offered some clarity. 'Chasing after. You know? Fancy.'

Mel struggled to contain her embarrassment. She wasn't about to let Chinny know her motives for lurking in the corridor by the kitchen. But there were very few options open to her to explain her reasons for loitering. She ended up nodding her head at the entrance into the kitchen, which persuaded Chinny to subtly peer through the door. Somehow this went unnoticed by Ali and Robert, and the lairy teenager wound his neck in with a sudden jerk. The expression on his face immediately indicated that there was a story to be told.

'What?' demanded Mel.

Even though it was delivered in a whisper, the sharpness of the delivery caused Chinny to vacate his smiley expression to one of surprise. It was his turn to nod his head, indicating for Mel to follow him towards the garden.

It was difficult to be inconspicuous outside, and Derek saw Mel come out onto the patio area. He beckoned her to go across to him.

'Hang on dad, I'll be there in a minute,' she called back to him.

She turned around to find Chinny nowhere to be seen. She surveyed the lawn for the easily recognisable grin, but to no avail. She glanced over to the alley way at the side of the house only to be presented with a comical scene. There seemed to be a head with no body attached to it, peering from round the edge. A hand then floated up, beckoning her over. The two of them camped at the far end of the passageway behind the dustbin.

'Hmm, very interesting,' he said rubbing his chin as if there were an imaginary beard.

'Keep your voice down. What is?'

'Those two. Seems to be a bit of a habit them being hidden away in a hush and me finding them.'

'If you keep talking in riddles, I'm going to thump you. What do you mean? That's the first time they've gone in there.'

'Nah, there was another time at school. I was doing the lighting backstage for the end of year awards. That's when they announced the head boy and girl for next year.'

'So, what?'

'I got bored so started mucking about with Harris. I crept off to hide 'cos I was going to jump out on him. I love dicking around backstage, you have to be careful not to be too loud or you'd get caught by the teachers.'

Mel was unimpressed with his childish antics. She dropped one hip, and the look of impatience was embossed on her face. Chinny's smirk disappeared and he continued.

'When I got around to the side curtains, there was Ali and Greeny. They were hugging.' He started sniggering. 'I thought I was gonna piss myself laughing. They started to unglue themselves from each other, so I stooped down and crawled backwards out of view. I got back to the lighting desk before they would have seen me.'

Mel frowned. 'Why were they hugging?'

'Dunno, she didn't look upset from what I could see. They were called on stage just after that, so she couldn't have been crying or anything like that. I reckon they fancy each other.'

'You can't say that just 'cos they were hugging.'

'You weren't there. He had his forehead perched on hers looking into her face. Looked pretty loved up to me. I've seen 'em before having private little chats as well. They spent a lot of time together helping bin-dipper boy as well – a lad called Oli Gemmill.'

'Yeah, Ali told me about him.'

But she most definitely hadn't told her about *that* cuddle. That was a pretty big omission from the conversation between them at Ali's house recently. It now made sense why she seemed to hold back when they were talking about how the head boy might support her. It appeared he had already become a little more supportive than Ali had dared let on.

As Mel was mulling over what she had just learned, Chinny was ill at ease. She was staring blankly at the floor. Even for a lad of limited ability to judge a social situation correctly, it was not difficult to sense that Mel was agitated at what she had learned. Chinny was puzzled – he was only trying to have a laugh, and to stir things up the way always did. He took the lull in conversation as the opportunity to make his way back round to join the other guests.

'I'll see you back round there in a minute yeah?'

'Bastard,' Mel muttered to herself and gritted her teeth. Her head was spinning with more questions than answers. Why the hell had Robert concealed this dalliance too? She was angry that he had gone along with their recent flirtation knowing that something else was brewing with another girl. She didn't understand what was going on and it made her feel vulnerable. Her two mates had frozen her out from something that in her opinion they ought to have told her about. If they were hugging in secret, there was something being concealed. She was desperate to know what it was all about.

In the parallel timeframe that occupied Mel and Chinny, the conversation between Ali and Robert revolved around their plans – or lack of them – for the future.

'Why don't you think about doing the work experience option for your enrichment next year, Ali? That might give you some ideas.'

This was a mature and measured response from Robert. He was hoping to undertake a work placement himself on Wednesday afternoons when students were tasked with developing their skills to enhance any future applications for higher education or employment.

'Yeah that's a good idea. Do you remember those meetings the school set up to help Oli? It had loads of different organisations going along. I'd like to do something like that. Not sure I'd be able to though.'

'Why not? You'd be ace at that.'

'I think all the stuff they talk about is confidential, things only professionals are able to know about.'

From out of nowhere, Robert found his flirting legs.

'You can come and care for me if nothing else works out.'

A mutual, cheeky smile of affection was aimed at one another, but Ali barely had time to play on his suggestion before Mel burst into the kitchen.

'Hey, you two, this is where you've been hiding!'

'I didn't think we'd been gone that long?'

'Sorry Mel, it's my fault for cutting my finger.'

Robert stuck out his index finger as evidence.

'Nice plaster. Couldn't you manage to put that on by yourself you wimp? Ali, I think my mum wants to say a few words. Sorry but you might have to put up with being stared at for a short time. We'll be there though won't we, Robert?'

He nodded in agreement at both girls.

Ali coped with Poppy's extravagant praise admirably, and even attempted a few words of her own. Typically, she parried some of the acclaim onto others who had helped Poppy in equal measures, using the opportunity to display her warm feelings towards Robert by expressing her gratitude to him for his help on the day of Poppy's collapse. That got his heart racing in expectation that perhaps their feelings *were* in tune with one another, and yet he remained hesitant as to whether he was reading the signs correctly or not.

The party concluded and was warmly appreciated by all who attended. Poppy had paraded as if everything was back to normal, inviting many compliments at how well she was looking considering the trauma she had overcome. She managed to mask the tiredness she felt, but it did not fool the community nurse who had been there during the latter end of the afternoon to monitor Poppy's well-being. The nurse was very discrete, but from a distance was able to scrutinise Poppy's social exertions. Once the guests had departed, some bed rest was swiftly encouraged, preceded with a reminder to take her medication. It was a true indication of how tired Poppy was that she didn't resist the suggestion.

For the trio of friends, there were two significant developments resulting from the get-together at the Burchell residence. Firstly, Mel had seen another side to Robert when he was in Ali's company. He behaved differently like he was in awe of her. He was more selective with his immature humour, and it was obvious that he liked her – a lot. Mel was grappling for reasons why this affected her so much, and why she was uncomfortable to think about Ali and Robert being alone in each other's company. She wondered how she was going to be able to overcome this.

Secondly, as Ali stood talking to Mel and Robert after the speeches, the community nurse went across with a proposition for her. On her way to the lavatory the nurse had overheard Ali in the kitchen talking to Robert about ideas for work experience. She offered Ali the opportunity to shadow her, and to accompany her when she visited Poppy. In that way she would get an insight into the network of professionals that helped to support patients in the community with specific difficulties. Despite any prickly feelings she was privately storing, Mel championed the idea immediately, excited at the prospect of her mum getting to spend some time with Ali. What she had not factored into the equation, however, was that this would also mean spending time nearer to Robert, and inevitably the two of them would meet up at his house after her placement on Wednesday afternoons.

12

For the staff at King Alfred's Comprehensive School the academic year began as frantically as ever. Teachers flapped with techniques to remember the names of their new pupils and to become accustomed to lessons with different classes. Clean, new books were distributed with the anticipation that the drying ink on the pages inside would reveal the kids' true talents.

While there were the same negative behaviours from a predictable few, from within the monotony of an academic timetable there were always moments of sparkle that made the complexities of the job worthwhile. They might not be the rewards recognised by some people in the world of work and were anything but a financial kind, but to the trained eye those moments were real gems. If the teacher could inspire their pupils to unleash their imaginations, then the work that followed could throw up those glittering surprises from the most unexpected sources: a page of writing from the one that never usually tries; a confident voice from the one who would never volunteer to read; the correct answer from the one who through self-doubt prefers to stay invisible; homework completed and on time from the one not prepared to sacrifice their ideology that school is a waste of time; a genuine look of pride from the one who never achieved an 'A' grade before. The life of a teacher never a dull moment or devoid of a fresh challenge.

Within a single morning the long holidays that had stretched over the lazy weeks of the summer seemed like memories deep in the past. The faint reminder was the warmth of the sun in a cloudless, blue sky, which teased teachers and pupils alike as they could only view the vista from the confines of a classroom window. It was, in some ways, a blessing then that rainfall ensued at the end of the first week, as it felt like normality had stamped its authority once more.

The newbie tag quickly wore off for Mel. She was adept at the art of adapting, settling into her classes and social groups like she had grown up alongside the other students. She hadn't anticipated it being quite so comfortable but given the genes of her parents it should have been no surprise that she was destined to be a resilient person. Though Ali and Robert did their best to smother her with care and guidance, Mel made a conscious decision to be as independent as possible. If ever the pressure of school versus home life came to the boil, they were of course a nice comfort blanket to have at hand, even if a layer of secrecy had recently been uncovered forming on the surface of their friendship.

The head of drama, Mrs McKenzie, was quick off the mark in getting an announcement round for all tutors to read out regarding the Christmas production of Oliver Twist. Mrs McKenzie was affectionately known as 'Meltdown McKenzie' to the sixth formers, owing to her being prone to becoming increasingly short-fused the closer it got to the opening night of a show. Pupil tittle-tattle suggested that Mrs McKenzie became stricter so that she could hand out more detentions, and then use the kids in those detentions to help on last minute snagging for the show.

But it was a rather public stand up row with a senior staff member that was testament to her nickname. While on his routine duty walk around the school, Mr Randle noticed a hive of activity in the school hall. He tried tactfully to question McKenzie on the academic merit of using pupils in her lesson time for painting scenery, and for his pains the deputy head was lambasted. Fortunately, she refrained from turning the air blue in front of her class, but by the time the said staff member had time to find his voice again he chose sensibly to decline the opportunity to probe any further and exited stage right promptly.

Many fifth-year pupils watched in admiration as 'Meltdown' reduced her colleague to a gibbering wreck for daring to question her judgement. Not that she ever struggled to gain the respect of the children in the school, but the episode was hot gossip for some considerable time for staff and pupils alike. Mrs McKenzie certainly cared deeply about putting on the best show possible.

The drama department was essentially an annexe, equipped primarily from funds raised through past productions. Some assemblies and smaller productions took place in its compact theatre, but larger shows such as musicals were usually staged in the main school hall. The school had a reputation for putting on excellent performances, and the drama department was a vibrant area of the school. Its popularity amongst the pupils was such that it never struggled to cast for roles.

The area where it lacked vogue was behind the scenes. Pupils generally needed to be coaxed into becoming backstage technicians. There was some disparity in personality types between those pupils performing and those in charge of scenery, curtains, and lights. Nonetheless, the tasks performed by the sometimes-cobbled-together backstage team were no less important or effective than their counterparts treading the boards.

It was a welcome surprise that a sixth form student not taking an A Level in drama wanted to volunteer for backstage and lighting duties. Mrs McKenzie was quite overwhelmed by the student's enthusiasm, which verged on being insistent. Then again, Mel was too new at the school to know it wasn't seen as being cool to be one of the techies. When Ali and Robert found out about their friend's intentions, it amused them. They thought it was commendable that Mel was getting stuck into school life, but it wasn't what they expected her to be interested in. At that point they had no reason to be suspicious of her motives.

Mel disguised her reasoning, claiming she wanted to be involved in something out of her comfort zone and entirely different to her regular studies. Ultimately, it was a smoke screen to be able to address the discontent in the thoughts and over-imagination of her mind. Clearly, Robert had already attempted to express his feelings for Ali previously and that had been awkward enough to listen to. But she wasn't prepared to ask or confront her two friends about her suspicions that something had developed between them without concrete proof. Instead she proposed to take a covert response to the situation. It would take someone with too much thinking time on their hands and extreme cunning to rumble her plan. She ought to have realised by then that such a person did exist – Chinny Jewkes matched that description perfectly.

Robert found academic study laborious. It wasn't so much the difficulty of the work; it was more the commitment to the endless stream of homework and organising his own time to study.

'I'm thinking of leaving sixth form, Miss. The thing is, I don't feel like I belong here and just don't like what I'm doing. I'm behind in all my subjects and my work is crap. I hate going to lessons and just don't want to be in classrooms most of the time.'

Mrs Irvine was another member of staff whom students thought of fondly. There was no better evidence of that than her being labelled with a nickname. She was referred to as 'Insomnia Irvine' owing to the wide eyed, fixed expression of someone possessed with fighting their tiredness. The sixth formers mocked that she worked so hard that she had no time to sleep, and the consequences for which was to have such a stare. Students found it difficult to maintain eye contact in conversations with Mrs Irvine, but she was completely approachable. She was a no fuss lady who cared passionately about students fulfilling their potential. She would go out of her way to ensure that they were successful in applications for their chosen post-eighteen plans. Robert sat down with her during one of his free study periods.

'I'll tell you what I know shall I, Robert? Some of your

teachers have spoken about their disappointment in you – the lack of effort and the unintelligent work you've been producing.'

'Pff, say it like it is Miss, you're wounding me.'

'Sorry to dent your ego Mr Spitley, but yours is not a unique speech. You're one of many who feel like they're the victims. Sixth form is hard. Fact. But I'm happy to work something out with you to get you back on track.'

Mrs Irvine felt the need to stick the boot in so that he could appreciate the need to raise his own expectations and to crawl out from the rut he'd fallen into – or get into the real world by making an informed, alternative choice.

'They're not doubting what you are capable of. It's not easy being the underdog when you've often been the outright favourite. You're used to being at the top end of the ability scale in your classes, not struggling with lower grades. But you'd be letting yourself down by just bolting, especially as you're a lad more used to being a game changer.'

Mrs Irvine's calculated reference to a sporting situation certainly resonated with Robert. 'Insomnia Irvine' became more like 'Inspirational Irvine' and a practical discussion ensued about the future which put his current studies into context. His eyes were opened up to the possibilities of pursuing an engineering enrichment programme as part of his studies, and also to the options available after sixth form that didn't necessitate the need to go to university on a full-time basis. Thirty minutes later, one head less scrambled. Motivational batteries back on recharge. The potential torture of the academic challenges suddenly made sense for the goals that Robert had begun to set for himself.

The academic year rolled on relentlessly. Rehearsal schedules for the school play intensified, and 'Meltdown McKenzie' began her metamorphosis from the cool and hip to the prickly and frenetic. Mel became a dab hand at the control panel backstage. She learned how to maximise the value of the stage mics and understood how to mix the lighting to set the appropriate mood for each scene. She was regularly called upon to apply her new skills for assemblies too, and not just those involving the sixth form.

Chinny Jewkes started to sense an ulterior motive when Mel began repeatedly expressing an interest in being involved at the termly address. This was when periodic awards for achievement and attainment were presented, and all kinds of positive progress was highlighted and acknowledged – from sporting endeavours to fundraising for charity. The head boy and head girl also fulfilled their duties by making a statement on behalf of the students. That had started to play on Ali's mind within the first week of term. She and Robert sat next to the head of sixth form and any other dignitaries at all assemblies, which is when Ali would be agonising over the thought of being up in front of that microphone. She often drifted off in those assemblies to begin calculating the number of days, hours and minutes until her pending moment of doom, and began trying to think of all kinds of excuses for not being there on the day. Robert snatched a glance on occasion and could see her preoccupation. He instinctively knew that she was fretting about the presentation they would be delivering.

Writing the words to be spoken came easily to Ali, and as it was done in conjunction with spending time with Robert, it never felt like a burden of duty. He always made light of the fact that they would be on a platform together, and never patronised her nervousness. He always offered reassurance – although not to the extent that he did in the closing assembly before the summer holidays when they were introduced as the head boy and girl to their peers. On that occasion they had found themselves in the wings of the stage, obscured by a partially closed main curtain. In hushed tones Ali began to relay her anguish to her partner.

'Robert, I can't go on.'

'What d'ya mean?'

'There's no way I'm going to walk out there in front of everyone and speak. I can't even move my feet.'

'Don't be a doughnut, Ali. We're going out there any minute now. You can't just not go on.'

He went to play act with her and grabbed her hand.

'Jeez Ali, you're actually bloody shaking!'

'Aren't you cold, Robert? I'm freezing.'

It looked as though she was shivering, but it was more like spasms. They could vaguely hear the lighting techie lads messing about backstage and snorting to disguise their giggling. Although they were out of sight and presumably couldn't see Ali and Robert, it diverted their attention sufficiently enough to snap the fretting girl out of her moment of anxiety.

'I've got your back Ali, we're going to be a team out there, so you're not alone.'

'It's not that... although, thank you. I, I... I'm just shitting myself because I'm rubbish at speaking in front of other people.'

'Well you've got to, Ali. Just think that you're only speaking to me. I'm not so scary, am I?'

Without prompting, they were in each other's embrace. It was almost like they had both been sent the same subconscious message because it was spontaneous and just felt right. No, Robert undisputedly wasn't scary. Ali's mind completely flushed of all the angst she had been feeling. Robert delicately pulled away from her slightly and leaned his forehead onto hers so that they were able to look at one another. The understanding between them through their expressions was as though they had been soulmates forever. He raised his eyebrows which Ali instinctively knew was him asking if she was ok. Automatically she smiled and nodded, or at least tried to as it ended up with her slightly butting each other, which made them both snigger and blush.

Their solace was over. Minutes later the double curtains were opened to their maximum as the two school seniors were introduced and invited onto the stage next to a number of senior staff. Naturally, her peers merely assumed that Ali's blushing was inextricably linked to her embarrassment at having to speak in front of a packed assembly. How ironic it was that her sheepish posture was the result of her battling to control her racing heart that had been instigated by a solitary person.

13

There were few people that could be trusted less with gossip than Chinny Jewkes. As much as he was a good mate to have a laugh with Robert was grounded enough to realise that his friend always went too far with his version of fun and was nothing short of unscrupulous. And yet bizarrely, Chinny was at the centre of unfolding drama for which there was no official rehearsals for the cast. Not only had he been privy to Ali and Robert's stage side shenanigans, but then there was a raking over the coals by Mel before term started regarding that burgeoning relationship.

Previously, his over-imaginative mind had been the root cause for his flirtation with exclusion from school, but even he could sense the quagmire developing between Robert and his two girlie pals. It was just not in his make-up to leave this alone, and he couldn't resist immersing himself further into this entanglement of friends.

Chinny felt intimidated by Mel. She was confident and popular with her peers within weeks of her arrival. He wouldn't step on her toes by asking about those increasingly desperate pleas to be involved with the upcoming termly address. He feared Mel's rebuke and the ripple effect of consequences for upsetting a popular student. Instead he intended to confront Robert.

Chinny had a tarnished reputation because he enjoyed publicly humiliating people, creating maximum embarrassment through mass exposure. He seemed not to have any morality. Uniquely for Chinny, on this occasion he did this with sublime subtlety, tackling Robert by himself after a workout at the school gym. There was the usual macho banter, before Chinny seized his chance.

'What the feck's going on with you, Ali and Mel then

Greeny?'

'You what? Where the hell has that come from, you dick?'

Matching Chinny's less than politically correct language did not wrestle the advantage in Robert's favour as it might have done normally. His maverick friend was relentless in his pursuit of unearthing the plot between the trio, and Robert instinctively went into pass-it-off mode.

'You know exactly what I'm on about, Mr swing-your-pants-in-two-directions.'

'Chinny, you're being a complete twat as usual. We all know your bollocks are bigger than your brain, but it'd be useful if you could think before you speak.'

'Dude, I saw you and Croftsy getting it on.'

'I don't think you did.'

'Oh yeah, before you went on stage at the end of year assembly. You were waiting in the wings, getting jiggy.'

'Like I say, I don't think you did.'

'Greeny, you were so close to her it looked like one person. It took me a while to work out it was two people loving it up!'

'You arsehole! Firstly, I should give you a slap for spying on me. What was that about, you stinking little pervert? Secondly, Ali's my mate and mates look out for each other. She was going to do a runner rather than go on stage. She hates being looked at by loads of people. I literally had to rugger tackle her or else she was gone. And then I just calmed her down.'

'Not what it looked like to me.'

'You're right, it's not what it looked like. You ask anyone who was in assembly how embarrassed Ali looked going on stage.'

'You were holding her.'

'Of course I was – to calm her down. It worked didn't it?'

Chinny frowned. The case for the defence did seem tight and logical.

'If that's all it was, then why is Burchell so bothered about it?'

Shit, that's a good one, Robert thought. Why was she bothered about it? He assumed Chinny had said something to Mel and given his version of what he saw. Which, to be fair, was probably more accurate than the bullshit that Robert had just served up.

'Did you tell her, cretin?'

Chinny nodded. 'She was listening to you two jabbering in the kitchen the other week at that house party thing. She got the feeling something was going on between you two, and then she interrogated me about it.'

This was beginning to test Robert to the limit. He wasn't about to give away anything to Chinny, and besides, he didn't even know himself what, if anything, was going on. His heart rate felt like it was beating at the same rate as when he was on the treadmill. He wanted to know what the hell Mel was playing at, but he would need to blunt Chinny's grinding axe first.

'Look mate, I don't know what's going on in your head, but your circuit needs a bit of rewiring. Me and Ali are really close to Mel after what happened with Mrs Burchell. But I've not said anything to Mel about Croftsy nearly freaking out at the assembly cos it's something that happened before she was living in Winchester. No wonder she was keen to know your slimy take on what you thought you saw. Everyone likes a bit of gossip, but that's all it is.' Robert was gesticulating to help reinforce the words he was delivering. 'We're good mates – like me and you are. We work well as a team, otherwise Oli Gemmill would still be looking like a homeless bloke poking around through bins. And all that stuff that went on with Mel's mum in the summer? Well yeah, me and Ali do chat about that you know – it was a scary situation for us to have been in. We thought Mrs Burchell was going to die. Ali just plays it down, and keeps it all in – but when she wants to open up about it, is it any wonder it's me she speaks to?'

Pacified for the time being, Chinny knew this wasn't him

getting something so fundamentally wrong. He refrained from telling Robert about Mel's desperate attempts to work the backstage area for the next termly address. Instead he would connive in her attempts to catch them in the act, if in fact that's what she was trying to do. And it didn't stop him from striking up a similar conversation with Ali in the sixth form common room.

Chinny was becoming quite the detective working diligently to acquire new evidence. Care was taken not to broach the topic in the company of others as he hoped this would encourage Ali to blab – and this she did. Unable to quell the waves of questions he threw at her, Ali collapsed at the first hurdle being the worst liar that ever lived. Chinny was able to uphold his suspicions: Ali liked Robert and wouldn't mind if something was to happen between them, but nothing was at that time; she was sure he liked her too, but they hadn't really talked about it properly. Chinny was hardly the person she would have picked to open up her heart to, she didn't really know him at all. In fact, it didn't matter. The old adage about telling secrets to strangers prevailed. In a quite a perverse way she felt relieved, excited even, that she had actually expressed her feelings to someone other than her own conscience.

During Chinny's cross-examination, it came to mind that if she felt alright telling him how much she liked Robert, perhaps she ought to speak with Mel about it after all. That idea was quickly retracted once her friend had been accused of spying on them at the summer party, and worse still, implicated in plotting to spy on them again at the termly address. She recoiled in horror upon hearing Chinny's supposed story of catching Mel outside the kitchen, and his subsequent discussions with her. It took some convincing to believe that everything Chinny had to say was correct.

'Look, I've been more than honest with you, dim wit – made

myself look like a complete banana no doubt. There's no need to rub it in and try to make me look even more foolish.'

Chinny was insistent about what he was clued up about.

'Explain to me why I would make that shit up?'

'Because you're a complete stirrer. That's what you do – you enjoy it.'

'Can't deny that. But if I really wanted to take the piss and stir it up nastily, I'd have done this in front of Greeny and Burchell, wouldn't I?'

Ali couldn't bring herself to look up at the imp sitting next to her. His protestation sounded sincere enough. She pondered his disclosure, the information now blowing a gale through her mind. It all seemed like a hyperbole, and consequently the whole thing felt cringeworthy. She picked at her nails for a short time before delivering her own verdict. She had given in meekly to the situation concerning her and Robert, but she was far more robust in her analysis of this potential tinderbox.

'Look Chinny, Mel is my best mate. I go round to look after her mum every Wednesday afternoon for my placement for God's sake. They treat me like one of the family. I think she only wants to do the termly address stuff cos me and Robert are her pals, and she wants to be involved too. She probably feels a bit left out. You know she's a bit of a character, so she was just messing around when she was trying to eavesdrop on us at the party. There's no way she's jealous of me and Robert – there's nothing to be jealous about is there? Well, not really. Not yet and probably won't be. And why wouldn't she have spoken to me or him if she was jealous or unhappy about something? I can see why you think there's more to it than that, but yours is a blurred version of the reality.'

Some self-doubt crept into Ali's mind even as she spoke her words. Had she overlooked the relationship between the three of them? Were things more obscured than they appeared to be?

Chinny offered no response and mulled over the possibility of

Ali's considered appraisal of the situation. Even he didn't feel compelled to drag one of his best buddies, Robert, through the mud. Besides, Ali was a nice person and had begged him not to blurt the gossip out. There was also the small matter about how Mel would react, and that made him nervous. He would lay low and watch this unfold from a distance. Ali was not convinced that Chinny was going to keep shtum, but there was no way she was going to say anything to Robert or Mel. She walked away from the common room feeling like an object being thrust at high speed and being hit by debris coming the other way.

14

On the morning of the termly address, Mel was handed a message by her form tutor, Mr Evans. It was from her sociology teacher, Mr Simpson. The note was marked 'Urgent' on the front and was short and to the point. 'Please come to see me in my office during registration today,' it read, with no indication of what it was about.

On her way to his office, Mel could only assume that she had somehow failed to meet a submission deadline. There was an awful lot going on at home in respect of care for her mum and the building work on their extension. She was usually so methodical when it came to organising homework, but it was just possible that something had passed her by.

Mr Simpson was also the head of fifth year pupils. To most kids he was better known as 'Squint Bags' Simpson. Whenever he spoke, or listened for that matter, his eyes would narrow to the extent that they looked like cracks. It was as if a bright light was being constantly shone into his line of sight, and consequently children felt like they were on the receiving end of a good telling off purely because of the way he looked at them. It was a most patronising if unintentional mannerism, and as he squinted the dark patches under his eyes concertinaed to form what looked like dustbin bags. Mel hadn't connected with him in the same way as with her other teachers and would endeavour to avoid eye contact with him at all costs during lesson time. She knocked the door to his office which was slightly ajar and waited for a response. She nearly jumped out of her skin when she was approached from behind by Mr Simpson who was on his way back from the school office.

'Ah, there you are Ms Burchell,' he began. 'Do come in. Now then, Mrs McKenzie talks very highly of your backstage technical abilities, Melanie. That's why those skills are needed in the school hall later for some very special dignitaries.'

He eased himself onto his oversized faux leather chair behind his desk. Dignitaries? Mel couldn't help thinking that was overstating the role of the head boy and head girl by some margin, but she went along with it.

'Sir, I'm a bit confused because I thought I was always meant to be in the school hall doing backstage in period three?'

'Yes, that's right, you are. But it'll be me leading an assembly in the hall now, not Mrs Irvine.'

'Oh, ok. So, Mrs Irvine isn't speaking in the hall then?'

'That's correct, Ms Burchell.'

His eyes became squintier than ever as he over-elaborated the 'Ms' so that it sounded like a fly buzzing.

'I'll be kicking things off, and then Mr Maxwell will do a piece using the projector.'

'Anyone else, Sir?'

'Well I don't want to give it all away, but yes there will be a surprise or two. Can you come to the hall at break time to agree the lighting arrangement?' Mel nodded. 'Very good, I'll see you then.'

Maybe she was over thinking things, but this seemed odd to Mel as she was sure Mrs Irvine would usually be leading the address. What was Mr Maxwell doing there? Perhaps she was going to arrive later and speak at the end. Although confused by the change of agenda, at least she was still going to be in the backstage area. The plan had not been derailed. As long as she kept a low profile, Ali and Robert would not suspect that she was consumed with prying on any arrangements for another moment of secret intimacy.

Mel went to the hall during break-time to make sure that the control panel was operating correctly, and to make sure that site services were not needed for any replacement bulbs. The last thing she needed was to be preoccupied with an outage during the assembly. She had already collared Vince Mitchell on her way to lessons that morning. He was one of the Chinny gang, and also a back-stage techie who was used for assemblies. Mel instructed him to arrive early at the hall as well.

'I can't. I'm supposed to go to the drama theatre instead now.'

'What are you on about? Don't know where you got that from, but I had to go and see Mr Simpson this morning; he definitely said he needed technicians in the hall.'

Saying the name of that member of staff was the cue for several adolescents to childishly grapple and pull at their eyes to imitate 'Squinty Simpson'. Mel scowled.

'Have you finished?'

Like the other lads in the gang, Vince was very wary of Mel and snapped out of his tomfoolery promptly. They were daunted by how self-assured Mel was, so much so that they would even take her word over the message that went round to all sixth formers that morning, instructing them that the termly address would now be taking place in the drama theatre owing to a Duke of Edinburgh presentation ceremony in the hall. Mel wasn't to know that – she had exited her form room to find Squinty long before the morning messages were read out by Mr Evans. She hadn't thought to ask anyone if she had missed anything from tutor time. Her mind was so preoccupied with executing her plan that she was in danger of being in the wrong place at the right time.

'Be there at break-time,' she demanded as she turned to walk down the corridor. There were no objections thrown back at her.

Vince arrived towards the end of break citing two problems for his lateness. Firstly, he needed to grab a sausage roll from the canteen because he 'was starving'. Secondly, he had bagged himself a detention from Mrs Irvine. She had asked him to go along to the drama theatre to get ready for the assembly. He remonstrated with her that he had to go to the hall instead. The fact that he did this while chomping on his pastry treat only shortened the fuse of patience that the head of sixth form was trying to maintain. She didn't understand the obstinate determination he presented to avoid the duties that he had carried out numerous times previously without such fuss.

'I kept telling her that you had told me that Squinty changed the plans, but she was having none of it. She told me to get out of her sight.'

'Why was she telling you to go to the drama theatre? Simpson categorically told me it's in the hall, you'll see. Typical teachers – rubbish communication. Let them sort it out.'

They were taken by surprise by the arrival of Mr Simpson through the rear stage door.

'See Mitchell, I told you.'

As he proceeded to glare at the two students it was obvious that he had been privy to some of their conversation.

'Ah there you are Ms Burchell. And Mr Mitchell too?' Squinty pretended to look surprised. 'How honoured we are to have your presence as well, Vince. Does Mrs Irvine know you're here? Wouldn't want you getting into any trouble, would we?'

Vince didn't have the gall to say otherwise, or to explain the incident at break-time. Instead he just nodded. Mr Simpson gave a dubious squint at Vince, and then checked his watch.

'Alright you two, listen carefully then. So, main lamps as the stage party arrive, and then the two spotlights when a speaker is introduced to the reading stand. That will include anyone going onto the stage from the opposite wing to you. Can we close the main curtains to about two thirds please? And I want the lights in the audience area to be partially dimmed. However, for the awards that will be given out, could you please put the lights in the hall back on fully? Probably sounds more complicated than it is. That understood?' He hurried through his instructions before disappearing to supervise the entrance of the stage party.

'What awards, Sir?' asked Mel.

'Duke of Edinburgh.'

Mel looked baffled, as this was not something that Mrs Irvine had mentioned. Although it did make sense of Mr Simpson's conversation with her earlier in the morning, regarding Mr Maxwell doing a talk. The physical education staff led on this initiative in the school. Robert had gained the silver award last year and had been asked by Mr Maxwell to complete the gold challenge as part of an upper sixth form enrichment programme.

The backstage area in the hall was dimly lit at the best of times, and the curtains being partially closed made it quite a lot darker than normal in the wings. They quickly tested the main lamps which illuminated the area where the stage party would be seated and speaking, and the lights shone intensely through the gap where the curtains were still apart. The channelled light formed what looked like a solid, white barrier, so that it was difficult to see clearly across to the other wing. That was a bonus in Mel's attempts to remain furtive.

The bell went for the end of break, the cue for Mel to take her place at the control panel. While waiting for the hall doors to squeak open for the students to make their way to their seats, they heard the muffled sound of commotion along one of the corridors. Then, undeniably, the full force of Mr Maxwell's lungs could be heard. He was a sports teacher whom no one with any sense ever tried to take advantage of, and he had a nickname owing to an optical deficiency too. The children at King Alfred's couldn't be accused of not paying attention to their teachers, but some perhaps needed to channel their efforts towards listening more to learning opportunities rather than amusing themselves with the anomalies they discovered in their teachers' appearances. His nickname was 'Blinker' as he suffered from dry eye. The difference with Mr Maxwell was that it was not a name you heard pupils prepared to band around liberally in the same way that others were. Blinker took exception to any form of mockery pointed in his direction – it was not pretty to witness a senior pupil in the school reduced to tears for slight of mouth.

'Gurpreet Chandra! Where on earth do you think you are going boy? Get to where you need to be!'

Vince turned sharply to look at Mel. 'That's Guppy. What's he up to?'

He poked his head around the main curtain only to find that both entrance doors into the hall were still closed with no sign of the students. As Guppy and his collaborators had regularly been rumbled by teachers for being involved in some sort of scheming, they didn't give it a second thought, and put it down to general pratting around in the queue to get in.

The control panel was located inside the right-hand wing of the stage. The technicians were used to having a restricted view, but with the curtains mostly closed they could barely see the front of stage. The shuffling of feet and the clanking of chairs being sat upon announced the arrival of the audience. Mel and Vince ensured the main lamps were beaming onto centre stage and waited to dim the hall lights. The glare of the stage lamps meant that Mel could barely make out the figure across the stage waiting in the opposite wing. She could see the outline of a dress, and the glint of a necklace, and guessed it must be Ali. It was customary for the head boy and head girl to wear formal clothing for the termly address, acting as role models for their peers. The first address was usually given by Mrs Irvine, but on this occasion, it seemed the duty had been passed onto Mr Simpson. Vince turned to Mel and whispered.

'Is Insomnia doing a talk in here today?'

'You know what, I haven't a clue anymore,' replied Mel, who was transfixed on the silhouette opposite. 'Vince, you'll be ok by yourself for a minute, won't you? I'm just going over to the other side to see Ali, I'll be back before the presentations start, but don't forget to put the hall lights back on if they start before

I get here.'

Mel wasn't really asking for Vince's approval; she would be going across regardless of what he said. He couldn't help but wonder why she thought Ali was backstage, and why Mel was prowling like a cat as she crept towards the back of the wing, and then to the extreme rear of the stage where the backdrop was.

To avoid any chance of her movement being detected, or any tripping over, Mel got down on all fours and crawled behind the backdrop. The darkness disguised the occasional ripple of the curtain caused by her movements that might otherwise have been spotted by any wandering eyes in the main hall seating area. Her knee jolted and got stuck within a couple of shuffles. She reached down to find out what had halted her movement, thinking it might be blue tack as it had stuck to her jeans. But as she pulled at it, the sickly, artificial stench of chewing gum wafted up her nostrils. 'Bollocks,' she muttered under her breath.

Her mind was skipping because she knew that time was against her. She didn't know at which point Ali and Robert were due to join the stage party for their address, but it could be at any moment. Completely randomly she started singing to the chorus of 'Three Little Birds' by Bob Marley in her head, assuming it was a subconscious attempt to calm herself down.

She crawled forward a couple of metres further before her swearing went into overdrive once more, after inadvertently pressing the palm of her hand onto either a drawing pin or staple. As it pierced the thin, translucent piece of skin, she knew it would be bleeding. Mel raised her hand to her mouth and used her tongue to clean the area that had been injured, and as she did so, listened to Squinty speaking. Kneeling statuesque-like behind the backdrop, she heard him pass over to Blinker Maxwell. It was time to hurry, and despite the darkness and obstacles, she made it to the back of the opposite wing. Mel needed to remain as covert as possible if she were to have any chance of catching her friends in the act. For Mel this would feel like being cleansed, but also the start of a period of many questions about trust and truthfulness.

In front of her she could make out curtain drapes and crouched besides a ground row. There were other pieces of scenery conveniently positioned for her to carry out her discrete observations too. Despite the murkiness, she could make out that they were the shapes of coffins, and knew it was for Sowerberry's funeral parlour in Oliver Twist. There was a thud from a door closing in the backstage area. The corridor that led to the changing rooms and wardrobe was also accessible from the head teacher's corridor, so the sound of someone approaching was easy to detect. The person was wearing rubber soled shoes because they squeaked with each step and it echoed faintly in the corridor. Then there was the tip-tapping as the person made their way up the stairs leading to the stage left wing.

Mel ghosted across to the next drape in front of which Ali was already waiting. As the owner of the footsteps walked in, she hid behind a Dickensian milestone, which emulated perfectly that Mel had come a long way on her own journey of discovery. Mel merely assumed the besuited, shadowy figure must be Robert as he moved towards his counterpart. This was it. Mel cranked her neck hastily round the silky material in front of her, and as if rehearsed watched as the guy leant in and kissed the girl on both cheeks. Taking hold of both of her hands, he pulled the girl towards him so he could whisper in her ears.

'Gotcha!' or so Mel thought, before losing control of her balance. She had stumbled on Fagin's box of stolen treasure, scattering the contents. In unison the couple turned towards the source of the clumsiness in the shadows behind them and let out a terse 'Shush!' That was the spark that caused the keg to explode. An eruption of raw emotion flowed from Mel as she lambasted the pair in front of her, momentarily forgetting the circumstances for them all being backstage.

'Don't tell me to shush you sneaky little bastards. I know

exactly what the pair of you have been up to. Why the hell didn't either of you tell me you were seeing each other, eh? You've hidden it like a dirty secret, and do you know how that's made me feel? Like shit – that's how; like I don't really matter when I'm supposed to be your mate. Well perhaps Mr Perfect should tell you about the time that me and him had a little bit of sparkle together. So, shove that up your arses. I'm pissed off with both of you. Oi, are you listening twat heads?'

Mr Simpson was alerted to the kerfuffle by Vince waving to him from the edge of the main curtain, but he had already heard the increasing volume of the tirade of abuse being banded around behind the grand drape. A good deal of fortune existed for all concerned; Mr Maxwell was showing a video on the projector screen at the time, the sound of the media largely masking the disturbance. The masses in the hall were therefore oblivious to the commotion behind the proscenium arch.

Vince was ordered to close off the main curtains. What was usually a graceful meeting of fabric instead became two ends crashing into each other in Vince's frantic attempt to close them quickly. Mr Simpson then instructed him to turn on the emergency strip lighting.

As the lights flickered on, several sets of eyes took a brief moment to focus having been shrouded in different shades of darkness for some time. With vision mostly regained, Mel baulked on discovering that who she thought was Ali and Robert were in fact the Mayor and Lady Mayoress of Winchester, in full ceremonial regalia. They had been delighted to accept the invitation from the school to hand out the Duke of Edinburgh awards to the successful participants. The school had chosen not to disclose that information to the children. Instead they were told that they could expect some surprise dignitaries. The two elderly officials stood looking at Mel in shock and horror, clasping each other's hands. When the light revealed the identities of the people in the wings it was difficult to ascertain who was more disturbed at the revelation.

Mel's mouth dropped and losing control of her senses she found herself bending her knee to curtsey as if she was in front of royalty. A squinting Mr Simpson had by this time made his way into the wing and wore an enraged expression, having heard the majority of her outburst.

'Get up Burchell. You're morphing from outrageous to ludicrous.'

Mr Simpson shook his head in disbelief as the crazy student enacted her confused attempts at protocol.

'Moment of sparkle? Good grief, I have never laid eyes on her before and have never been spoken to with such disdain, Mr Simpson. Did you hear the deluge of smut and accusation that this young lady has thrust at us?'

'Yes. Yes, I'm afraid I did. Mr Mayor and Madam Mayoress, could I kindly leave you in the capable hands of Mr Maxwell here, who will be delighted to introduce you to our expectant audience anon?'

Squinty's elaborate attempts to calm the predicament were lost on his guests who remained bemused by the unwelcome situation they found themselves in. He briefly exited the scene to brief Mr Maxell on developments, while the projector displayed images of pupils grappling with compasses. How apt this imagery was, as on his return behind the curtain an extended arm and sharp point clearly indicated to Mel in which direction she was to walk. As she set off towards the corridor that would be a walk of shame, she felt compelled to say something.

'Very nice to meet you both,' she mouthed to them as she turned her back to leave the distressed pair.

As Mr Simpson marched the shamefaced sixth former to the head teacher's office he was fuming, ranting how her conduct had been disgraceful, and that she was an embarrassment to herself and the proud reputation of the school. The gravity of what had happened hit hardest when he asked, 'how are you going to explain this to your parents?'

The closer it had got to the assembly, the more Ali's nerves began to jangle, but what came across to the sixth formers in the audience on the day was a smart speech given by a composed student. Unbeknown to Mel, her hunch about her pals was spot-on. Robert *had* arranged to meet with Ali, but neither in the wings of a dingy school hall nor the cramped theatre.

'Well Croftsy, I've not been around this side of the school since rumbling matey boy Oli.'

'No, me neither. And coincidentally, he was a nervous wreck when he was here too.'

'Aha, but we succeeded in calming his fears, so I reckon this'll be a breeze for you.'

There was a recurrence of arms being wrapped around one another, one pair belonging to the recipient of some much-needed reassurance.

15

The jungle drums were beating loud and sounding out a rhythm of disbelief amongst the population of King Alfred's. Incredibly though, neither the school nor the Mayor's office were approached by the local press for comment, and the Burchells didn't have to endure further embarrassment of the misdemeanour by being dragged through the pages of the local rag.

Mel avoided a permanent exclusion thanks to the intervention of her parents. Poppy would never ordinarily dream of using her illness to gain any advantage, and on this occasion wrestled with her faith. She used the 'on death's doorstep' card sparingly, but in choosing to do so it pricked the conscience of the head teacher. This most devout mother wanted nothing to scupper her daughter's education. Mel felt obliged to send a letter of apology to the senior leadership team at the school, and another to the officials whom she had deeply offended. It was a sensible and appropriate course of action that went some way to redeeming herself to the recipients. That left the most difficult task for Mel which was closer to home.

Mel had to be honest. It was going to hurt her emotionally and obliterate any remaining pride and self-respect. To do otherwise would never result in a credible explanation. Besides, Poppy had received a near complete transcript of the provocation gleaned from conversations with the school and Mel herself. Inevitably, Poppy wouldn't rest until she had unpicked the motivation and circumstances behind her daughter's inappropriate actions.

'Child, your wall of dignity has some cracks. To repair it you must put truth in your mortar if it is to regain its strength.'

Mel decided the best policy was to hit it head on.

'I thought Ali and Rob were going to be making out in the

wings, not the ruddy Mayor and his Lady.'

'How on earth did you come to decide that they would magically be in the same place where you were?'

'Just take it from me that someone told me they had seen them do this before.'

'And you believed this tittle tattle? Could you not see that you were being set up, Mel?'

'It wasn't like that mum, and besides there were other things that added up. I know I'm in the wrong here but give me some credit. I'm not a complete fool. I've seen them together and when they're alone they look different to how mates usually hang out.'

'So, you were going to peep on them to make fun of them – to catch them out?'

'Catch them out – yes. To make fun – no.'

Poppy lowered her tone and asked her next question slowly and deliberately.

'You jealous of it?'

Mel was dumbfounded and froze to the spot. Her mum had nailed the issue – the very conundrum that had enveloped her thinking since learning that Robert liked Ali.

'I'm not sure Mamma. I don't even know if Ali and Rob are actually seeing each other.'

'You did use language that disgusts me daughter, but I see so much passion in your efforts to find out the truth. You don't know your own feelings, and maybe you don't like it that those two do know what it is to want to show affection for someone else. Is that what's eating away at you so much?'

Mel skirted round the question.

'It's the not knowing what's been going on between them – the secrecy.'

'But you said you don't know whether they be a proper couple together, right? Why is your mind so tangled up about what might be?'

'I feel a connection with Robert, there's something that makes me feel special when I'm with him.'

'That's what having a good friend should feel like Melanie, it is a gift to have a bond with someone who looks out for you.'

She wasn't sure whether her mum was reading the signals properly after all. Mel hadn't invented what happened with Robert that night in the summer, when they shared a real and tender moment, but she didn't want to start gushing about it only for her mum to pick it apart as being something she had overinflated in her mind.

'It doesn't feel like that with other lads that I'm friends with mum.'

'How does he feel about it?'

A tear trickled down Mel's cheek, and she looked up at her mum. 'He likes Ali.'

This was an unfamiliar situation for Poppy to be in as a mother, and even for a woman blessed with the wisdom passed on from her own mamma it was a challenge to muster up something profound for her distressed girl.

'Melanie, him not for you. You only see light where I see shade. He bring heavy winter skies that will not mix with your summer sunshine. You be opposites. Stick with him as a friend, and he not let you down that way.'

They weren't the words Mel wanted to hear. She didn't want to agree with her mum, and the chord that had been struck sounded flat. Still she continued.

'This triangle you be a part of have very harsh angles, Melanie. I see a boy and girl who know what they feel but cannot tell each other – and fight the temptation to confide in the other person in their triangle. Don't go trampling on ground already trodden on. All this time you do everything but the one thing you should have done.'

'What mum? What should I have done?'

'Ask them both, to their faces – separately.'

Blunt, simple, and impossible. This reality stung Mel.

Striking up that kind of conversation with Robert and Ali required some gut wrenching that she wasn't sure she'd be capable of contriving. She pondered on how her mum was so intuitive about Ali and Robert. It never entered her mind that perhaps on her weekly visits Ali had developed a bond with her mum that would allow Poppy to understand exactly how Ali ticked.

Poppy knew far more about this muddle than she was prepared to reveal. It felt cruel to be as guarded as she had been, but by being tactful she hoped Mel would be able to own the resolution – be it positive or not.

'What should I do now mum? How am I going to deal with the questions and the rumours?'

'Pickney, why you damn yourself for one mistake? What's already happened isn't changeable, and whether good or bad it's an experience to learn from. What's happening now should be you showing everyone the lessons you've learnt that make you a stronger person. But what is going to happen to you, the unknown, that is the most important thing as that is what will define you. The future still be in your control girl, you still got choices.'

Poppy picked her daughter off the floor with a range of advice that made sense to her, and some of it was quite unexpected.

'Go and make your peace with your friends but play caution with the facts. That be the recipe for much pain and loss if you share an honest story.'

Mel knew her mamma as a woman of Christian values and wondered whether she might have advocated something along the lines of a public trial to cleanse the sins away. But rather than being shocked at her mum's suggestion of giving out half-truths, she ought to have known better by now that her uncompromising loyalty was first and foremost to her children – and if that meant challenging God's own expectations, Poppy was prepared to do it and have that out with the Lord at a later date.

Robert and Ali were both independently anxious to understand Mel's motives for striking out at two VIPs. It didn't take much initiative to realise that it was a case of mistaken identity. She surely hadn't set out to offend two officials. Without fully engaging in Chinny's rhetoric regarding Mel's obsession with assemblies, they did presuppose that there could be some validity in what he had said. There was the very real possibility that for all his faults Chinny had been speaking the truth about their friend's reasons for being in the assembly in the first place.

However, Mel was creative with her version of 'wing-gate' to them both, turning the table on Chinny. Her explanation for the verbal abuse of the Mayor and Mayoress was that she had every reason to suspect that it was Chinny and Guppy messing around. Both had eavesdropped on her instructions to Vince on the morning of the assembly, and 'Blinker' was heard yelling at Guppy for some kind of antics before the assembly started. Was it any wonder that she became suspicious, she remonstrated?

It remained Mel's most closely guarded secret that she hadn't realised she was in the wrong assembly and in the wrong venue. Her version of the circumstances might have sounded more reasonable if Vince hadn't been there to witness the whole event. He was obviously going to speak about what he saw and heard with his mates. Vince was the centre of much attention with the vultures keen to pick away at any pieces of scrap he could throw out. People could be forgiven for thinking that Vince was exaggerating and at worst spinning a story. But no one could ever remember a sixth former being under consideration for permanent exclusion, so there must have been some credibility to his story. The dialogue that he claimed to have heard was different to Mel's explanation, and that got picked apart by Chinny when he spoke with Ali about it.

'Fair enough, Croftsy, if you want to believe what she's told you. But ask yourself why Burchell told Vince she was going across the stage to see you, and then to get there like she was a camouflaged marine on a secret mission?'

While others effused about the time Mel Burchell humiliated Winchester's Mayor, Robert lacked his usual calmness whenever the subject came up and would remove himself from the vicinity of the gossip. He certainly rebuffed any attempts Chinny made to broach the topic with him, and on more than one occasion it seemed the spat would end in fisticuffs.

The consequences of Mel's unusual and protracted attempts to reveal the extent of Ali and Robert's feelings for each other seemed like it had been a most unsatisfactory episode for everyone concerned. Suspicion and distrust emanated amongst themselves, without it ever revealing itself to completely wreck the weakened bond between them. Publicly they all carried on regardless. The fact of the matter was that their peers were always having quarrels, with fallings-out, and then kissing and making up. Why should their situation be any different? They still spoke to, and between, each other but inevitably there was always an elephant in the room too.

In any case it was difficult for Ali and Mel to distance themselves from each other because they were intrinsically linked by Poppy. As next-door neighbours it was geographically impossible for Mel and Robert to form a barricade. As for Robert and Ali, a wedge did begin to insert itself between them, which was as unexpected as it was unwelcome. It was never discussed, but a period of zero flirting was automatically an understood rule. And so, another opportunity was about to pass them both by, just when it seemed that their feelings for each other were going to unravel themselves and blossom properly. Just days beforehand it seemed likely that they might finally allay their nervousness and start going out with one another – and finally admit to each other what everyone else had assumed anyway.

16

Mary Ainscow's main job as an accounts clerk paid well enough, but it was dull. As luck would have it, she was only contracted to work for three days, so didn't have to endure the monotony of the role for longer than was necessary. To help compensate for any financial shortfall, she had acquired a job at Bar End working men's club. As Robert was at an age where he was largely independent with his own plans and circle of friends, it was some light relief for Mary to get out of the house, albeit to make some extra money. Those weekend shifts introduced her to a completely new world of social diversity. It was often littered with invitations to live it up and go wild, especially around December, though she rarely entertained those proposals.

Having been stung by the heartless antics of Robert's dad however, she was always hypercautious about getting entangled in another relationship. Her sense of trust was egg-shell vulnerable. Any emotions she harboured for that chapter in her life were always more likely to be exposed and raw during the run up to Christmas. There could never have been a right time for Robert's dad to abandon his responsibilities, but choosing to walk out – or rather sneak out as it happened – at the time of the year when families traditionally spend more time together cut a deeper wound than was necessary.

Working at the local club was like being granted the role of regional agony aunt, judge, and jury. It quite simply gave Mary an insight into a deep well of secrets, gossip, sins, and accusations. Inevitably the stories leaking from King Alfred's Comprehensive School gathered in notoriety in some parts of the community, and the Chinese whispers stretched as far as the town's clubs and bars. Mary had long grown used to treating such speculation with a pinch of salt, but the one about the Mayor in the wings aroused her suspicions about why Mel Burchell had been so fiery. For sure, Mary had teased Robert previously about his closeness to Mel but saw nothing other than friendship in the time he spent with Ali. Robert's nonchalance, though, further fuelled her own belief that there was some substance in the suggestions being banded around that Mel had fully anticipated to find a couple of students in the wings – and not any decorated officials.

Mary suspected her son was possibly in the middle of a tussle for his affections, but she didn't need to be any more forthright with him. Robert sidled up onto the couch next to his mum one evening. He had grown a longer fringe in the last year and it flopped across his brow covering his eyes. Mary laid her right arm over his shoulder and brushed it back over to the side of his head. Robert had no problem confiding in his mum; his first crush, his first kiss, his first fight, his first detention – who else was there for him to turn to?

'Something bothering you, big man?'

'I don't know what's going on mum.'

'Start by telling me things you think you might know then love.'

Robert wasn't sure which of the bits he knew were reality, and which bits he just wanted to be true. Only once had he attempted to explain to anyone how he felt about Ali, and that imploded in a way he didn't expect. Here was an opportunity that he didn't want to let pass him by. It might have been his mum, but she had a good pair of ears on her.

'The thing at school with Mel was just weird. She's sat me and Ali down and tried explaining what it was all about, but I couldn't say for sure whether she's making it up.'

'What's your gut feeling telling you?'

'I'm into Ali, and I think she's into me. Some people reckon Mel isn't too keen on that, but she's never said anything to me. It's just...' Robert contorted his lips in a pout as if to protect himself from any hurt from what he was about to say.

'Just what, Rob?'

'The kind of people stirring it up – I wouldn't normally give a toss about. But there might be some truth in what they're flapping about.'

'How would you know though Rob, you weren't there in that hall.'

'True, except...' he paused, and his mum looked puzzled. 'We *were* originally meant to be in there, and it only got changed on the morning of the assembly. Maybe I'm not imagining things after all. The thing is mum I didn't need to be in the hall to know Mel might be sweet on me. I can't really explain why it happened but there was a little moment with her back in the summer. No offense, but I don't want to say any more about it.'

Mary smiled. None of this was a real surprise to her.

'Look Robert, if it were me and you started giving out the advice, I'd probably do everything I could to do the opposite, so I doubt you're looking for me to give you a solution.'

He *was* actually but didn't want to interrupt his mum in mid-flow, and risk her losing her train of thought and missing out on something shrewd.

'All I would say to you love, is be honest to yourself and be honest with those girls. Seems to me things are a bit uncertain between you all. Perhaps you're not being as clear as you could be with either of them?'

While they snuggled up watching a film together, Robert was playing out a cast of his own in his mind. He repeated his mum's words over and over in his head, trying to imagine himself in front of Ali and Mel being honest. He was struggling to see how he would be able create a happy ending for all three characters.

Though Ali, Mel and Robert saw relatively little of each other during the festive season, the triangle of mess would be given a helpful opportunity to reconfigure at a carol service hosted by

Poppy's local church. Mary had to decline the invite to attend as she was already on the shift rota at the working men's club, and Robert was never likely to take up the opportunity himself to share his vocal capacity despite the best efforts of Poppy to persuade him otherwise. The promise of mince pies and mulled wine could not seal the deal either. The Crofts' on the other hand were only too pleased to offer their support, and Ali's close association with Poppy rendered it impossible for her to find an escape route.

The service interlude gave Ali and Mel an opportunity to peel away from the rest of the congregation. They greeted each other with a warm hug, which belied the icy blanket beginning to form outside. Crystals were gravitating towards the stained glass as if they had been sprayed on with glitter and were forming shadows in the corners of each pane. The cheeriness of the carol service seemed to influence the girls, initially concealing any fractures that might have existed between them. They talked excitedly about their plans for Christmas Day, and perhaps intoxicated by the cosy, fuzzy feeling generated by the festive season, Ali began jabbering nervously. Her usual lack of self confidence in social settings was once more snapping at her heels, and it caused the thoughts in her head to jumble like the drum of a washing machine.

It was impossible to build a dam for too long to block out what had gone on in the previous couple of weeks, and the curiosity to know what had really happened began trickling through. Ali was neither thinking about what she wanted to say, nor listening properly to Mel's replies, caught somewhere between the words and the sound of her voice. The only way she could register what was being said was by repeating her friend's responses, word for word. It didn't take long for Mel to catch on to what was becoming an unorthodox conversation.

'Ali, you're either taking the piss out of me or you've been sipping at that mulled wine.'

'Sipping mulled wine. Eh, what do you mean?'

'You're still doing it.'

'Still doing it. Doing what?'

'Every time I speak it's like there's an echo in the room when you respond.'

'Echo in the room, right.'

Mel stood statuesque. Her arms were outstretched, gesturing like she was exasperated and had no idea what was going on. This was compounded by her stare, two wide eyes almost straining out of their sockets. Unable to look at her gawping friend in the eye, Ali's head drooped in the direction of the flagstone flooring and activated what was in the back of her mind all the time.

'Mel, I no longer believe a word of your story about the incident with the Mayor.'

Mel certainly wasn't expecting the bluntness of Ali's comment, particularly as she had failed to articulate anything properly in the minutes beforehand. Just as she tried to interject, Ali stopped her in her tracks with an equally impressive follow up.

'What you said, your explanation – I know it was probably a pile of crap.' Mel looked vacant. She was impressed with the conviction that Ali spoke with, as if it had been a speech she had rehearsed. 'I also want to say something else to you and I'm not looking for you to say anything back. I should have told you that I do like Robert. A lot.'

'So? What makes you think I'm bothered about that?'

It wasn't possible for Mel to say nothing, but her question was riddled with irony given the recent bout of backstage stalking. It was Ali's turn to gesticulate with outstretched arms.

'Do you need me to answer that? You like him too don't you, Mel?'

Mel froze like the icicles on the old guttering, stretching out from where it had been dripping under the roofline. This was a loaded question that needed addressing but she skirted around it. Instead of offering an answer of any sort, she turned the spotlight smartly back onto Ali, snapping like one of the icicles had been savagely wrenched from where it had formed.

'How do you know he likes you?'

Ali could have chosen any one of a number of examples to illustrate Robert's fondness for her: the stage-side hugging, the rendezvous by the bins (although she didn't think getting up close and personal by some smelly trash would sound overly convincing), the on-going flirting whenever they spoke. She wanted to say the right thing, something convincing. But with her mind racing, she wilted under the pressure. Instead, Ali recounted her experiences with Robert at two different parties before the end of their fifth year at school.

'He'd asked a few of us along to a football presentation evening at the local club where his mum works. He'd been drinking cider at his mate's house before it started, and somehow managed to get hold of some more beer at the club. Anyway, he was really drunk and went outside to throw up. It was terrible. I knew his mum would kill him if she saw him like that, so we used the cloakroom to lie him down for a bit. There were people coming and going. There were some fruit machines around the corner, so I got a couple of his mates to stand by them as lookouts, and to act like a screen. We got him some water and put his head down on my lap, using our coats to make a pillow. I kept saying he'd be ok, and to just rest. He slept for about an hour and was ok when he came around, but his eyes were all bloodshot. We told his mum that he'd been sick after he'd eaten an egg batch at the buffet, and that we'd walk him home – which we did. He reckoned the sleep rescued him, but we couldn't believe he'd managed to drop off on the cold, hard tiled floor. Before I left him, he said that it was me stroking his head that calmed him down enough to go to sleep.'

Mel listened keenly, waiting to interrupt to throw in her

observations.

'We know only too well that you're a caring person, Ali. He was off his face and you were a brilliant friend looking out for him. But what he said doesn't mean he fancies you.'

'Hang on a minute Mel, let me finish. A couple of weeks later, on the weekend before we broke up for summer, a few of us were invited along to a party being held by a sixth former. His sister, Zoe, was in our year. She thought me and Robert were cool for what we did for Oli Gemmill, so she said a few of us could go along. I went along with Rob and his mates – the popular kids. The people lived on a farm, and the party was in one of their barns. Their parents would occasionally look in to make sure everything was ok but loads of people in our year were helping themselves to the booze. Funnily enough, Robert didn't drink though – learnt his lesson he said. Anyway, Zoe got absolutely wasted and started throwing up everywhere. Her brother was going mental at her saying their dad would end the party if he saw her like that. Robert stepped in. He took her behind the barn door where he used some hay bales to lie her down on. He sent Chinny off to get some water and asked a couple of us to keep an eye out in case her parents came round. He kept telling Zoe she'd be ok and stroked her head while she went off to sleep. Mind you, her mum did find out. She got Zoe to bed before her husband found out, fortunately.'

'I think you need to worry about Rob fancying Zoe if I were you, Ali.'

Ali tutted. 'Don't you see? He looked after her by doing the same thing that I did for him when he was puking up? *Exactly* the same.'

'Is that it? Nothing actually happened with you and him during the party?'

'We were kicked out. I think they thought we were the ones that got Zoe drunk.'

Mel clapped.

'It means nothing, Ali. It was just a coincidence. Rob's a nice lad, and, like you, he'd help anyone who was struggling.'

'No way, Mel. That's an easy way to explain it if you hadn't seen it yourself. It was the way he looked at me. Every time he did something that I had done for him he looked up and smiled. He deliberately did things the way I'd done it. I kept thinking that I knew what he would do next, and then he did it.'

Mel was wearing a disbelieving smile.

'Your thing isn't even a thing.'

'I don't care what you think Mel, you weren't there. You ought to believe me instead of scoffing.'

Mel thought better of making this a more difficult situation than it was already becoming. There had been no prior indication that Robert was going to be the centre of their discussion that evening, and aside from that she was continually torn by the not-insignificant fact that she loved Ali as a friend. It was hypocritical of her to castigate Ali when she seemed far more adamant about her feelings than Mel did.

'Ok, let's say I do believe you. Then why the hell have you two just not talked about it openly with me?'

'I don't know, Mel – probably because this has been going on before you even came to Winchester, and it's still... complicated.'

'You're damn right. If the feeling was mutual like you reckon Ali, why the hell aren't you already together? Do you think you're misunderstanding where he's coming from?'

'No,' Ali answered with much certainty. 'He's a popular person, I'm not. I don't know if I'm good enough for him.'

'Well, it's just not normal.'

'I don't want normal, I want... special. Something worth waiting for. It's just the way the chemistry between me and him works, I suppose.'

Given that both Ali and Robert had separately told Mel they liked one another, this was a situation that looked like she'd tried to hijack, a plotline that had been positively developing – not festering as Mel had perhaps hoped. There was no malice in Ali's explanation, but it made Mel feel like an outsider. Above all, there was a determined belief in Ali's words, much to the annoyance of Mel. It was cruel of her to expect Ali to prove her case. Mel knew full well that there was a definite connection between Robert and Ali. She only had to recall Robert telling her he liked Ali to know that. She just seemed to have conveniently parked that in the 'try to forget it' file in the back of her mind. She had also witnessed at first-hand how effortlessly they connected when they were alone. Despite the uncertainty about her own feelings for Robert, or vice versa, Mel realised she had to leave this alone.

Mel was strangely subdued on the way home in the car. She pressed her forehead against the window and peered out at the lights shimmering in the town centre. Mel wrapped herself inside a private bubble, deliberately opaque at the edges so that she could block out what she didn't want to see. A car pulled up alongside them at the next set of traffic lights blocking her view. In the back she could see a little boy, no older than five, playing with a toy dinosaur. He looked out of his window at Mel and mouthed a huge T-Rex roar while bashing the toy against the glass. Inexplicably, Mel found herself spontaneously roaring back at the child, drawing a smile from him and some shocked glances backwards from her parents in the front seats. The boy grabbed a teddy bear from beside him and waved the paw at Mel. She mouthed 'Merry Christmas' to him as the car edged forward and he beamed back at her.

Some minutes later she could hear her parents lambasting 'some hooligans' and momentarily looked beyond the hazy film of her bubble to see the shattered remains of a bus shelter panel strewn across the pavement. Tiny pieces glimmered like jewels, surrounded by larger shards shaped like blades. Mel imagined that such destruction must have been caused by someone very angry and with much force.

'You don't know it was kids, dad – probably some drunk, middle-aged blokes on their way to the kebab shop more like,' she retorted.

But she was mindful that anyone with enough determination could cause much damage, especially if they had felt aggrieved.

No sooner had she finished her defensive riposte than the Crofts' pulled up alongside in their car. Ali's forehead was leaning on the back window too, and she was drifting in a bubble of her own. The girls' eyes met, briefly locking onto the inner dark roundness that reflected their own souls. Far from being antagonistic, their stares drew out a warm smile of reconciliation. As the lights began to change, Ali cupped her hands to imitate a heart shape and whispered 'Happy Christmas' to her friend. Mel instantly whispered back 'I'm sorry. Merry Christmas.' It was as close as Mel would get to giving her approval of Ali and Robert getting together. It was also the last Christmas she would be able to spend with her mum.

17

On the day of Poppy's funeral, the unseasonal conditions and murky skies were indicative of the moodiness felt by those who knew her. They didn't need reminding that downpours were the unwelcome contrast to the conditions that she enjoyed most. The rain had been relentless in the area in the preceding couple of days, spoiling the plans for enjoyment and relaxation of many. The churchyard was sodden, making the structure look dreary and uninviting. The dark hearses in the cortege punctured through the lines of mourners queuing outside like a bead of oil dripping slowly down the sides of damaged machinery, the indicative signs that the individual parts turning inside were beginning to fail.

Inside, the priest attempted to relieve the sombreness emanating from those present at the church by encouraging people to celebrate the colourful memories they held for a much loved and respected woman. And then it was Derek's turn to deliver his eulogy, fighting bravely to hold back the tears as he stood to face the wall of grief engineered through the mass of faces in front of him. With so many people standing at the back and at the sides it felt like being in a sell-out concert hall. He gained some strength from realising that Poppy had touched the lives of all those faces in front of him in some way.

'Have you seen those huge grey clouds out there? Mucky, as Poppy would say. You can just imagine her having a verbal ruck about it up there in her place next to the big man. She'll get him to see her way of thinking soon enough.'

The humour was merely a brief respite. Derek looked at the coffin and bit his lip.

'Or maybe it's some kind of reverse psychology thing, her way of letting us know how mad she is, that leaving us now was the last thing she wanted to do.'

Other than Derek's voice, the only sounds that were audible when he paused were the odd cough or sniff of people fighting with their emotions, and the tap-tapping of raindrops being blown against the stained glass. Many hours had been spent poring over the words on the page of notes which he now looked down onto. Derek wanted them to be right, not understated. Mostly he wanted them to be words that engaged his children in being proud of their mum. He had the congregation nodding and smiling at the memories he relayed, before delivering his final thoughts.

'People may ask how I could stand here and say these things to you without falling apart. I will say, how could I not say these things when this is the best opportunity I will ever have to do so? There's a date out there with our names on it, so every minute is precious with those that matter to you. That message cannae be emphasised enough to you all from me and my kids. You will know the intensity of the pain we all feel right now, and how hard it is to let her go. So, let me say that we don't intend to let go. We will remember her the way she was, not how it is. She dug so deeply into all our lives, so although she might not be here in person, it doesn't mean she is not still with us. She would talk about her family using words like 'pride' and 'love'. Well I hope you will agree with me that these are words befitting of how we will remember Poppy also. I guess heroes come in all kinds of packages, and that's what she was to me.' He nodded at his two children; their gazes fixed upon him through smudged red eyes. 'No doubt she was other people's hero too.'

A candle by the alter fizzled out, and a wispy cloud of burnt wax drifted towards Derek causing him to puff out his nostrils as he inhaled a lung full.

'My rage at how cruel this is won't move on like the weather will, but I guess it'll change guises like the seasons do. And yet, Poppy would say that everyone has suffered enough with her

131

passing, and she wouldn't want that to continue. She would far rather you go away and be happy, not grieve; live your life to the fullest and not let this get you down or get in the way of you doing that. It breaks my heart to say goodbye, but I have to, even if I don't want to. Of course, we spoke about the possibility of her leaving us unexpectedly, and the effects that would have. But I remember clearly Poppy suggesting one way that people might cope with such loss. So, I will leave you with this instruction from her…'

Derek wagged his finger, and the congregation chuckled knowingly that Poppy would expect it to be done.

'Poppy's own view about a song was that if it were any good it'd make us see a person, a place, a memory. She would say that when we play music, to hear and to listen is to see and understand. The Lord knows she heard enough tosh coming out of Lewis' room to be an expert on this subject!'

The light-hearted banter and mockery in a moment of such torment didn't feel out of place. A wave of laughter spread from front to back and managed to draw smiles onto the faces of his kids.

'So, this was one of her wishes: when you leave this place today, take a mental note of the *very first* song that you play. It doesnae matter whether you like it or not; it might make you laugh, or cry; it could be ironic or poignant. Whatever the song is, whenever you hear that tune in the future, turn it up loud and take that moment to remember our dear Poppy, ok?'

Derek turned to look at the beautifully ornate, white coffin. He reached out to touch it. His fingertips glided over the smooth, flawless, polished surface, and onto the delicate petals of the spray adorning it.

'I love you so much Pops.'

Some people smiled, others sobbed, but all were touched.

Derek's own attempts to hide the tragedy of losing the love of his life fooled everyone. When he flicked the radio on back at home, he simply froze as he listened to 'The Sun Ain't Gonna Shine Anymore' playing through the speakers. Tears gushed as he thought back to the rhetoric of Poppy's message conveyed to the congregation; about the things they might feel when they listened to their first song after the service.

'Ha, full house,' he muttered to himself. 'I see ya Pops.'

18

There were allowances for below-par performance, poor behaviour, and a dip in attendance, but there came a point where the school could no longer defend Melanie Burchell's antics. The warning signs that Mel would endure a meltdown were already evident at the end of the funeral service, and at the wake. They were subtle – but they were there. As friends gathered alongside and around to support her, she was unusually flippant for a daughter grieving for the loss of her parent.

'That's that then,' she said, impersonating someone dusting off their hands.

No one said a word, it wasn't a time to judge. But it made them feel beyond uncomfortable.

The sixth form were completely understanding of her circumstances at home, and with Derek's agreement they ensured that support in the form of bereavement counselling was available if Mel ever wanted to access it, but it would have to be her choice to do so. However, within a four-week period at the start of the new academic year, Derek was being contacted on an almost daily basis with nothing other than negative feedback about his daughter. He was struggling to know how to deal with her volatile attitude, which followed a gruelling summer holiday in which family life began to tear itself at the seams, distraught at their loss. He was tempted to ask the obvious question, 'what would your mother say?' But because his daughter's rebellious behaviour was a reaction to that loss, he realised that it would be underhand and overly hurtful. Above all, Derek also knew that Poppy would never approve of such a tactic.

Although the coroner's report itself told them nothing new about the state of her diminishing condition, it did identify that 'the deceased experienced complications that would have been difficult to predict'. That she would have been thinking about nothing other than her family wasn't the least crumb of comfort for them. The candid reality that she had been convulsing for some time on a cold, concrete floor cut Mel to pieces inside and the possibility that Poppy might have suffered only served to exacerbate the painful feelings of guilt for her. She blamed herself for dawdling at the end of school rather than getting home to help her mum. And though Mel was instructed that it would have made no difference, these were words that she simply didn't accept. She continued to be crippled with regret, and sometimes in a state of distress and complete mental distraction, Mel would set a place at the table for someone that wasn't coming home for tea.

Derek was concerned about the depressive signals being given out by his daughter, and he felt like they were running out of options. With little sign of improvement, he decided to give his children some pre-prepared bundles that Poppy had put together when they had first arrived in Winchester, hoping that it would be a catalyst for healing their hearts. With the funeral barely a few weeks past, Derek had contemplated that it was too soon to do so, but he was losing the bond with his daughter, and that would break Poppy's heart.

Poppy had considered leaving her loved ones with something personalised on many occasions, but usually put this off as she didn't want to tempt fate. However, she had been forced into a rethink after collapsing within hours of being in their new environment. She never set out to be in denial of her own mortality, though she would do and say everything to not let it undermine her existence. The nightmare possibility of her life being taken suddenly and not being able to say 'goodbye' properly to her loved ones constantly disturbed her. While she refused to write any kind of will, her affectionate thoughts were embedded in handwriting to counter the potential of the unexpected.

Derek tapped on Mel's bedroom door but had presupposed that she wouldn't answer him. He gently turned the handle and walked across to where she lay on her bed with her back to him. He laid his hand on her shoulder, but she jerked it away from him.

'Look love, your mum told me that if anything happened to her...'

'You mean if she keeled over and abandoned us?'

She was so very difficult to speak to, taking any opportunity to cut in with a bolshie comment, but he persisted.

'Something personal has been left for you. She wouldn't even tell me what this was about, so I have no way of knowing whether this is going to help you or not. But whenever we talked about what might happen to her, she always reminded me that I had to let you have this. I hope it doesn't upset you darling, but I just want you to know...'

'You can go now, dad, thanks.'

The terse interruption made Derek realise he had probably outstayed his welcome. He placed the small bundle on the pillow next to her head, and as he did so he couldn't help himself but put his hand through her hair a couple of times. She did not flinch this time and, satisfied that he had made the tiniest bit of progress to win her over, Derek slipped back out of the room.

It took Mel some time to zone back into the present from whichever dark place she had cast her mind. The anxiety that had begun to embed itself in her emotions had caused her to start biting her bottom lip. It was sore and bloody, and when it dried, different layers of skin were exposed. Mel reached across to her bedside for some balm to soothe the pain, and as she did so the bundle that her dad had left her came into view. She stared at the package as she rubbed the ointment onto her bottom lip and smudged the gloop around using her top lip.

The items were wrapped in bright orange tissue paper and secured using a similarly vibrant coloured ribbon. Mel undid the bow and removed the protective layers. Underneath she discovered that the bundle was draped by a folded layer of canvas. She lifted this off to expose three small picture frames and an envelope. It was only when the canvas dropped to the floor from her bed that Mel realised the secret it had been concealing underneath the tissue paper wrapping. Because it had been folded, she did not notice the artwork painted on the reverse side that exposed itself when the canvas unravelled upon hitting the floor. Mel picked the small rectangular material up and rubbed her index finger over the oil painting. It looked like a silhouette with dark blue, grey and black colouring, and she could make out that it was a beach scene bathed in moonlight. In complete contrast, the picture frames had been coated in buoyant, vivid colours that made Mel recoil. She thought they looked tacky. The objects were set to one side and a letter was taken out from the envelope, which Mel read quietly to herself.

Dearest Melanie, my sweet girl. If you be reading my notes, then I have moved to another place to watch over you for now. Don't you ever think that I'm gone from your life, I will be wrapping you in my love every single day. If you think about me then I already be there by your side. Don't be sad for what has happened – I loved my life.

I want you to love your life too Melanie, really live it. Don't put pictures in these frames that I want you to have, put memories in them. Don't put something in to fill it for the sake of it. Put something in that you look at and can remember what it feels like, looks like, sounds like, and smells like. Surround yourself with things that take you straight back to that time and place. A proper memory should stay alive. If you can do that then I can rest knowing that you are happy. Don't be cynical about my illness, acrimony won't lead to any good, and it repairs nothing. Though my heart was poorly, it never leaked away my love for you and my precious family. Tears taste bitter for a reason Melanie, they not meant to slide down a sweet face.

Enjoy the precious time that you have on God's earth. I only wish I could have spent more days with you, but I cherish the ones that I did – my love for you will last for eternity, child. Becoming a mother was the most amazing thing that ever happened to me. Love your family always – take care of your father and hold Lewis by the hand often. Be bold, be brave, be colourful. Go out and discover what the world is about.

Mamma x

Mel's thoughts about the letter were erratic. On the one hand, it all felt so cruel and final, but on the other it contained the same wishes that her mum would have spoken about had she still been alive.

Her brother had a letter that contained a similar sentiment about living and loving his life. But Poppy also asked Lewis to take an ultimate trip when he felt the time was right – back to her homeland to scatter her ashes in her favourite place. For that he would need to get his father's blessing, and to talk to him to understand where she came from in the truest sense of the phrase. This irked Mel to think that she would trust him over her. Although she was given her grandmother's precious painting of Darkwood Beach, Lewis was being asked to go and see it in person. There seemed no correlation in fairness between that and some crappy frames.

Mel would goad her brother regularly with 'I'll swap you'

taunts. She had become self-righteous, and rather than trying to understand logic, Mel let things that she didn't agree with irritate her. However well intended, taking advice was something that Mel began to resent, and consequently a great wall of stubbornness grew around her. She missed the person that was best at providing enlightenment. It just didn't work coming from anyone else.

The hangover from her loss saw Mel become withdrawn from Ali and Robert, as well as her own family. During her first half-term in upper-sixth, the extent to which it had affected her was realised when Derek attended a meeting with the senior staff at the school, at which they reluctantly issued Mel with a final warning. Failing to follow an action plan devised by the staff would result in her permanent exclusion. This was not what Poppy had intended when suggesting Mel be bold and brave.

Then, the rapid decline in Mel's capacity to be a decent human being was halted as suddenly as it began when an appointment letter arrived from the hospital. The extreme anger that represented her grief was instead replaced by acute fear. Owing largely to the sudden demise of their mother, the specialists at the Royal Hampshire felt compelled to act immediately in assessing both children for any change in their physical make-up. Mel's reaction was to suddenly cling onto anyone and anything she could, her turbulent persona suddenly transformed into a needy individual. Without allowing her dad to see every demon in the vault of her emotional turmoil, she was at least able to talk openly for the first time about how losing her mum had made her feel instead of pushing him away. The line was drawn at the suggestion of formal counselling. The fact that she was struggling to eradicate the picture of her mum lying helpless on the floor remained a scar and a secret, that nightmare scenario playing over in her mind but hidden from everyone else.

Mel apologised to her teachers and embarked on a quest to

cradicate the image that she had created of herself as an underachiever. She finally turned to her friends for support, who were only too willing to welcome her back with open arms. Robert knew what it was like to lose someone close, and watching Mel go through this torment rekindled some of the anguish that he had felt as a young boy when his father left. It wasn't something that he had dealt with sufficiently to stop it resurfacing from time to time to make him wobble emotionally.

Mel never set out to take advantage of the kindness that was bestowed upon her by Ali and Robert, but so overjoyed at being able to use them to block out the fear of her appointment that she didn't let any opportunity to see them outside of school pass; even if it were a quick cuppa round at Robert's house with his own mum – in fact, especially if it included his mum.

The siblings reacted very differently once the screening of their health had been completed. Lewis instantly forgot about it, not wanting to paw over the details, while Mel couldn't – or wouldn't – get it out of her mind. She was beginning to endure the worst part of the medical intrusion – waiting for the results. Although her dad and brother understood perfectly well what she would be going through and what it meant, she still felt alone. She needed someone special to be able to talk to, to be able to share feelings with; someone that could fill the void left by her mum. Quite impulsively, Mel decided to do something about that, she wasn't going to go through the trauma of waiting for her results by herself.

19

As Mel headed into the October half-term break, any social distractions with her friends were a positive deviation for her thoughts. Robert's eighteenth birthday party on the first Saturday of the students' week off was going to be one of the highlights of the year. Mary had used her network of contacts at the club to arrange for a small marquee to be erected in their back garden. She had been offered the use of the function room at the club but had declined the kind offer. It still rankled with her that Robert had got embarrassingly drunk at his football awards ceremony in that venue, and the idea that he and his mates might end up in the same state again was something she would rather deal with on private premises, not in a public bar. Robert wanted to invite more people than was feasibly possible to fit into the house and marquee. That was the problem with being so popular - it was difficult making the decision on who not to invite.

He was delighted that Mel was in a better frame of mind and would be attending. He thought it would be a good opportunity for her to forget about her woes and to enjoy herself. The discussion she had started with him earlier in the week about being petrified of waiting for her screening results concerned him though. Robert didn't feel he was best placed to help her with that, but as she had instigated the conversation with him when they were alone, he felt obliged to be the best friend he could.

'There's no point worrying about something that hasn't even happened yet, Mel. Focus on what is important in your life and don't let anything stop you from being happy.'

To Robert, he was just trying to find the right words to say as an understanding mate. To Mel, he understood it. He got her, absolutely spot on. His words resembled those of her own mum's.

Both Ali and Robert had watched in disbelief as their friend deteriorated in the aftermath of her mum's death. Ali had only privately relived the horror of that day, but she couldn't subdue her emotions forever. She had tentatively spoken to her ever-supportive parents, but it was when she was walking home with Robert that she spouted mostly. She always felt touched that he would walk her home even though it was in completely the opposite direction to where he needed to go himself.

On the afternoon they broke up for half-term, she opened up to Robert about the awfulness of seeing medics battling to save Poppy, and she literally cried on his shoulder.

'Oh god, it looks like someone's p'd on your top Robert.'

'Yuck, thanks Ali. Hope you've not snotted on it as well,' he laughed.

'I can't promise you that. Come in and let me wipe it off?'

'Don't worry about it.'

'Don't be silly. Come on.'

As Ali closed the front door, Robert sensed that no one else was at home.

'Are you sure your folks won't mind me being here?'

'Why? Are you planning to steal the family jewels?' mocked Ali.

'I might if I can find where they're hidden. Are you one of them?'

Ali blushed, and skirted round that comment.

'They know that we're best mates, so it's not like you're a stranger I picked up on the way home. Mind you, you are strange.'

There followed a bout of mock wrestling and giggling as Robert grabbed her by the waist and lifted her up off the floor. Ali's vertical lift sent her head towards the ceiling, knocking the faux crystal chandelier in the process. A line of plastic beading held on by a small metallic ring was pulled and the delicate attachment snapped loose from the main body. Ali hung in mid-air with the beading dangling on her forehead before she alerted Robert with a tap on the shoulder to let her down. Ali put her hand up to her open mouth and muttered 'oops' as she looked at Robert. He couldn't help himself and was in hysterics.

'You crack me up, Croftsy. You got any step ladders?'

Using a stool from the kitchen to stand on, Robert was able to reach up and pinch the deformed metal ring back into a circular shape, and back through the hole on the chandelier frame where it had broken away from.

'Thanks, Greeny.'

'No worries. Always seems to be a bit of a drama when we're together. What's that all about?'

'Must be a sign.'

'Saying what?'

'Dunno, a warning maybe?'

'That I should run away while I've got the chance?'

'You should be so lucky, big head.'

They stared at each other without it feeling awkward. Robert caved in first.

'I'm tired of going around in the same circles Ali, aren't you?'

Her voice quivered as she answered.

'Yeah, but I'm no good at this. I'm scared. I don't even know what to do or say to move it on, Robert.'

'I don't either. It seems like you're always just out of the corner of my eye, never quite in view, and yet you're all I want to see. I'm such a moron. You must think I'm pathetic.'

'No. No I don't. That's a lovely way to put it. I just hoped that you weren't messing me around because I'm so gullible.'

'I'm not! Honestly. I wouldn't do that. *Definitely* not to you.'

Self-doubt crept into his mind followed by a short silence that began to feel ominous. It prompted Robert to adopt his regular mode in deflecting a tense, negative situation with some light humour.

'Tell you what, why don't you write me a letter.'

This prompted Ali to widen her eyes at Robert in disbelief, as if he had just insulted her. Robert started to snigger because she knew exactly what he was referring to. During the lower sixth, Vince Mitchell had flirted regularly with a student called Belinda Tomlinson. He would be crude with her in the common room, and even more so at parties. Belinda was taken in by his smutty humour, but she read more into their friendship than he did. She really liked him and mistook the signs that the feeling was mutual. She began to let her feelings be known to her friends, hoping that the whispers would reach Vince and his chums.

Belinda was not shy at coming forward, and told Vince herself that she fancied him, but was confused why his response was less than enthusiastic once she'd put herself out there. Vince chose to manipulate the situation, knowing that he was leading her on, but not thinking for a moment about the consequences his actions would have on her. He told Belinda to write 'one more letter' knowing full well that she would deliver an outpouring of mush on several sheets of paper – proper writing paper too, not on a lined A4 student notepad. She excitedly handed him the envelope in which she had placed the words of someone smitten by the recipient.

Vince read the letter in the company of his cronies. His childish and callous response tore the girl's heart apart, mocking her by saying that he had literally wanted a single letter from the alphabet, and as she had failed to do so, he was no longer interested in her. Not once did Vince feel any shame or remorse, while Belinda had to endure the embarrassment of rejection in a very public arena. Some protested there was a funny side to it; most thought it cringeworthy and felt sorry for her.

'I'm actually serious, write down how you feel rather than saying it, and then that'll help me to tell you likewise. If you take the time to write down what you feel about me then I'll know you absolutely mean it.'

Robert hadn't explained it very well to Ali, but he needed her to make that first move, because he couldn't stand rejection. It was something he would far rather be immune to, but he retained bitter memories of being stranded by someone special he had once trusted.

Ali blushed.

'Alright. I can do that. But how do I know that you're not going to do the same as Vince?'

'Because… it's the birthday present I'll look forward to getting the most tomorrow.' Robert was definite in his response, and Ali could tell that he meant it. 'Besides…'

'Besides, what?'

He didn't answer, instead taking a step forward to plant a kiss on her lips. And then time slipped by unnoticed.

'You got any marshmallows?' Robert asked.

Upon being directed to a cupboard with biscuits and other packets of goodies, he proceeded to make some hot chocolate while Ali regained her composure and flattened the crumples of her clothing. When Ali came downstairs, the conversation lightened as it centred on Robert's birthday, and the pair childishly made moustaches of cream as they sipped on their drinks. Robert couldn't have timed his mischief worse, as Ali's mum arrived home and appeared in the kitchen. He attempted to wipe the sticky mess away while greeting her, but it was impossible to cover up.

'You could drink some of that as well Robert if you'd like,' she said sternly. 'Can you clear those marshmallows up when you've finished Alison please? I've just got to nip out again, down to the supermarket to get some ingredients for stroganoff. Horrible place at the best of times.'

Mrs Crofts didn't seem in the best of moods and was more than a little apathetic to find Robert clowning around in her kitchen. She was just the same on her return, so the lad politely gave his excuses and made a sharp exit soon afterwards.

'Have you wiped the spills off the working surface Alison?'

'Just doing it.'

'I've been out the house forty minutes, what on earth have you been up to?'

Ali hid her face from her mum so that she couldn't see her reddening and changed the focus of the conversation.

'You could have been a little bit politer to Robert, mum.'

'Hmm. I just wasn't expecting to find a juvenile with cream round his mush when I got back, that's all. What was he doing here anyway?'

'He walked back with me after school to talk about his birthday party.'

'Took the scenic route home again, did he?'

'What's that supposed to mean, mum?'

'Well, he walks up here with you, which is the wrong direction for his own house, so I'm left wondering whether there's something going on between you two?'

She started blushing.

'He's a really good mate, mum. And anyway, what if there was something going on? I really like him – don't you?'

Mrs Crofts deliberately fell silent for a few moments, and that riled Ali.

'He's not the kind of lad that I would have expected you to like, Alison.'

'Well, tell me one thing about him that's bad then. If you ask around, I bet you'll only ever hear good things about him. He's looked out for me more times than you know. He's been there when there's been really awful things going off, you know that.'

It was true. He seemed to care for her daughter so there was nothing that Mrs Crofts could do to retaliate against such an impassioned argument. That evening though, Ali struggled to empty her thoughts out onto the blank sheet in front of her. She felt tense between her rib cage following her defensive encounter with her mum. It was well after her parents had turned the landing light off that she finished writing the words that she hoped would connect with Robert more deeply than ever before. In stark contrast to Belinda Tomlinson, she did not need pages to express herself. Ali concluded that she had more to say with fewer words, that had greater meaning.

20

Mary specifically asked Robert to make sure that no one turned up before seven o'clock, not even his football team buddies intent on necking some cheap cider en route. The knocking at the door an hour earlier than the commencement of the jollification was met with an irritated response from Mary.

'Bloody hell Robert, didn't I make it clear that no one was welcome before seven?'

She was just putting the finishing touches to her nail varnish and was blowing on her fingers furiously as she scuttled down the stairs to find out which nincompoop had not read the invitation correctly. Mary was not about to deface her cosmetic efforts, so she placed her arms behind her with the palms of her hands facing upwards and resembled someone imitating a swan. She pressed her chin against the door latch and pushed it in a clockwise direction to unlock it, and then used her right elbow to ledge it open. Up to this point there had been no response from her son, who was in the shower singing merrily to himself. He was oblivious to the early arrival until Mary tapped on the bathroom door.

'Robert, there's someone here already.'

'What? I told them not before seven, mum. *I'm* not even ready yet. Tell 'em to get lost for an hour.'

'Shush! I don't think it'd be nice to do that to her, Rob. Just try and be quick getting yourself sorted please. I don't want to be the only one entertaining your female friends.'

Robert stood gawping in the mirror. His scarlet face caused by the warmth of the water masked the blushing that had begun upon hearing that it was a girl that had turned up early. It had to be Ali bringing him his present and maybe 'the letter' before any other guests turned up. Perhaps they would be going out with each other properly in front of everyone tonight, he thought. The muffled tones of females chatting together downstairs could be heard as he got changed in his bedroom, spraying so much deodorant that it briefly formed a cloud that engulfed his upper body. He glanced at himself in the mirror, puffed his pecs and psyched himself up as if he were going into the most important game of his life. In reality, he probably was.

Ali had been desperate to get along to the party as quickly as she could, in the hope that she would see Robert to give him his present before anyone else arrived. She wanted the chance to let him read her letter, and for him to show her that he felt exactly the same way – though he already had, if the other day was anything to go on. It was one of those afternoons where she could feel it in the air that something was afoot, and fate was falling into line. Although she stuck her big toe through one pair of tights, that was the only mishap in getting ready for the party – up until her dad was turning into Wood Street and she realised she had forgotten the letter. Ali took in a large intake of breath, which scared the life out of her dad who jumped and twitched at his steering wheel. He pulled over in a bus layby, prompting the bus driver directly behind to sound his horn at the illegally parked driver.

'What's the matter Alison, are you ok?'

Ali pressed her cheekbones with her fingertips, staring at the footwell. She struggled to get any words of explanation out.

'Dad, please just trust me and don't ask any questions. I've forgotten something at home. Can you quickly take me back, so I can get it?'

'Or I could drop you off at Robert's, and I can bring whatever it is down to you shortly?'

'No! Thanks, but I don't want you to do that dad.'

Her letter was sealed and hidden in the side of her wardrobe. At the far corner of the base where her shoes were neatly stored, there was a gap to the wall in which she kept some things very privately. There was no way that she was going to tell anyone about that. Besides, it would only invite inquisitive and unwanted questions from her parents about what she was being so secretive about, and the last thing she needed now was any kind of hassle.

It was busy in the town centre with people making their way home from an afternoon of shopping or going out in the early evening. Mr Crofts navigated his way through the traffic, doing his best to avoid congestion. As he drove, he was commentating to Ali on his chosen route, justifying why he chose to go up one street particularly rather than another. He thought he was helping to avoid her getting any more uptight than she looked. Conversely, a middle-aged man divulging his knowledge of Winchester's one-way system irritated the hell out of Ali, and so she tried to zone out by looking disinterested.

By the time Bryon Avenue was in sight she had already undone the buckles to her court shoes so that they could be quickly kicked off as she darted upstairs. She slipped the envelope into her clutch bag and grabbed her deodorant for one final spray before they left again. She didn't want to spend time undoing her dress, so carefully placed the can under her armpit. Unfortunately for Ali, the direction of the nozzle was pointing away from her skin, and instead soaked the material around her ribcage. She rubbed frantically at the wet patch which achieved nothing other than to help smear the grey looking stain that began to appear as the liquid dried. She grabbed a damp flannel from the bathroom and stroked the affected area. As it started drying it was less obvious than it had been, faint enough not to notice in a darkened marquee. A couple of sequins had been pulled off from the vigorous cleaning operation, causing the dress to snag slightly. Ali used her nail scissors to trim the loose threads left hanging.

Ali was delighted that her dad knew how to locate the accelerator pedal after she had hinted that she was going to be late. It had been some years since Mr Crofts last took to flirting with speed limits in the way he did to get Ali to her destination on the other side of town. Rather than lamenting on the impatience of his daughter, he rather enjoyed his excursion and putting his BMW through its paces.

Ali had checked her watch frequently on the journey and was content enough that she had made it to Robert's house just before quarter to seven. As she stood in the road watching her dad disappear at a more sensible speed, she could hear the dull thudding of music and guessed that it was coming from the back garden where the small marquee had been erected. A friend of Mel's brother had offered the loan of his decks, and Lewis had volunteered to play the tunes to keep the guests swinging their pants. He was obviously taking it seriously, Ali thought, if he had turned up early to check the equipment.

She reached into her clutch bag and placed the letter on top of the present that she had bought for Robert. He was going to be impressed with her gifts. She had dipped into her savings to buy him a new Walkman, much to the disapproval of her mum. This was one secret that she couldn't put away in her wardrobe hidey-hole without her mum finding out, because Mrs Crofts needed to get the money out from Ali's account as she wasn't able to do so herself until she was eighteen. Ali had argued that it was a special gift for a special birthday – he'd only be eighteen once, and she was convinced that he would go out of his way to get a lovely present for her birthday. And besides, if they were going to be an item, it was a good way to show her affection for him. She just hoped he would be as impressed with her letter.

Ali noticed the gate was open at the side of the house and went into the kitchen through the side entrance. Instead of being received by Robert or Mary, she was pounced on by Zoe McCullagh.

'Hiya Ali!' she squealed, in her enthusiastic, high-pitched tone.

Ali was completely taken back and realised instantly that her plan to spend some time with Robert was scuppered.

'Oh, hi Zoe. How come you're here so early?' she asked with some irritation.

'Dunno really, I think my dad's going out, so he dropped me off. I've only just got here, but Mel Burchell's been here ages.'

Ali's stomach spun. She walked round to the lounge to find Mel in conversation with Mary, with the latter helping to straighten her hair. Ali quickly deduced that this was perhaps something Poppy would have helped Mel with, and in the absence of female intuition at home she had obviously sought some intervention from Robert's mum instead. Or, at least, that's the explanation that Ali had hoped was correct.

'Ooh that looks intense, Mary.'

'Hello Ali, how are you?' the impromptu stylist responded.

'Good thanks. Looking good Mel!'

'Hiya Ali, I'll be done in a few minutes. I'll come to find you.'

'Sure. Where's Robert?'

'Probably stashing some alcohol somewhere Ali, do you think you could keep an eye on him tonight? I could do without having to clear up puddles of vomit.'

Ali giggled.

'I'll do my best. It's his mates that you'll probably need to keep an eye on though, Mary. It'll be the first thing I'll talk to him about when I find him.'

'He said he was going to help Lewis set up the decks in the marquee,' said Mel, looking at Ali through the reflection of her hand mirror. 'You look lovely, by the way.'

'Oh thanks – so do you. See you when you're done?'

Ali managed to avoid being trailed by Zoe as she ghosted through the kitchen again, and outside via the side door. As she stepped into the entry, she could hear indistinct voices and intermittent music one way, and the sound of a car pulling up outside the house the other way. Other guests were beginning to arrive. As she turned left and started heading to the entrance of the marquee, a sharp breeze lifted the envelope she had placed on top of Robert's present, and carried it onto the floor alongside the fence that bordered the neighbours. Ali approached the letter and stooped down to try and grab it juggling the present in her other arm. But each time she went to lay her thumb and fore finger on the corner it teased her by turning over like a cartwheel in the gusts, landing a couple of feet further away. It bounced off the dirt in the borders and ledged against a panel of the picket fence.

By this time, Ali was parallel to the marquee and could see the colours of the disco lights shining through the plastic windows. If she was going to repossess the paper projectile, she had no choice other than to step on the dirt in the flower bed. Without much thought for the consequences, Ali sank her right foot into the mud, which immediately seeped over the front of it. She tried to stop it sliding any further, but as she reached forward there was nothing to stop the damp, soft soil from pushing up over her shoe and onto her ankle. The closer she moved to grab the envelope, the more the wedge pressed into the mud, so she tugged her foot back out of the gloop which did everything it could to retain the heel. Ali tried to subtly scrape the excess mud onto the path, but by this time she could feel eyes burning in the back of her head, as young party goers were peering through the kitchen window at her peculiar behaviour. She stared back at those trying to target her for a good teasing. When she looked back down at the flower bed the letter had blown through the gap between the panels and disappeared onto the Burchell's lawn next door.

She had two choices: either let the letter fly off and hope that Mel never found it which would be calamitously embarrassing all round if ever she did. Or she could sneak round to the neighbouring property to nab the letter and hope that no one would notice.

She put her head down as she passed by the kitchen entrance, like how she went hurrying through the corridors at school. Her great escape had been rumbled by Simone Birtles and Brett Etherson.

'Oi, Croftsy! You must be the only person on the planet who leaves a party before it's started!' snorted Brett before Simone added her own contribution.

'Ali that was hilarious, you scampering after Robert's birthday card and it blowing away.'

'It's got some cash inside, so I can't let it get wet, can I? I'm just going next door to get it. I'll be back in a minute or two Brett if you want to count. Can you get past twenty these days or are you still retaking maths at college? I'm sure Simmy will help you if you get stuck. Then again…'

They had ruffled her feathers – and sequins – so Ali's sharp put-down was somewhat out of character for her, causing Simone and Brett to look at each other in shock. She didn't wait for a reply to her sarcastic dig at the pair, and instead found herself reluctantly walking towards the entry of another house.

There was no gate at the side of Mel's house. It had been left open to allow easy wheelchair access for Poppy, and so Ali had no obstacles in her way to reach the lawn. Though she knew Mel and Lewis were already at the party, she took a quick glance round at the back of the house to make sure Derek was out of sight. When she was sure the coast was clear it took her a matter of seconds to scan the garden for the white envelope causing her so much bother and started prancing towards a white spec at the top end. It had lodged itself underneath the raking arms of a mature hosta. Ali snatched it before it became any more of a nuisance and hurtled back over the lawn in the direction that she had arrived.

She had retained a stooped position throughout her mini adventure, but as she straightened up on her exit, she noticed Derek staring down on her from an upstairs window. She could have no idea how long he had been standing there and didn't want to wait around long enough to give any sort of explanation. Ali casually gave him a polite wave as she reached the entry again, and once she was out of Derek's gaze rested her back against the side wall to take a quick breather, and to brush off any remnants of soil attached to the envelope.

The early evening dew on the grass had smudged the ink on the front and exacerbated what was already a soggy pair of tights, but at least it had stayed off her dress. Ali intended to get straight to the bathroom at Robert's house, and remove the tights before anyone noticed. The coarse brickwork behind her clung to her dress as she went to move, and once more the dress was snagged, this time behind her right shoulder. But Ali was so intent on getting back to the party that she was oblivious to the short strands dangling over her back.

The kitchen was the focal point for guests arriving at the party, where they were able drop off their gifts, grab a drink, and start to socialise. The mass of revellers camouflaged Ali's re-entry, and was a smoke screen for her to be able to drift unnoticed towards the cloakroom off the main corridor. She paused at the kitchen table to place her present and birthday card amongst the others, then took a few paces before realising that her letter was still on top of the present with the card. Turning back erratically, Ali pounced on the envelope before anything else sinister happened to it. There was a shifty look about her as she took a glance over each shoulder, but no one saw her claim her prized asset.

'Yuck, what's that rank smell?' Everyone's attention was grabbed by Zoe, standing in a group close by. 'Has someone dropped their guts?'

The pungent smell was not lost on Brett either.

'Ugh, that is minging. C'mon, someone own up.'

Inadvertently, Ali started to bulge out her nostrils to identify the source of the putrid smell that was wafting through the kitchen. In small degrees of revolution, she turned her neck to examine the air quality around her – first one way, then the other. Her senses began to drag her head towards the floor, and the realisation that the sole of her shoe contained the root cause of the less than fragrant odour was predictable and typical of the evening that she was having. Ali knew that she must have had cat shit clogged up on her shoe, and this was the consequence of foraging through undergrowth and plant beds. Her letter had wreaked havoc on her appearance. Accompanying her sodden and muddy tights, she now had the remnants of a cat's gut glued to her foot.

With the rest of the kitchen poking fun at each other for suspecting that someone was responsible for a very fruity fart, Ali planned her escape route to the cloakroom. If she had planned to slip away inconspicuously, it didn't work. To avoid treading any of the excrement onto the floor she walked with her heal arch lifted and the weight carried by the ball of her toe. This made it look like she was limping, and Brett noticed her head bobbing up and down as she headed towards the toilet door.

'What's up with your foot, Croftsy?' he shouted across to her.

Ali didn't pause or turn around, as she would inevitably find a sea of expectant faces all waiting for an explanation that she would find difficult to provide without being honest.

The desperation to ensure there was complete privacy meant she tried the door handle of the loo several times to make sure it was locked. Ali stuffed the grubby looking envelope into her clutch bag and slipped off her shoe. She grabbed reams of toilet paper and used this to remove the excess crap from the heel. Her breathing was erratic, using short, sharp breaths so as not to let her senses admit what she really was doing. This was truly horrible. It stank so bad that she felt as though it would leave stains in her nostrils, and she did everything she could to avoid retching.

The toilet paper was not as effective as she hoped as it began to smear the mess rather than effacing it. Ali knew she needed to be assertive to get this sorted out. Knowing full well that it was disgusting to do it, she grabbed the bar of soap anyway, wet it slightly, and rubbed it against the affected area. The bar was mostly worn, so the edges were useful to get right into the groove between heel and sole. Then, she held the shoe over the basin beneath the mixer tap and pulled the lever in the hope of using the water to remove the excess soap and gunk. The tap was yanked too far, causing the water to rebound off the shoe and splash back over her. She quickly pushed the lever off again and started spitting into the basin where she had been splattered with the residue. Looking up in the mirror it was a struggle to recognise the image that was looking back at her. She had literally been pebble dashed – her hair, her face, her clothes. This was surely what despair felt like, looked like, smelt like. Her heart was pounding with dread. How could she entertain the idea of letting anyone – let alone Robert – see her speckled in shit?

It took a significant amount of time to get to a point where Ali was ready to unlock the door. Her tights had been used as a cloth to wipe away as much of the rancid excess as possible. Although they were dirty at the ankle area, they were okay further up, and they proved to be effective at absorbing the vile faeces. She wiped down the basin too and flushed the remnants of the bar of soap down the loo. She felt like she would die from embarrassment if she were to leave behind any traces of her misadventure for someone else to discover. She would never be able to live this one down back at school if that happened. Once Ali had unhinged the lock, she slowly clawed the door open. The first and, thankfully, only – person she saw was Simone who was dancing from toe-to-toe.

'Blimey Ali, how long do you need to take a leak? Hope you've not laid any cable in there as well. It smells a bit whiffy.'

'Hang on a minute, Simmy. I'm not quite finished yet.'

'What's that supposed to mean? I'm desperate to go. Been hopping around out here for ages.'

'I need you to do something for me first.'

'Get stuffed Ali, let me in.'

'Go and tell Mel I need to see her.'

'No chance.'

'Well you can forget coming in here until you do.'

Simone looked shocked; it wasn't like Ali to be bolshie. And then she saw the mess she was in.

'What've you got in your hair?'

'Go and give Mel the message.'

Reluctantly, and still wriggling with the feeling that she was going to wet herself, Simone dashed off through the kitchen and outside to the marquee. A few minutes later she returned and tapped the door.

'It's me, let me in.'

Ali opened the door and peered out.

'Where's Mel?'

'She's in the marquee, dancing.'

'Well did you give her the message?'

'Yeah – you saw me go.'

'Where the bloody hell is she, then?'

'How do I know? I told her you needed to see her, and she was like "ok, tell her to come out to the marquee."'

'Simmy! You are ten chips short of a portion. I meant for you to get her to come here. Go back and tell her it's an emergency.'

'I need to piss Ali, or I'm going to do a puddle right here.'

Ali let Simone into the cloakroom to relieve herself but wedged the door open so she couldn't lock it. She could hear her moaning about no privacy, and that there was 'no soap to wash her frigging hands'.

'Are you done?' Ali asked impatiently.

'Just hang on, will you?' remonstrated Simone.

Ali opened the door regardless to discover her hostage applying a layer of mascara on top of the thick coating that already existed. Without moving her head from the position that it was locked in to create eyelash perfection, Simone looked at Ali out of the corner of her eyes and got the very heavy hint to hurry up. She threw her make up pieces into her bag and gave Ali a filthy look as she squeezed by in the tight space offered by the cloakroom. Her parting shot at Ali was sharp.

'I'll get Mel, but you owe me big time. I've seen a different side to you tonight Ali, does Rob know what a cow you can be?'

A short time later, Mel came down the corridor singing a tune that she had been dancing to in the marquee. She was clearly tipsy and wore the kind of alcoholic smile that looked like a mask. Ali succeeded in convincing her giggling friend to go into the confined surroundings of the cloakroom, which was quickly becoming Ali's private office in which to conduct her business.

'Mel, please calm down just for a minute. Look at the state of me!'

'Shit. No seriously, you stink of shit!' she snorted.

'I know, and it is. It's a long story and I don't have time to explain. I've got to get home; I can't stay at the party looking and smelling like this.'

Mel looked her up and down and stopped acting foolishly once she had recognised the tragedy of this surreal situation.

'What do you want me to do for you, Ali?'

Ali reached into her bag and pulled out the scruffy looking envelope.

'You're the only person I can trust to do this for me, Mel. It's unbelievably important. See this letter? I need you to give it Robert as soon as possible.'

159

'Ok, I'll go and do it now.'

'No, not until I've gone.'

'Why don't I get him to come down here to speak to you?'

'No, Mel. I don't want him to see me like this. Do you know how wounding it would feel to have to expose yourself this badly to people you care most about?'

Mel did know how that felt, having been defenceless in her explanation for stalking Ali and Robert.

'He'll be expecting that Mel, please make sure he gets it and no one else.' Mel nodded. 'I might be back later if I can get changed quickly enough, so I'd better call my dad to come and get me. Would you be a look out while I go into the lounge to use Robert's phone?'

Mel kept Ali company while she waited outside for her dad to arrive, who seemed to take an extraordinary amount of time to get there.

'I'm really sorry we've not had the chance to catch up for ages, Ali.'

'Blimey Mel, you've had hell round to visit you and it overstayed its welcome, so I'm not at all surprised. I'm sorry too. Whenever you're ready for a good natter just call me. We could organise a sleep over at mine if you want?'

'Maybe. I need to get back in tune with myself a bit more first, you know, get my head around things a bit better before I start off-loading to you – or off-loading to anyone really. The thing is, people mean well and all that – but I just don't need thousands of pieces of advice right now, or pity.'

'It is difficult to think about you and not feel sorry about the whole situation, Mel. I'm sorry, I don't wish to be morbid. Look, you get yourself back in there and have a good time tonight – you deserve it. Hopefully see you later.'

When her dad finally arrived, Ali provided no answers to the questions he asked about her appearance – would he even begin to believe her anyway, she wondered? Then he would want to know what the significance of the letter was, which was something she was hardly likely to want to digest with her old man.

Ali had anticipated getting home, getting showered and changed, and making her way back to the party again. It took a little bit of time to invent some dross to tell her parents, but eventually Ali thought she had blagged an explanation to pacify them that didn't involve letters or Robert. Conversely, it didn't involve too much brain power on Mrs Crofts' part to realise that her daughter was never going to win any awards for fibbing. But seeing the distress carved on Ali's brow, she knew better than to start pulling the tale apart.

Convinced that the putrid smell was still in her hair after the first wash, Ali proceeded to shampoo it three times. Her fingertips were red raw by the time she had scrubbed them with the nail brush, and what had started as a new bottle of shower gel at the start of her bathroom fest was reduced to remnants by the end. Whether she believed it or not, Alison Crofts was as clean as a daisy.

Swathed in her towel and bath robe she sat on her bed agonising over what to do next. It was just before half-past-nine, mid-point of the party. It was probably going to take her at least an hour to get ready and down to Robert's house and then there would be only just over an hour left. Was there any point in going down that late? Would Robert be drunk by then and not want Ali to be crowding him while he hung out with the lads? Would she feel like a spare part because everyone was already in a party spirit and she would not have even warmed up by then? Most importantly, would Robert have read his letter? If so, what if he didn't feel the same way? If not, well why not? Ali bent her legs and buried her head between her knees, rocking anxiously as she did so. Her head was full of questions and just couldn't decide what to do for the best and started crying. The next thing she remembered was looking at her clock at two o'clock in the morning, and her stomach feeling like it was in knots again as she realised the party was now well and truly over.

21

After Ali had left with her dad, Mel returned to the party. The conversation with her friend had triggered a bout of anxiety about the results that she was expecting from the hospital within the next six weeks. She looked at Lewis, the crowd pleaser, cranking up the sounds that were causing euphoria on the dance floor and realised that he was getting on with his life. Mel felt emotionally isolated, and it scared her. She didn't want to be alone. She looked down at the envelope that Ali had given her and scanned the marquee for Robert. It didn't take much craning of her neck to identify him, being hauled around on the dance floor by his mates. Their arms were linked together as if they were performing some sort of Greek line dance to 'Don't Look Back In Anger' and then 'Three Lions' which ironically made many of the lads look back in anger at the despair and disappointment of the Euro '96 tournament. Mel didn't think it looked like he was there voluntarily, or that he was particularly enjoying the experience. She sidled up next to him and grabbed his attention over the thudding of the music.

'Nice dancing, Rob!' She had to lean in, up close to his face so that he could hear. He placed his arm round her so that he could give her his full attention, and it felt nice being this near to him.

'Get me off this dance floor, Mel!' he replied, wincing.

'You alright?'

'Yeah… No! Not had enough cider yet to get up and dance.'

'Well at least you aren't throwing up.'

'That's true. Hey, listen, where the hell is Ali? She reckoned she was going to be here early, but I don't know if she's even turned up.'

If Robert hadn't asked about Ali's whereabouts while Mel

was having some time with him, she would have voluntarily explained her absence and handed the envelope to him there and then. She went to give him a straight answer, but her efforts faltered, and she kept the hand that held the envelope tucked discretely behind her back.

'I saw her ages ago, but not got a clue where she went.' Robert frowned at her, deep ridges forming on his brow. 'How about grabbing a beer from the kitchen, she might be inside with your mum?'

Mel waited in the kitchen while Robert explored downstairs for signs of Ali. While she poured some cider into two disposable beakers, she could hear him talking to his mum.

'She was here at the same time as that other girl – Zoe. She came into the living room and said 'hello' while I was helping Mel with her hair and make-up and asked where you were. I thought she had found you in the marquee?'

'Nope, not seen her at all. Weird. Are you sure she was here?'

He huffed and puffed and disappeared upstairs to his bedroom, struggling to think rationally, not helped by the booze that he had already consumed. He automatically jumped to the conclusion that she had rejected the idea of going out with him. If she couldn't speak to him in person previously about her feelings when she *did* want to go out with him, she was hardly going to find the courage to do so now that she was looking for an exit clause. Robert's confusion made his head hurt, and he could feel his frustration turning to anger. He felt completely let down.

Mel sipped at the sweet tasting cider. She stood peering out the window at the flashing lights in the marquee, with the pint pot pressed to her chin. Mary came into the kitchen.

'You ok love? You look like you're cooking something up deep in thought like that.'

'Just taking a quick time-out. Are you coming into the

marquee for a boogie, Mary?'

'Not to that rubbish. I'll be having a word with your brother to ask him if he's got anything decent to play.'

'Where's Rob? I've poured him a drink here.'

'Ooh, he's gone off sulking because Ali isn't here. I haven't a clue what's going on between them two, do you?'

'Same as you, don't know.'

'I can't work out what the problem is, how difficult can it be to ask a girl out? He really likes her. Can't you put a good word in for him? Right, I'm just going to do some surveillance outside to make sure no one is up to no good – if you know what I mean.' Mary winked at Mel. 'If you see that lad of mine before I do, tell him to get his backside back out here.'

Once Mary had begun her rounds to tame the unruly, Mel gulped the contents of the pint pot down in one. She slipped away from the kitchen and went to stand down the side entrance of her own house next door. If Ali returned to the party at any point it would be impossible for Mel to provide a rational explanation to her or Robert for not giving him the letter that she been asked to deliver. Ali had entrusted in her to get the envelope to him, but Mel was about to betray the faith that Ali had placed in her. The intrigue was too much, and it had reignited her dark side.

It was clear to Mel that for Robert to have become so disturbed about Ali's absence, the letter must contain something of significant emotional magnitude. Even though she felt disgustingly guilty to do it, Mel ripped open the grubby looking envelope. She did so with her hands operating to her left side while her head was turned to the right, so the deed was out of her own sight. She tried slipping out the contents with her thumb and forefinger, but the notepaper seemed jammed on one of the edges of the opening, as if in protest at the illegitimacy of the current ownership. Mel scooped her hand inside and grabbed the contents roughly so that the letter was partially screwed up by its forced exit. She took a minute to compose herself, and once she was satisfied that she was not being watched she unravelled the neatly folded note. Her eyes fixed onto the neatly written words, and she whispered the content to herself as she read it through.

If you've got as far as opening my letter, Robert, then I hope you are smiling that I've stuck to my side of the bargain! A wise woman once said to me that it wasn't important to be popular if you were the favourite of just one person. With you there's nothing I need that I haven't got. My personality might not sparkle but look for the glow that I have shining for you in my heart and it will make up for that. I want to be your someone whenever you think there's no one. There's this song that my dad listens to that says, 'only with you, life moves so fast' and that's how I feel about you. You make my head spin, and time just runs away. I'm never more comfortable than when we're together. Please tell me that you feel the same, so that you and I can become us. Ali x

Mel lowered her hand and stared glumly at nothing at all. She had knowingly sabotaged their attempts at togetherness and was culpable for trampling on the hopes of her friends. Where Melanie Burchell was concerned, there was a fine line between respect and raging jealousy, so no one would ever understand the rationale of what she was about to do. Not only did she have a void in her life, but she was suffocating from fear of the destructive effects that the same disease that killed her mum might cause her.

Mel completed the short walk back round to the party and was greeted with a scene of chaos in the kitchen. Vince Mitchell was puking up in the sink, being comforted by none other than

Belinda Tomlinson, the very person he had chosen to publicly ridicule. How the tables had turned. He would struggle to play it down with his mates that he was the first person to chunder at the party, not at all classy for the cool image that he supposedly wore.

Mary was speaking to Vince's dad on the phone in the corridor, insisting that he was collected from the party at once. Understandably, she didn't sound particularly happy. Zoe McCullagh was sitting at the small round kitchen table sobbing, the result of being repeatedly wound up with the nickname 'McCull-yuck' for the suggestion that she was the origin for the foul smell that could still be detected in the room. Robert was nowhere to be seen, so she turned to go and find out if he had reappeared in the marquee. Mel turned sharply to walk out of the side door, not looking where she was going, and promptly barged into someone coming in the other way.

'Hiya Mel – you drunk or something?'

'Oli. Sorry, I was on another planet. Must engage brain when walking.'

'No worries – it's becoming one of my better habits bumping into you. How is everything?'

It was not meant to be a loaded question, and Oli couldn't know how complicated it would be to answer truthfully. So, Mel chose to swerve round it.

'Don't suppose you've seen Robert?'

'He's in the marquee. I'm getting myself a drink – do you fancy one?'

'Er, yeah – thanks, that'd be nice. Look, I never really had the chance to thank you for reaching out to me that time.'

'Don't be daft. Anyway, someone needed to protect them pigeons.'

Mel smiled and placed her hand on Oli's shoulder as she slipped past him into the side entry once more. Mel wasn't on the look-out for just anyone with whom she could offload the weight of fear and doubt to – otherwise she may not have overlooked the noises being made by Oli. He liked her, but she was not reading any of the signals being given off. Even at this point, her spiteful actions in relation to Ali's letter could be curtailed. Oli was a credible person with whom anyone could trust to help them deal with the havoc currently raging in their lives, but she wasn't to ever know that if the time wasn't taken to get to know him. It simply wasn't a choice she would even have contemplated making once her compulsion kicked in to set her radar on Robert once again. It had to be him.

The birthday boy was not difficult to spot inside the marquee. The influence of booze and the Stone Roses produced dance moves consisting of swaying from one foot to the other, nodding head to the beat, eyes closed for concentration and an occasional demonstration of how to play an air drum. It wasn't a pretty sight, but Mel had never been happier to see her friend. She manoeuvred herself through the excited masses on the dance floor next to Mr Popular, and unashamedly flirted next to him salsa-like. Mel looked at his red face and sweaty brow, and noticed his shirt was half hanging out over his belt where it had been tucked neatly into his jeans earlier in the evening.

Though the marquee exhibited mass elation from the partygoers, Robert's inner-self exposed a forlorn soul. This was lost on the people raving around him, far too lubricated to notice such detail. But Mel could see it, and she sensed it was her opportunity to pounce.

'Oi! Birthday boy. You gonna dance with me or what?'

Robert opened his eyes, screwed his face up and shrugged his shoulders.

'What's up?'

'Ali.' replied Robert.

It was the obvious and predictable response, and yet it rankled with her. The temperature in the marquee made it feel like a sauna. The tarpaulin had soaked up the warmth of the sun from earlier in the day, and now it was being topped up by the exerts of sweaty teenagers. The steamy atmosphere caused a bead of sweat to run between Mel's shoulder blades, and it felt uncomfortable. She needed to get out for some fresh air.

'Do you want to fill me in? C'mon, let's grab a breather outside.'

A lubricated and miserable looking Robert did his best to explain the situation, while Mel pretended to listen attentively to his doom and gloom ramblings.

'Did you speak to Ali?' he enquired.

'Yeah I told you. I saw her earlier after your mum had done my hair.'

'Well what was she like?'

'What kind of question is that? She was like what she's always like.'

'Did she seem edgy? Did she ask anything about me?'

'To be fair, Rob, she did ask where you were. Me and your mum said you were in the marquee setting up.'

'Well she didn't look very bloody far did she? She left without even wishing me a happy birthday. What kind of person would do that, let alone a friend?'

'Dunno Rob, maybe you need to read the signals that gives off.'

'She was supposed to bring me something today. She's all mouth and no function,' he muttered.

'Action.'

'Eh?'

'All mouth and no action. That's what the phrase is, you doughnut!'

The error made them both snort.

'Whatever. I just don't get girls; I'm doomed to be a single bloke.'

'If you just stop your moaning for a minute you might still

have a chance to get off with me.'

Mel didn't wait for the confused looking Robert to work it out. She wrapped her right arm around his shoulder and pulled him towards her. The fact of the matter was that Robert was a complete sucker for a confident girl, someone that surprised him with such conviction. It was what had attracted him to Ali, and now Mel was pulling the same strings. To him, Ali had failed to deliver on what she had promised, and he read that to be that she wasn't really that serious about getting together with him after all. Completely unaware of Mel's subterfuge, he had every reason to believe that he was doing nothing wrong by giving in to her advances. The volume of alcoholic intake caused him to lose any inhibitions, and they kissed – oblivious to the prodding, nudging, and whispering gossip of their peers in different directions. They were hardly trying to be discrete.

Predictably, it was Chinny Jewkes who broke the moment.

'That's disgusting, you two. Get a bloody room.'

It wasn't his intention to do so, but Oli lingered and stared when he saw the pair smooching away. He carried the two drinks he had collected into the marquee and tried desperately not to look back at what others were pointing at.

When they broke off from each other's lips Mel rested her forehead on Robert's, and they smiled at each other.

'Good,' said Mel.

'What is?'

'Well that's put a smile back on your face. It's your birthday matey, time to start enjoying it!'

22

Ali sat on the cold, damp bench at Coventry railway station, waiting for her connecting train back to Winchester. The drab concrete infrastructure did nothing to shelter her from the bitterly cold air weaving its way over the platform and between the tracks. Frost and a dense fog had begun to set in as forecasted and had somehow contributed to creating havoc on the rail network in the Midlands. It was causing Ali a huge inconvenience, as she was heavily delayed on her journey back from York where she had attended an interview for a place on a degree course in social policy. It had been a long and tiring day, with her journey beginning before 6:00am. She was cold, hungry, and fed up with public transport.

Ali watched the departures screen intently and balked each time the estimated arrival time grew later and later. She didn't think for a minute that she would regret turning down the offer of a lift from her dad, but the idea of being in a warm car travelling home – irrespective of the lame conversation that might ensue – exacerbated her feeling of despondency. This was scheduled to be the last train heading to Winchester, and Ali was becoming increasingly anxious that it would be cancelled. Even if it did arrive as indicated on the screen, the two-hour journey would mean getting back after midnight.

She couldn't see a single other passenger on the platform, so she didn't want to go into the waiting room. In there she would be out of sight, and her parent's instructions were to be careful and to keep her wits about her 'at all times'. Here she was, alone, waiting for a train that didn't want to arrive; in a city she knew nothing about; on a murky and unwelcoming platform. On top of that, there was the small matter of an interview for university that she felt went awry. Ali felt she waffled when asked about the importance of client confidentiality, and thought she overused the example of Oli Gemmill in relation to people's welfare rights. The more she went back over her answers in her head, the more she exaggerated how unfocussed her responses had been. She wondered whether the day could have been scripted any worse than it had felt.

The guard appearing through the mist looked like he had been conjured up by the grey mass. He appeared from nowhere, whistling, and winked at Ali as he strolled by in readiness for the arrival of the overdue locomotive. Without being able to see more than a few feet in front of her, she was puzzled about where on earth he'd been, and what he'd been doing. Ali pulled the collar of her coat up as far as it would go and burrowed her face and neck into her scarf, but each time she felt snuggled by its soft fabric, another breeze would blow through the station, cutting through her like the sharpness of a blade. To suggest that Ali felt gloomy like the weather was a complete euphemism.

Dark thoughts began to cloud her mind, dragging her emotions down to a depth she wasn't used to. She began contemplating if this is what it felt like to be dejected, before recalling the immediate aftermath and subsequent fallout from Robert's party. Harassed though she may have been from the challenges of a getting to a university in the North, this unpleasantness paled into insignificance compared to that other entanglement – and the ill-feelings that continued to linger following it. She sat and stared into space, torturing herself with every detail of the morning after that eventful evening.

Ali had woken up with a startle that morning. She sat up disorientated, but as soon as she had gathered herself, she began to recollect the cruelty delivered by fate a few hours earlier. Her head became flooded with questions just like it had before crashing out. How could she have fallen to sleep? Why did her mum or dad not nudge her to get ready for the party? What did

Robert think of her letter? Was it safe to tell people she was his girlfriend now?

Ali felt clammy. She had fallen to sleep without removing the towels she wrapped around herself after showering, and this was becoming more uncomfortable now that she was beginning to feel agitated too. She glanced round at her alarm clock to see that it was already almost ten o'clock. She got out of bed with some urgency and was downstairs changed with lippy and mascara applied within minutes. Ali was on a mission. Her hasty plan to bomb it down to Robert's house was met with disapproval and concern from her mother.

'Why on earth are you going so early? He might not even be awake yet, and probably hungover if he is.'

'It isn't early mum; it'll be nearly eleven by the time I'm down there.'

'I just don't understand the necessity to be dashing down there when you saw him at the party last night.'

'Well if you would have been a bit more supportive last night I might have got back to the party, avoiding the need to be scampering round this morning.'

'That's not fair Alison. For a start, we played taxi whenever you needed it. I told you how sorry we were about what had happened to you, it was a horrible experience. What else were we supposed to have done, love?'

'I'm sorry mum, it's not your fault. I know you're only looking out for me, but can't you remember what I explained to you last night? I didn't even see Robert to speak to, not even to wish him a happy birthday. I need to explain to him what happened.'

'Wouldn't Melanie have told him the problems you had?'

'I hope so.'

Without more than a couple of bites of her toast, and ignoring the protestations of her parents, Ali was moving briskly in the direction of the town centre. As she peered down the High Street, she thought she recognised a lanky figure at the bottom end. She became less sure when the person seemed to do a U-turn to walk back the way they had come, and then darted into the nearest shop doorway across the road to avoid her. It was odd behaviour, but when Ali realised that it was Lewis, she put his suspicious reactions down to his quirky character. With a grin on her face and sarcasm in her voice, she shouted across the precinct, letting him know that she had caught sight of him.

'Hiya Lewis.'

Once he realised that his pathetic attempts to avoid detection had failed miserably, he gave a quick wave without ever making eye contact and dashed off. Ali walked on with a puzzled expression. She got on fine with Lewis usually, so at the time she couldn't understand why he had acted so peculiarly.

When she reached Wood Street, Ali remembered how she started to walk faster, but it seemed to make little difference in getting down the long, winding road. The trees that lined the street on both sides of the road were stripped bare of their foliage, and with no wind the exposed branches remained still like sculptures. When she approached the straight stretch where Robert's house was, Ali felt her heart knocking at her rib cage in anticipation. She remembered breaking out in a smile right before the wind was taken right out of her – as if someone had landed a roundhouse kick in her midriff. She literally gasped for air as she watched Robert and Mel walk out onto the path, and head towards the end of the street that led to Aethelred Hill. She didn't stalk them but stayed rooted to the spot like one of the lime trees next to her. Whereas Lewis had earlier tried to become invisible and to avert attention, Ali did nothing. Completely oblivious to her presence, Robert and Mel were deep in conversation, giggling and holding hands the way only a boyfriend and girlfriend would. They didn't look round, the only thing that seemed to be of interest to them both was each other.

Even as they were beginning to walk round the bend at the top of the road, Ali remained motionless. She tried to comprehend what had happened and could only conclude that upon reading her letter Robert had completely backed away from wanting to get involved with her. Instead it seemed that his preference was to be with Mel. He'd hidden that one very well, she thought. Naturally she felt confused, let down, and disappointed by the shambolic situation. Bitterness became a new and emerging emotion in Ali too. Before going back to sixth form after half-term, she had cried to the point where her ribs hurt. The raking over all that had happened caused her tummy to bubble up, spin, and tumble over every few minutes like a lava lamp. There seemed no way to control it.

The replay was disturbed by the tannoy announcing that her train was due to arrive. Warm tears had filled Ali's eyes; the cold air kissed the edges of the teardrops and caused them to be dragged over her eyelids. Once on the train, she found a spare couple of seats for herself. She obviously wasn't in the mood for a natter with fellow passengers. She leaned her head against the side of the carriage, and looked out into the darkness, which was interrupted at intervals by streetlamps or the glow of lightbulbs in houses and other buildings. The momentum of the train made her feel dreamy, and she was soon deep in her thoughts again.

Ali made no further attempt to contact either Mel or Robert for the rest of half-term week. Unsurprisingly, neither did she receive any contact from them. If it were not for the homework that she had to complete, Ali would have barricaded herself inside her room at home. However, to produce an essay on 'the functionalist view of the role of family in society' some research was required at the library.

Ali considered that Thursday might be the quietest day, not mid-week, and not the day before or the day after a weekend. She had hoped that by arriving when it opened at nine o'clock, she would avoid anyone she knew. Her plan was to find a seat at the back, obscured by book aisles, and as far out of view of the public as possible. She executed her plan perfectly, finding a table with a partition screen that added further privacy. What she hadn't banked on was bumping into anyone else from her sociology class looking for the same information to cite in their essay. The girl at the opposite end of the sociology reference aisle did a double take, before gawping in astonishment and making Ali feel most uncomfortable.

'What do you want, Tommo?' whispered Ali.

Belinda Tomlinson puckered up her mouth, tilted her head forward and pretended to imitate puppy eyes.

'You ok, hun?'

'Not really, I'm finding this essay hard. What about you?'

'Blimey Ali, you do know about wotsit don't you?'

Ali withdrew her eye contact and started thumbing through the textbooks on the shelf nearest to her. Tommo tried a more direct approach.

'Rob got off with Mel at the party – I thought you two were like, an item?'

It was difficult for Ali to hear this affirmation of Robert's rejection, but Ali just shrugged her shoulders.

'He knows I liked him; he's made his choice. That's the way it goes, I guess.'

'Yeah but I heard him muttering...'

The gossiper was cut short. 'I don't care Tommo. I just... don't have... just... want to forget about it now. There are more important things going on in the world.'

It would have been difficult to have included more lies in a single sentence. If Ali had made a list of people who she would prefer to avoid, Belinda 'Tommo' Tomlinson would have been on there. Belinda was a nice girl, ordinarily completely inoffensive. However, to be comforted by a girl who had also suffered the embarrassment of a communication breakdown via a letter was just too much to handle. And Ali didn't want to feel as though she was in quite the same, lame category as Tommo anyway. What she really wanted to say to Belinda was to sod off and mind her own business. But that might have been slightly harsh. Tommo wouldn't be the only person to assume that Ali and Robert were the ones supposed to be going out with each other.

Ali had wondered what other people's reactions would be when the term restarted. She planned to be as inconspicuous as possible entering the school, but this strategy wasn't helped on the first day back by the laddered tights she wore which were always going to be an invitation for a snigger. She had imagined there would be sixth formers huddled into corners, hushing as she passed by, amusing themselves at her expense. But to her astonishment, she slipped under the radar and into her form room for registration without so much as saying a word to anyone. The bonus for Ali was that she wasn't timetabled for maths on Mondays. It meant that she avoided any direct contact with Mel and Robert, but it was a reprieve that couldn't last. The only reference to what had happened came when she inadvertently bumped into Chinny Jewkes on her way to grab a sandwich from the canteen during her afternoon free period. Not known for his subtlety, he provided a verdict on the matter irrespective of whether it had been asked for.

'No disrespect to Mel, but I reckon Greeny's been a dick.'

The voice of no authority on relationship matters didn't wait for any response. His outburst continued to cause a wry smile to break out on her face whenever she thought of it though, and she caught her own reflection of doing just that as the train passed through tunnels not far from Winchester.

Ali arrived late to maths in that first week, knowing that by doing so she would avoid the awkwardness of needing to speak to Mel or Robert in the queue to get into the room. The door to the classroom was at the rear, meaning she could take her place at the back of the room rather than being watched by those she wanted to avoid positioned near the front. What she hadn't factored in was the sarcastic comment of her teacher, Mr 'Whinge-bag' Williams.

'Is there any chance that you might make it to one of my lessons on time at any point this half-term, Miss Crofts?'

The heads of her classmates turned around in unison in her direction as if rehearsed, and while she spent an unusually long time unpacking her books and pencil case from her bag, she felt the full weight of everyone's stare.

The only exception was Robert. On returning to school he found it incredibly difficult to look at Ali, whether it be in a lesson, or in the common room, or simply in passing through the school down a corridor. Contrary to what Ali suspected his persona might be like for ignoring her romantic invitation, it wasn't one of guilt. That was only her conjecture after all. As he knew nothing of the letter, his reactions were those of a lad who found it difficult to stomach that he had been rejected, jilted, dumped, blown out. There was no indignation, he just couldn't contemplate looking at her the same way now that she wasn't to be his. If ever he did catch sight of her, he still couldn't find it in himself to think negatively. As for Mel, up to this point there had been a conscious and mutual ignoring of each other, which caused an icy tension in the common room.

The train conductor announced the next stop, and a weary Ali gathered her things together from her seats. For all the upset, she felt in control by being able to analyse what had happened, and on this occasion, it helped to fill the time spent on a freezing cold platform and a late-night journey home. Trying to forget it and block it out would feel like letting go, and she didn't feel she could do that just yet. She remembered a conversation that she had with Poppy on one of her Wednesday afternoon visits. Never one to be short on wisdom, Poppy offered her own insight into the damage that love could create.

'At some time in life you will let someone steal your heart, Alison. So be careful not to crash, because if you do your heart is not like the shell of a car. If it gets dented, it's difficult to re-shape.'

As she shuffled along the platform towards the exit at last, Ali knew there would have to come a point where she came to terms with the situation, and realise the facts were not going to change. With Christmas on the horizon, it had crossed her mind that the new year could be a chance for a new start. But for now, the challenge was to drag herself through each day with the harsh reality of a relationship that had misfired, and not give any indication to her peers how affected she really was by it.

23

The rules at King Alfred's Comprehensive were as fundamental as in any school; no running in the corridors or on the stairs, and in this case keep to the left-hand side. With forty minutes left until they all went home for Christmas, there was no semblance of children walking to lessons in an orderly fashion.

Somewhere amongst this chaos, two girls were stooped on the floor, hastily picking up work sheets displaced from a work file. Ali was attempting to behave naturally while all around them youngsters scampered along random routes making it near impossible to dodge one another. Though she gave the impression that she wasn't really bothered, Mel was listening intently. The give-away was her eyes rolling at Ali's suggestion of reconciliation, and her apparent newfound status as peacemaker. Ali knew she was already up against it, but she had come this far, and so persisted.

'You just don't realise how badly my heart shattered; I've been hurt more than you can ever imagine. I'd be lying if I said otherwise.'

'You just have to accept it's the way it was meant to be, Ali.'

As she looked to the floor, Ali meant to snigger to herself, but unwittingly her breath got trapped at the back of her throat and she unwittingly let out a nasal puff which sounded like she was mocking Mel. She gasped when she looked back up to see Mel looking at her scornfully.

'What's that meant to mean, Ali?'

She moved her mouth from one side of her face to another nervously as she tried to find the right words to explain. 'It's just your mum said something opposite to that.'

'You spoke to my mum about Robert?'

'I spoke to your mum about lots of things when I did my care placement. She liked knowing things about us and liked telling me stuff about you.'

This riled Mel.

'Like what?'

'Erm, gosh, I don't know. Like when you were younger – the time you bought her a purse for her birthday with your own pocket money. She said you had asked the old church warden ladies whether it'd be a good idea, and then by yourself you went into town and got this grey, rectangular, cheap thing from Woolworths? She said it wasn't something she would ever have chosen to use when she went out, but she adored it because of the thought you'd put into it. So, that's where the stamps, spare keys, passport photos, buttons and things like that were put – in a drawer in the kitchen at your old house.'

Before a stunned looking Mel had any time at all to respond, Ali had reached down to her own file and offered her friend the gift wrapped present.

'It's not a purse, by the way,' she said trying to lighten the topic of conversation, not suspecting its reference to the preceding anecdote might cause offence. 'When you open it on Christmas Day, I just want you to know I was thinking about you, and that I want to think back to a time when you and I could chat with each other for hours and hate it when it was time to go.'

Mel felt verbally mugged. In different circumstances, receiving a Christmas gift from a friend would have led to the type of over the top, immature jubilation that teenagers typically display when they get a surprise. But this was not one of those fist pumping, arms waving opportunities. It was an embarrassing moment for Mel, and completely unexpected. Ali had become an outcast from her inner circle of mates, alienated by her liking for a lad high on popularity stakes, and who continued to believe she had shunned him. And yet there in front of Mel, stood the very same Ali Crofts, spouting niceties about their relationship, despite being on the receiving end of more crap than can be found in a field of cows. Mel took the present off her, with the elaborately curled ribbon dancing around the bow on top. She was numb to Ali's kindness because she was desperate to know what else her mum had said.

'I think I know my mum better than you, Ali. She absolutely loved Robert.'

'Yeah, you're right, she did. She called him an 'unrecognised hero' for his help on the day she collapsed by the cathedral.'

'Did she say anything about me liking him after that backstage debacle?'

Ali pleaded her innocence. '*I* never said anything to her about *that*, but it didn't stop her from having an opinion on the matter anyway.'

'Which was?'

'She thought he wasn't a bad match for you, just not 'the right one' – her words, not mine.'

Mel looked devastated on learning this. She recalled a recent conversation where her mum had implied the exact same thing, but at the time Mel chose to dismiss it as her mum just trying to protect her. Mel now knew that Poppy meant it.

'Anyway Mel, it's not your fault, he made his choice. He read my letter and decided I wasn't for him.'

Mel looked away, screening the guilt of knowing that Robert had no idea a letter even existed. More than that, she was itching to know whether Ali had ever spoken to her mum about liking Robert. It was a question she would have to refrain from asking, but little did she know that a conversation of that very nature had occurred.

The topic of relationships was first raised by Poppy during an early spring outing alongside the river Itchen. She liked Ali to take her out in her wheelchair for some fresh air and freedom, and they would often pause at the weirs to throw crusts to the ducks and swans. Astute as always, Poppy sensed the ticking of Ali's inner thoughts, and invited her to open up.

'Oh, it's nothing Poppy, honestly. Just teenage stuff.'

'You in a different generation to me, but I remember boy trouble when I was young too, you know.'

Ali's eyes bulged in disbelief.

'How do you know it's about boys – I never said that.'

'No one has secrets you know, Alison. Everyone has things that they hide away in their head, until they find the right person at the right time to tell it to. The burden of carrying something around that weighs heavy in the mind is too much for one person. It always comes out. Besides, do you know you've started nibbling on that stale loaf that be meant for them birds? It not take me too much to see a girl occupied with a dilemma. I can't promise to pour you a remedy, but I be here to listen if you want me to, child.'

Ali sat chewing her cheeks, something she always did when she was deep in thought or anxious about something. 'I don't know how to tell a boy how much I like him – or whether he already knows, or whether he likes me.'

'If you're fighting with it, that's when you know it already means something. Anyway, Robert already know he feels the same way about you, girl.'

Ali looked freaked out. 'How on earth do you know it's about Robert? Has Mel said something?'

Poppy chuckled. 'I hear nuff from my daughter for sure. But I see the way he stare at you at the party last summer. That the look of a soul mate. This one is easy. I not need to reassure you that he right for you Alison, you already know yourself.'

A brief pause ensued, with the silence disrupted by the splashing of ducks flapping across the water aggressively at each other for the rights to the scraps of stale bread that the two of them continued to lob into the water.

'Maybe you're right, Mrs B. It's got a fifty-fifty chance, so

I'm only half expecting it to fail.'

Not usually known for her quick wit and humour, Ali's response had Poppy in fits.

The decibels along the network of corridors had lowered to near silence now that the drama of lesson changeover had concluded. As the start-of-period bell rang, the natter of children was replaced by the hum of adult voices conducting their final lesson before the early closedown of the school day. The meeting between the two girls in the hub of the school might have been a convenient enough situation for Ali to premeditate, but there was some resistance from Mel to kiss and make up. Mel hadn't enjoyed keeping Ali at a distance, but it had been necessary to be able to deal with the dirty secret.

'Look, this doesn't seem right – after what's gone on do you really think you should be wasting your cash on me, Ali?'

'After everything that's happened this year, this is the very reason for making sure that you know I haven't forgotten we were – are – mates.'

'This is very difficult to accept.'

'But wouldn't it be even more difficult if we didn't try? I'm not asking for you to change anything, other than don't avoid me. What do you think?'

Ali put her arm around Mel and hugged her, whether she was a willing party to it or not. Ali smiled sweetly, picked up her folder and scuttled down the stairs. She expected nothing in return, but just as she reached the bottom step Mel shouted down to her, sealing the compromise.

'Ali! I'll see you soon, ok?'

Unbeknown to Ali, there were other less obvious reasons for Mel's reluctance to indulge in harmony. In the time that had elapsed between Robert's party and now, she had watched her dad falling apart. Not only had Derek struggled to comprehend the loss of his wife, but the rumoured takeover at work led to inevitable redundancies as the operation was scaled down. Although he had been encouraged by senior management to compete for his position through a formal interview process, he didn't have the stomach for the fight to retain his job, and instead received a modest pay-off. His self-respect began diminishing at an alarming rate along with their fragile finances, and he openly dreaded the prospect of Christmas this year. He was crushed under the weight of expectation of his responsibilities to 'carry on' for the sakes of his kids.

With no plans made to enjoy the upcoming festivities, the hopelessness of the situation was best reflected in Mel's response to it. Using her own money, she bought her own gifts, and wrapped them complete with tags as if they were from her dad and brother. For days afterwards, she pestered and nagged them both, trying in vain to recuperate the amount spent so that she wasn't out of pocket. Then, it was Mel who dragged the artificial tree and decorations from out of the loft and neatly placed the presents underneath to portray a scene of normality. She didn't want Christmas Day to be affected by the dismal nothingness that had been fermenting in the household. Not this day, not a day that her mum held so precious for her family.

Any spare cash that Mel had scraped together was used to buy a present for Robert: two tickets for the Manics gig in Reading the following April. She knew he'd be totally floored that she had managed to get them. But despite the financial restraints the family were under, Mel had now involuntarily committed herself to returning the favour of getting a gift for Ali. The challenge to begin anew with her friend had come at an awkwardly imperfect time.

24

Mel could hardly be resentful of Lewis accessing a large chunk of their father's redundancy pay to fund his journey across to Antigua, when her own blood tests were clear and his showed up one or two 'anomalies'. The uncertainty of the results prompted Lewis to be forthright for once.

'My life has been useless here, just bobbing along with no clear direction. But I've learnt some stuff in the building trade, and I've loved being involved with security at music festivals. I'm pretty sure I could put those things to some use over there. Anyway, Cousin Lawrie has already said there's work at the shipbuilders in English Harbour. I'm not going to rot away over here. If my health is going to get worse at any point, so be it. But I wanna live a bit first, like mum told us to. Besides, I've got to deliver on a promise to get her ashes into the sea at Darkwood Beach.'

His passionate and forceful delivery convinced Derek that his son finally talked the language of a man with ambition, and it secured Lewis the money he needed for the trip.

Mel felt that the least he could have done, though, was to support her enthusiasm to create a sense of unity at Christmas. For Derek, it was going to be unbearable waking up on a day that was usually orchestrated by Poppy. The more he analysed the family's current predicament, the greater the anxiety he suffered. He knew perfectly well that he was lacking as a role model for his kids, and that it was the antithesis of everything he and Poppy ever believed in. He was letting himself and everyone around him down but lacked the ability to deal with the hardship as he had no belief in his abilities to deliver a stable home life. He was a bloke on the verge of defeat with no idea about how to devise a plan to stop the slide towards it.

In her job at the club, Mary had witnessed her own fair share of characters in desperate circumstances, unwilling to accept help or advice however well intended. Derek's plight had familiar undertones, but the context was more personal. Mel had confided in her about the situation at home, shedding tears on numerous occasions with both her and Robert. Mary set about ensuring Mel's own welfare was secure with her subtle questions, and in doing so she was insistent that the family were her guests for Christmas dinner. There were no spiteful reactions or lashing out of someone too proud to admit they were on their knees. Derek was full of gratitude that someone was willing to rescue the situation – albeit briefly.

It took some coaxing, but despite their objections, Mel managed to get both Derek and Lewis out of their slumber on Christmas morning. She delivered good on her promise of a bacon sandwich, which helped to alleviate the miserable expressions on the faces of the two blokes when they first appeared. If it were not for Mel's tenacity to make it happen, the scene in the living room would have been one of desolation. But her efforts had made it feel nothing short of warm and fuzzy, just as though Poppy had organised it herself.

There was a silent reluctance on Derek's part to accept the role of present distributor, knowing full well that none of it was organised by him. Nonetheless, he tried to be as enthusiastic as he could muster up. For Derek and Lewis this was fascinating, as they were surprised by every gift that was opened. A bizarre scenario followed. Mel thanked and hugged Lewis for 'his' present, to which her brother replied with the straight face of someone with no scruples that she was welcome. However absurd the morning may have appeared from the outside, it gave the Burchells some definition on the first key date without Poppy, so much so that they were able to talk openly about missing her. It galvanised them to ensure the day was enjoyed as she would have wanted it to have been.

The only thing weighing heavy on Mel's mind now was getting a present on par to the one received from Ali, a beautiful silver-plated compact make-up mirror, with the inscription 'Love from Ali, Xmas 1996' on the back. Poppy had taught her children the adage about not giving to receive, but Mel's cluttered conscience would feel some relief if she could reciprocate the gesture. She'd been unable to cobble together any amount of money that would buy even a token gift. It was scraping the barrel when she started to consider recycling one of her own presents or taking something that was unused, or maybe received at some time in the recent past. There was very little that would constitute being worthy of passing onto someone else, apart from a make-up bag that Mary had bought her. She really liked it, but reluctantly re-wrapped the luxury item in its original paper. However, on its own it did not feel remotely enough.

Mel sat on her bed desperately thinking about what to do. That's when her eyes fell upon the three striking photo frames that her mum had left for her. Poppy's sentimentality alone didn't make Mel suddenly cherish them; she felt no real attachment because they were simply not her taste. She could see that they held no monetary value, and that made her question whether they were worthy of redistributing as gifts. She was running out of options – and time. The family were expected next door at one o'clock and it was already on the way to midday. Mel made the executive decision to keep one of the frames, and to give one each to Ali and Robert. The colour scheme was almost identical on each frame, so there was no exact science applied to the decision-making process about which one to give to who. Mel placed the one she was keeping into the drawer of her bedside table, and hurriedly wrapped the others by reusing the paper that had come off other presents.

It was Ali who opened the door at the Crofts' house; her mum was too busy flapping in the kitchen to ensure there was perfectly cooked poultry, while her unflappable dad soaked up some peace and quiet from the comfort of an armchair. He knew better than to make a pest of himself in his wife's domain while it was so intense. Ali virtually jumped when she saw who it was standing underneath the porch. Mel was the last person she would have expected to be there on Christmas Day. Her lukewarm reaction was completely unintentional, but her instinct was to feel uncomfortable about her being there unannounced, so she struggled to be welcoming.

'Oh, hi Mel. Wow, er what're you doing here? I mean, it's ok, I just didn't... did we make a plan for you to come round? Blimey, is everything ok?'

'Merry Christmas Ali, sorry this is cutting it a little bit fine.'

Mel proudly held out the present, with the shiny red and gold paper looking no worse for wear having been recycled.

'For me? Thank you so much. Look, please come in.'

'I won't if you don't mind, I've got to get back quickly. Mum really loved Christmas Day, so I guess I just wanted to pop by to see you. If I think about her, I usually think of you too.'

'What a lovely thing to say. Please Mel, just for a minute. Let me at least open my present.'

'Ok, please don't think I'm being funny if I just wait in your hall then, Ali.'

The girls shuffled from the porch into the hallway.

'Did you like yours?' asked Ali.

'The make-up mirror? Yeah, it's gorgeous, I love it. You've spoilt me; it must've cost a lot of money. Look, mine really isn't very much Ali...'

'I just wanted it to be something pretty for you. And don't be daft, you shouldn't have gone to the effort of getting me anything, it's not expected – and I'll love it no matter what.'

It was difficult to determine who felt more awkward as she opened the package, but Ali was truly brilliant at saying the right thing to appease Mel.

'Aww, I will definitely reserve that for a nice pic of me and you, Mel. The colours are stunning and vibrant, just what's needed while the winter is dull and gloomy.'

Suitably reassured, Mel turned to make her exit back to Wood Street. As she reached the front door, Ali alerted her to something that had fallen on the floor.

'Mel is this letter yours? I think it fell from the wrapping.'

Mel looked confused. Her heart was in her mouth as she took hold of the letter and gently turned one of the edges over. She could see immediately the handwriting was that of her mum's, and hastily shoved it into the back pocket of her jeans without offering an explanation.

'Oh, yeah, thanks Ali. It's from my bedside table, must've got caught on some sellotape as I was wrapping your pressies last night.'

In truth, Mel had no idea what the letter was but had been panic stricken in thinking it might be the letter that Ali had written to Robert. She made a conscious decision to do something about that when she got home later in case it tried to reveal itself at some point, and that would surely cause havoc. She wasn't sure why the evidence hadn't been destroyed before now, but where it had been concealed had been forgotten.

When Mel reached the end of Ali's street, she glanced behind before pulling the note back out from her pocket. She was naturally intrigued to know what it said and started to read as she walked. Her footsteps were erratic as she did so, occasionally slowing to a standstill while she tried to take in the words, re-reading the sentences to fully understand them.

My darling child, I cherish the time I have spent with you and regret not a minute of wrapping you in layers of our love. To love and be loved is so precious. Love is very powerful, so let me tell you to handle it with care.

Tripping into the pot of honey doesn't have to cause a mess, but that's the easy part. Mind how far you fall in, in case it doesn't taste as sweet as you expected it to. Love that fades away still has the strength to cause regret that could nag away at you and linger in your mind if you allow it to, making the past difficult to let go of. And temptation? Well, that be an axe that can fell anyone, a storm from which it can be difficult to find shelter from. Be wary and steer clear of it.

Life is like a timetable of lessons. One day it's full of favourites that you enjoy and understand, the next day you might be left completely confused by people you don't understand. But baby, as Nana Azalea once say to me – ration your frust, and don't be strangled by these harsh lessons you will encounter. Discover how to nurture love's capabilities to overcome sadness. Never feel you are in someone else's shadow my child. Be a shining light yourself, a beacon of determination to glow in the darkest hours.

Love Mamma x

Mel had no idea where the note had come from but suspected that it must have been with the other letter she had read, amongst the bundle created by her mum. As Mel had taken an instant dislike to the frames, she didn't exactly paw over them for very long, so she concluded that's why the note was missed. It left her wondering whether her mum had the foresight to write the letter in advance, recognising a deterioration in her own health. It felt so weird, like she was being talked to from the grave, as if Poppy had knowledge of the predicament Mel had been in with Ali and Robert. She could feel her back and arms tingling because these words spoke volumes for how Mel had been finding the struggle to get by without her. Whatever the reasoning behind the writing, this most unexpected paragraph of words was priceless. It was the loveliest of presents because however short lived the moment might feel, her mum was around on Christmas Day after all.

It felt properly festive with their neighbours, which was precisely the air of normality that Mel had craved for. Mary had whipped up the joviality as the perfect hostess, being well practiced in how to work a bar propped up by a multitude of personalities. She could draw a smile out of the town's grumpiest, rudest losers and show grace and compassion for someone genuinely down on their luck. Her ability to get under the skin and really know people for who they were, and what they had experienced and suffered, was powerful. It earnt trust and respect, and inevitably she was the barmaid with a big heart that everyone wanted to socialise with. She was in her element putting everyone at ease and making the Burchells feel welcome.

'Flippin' 'eck! That's totally amazing!'

Robert's screaming caused everyone to stop what they were doing and converge their attention on the jabbering wreck of a boy sitting in the middle of the floor in the living room. His jubilation was infectious, causing everyone to break out into smiles and chuckles. He held his present at arms-length, staring at it quite trance like in disbelief. He was almost shaking at the realisation that he was going to see the sold-out gig. He fingered the tickets for what seemed an eternity, viewing the lettering and picture design, and then broke off from his trance momentarily.

'I'm going to see my favourite band, with my favourite girl! Can someone pinch me; is this real?'

Mel pinched him.

'Yeah, and afterwards you can put a photograph of the gig in your favourite frame, if we can smuggle a camera into the concert hall.'

Robert looked down at the frame, commenting on how he

liked the psychedelic colours on his other less amazing gift. Mel felt enormous relief that those offerings to Ali and Robert had been so well received. At one point, she found herself looking to the sky out of the bay window and whispering 'thank you mum' for her part as the donator of the goods.

Mel wasn't to know the frames had been constructed by the hands of her grandpa and made out of driftwood washed up on the shore at Darkwood Beach in Antigua. Without ever showing more than the slightest bit of interest in them, she wasn't to know the secret that each one of them harboured, only to be revealed by the actions of someone imparting a photograph into the back of the frame. It was circumstantial now that the witnesses to the significance of those possessions would be two people that they were not intended for. Those heartfelt letters were destined to be lost forever.

25

Throughout the last weeks of January at school, Mel had been pestered about whether she was having a party for her eighteenth birthday. It would be another milestone without Poppy, and once again Derek was finding it impossible to deal with the fact that the person so instrumental in all their lives wasn't going to be there to celebrate it. It hurt all the more given that she had talked quite openly about the significance of her daughter turning into a woman, something so often celebrated in her native lands. Derek was seeing the morning hours less and less. At best, unkempt seemed to be the only style he could master. He was incapable of writing a shopping list let alone consider putting together a party for his daughter that could inflame the excitement of beautiful youth.

Thereafter, it was assumed that any celebrations were going to be low key. However, the jungle drums at school continued to beat out an alternative rhythm, that a party was being planned at Mel's house after all. Mel didn't deny the rumours that spread far and wide amongst the student community, and so the speculation grew. A party for her got talked about so much that whether there was a plan in place or not, people believed it.

Mel was starting to enjoy the thought that she might be the centre of attention, the feeling of being able to orchestrate an event based around her. Subconsciously, she started to crave it. Without ever confirming any such plans, an itinerary was formed out of whispers, the result being a larger than average number of students converging on the Belgarum Tavern, swelling the regular Saturday takings for a bar area usually populated by a sparse number of regulars. Predictably, stale conversation about flat ale was suddenly fused with exuberance and requests for shots and chasers, and for a brief couple of hours the walls of the bar at the old boozer were buzzing and rebounding the celebratory decibels of youths in their glad rags.

There was still nothing to repel the assumption that there was an after party to attend, and inevitably an impromptu gathering of the worse-for-wear followed at Mel's house – but not before hordes of party goers frequented the local Spar to raid a wide array of alcoholic preferences. There was the inevitable refusal to serve some youngsters who could not produce ID when asked to prove their age. It mattered little as there was always someone else willing to make the purchase for the people whose pride was dented at the suggestion that they looked underage. The assemblage was precisely the kind of get-together that Mel had insinuated previously that she would resist entertaining. There was no alternative in place, nothing of the nature that she supposed would have been the case if her mum was still alive, nothing to put her in the spotlight the way Poppy would have set about glorifying the occasion. Mel had simply drifted towards an option where it seemed she was being thought of and wanted – however selfish and fickle the intentions of those people may have been.

The invasion of hyperactive youngsters was met with no resistance by Derek, who only knew about it because Robert had tipped Lewis off, and in turn he had warned his dad. In any case, Derek had dumped and abandoned the inner strength required to remonstrate with his daughter. He wasn't amused with some of the reprobates he witnessed staggering through his hallway, but he entrusted Lewis and his mates to control the invasion.

Lewis had every intention of ensuring his little sis enjoyed herself, but also that his dad had as worry-free an evening as possible. The new decks that he had recently purchased were assembled ad-hoc, filling the air with thumping beats, announcing to the neighbourhood that a celebration was underway. When he had a vested interest in something, Lewis could be resourceful. He used his initiative to commandeer the help of three local blokes who he had got to know when he worked on the security entrances at Glastonbury. It would help to filter anyone intending to gate crash.

Making a move from the front of the house through to the rear was quite a challenge, as Mary found while squeezing past revellers who had chosen to camp themselves along the hallway, though firstly she had the task of satisfying the checks of the improvised doormen. The extended kitchen at the back was another bottleneck, where youngsters amassed to use the door to the back garden and to throw down some shapes to the music. It was also where many of them had chosen to park their tinnies and bottles of less regular concoctions. She caught Lewis' eye and mouthed 'where's your dad?' in his direction. With one headphone hanging on the side of his face and the other wrapped around the back of his head, he looked the part of a resident disc spinner. He pointed to the ceiling to insinuate that Derek had retreated to his bedroom away from the madness downstairs, meaning Mary had to plot a route back down the hallway, and then explain to one of the bouncers that she was the next-door neighbour.

Satisfied that she presented no threat of trashing the upstairs area, she was given clearance to go up and see him. The tapping on the door alarmed Derek. He jumped up from where he was reading on the bed and approached the door in expectation of finding a stray from the party. The door was opened aggressively, but Mary's smiling face was the last one he was expecting to see.

'You do surprise me Derek, I thought you'd be strutting your stuff downstairs,' she threw at him sarcastically. He didn't answer but his smirk told her that he appreciated the humour. 'Nah, not really. I thought you could do with being rescued old man. Fancy escaping for a cuppa round at mine?'

There were no complaints or resistance. His reactions were

acutely different to how he had been living life in recent days, overcomplicating otherwise straight-forward decisions in his incessant grief.

It was inevitable that an opportunity would arise for Ali and Robert to engage in small talk once more. It hadn't been easy to glance at one another in the confines of a classroom, a corridor or common room. That was likely to cause an emotional sprinkler to go off and activate the fiendish stomach churner to stir feelings of love and loathe together. Even now as the pair grabbed a drink from the kitchen, they were aware of one another but doing everything they could to avert looking up.

Given the sheer number of people milling around, it shielded them from any temptation to begin asking the unanswered questions that lay festering beneath the surface. Instead they leaned against the same work unit looking onto a swarm of people strutting to the music. Amongst them, Mel's arms could be seen flailing, and in one hand the contents of a bottle spilled over the top and down her hand. She licked it off, laughing childishly as she did so, lost in the merrymaking and oblivious as to who was with her. She certainly didn't seem to be craving Robert's attention.

The tension that existed between Ali and Robert was dampened by Chinny and Guppy tripping over themselves simultaneously, generating laughter from the onlookers. It was timely light relief, and though it was an effort to be heard above the din, Robert struck up a conversation.

'As my mum would say, he is such a dip stick!'

'Chinny? Yeah, she's right. And yet he's the only one that doesn't know it.'

Chinny remained oblivious to condemnation being dished out.

'How the hell does he think he's going to get a job after college? He's unemployable!'

'I'd like to be a fly on the wall at his interview.'

'I bet you any money he puts on some kind of stupid accent to disguise the common piece of muck he really is.'

'And I bet he uses lines from films to answer the questions because he thinks it'd be cool. He'll grow up someday.'

'He's got some catching up to do on the maturity front I reckon, but he's always good value for a laugh.'

The music continued to boom, making it difficult to hear a conversation without craning necks or lodging heads close together. That kind of invasion of space was hardly likely to sit comfortably with either of them.

'So, how're things with you, Ali?'

'Pardon?'

'I said. HOW. ARE. YOU?'

'I, I'm…' Ali paused and nodded her head towards the garden, insinuating that Robert should follow where there was a chance of holding a conversation without them having to shout or repeat themselves.

The night-time chill was an uncomfortable contrast to the steaminess inside the house and made their senses more alert.

'Did your mum tell you I saw her the other week, Ali?'

'Err, no. Where did you see her?'

'I was in the supermarket off High Street.'

'You, food shopping? Blimey, had you gone in there by mistake?'

'Ha, funny. My mum wasn't very well so I wanted to help out.'

'Oh no, is she ok?'

'Yeah, just a bout of flu.'

'Did you actually speak to my mum then? She hates spending more time shopping than she needs to – hates bumping into people randomly and exchanging pleasantries. I'm surprised she wasn't rude to you as well, Robert.'

Robert hadn't intended to use this as an opportunity to berate

Mrs Crofts, however much he knew she had a dislike of him.

'I just said hello really, she seemed to be in a hurry. Are we ok then Ali, yeah?'

She wasn't going to give him any satisfaction of knowing the hurt that had been tattooed onto her heart, and so avoided the loaded question. Instead, Ali looked deliberately past him in Mel's direction, as if to hint at the consequences of his decisions. But it wasn't as if Robert had ever rejected Ali, and he never got to know the full extent of her feelings for him.

'I hope you spoiled Mel for her birthday, Robert. Looks like she's having a good time tonight. You should go and join her really.'

'You know me and dancing, Ali, not a combination that works very well. So, tell me, do I know who it is that you've dressed so nicely for tonight?'

Though he asked his question in jest, there was a genuine struggle with his curiosity to find out if she had started seeing anyone else. Ali considered his question thoughtfully, wondering why he had manufactured such a question. There *were* other options making sounds in her direction, but she hadn't allowed anyone into her life like that. She turned to look at him straight in the eye.

'You'll always know him, Robert.'

She hadn't wanted, or expected, to expose her inner self to him like that, but he didn't grasp the cryptic nature of her response. The answer threw him because he wasn't expecting her to say anything at all – it was just meant to banter. He scratched his head and tried a different approach.

'Ali, I need to ask you something.'

Ali's heart was pounding in anticipation of being quizzed about the night of his party.

'I can't promise I'll answer it Robert, but you can try.'

'We're all heading off in different directions soon enough, to university and whatever. Do you want me in your life or not?'

Her response to the blatant and direct question that struck a chord deep inside was not rehearsed; it was purely instinctive.

'Not.'

With that short response, Ali realised that it was possible to break your own heart and the pain was unimaginable. The back of her tongue and the roof of her mouth ached from trying to stop her tears from pouring out. She had to tell Robert what they both needed to hear, but not what either of them wanted. It was just too difficult to contemplate how being friends could work while Robert's affections were pinned on someone else so close to them. Ali didn't resent Mel, but how different that might have been if she were aware of the extent of the damage the birthday girl had fashioned.

The last time Robert felt so redundant and vacant was when his dad walked out of his life. So distracted by the madness of his sadness, that he didn't see Ali exit. Right in the centre of his midriff, he could feel an acidic burning in reaction to Ali's rejection. He massaged the area between his ribs, convinced he was about to throw up. Robert had never imagined that she would have reacted that way, or that the pit of his stomach would be clenching like a fist at the thought of her not being around anymore.

Ali's sudden departure from the party was poignant, as she effectively left the lives of Mel and Robert for good. Mel was way too intoxicated to acknowledge Ali's good wishes as she left, and she was hardly likely to remember grabbing Ali's hand from within the scrum of fake sincerity flocking around her. Her friend literally slipped through her fingers and left without so much as a hug.

26

Robert's evening would swing from one personal trauma to another. With so many revellers packed into a relatively small area the party always seemed on the edge of getting out of control, but despite the huge quantity of alcohol intake, it did stay on the right side of ecstasy. Numbers started to dwindle, so that those who were left were camped inside only, much to the relief of the households in the locality who had suffered the pounding of bass lines for several hours.

Other than some inevitable spillages, the house had largely been respected thanks to the presence of Lewis' aides. It could only have been Dutch courage which possessed the girls to take it upon themselves to scale the kitchen table that had been pushed to one side for safety. Their antics didn't detract from the good-natured behaviour that had gone beforehand, and although it was just high jinks, the small posse cavorting on the tabletop risked some damage and potential injury. Robert did all he could to dissuade Mel from this over excitement – he knew it would be a regrettable part of the evening. He just couldn't understand her insistence on acting like a fool, ignoring his attempts to withdraw her from the mockery and scorn her behaviour was beginning to receive.

It drew the bouncers' attention almost immediately. Within seconds of rejecting their requests to remove themselves, the girls were involuntarily man-handled off, changing the ambience instantly. The scuffling and shouting caught Lewis' attention, and it brought an undignified ending to the tune he was playing. Instead it was his voice that the revellers could hear over the PA.

'Oi! That's my sister you dick, put her down!'

Apologies followed the confusion and misunderstanding that signalled the end of the proceedings. It wasn't Lewis' intention to aim aggressive abuse at blokes who had only been there to help and had delivered on their promise to ensure nothing untoward kicked off. Nor was it their intention to upset a mate and to embarrass the birthday girl. It didn't stop Mel screaming relentlessly at them, then her brother, and finally Mary and her dad. But rather than gaining the support of others, the spotlight began to fall on her own worrying behaviour as she continued to blame everyone and anyone for something or other. It was just the start of an episode of identifying scapegoats, and Robert wasn't exempt from that.

It had been a chaotic ending. After everyone had left, Mary didn't want to abandon Derek to deal with a frisky mare, so she and Robert hung around to ensure that Mel was calm enough to get to bed to start sleeping off the excessive amount of liquor she had knocked back, complete with a plastic bowl at the side of her bed in case she started to throw up. It was Mary who perched herself on the side of Mel's bed, while Robert lurked in the doorway. Mary stroked Mel's hair to help her nod off. While she pampered the teenage rascal, she felt something underneath her foot. Her eye was drawn to an envelope partially hidden underneath the drawer in the base of the bed but poking out enough to suggest it had been deliberately cast under there. Either that or it had been intended for the drawer itself. Instinctively, Mary reached down to pick it up. The card looked like it had been hastily thrown back into the envelope because it had been put in on its head rather than slipped in on its side, and so half of it was jutting out. Mary looked over to where Robert stood. He had taken a couple of steps into the room by now, having watched his mum retrieve the card from the floor.

'What is it?' he whispered.

'Looks like a birthday card.'

'You're not going to open it, are you? Just put it on the side for her.'

'Why not? People read each other's cards.'

'Yeah, but that one isn't downstairs on the mantel piece for everyone to see, is it? There must be a reason for that.'

'Don't you want to know who it's from, Rob? Aren't you a little bit intrigued why she's not shown this one to you?'

Robert didn't reply. His mum flipped the front of the envelope over and stared at the handwriting.

'I think it's from Poppy; must've been something she did in case…'

Tears welled up in Mary's eyes, before she began biting her bottom lip in a determined effort to stop the flood from appearing. That got Robert's attention and he walked across to the bed. He slipped the card out of her hand, and then out of the envelope. The only sound in the room was a gentle hush of Mel's breathing who was already in a deep sleep. Robert looked at his girlfriend snuggled up peacefully, his transient stare emitting sorrow. He passed the card to his mum without looking at her, and in turn she read through Poppy's message to her daughter.

I cradled you in my arms eighteen years ago, so overjoyed at the delicate petal I had me, scooped up in swaddling. I spoke many sweet words to you while you slept. I hoped and prayed that you would blossom into the young woman you have become. You breathe pure joy into these old bones. And now you going to celebrate this wonderful milestone in your life, with plenty more to come. I remember once on one of my birthdays, when me was but a pickney, Nana Azalea sat me on her lap, and she whisper these words in my ear:

"Years roll by in the blink of an eye, the journey to get here was not always kind, to the unhappy memories I can choose to be blind, and see only joyous ones at the front of my mind."

We came to England penniless, but our love and happiness could not be stolen. It's not what you have, it's what you do that matters – and who you choose to do it with is what makes it special. Better to be rich through your experiences than to be surrounded by material things. Use your birthdays to reflect and celebrate how far you have come, but also to plan tomorrow's dreams. Then don't let time be a barrier for you to go out and discover them.
Love, Mamma x

Even in the dimly lit room Mary could see that some of the ink had been smudged previously by a tear gambolling down Mel's cheek, and dropping down from her chin when it was barged into by another. Mary struggled to contain the lump that was pressing at the back of her own throat. She was thinking about the dilemma that Derek must have been in, not knowing whether the effects of those beautiful words on his daughter would be positively received or not, and yet at the same time knowing that he must ensure Mel received the card regardless if he were to respect the wishes of his sadly departed wife. She couldn't imagine the conversation that must have taken place between him and Poppy, where she would have made him promise to give the card to Mel should she not be around to do so herself.

Robert was lost in his own thoughts, pondering whether the card had been another trigger for her behaviour and spontaneity that evening, and perhaps the subsequent heavy drinking was a way to block it all out. Above all, he knew the impact those words had on Mel were the absolute opposite to what Poppy would have intended.

The moment of gentle calm ended abruptly when Mel sat upright and proceeded to violently empty the contents of her guts into the waiting bowl that Mary had wisely positioned at the side of her bed. The retching continued for a short time, the tears of self-pity a little longer – but eventually she had sobered up sufficiently to be able to doze back off without fear of a repeat episode. Upon resurfacing the next day, she experienced both guilt and remorse for her actions, but all of that was overshadowed by the feeling of a rock banging against her head as she suffered the most immense hangover.

27

Once Mel's birthday passed, Spring found itself in a hurry. Normality seemed to be bursting to life alongside the buds of plants and trees. Robert and Mel lived the dream by going to the Manics gig in April, before attending to the nightmare endured by every student, when they started to bury down the hatchets to revise from notes in tatty files ahead of their finals. To reach the promised land known as 'exam ready' needed a combination of minimal distractions and a well-planned revision timetable to guide them through. Or, at least, that's what was meant to happen.

In the subsequent weeks that followed, Mel started falling apart, and Rob found it increasingly difficult to help her pull through. She was riddled with guilt at trampling on Ali's dream, and then stood by and watched her friend take the flack for appearing to have led Robert on. That aside, her attempts to extinguish the demons that were unrelenting in cranking up the pain of losing her mum was like lopping a weed at the stem above ground level but leaving an untendered mass of offshoots entangling her well-being beneath the surface. Out of sight of others she was struggling to treat the negativity that continued to grow aggressively. She chose not to tend to the root cause of the problem, and so inevitably the undesirable behaviour resurfaced and was even more unsightly. She just hadn't dealt with her grief or faced up to life without Poppy. Until that happened, she would continue to slide down on a spiral of misery.

The consequence of her state of mind was that she lacked the nerve to execute even the most fundamental tasks in her studies. A positive and rational approach to revision deserted her, to be replaced with an irresponsible attitude and a significant increase in her desire to socialise instead. Robert was instrumental in getting her to cram in revision on days that he could influence her routine, but when he wasn't around to be a calming influence Mel would need little encouragement from her peers to get out and party hard. She would lie to her dad about the amount of work she was putting in and played on his fragile disposition by convincing him that it was perfectly normal to down tools regularly to avoid burning out.

Mel also blagged to those that capitalised on her generosity at the bar about the amount of studying she was doing, knowing that the wall of deceit was sure to implode at some point. Sensible was no longer an adjective that she could pin to her chest. Even as she drank her way through her study leave, she knew full well that she was screwing up her chances to pursue her long held goals of university and beyond. Having spent time researching for the right course, Mel gained a place on a business degree at the University of Nottingham and ensured that she was well placed geographically to be able to see Robert regularly. He would be living in digs in Derby with other apprentices who had been taken on at Rolls Royce. Both of their life choices came with conditions around grades, but when it came to it Mel just didn't have the nerve or self-belief to see it through. She did the minimum amount of revision required to be able to have a stab at the questions on her scripts.

By sheer chance, the History exam included questions that the class had previously answered in a mock, and for which they had all been given detailed feedback and notes from their tutor. Business mostly covered topics that she had previously been naturally proficient at. The maths papers were an entirely different proposition. Straight from opening the crisp white sheets in front of her, Mel struggled to sit still in her seat. She could feel the heat of her body radiating onto her face as she thumbed through to some of the latter questions.

Mel was writhing at the thought that her expected grade for

this subject was going down the pan – and with it the very real possibility of her plans of going to Nottingham. It was an excruciating situation, knowing that she was failing the paper in front of her. The unpleasantness she experienced didn't go unnoticed by the staff invigilating, who were not being particularly subtle about it as they stared and whispered to each other. They saw the agony etched on Mel's face as she attempted to confront questions that required the level of knowledge and skill that were commensurate only with a committed, and prepared, student.

The students leaving the exam hall after maths resembled a colony of ants, with activity in all directions. Some people followed each other uniformly out of the hall and onto the steps outside, where they screeched and gasped as they discussed the content of the exam. Others scurried randomly in different directions, quite deliberately avoiding any 'what did you put for that?' type conversations. Ali was in the latter group. She hated those vexatious questions and the idea of standing for ages, wasting time while everyone else ploughed over their answers. If someone had a different answer to her, Ali would mither about it for the rest of the summer. It would simply ruin the chance to have a well-earned rest as her stomach would be in knots everyday agonising over how she had tackled the question.

Conveniently, she had to slip away quickly to get on with revision for her last sociology exam, and besides, it would avoid any unpleasantness of being around Robert and Mel. She didn't so much as peep to see where either of them were, even though she knew the seating plan for the exam meant that Robert had been sitting two rows to her left and six seats behind during the exam.

In the hope that his stare would somehow tease her to turn around to look at him, Robert had glanced across at Ali while the papers were collected at the end of the exam. He was careful it didn't develop into a stare for fear that someone else in the hall would notice, and because Mel also happened to be in his sightline. At brief intervals over the previous two hours in the hall, he flicked his sight over to her seat and then up to see the look of concern on the faces of the invigilating staff. He pulled her to the blind side of one of the stone pillars by the steps to the hall and took the opportunity to discretely ask her about it.

'You ok, Mel?'

'Yeah, why shouldn't I be?' she reacted defensively.

'I could see you from my seat over the aisles and a few seats up from me. You looked a bit panicky.'

'Christ Rob! It's a bit disturbing that you had time to check me out during the exam. Don't you think it would've been more important to concentrate on your own work, you muppet?'

'I was and found the whole thing bloody difficult; some of it was impossible. Anyway, I wasn't watching you as such, I was looking up when I was thinking, and you had your hands on your head and kinda rocking it to and fro.'

That he had been able to read the distress signals irked Mel, and if it was easy for Robert to have realised the mess that she was making on her script then perhaps others had seen it too.

'That's just what I do when I'm trying to focus, and anyway for your information I thought the paper was fine. You need to stop fussing Rob. I don't need anyone to mother me,' was her lame response.

Mel had become accomplished in the art of bluffing, but Robert was neither convinced at her attempts to blow smoke over her academic meltdown nor her protestations about not needing her mum. If she scrutinised her last comment it would translate as a cry for help, and it was another screwed-up attempt to keep a stiff upper lip. But if ever Mel needed evidence that the conning needed to stop, it came in the form of her exam results in August, and rejection from her first-choice university.

28

Across town, Ali had already posted the official application papers to be able to reside on campus at York. She had seen Mel and Robert huddled in a corner at school on results day looking serious and had been concerned about whether it had anything to do with their grades. She had wanted to wish them both well but thought better of it when she could clearly see that Mel had tears in her eyes. Instead she made a beeline up to the pigeon trees on Aethelred Hill to soak up the view and breathe a sigh of relief that she, at least, had achieved her goal.

Though Ali was beyond excited at the prospect of being an undergraduate in another historic city, she would miss one of her favourite places. But there were memories embedded on the hillside that she would soon rather forget. It was there that she and Robert had once expressed to each other that,

'You and me time is my favourite time, anytime, and always.'

Maybe that was one thing that had been slightly misjudged, an oversight of the obstacles that could get in the way. Perhaps the simple fact was that remembering those words meant that she just missed being close to her friend. And just because she couldn't tell him that, it didn't mean she wasn't feeling it. Ali craved to feel differently once she was in York, and she was ready to go. But in the back of her mind was something she could recall that Poppy had once said about moving to Winchester.

'A new place will hide old wounds, but they still be there no matter what. It's what you do to disguise the scars, and who you trust to be able to show them to that helps you move on.'

Everything was still raw in Ali's head, and ordinarily her timid nature would curtail any knee jerk reactions. She knew it would be better to adopt the stance that it was good riddance to bad smells, but there was an urge to sprint back down the steep slope of Aethelred Hill and up to Wood Street to confront Robert about his indifference since getting her letter. If Ali could get anything that resembled an explanation from him then it would mean that chapter was closed and the next one could begin with no overhanging what-ifs or maybes. Besides, given that they were going to be miles apart in different areas of the country there was nothing to lose. She just wanted to know what it was in the letter that made Robert suddenly discard her like jetsam. She needed to know why he decided she and him couldn't become 'us'.

As she reached the bottom end of the town, Ali's spontaneous decision was halted in its tracks. Walking the opposite way towards her was Mary, who showed complete delight at learning of Ali's results by squeezing her in a big bear hug. The head of steam that had bubbled up in Ali dispersed, and she resigned herself to never knowing the truth. As they stood looking into one another's eyes, the smile gently slipped from Mary's face.

'Robert tells me you're not keen to see him anymore. Such a shame, but you go off and grab yourself a life in that beautiful city ok?'

Ali blushed. She wasn't sure how to respond, so nodded and smiled instead. She didn't feel uncomfortable knowing Mary's point of view, but neither was she going to get into a conversation about it. Instead, she shifted the focus of attention back onto Robert and Mel by explaining her concern after seeing the pair looking so tense.

'I could be wrong, but it didn't look like good news, Mary.'

Mel endured a torrid time through clearing. It didn't matter to admissions staff that Mel ought to have scored higher grades than she did, and in any case, that set alarm bells ringing about why she had performed so poorly. She blamed anyone and everyone that had taught her for her failures. Whatever the protestations, Mel failed to grasp the fundamental issue; she hadn't worked anywhere near hard enough to be able to score well in her finals.

Over the course of the next twenty-four hours there was a mad scramble to get onto a degree so that she could follow her beau to the East Midlands, and it meant a change in her preferred course. While her negotiating position was weakened by her results, a desperate plea and a phone interview with an understanding course leader led to an offer of a place on Business Management and Accounting at Nottingham Trent. Same city, different institution, but no change to being located close to Robert. It was received with relief rather than celebration, and while there was no finger pointing, patience and understanding were wearing thin all round. And Robert wasn't the only one holding back their inner thoughts about what the hell had happened to Mel.

Even before Mary was able to talk with him about her own concerns, Robert already harboured reservations about their future together. The evening after the frenetic attempts to get Mel into university, she and her son chatted together on the sofa the way they had done many times over the years.

'So, big man, you're selling out on me then?'

'What's that meant to mean?'

'You're sodding off up north to have a jolly, leaving me behind here to rattle between the walls.'

'Mum – for a start, it's the Midlands, not the north. Secondly, if I pass my driving test in September, I'll be looking to buy a car. Which means I'll be able to get home as often as I like.'

Mary paused to think.

'That's not quite how it's going to be though is it, Rob? Let's be honest.'

He looked at her bemused, the screwed-up expression an invitation for her to add some clarity.

'You won't be able to just go galivanting about in your car, 'cos you've got someone else to consider who is going to be expecting to spend a lot of quality time with you when you're not at work. You know that, right?'

It was Robert's turn to pause; he did know that, and it didn't sit comfortably with him.

'I'll come back as much as I can, and I'll come down *with* Mel.'

'Look, darling, you can come as often as you want, and with whomever you choose. But we both know it's going to be difficult to share your time out evenly like that. So, I'll say now – I don't want you feeling bad or guilty about it. As long as we can speak on the phone to catch up, I'll be ok with that. It'll make our meet ups very special, won't it?'

'I'm scared, mum.'

'What about? It's not like you.'

'Everything. Literally, everything.'

'Oh, c'mon Rob. Do you think you're the only one agonising over the great big chapter ahead of them? You've got yourself onto a prestigious apprenticeship through sheer grit, determination, and a whole load of other skills. They loved you at the interview, had no hesitation in offering you a position. It's going to be amazing learning new things and meeting new people.'

'I know, I know. It's not that.'

'And you've got your best mate living just up the road if you need a shoulder to cry on.'

'It's more likely to be her crying on my shoulder if she screws things up.'

Robert's chin was resting on his chest, he was looking quite forlorn.

'Are you going to ignore what I said.'

'No. I just don't think it's fair to tell you my opinion.'

'It is, that's exactly what I want. Please mum, tell me what you're thinking.'

Mary cupped Robert's chin in her hand, and gently lifted his face so she could look at him.

'Blokes often sow their oats in a number of fields, Rob. I'm not condoning that, and I don't want you messing girls around. But are you happy with your lot? I don't want you to be content with... one single, scrappy patch.'

'Is that what you think about her – scrappy?'

'No! I love that girl, whether she's with you or not. You're my son, I love you more. I just want you to be happy and if you're not that'd shred me inside. I just don't know if you've taken on a puzzle with no solution.'

She was right.

'She means so much to me, mum. I just don't always feel like we're connected, it's difficult to explain. She's imploded so many times over the last few months, I've not told you about most of it.'

'Do you think I'm stupid, Rob? I know she's been on a journey of chaos, and she's done well to pull through to this point.'

'I don't know if she has pulled through, though. She clams up about her mum, won't talk about how she's feeling about it, and changes the subject or has a crazy moment to block it out.'

'And you think her exam results were just coincidental, an unfortunate set of papers in each subject? Don't be daft.'

Robert sat up.

'No, I think you're right. I can't believe she messed up as badly as that.'

'And her behaviour at the birthday rave – a bit extreme for someone just letting their hair down, don't you think?'

'I know. But the thing is, I'm not just going to walk away from her, I'm not my dad – I'm loyal.'

That short dig made Mary wince.

'You are a lovely lad, and I respect you for that, big man. It's wonderful that you know what's right from wrong. But it sounds to me like you've thought about not being with her?'

'I just don't know if I'm what she needs.'

'You're kidding me, right? She obviously cares for you Rob.'
Robert paused.

'Am I being selfish if I say I don't know if I can handle it if she keeps melting down like she does?'

'No, of course you're not. It's really demanding stuff for people so young to deal with.'

'I want her to be the girl I know, and to keep away the intruder that seems to appear every now and again that takes over her personality.'

That was a conversation stopper. The only person that could prevent the intermittent intrusion of an erratic character was Mel herself. If she was unable to curb that, then it was difficult to know what mileage was left in their relationship, no matter how gallant Robert wanted to be about it.

Late September, and the back end of 1997 in sight. Some trees were already beginning to shell their foliage, and at the least, most were an altogether different shade of colour from even a few days beforehand. Ground frost was the early sign that autumn was knocking on the door, causing the leaves to begin curling at the edges as if to shield themselves from the sudden difference in temperature.

Change had been creeping up the whole summer on the next batch of freshers and those taking their first steps into the working world, and suddenly it was overpowering every thought and action of beautiful youth. Ali, Mel, and Robert journeyed north of their hometown, the excitement of unknown challenges awaiting them, and their nervousness hidden. The craving to hold a parent's hand for reassurance wouldn't be a unique feeling for someone leaving home for the first time, though there would be much bravado to disguise it for fear of being found out and never being able to play it down with their peers.

The triangle of friendship that was once held with such affection remained blunted at the edges. Far from being forgotten, it continued to play on each of their minds in some way. The trio began new chapters of their lives with the overspill of unfinished business from their former ones.

29

Mel's love life around 2011 was severely lacking; her relationship count had dwindled and for whatever reason her pulling power had diminished. Her abysmal efforts to land herself a man grew increasingly desperate. In one recent encounter, she pursued an unwilling contender around the bar area of a dingy club. Being well lubricated with pornstar martinis, any inhibitions deserted her as the man was cornered, and Mel began to slur her words at him.

'I don't think I caught your name.'

'And I don't think I said.'

His response was intended as a rebuff.

'Ooh, man of mystery.'

Mel let out a drunken cackle, before grabbing the bemused man's pint glass and licking around the rim in full view of him. Upon exuding her saliva, she shoved the pot back into his hand and goaded the man to drink from the glass dripping in her spit.

'It's try-before-you-buy night; taste me first before taking me home. Go on, take a sip.'

For a moment Mel's horrified victim was too stunned to speak but found his voice before she attempted to manipulate him any further.

'You're a fuckin' weirdo.'

As he delivered his scathing parting shot to the grinning, swaying letch he slammed the half-finished lager on the nearest table to the exit that he hastily escaped through. The bloke was nowhere near bladdered enough for that kind of challenge, and neither was anyone else. Unsurprisingly, Mel went home alone that night.

Crashing and burning was becoming an all too familiar feeling for Mel, and not one that ought to have been associated with an educated, pretty, young woman. Unsurprisingly, she didn't endear herself to work colleagues, appalled at the behaviour they had previously witnessed from their workplace superior. Invites to birthday celebrations and the like simply dried up as nobody dared risk being associated with the humiliation that followed Mel around on a night out.

As inexcusable as Mel's escapades had been, that self-indulgence was her way of dealing with the pain of the fifteenth anniversary of her mum disappearing from her life. This self-abuse occurred annually and seemed to have no let-up. But few people that knew Mel were aware of that; certainly not those who were likely to gossip about it in the workplace and then cut her out of any social plans. Periodically she had to contend with the build-up of having those tests to measure any hereditary development of her mum's myotonic dystrophy, and then dealing with the anxiety of waiting for the results. That was the worst thing – the doubt in her mind whether the next set of data was going to be life changing. No sooner would she receive confirmation from one test that she was clear than her attention would immediately turn to the next ones, even though they could be two years away. It was a rough psychological cycle to endure.

Looking back, it was difficult for Mel to pinpoint exactly what it was that triggered her curiosity to search for Robert through social media in the first place – though it was perhaps little wonder that she turned her attention to what she thought may have been safer ground after the stinging encounter with the guy in the club. She was single, and that was probably a primary motive for wanting to check him out – to see whether he had bobbed and weaved his way through the opposite sex to find ultimate happiness.

Mel remained unsure about what she wanted – professionally and romantically – and was probably curious to see if other people had figured things out more effectively than her. Her dabbling on social media was originally meant to be a toe in the water with dating sites, an attempt to clean up her image using a more orthodox method to find 'the one'. But she couldn't bring herself to go through the hassle of creating a bullshit profile, and to date guys that were good matches rather than the ones she really wanted. She parked the idea of romance, and instead decided it would be a much better idea to touch base with people she already knew, and maybe to make up ground with old friends.

She had been trying to work out the last time they had seen each other, and realised it was over thirteen years ago, in March 1998. The past was only ever intermittent in her thoughts, and it didn't always fill her mind with fondness for days gone by. If she dissected those flash backs correctly, she'd have remembered that it was a time that could throw up nothing other than bile memories. But somehow Mel had convinced herself that it hadn't ended as messily as it did, and perhaps her excessive alcohol intake that night had magnified the ill feeling that ensued. Wasn't she still blind drunk the next morning? Had their parting contained any less bitterness than it did, they may have been on speaking terms thereafter. Even now in adulthood, Mel continued to be a master at deceiving herself of reality. While she risked the wrath of Robert reminding her of what really happened if she pursued this internet track down, the stirring of nostalgic curiosity was too potent to avoid.

It was inevitable that the profiles of friends and acquaintances were rifled to uncover their wider network of associates. She dug deep; by chance, Mel had viewed the profile of someone who used to work with someone that was married to someone else who worked for Rolls Royce. It would surely have been too coincidental to find anyone else called Robert Spitley. His profile was severely lacking in personal details or photos, but it didn't take much effort when viewing his friendship groups to realise that this was him. It took a couple of weeks for Mel to receive a notification that her 'friend request' had been accepted and followed it up with an ambiguous note.

It's been a long time; I hope you're well? M x

At first, she just wanted to know about Robert and his life, not necessarily to be back in it or a part of it. The problem for Mel is that once a reply was forthcoming, she went into her renewed link-up with Robert feet first, full-on, and with no regard for how he felt about it. All those exciting feelings for him came flooding back.

Hi Mel, it was a surprise to hear from you. I don't go on this site very often, and I'm rubbish at keeping in touch with anyone – just ask my mum! She moved to the Cotswolds to run a boozer a long time ago, and I think that's when she lost contact with your old man. I haven't been back to the old town many times since. I stayed with RR in Derby for 8 years after finishing my apprenticeship, but recently moved down south again. Hope you eventually got through uni ok, and that you're settled with a good job. Best wishes – Rob.

Mel couldn't help but wonder if opening this channel of communication was just a start, and whether a floodgate of possibilities had been undone. She didn't set out intentionally to cause the resulting stink, but that didn't mean it wasn't foul.

30

Agreeing to meet Mel was done reluctantly, and after polite but persistent badgering on her part. Robert had managed to swerve countless generous offers of 'post-work drinks' and 'a bite to eat'. But the bombardment of suggested dates many weeks ahead into the calendar to 'help him plan around other commitments' meant the excuses ran dry. He immediately regretted letting it slip that he was living in Hampshire, as Mel then assumed that geography was no barrier for meeting in person. When the suggestion came to meet nearer his side of the county to 'make it more convenient' for him and his 'busy lifestyle' he felt backed into a corner.

Aside from that, there was the not-insignificant matter of considering what his better half would think. That put Robert in a conundrum as to whether to tell her or not, and suddenly it got complicated. He convinced himself that a quick cup of coffee was innocent enough and would be the remedy to stunt the flow of messages being received. This prudence proved to be misguided.

Pedicure perfect and with salon-styled hair, Mel began her journey to Eastleigh. That wasn't before another quick pit-stop at her wardrobe though, anxiously dithering about not wanting the colour of her top to clash with her nails. However inadvertent it was, Mel was behaving like someone going on a date. She still arrived at the main entrance to the park ambitiously early despite the pampering session she had afforded herself that morning.

The contrast with Robert couldn't have been more different. Though he'd travelled only a fraction of the miles that Mel had done to get to the park, he still managed to be late for the two o'clock rendezvous. His attire of choice were some jogging bottoms, which wouldn't have been out of place on a building site, and a matching top that was in need of a wash to remove the odour of work-out sweat. It wasn't done deliberately, but when he saw Mel, he felt significantly under-dressed and had underestimated the significance of this meeting to her.

Mel saw straight past the clothes, and was more concerned with seeing him, looking at his face, and not quite believing he was standing there in front of her after so many years. She let out a childish squeal as she ran towards him, high heels tip-tapping on the tarmac. Robert stood rigidly with arms at his side as Mel flung her arms round his neck. He had to take step backwards to balance the motion of her sudden launch at him, otherwise she would have been frolicking with him on the ground.

'Hello you! Oops, sorry you've dropped something.'

Robert took half a step backwards to look to the ground where the item had settled by his feet. Simultaneously they both reached down to pick it up, and caught each other's eyeline, momentarily causing them to pause. Mel smiled, before Robert was quickest to recover, and slipped the item back into his pocket.

'So, what's this stubble on your face then, eh Greeny? Looks strange on you.'

Robert frowned – he hadn't been called that in a very long while.

'You'd look better clean-shaven, chap.' Robert didn't reply. 'Wanna go for a walk around the park?'

'Nah, don't think I've got time really, not if you want to grab a coffee that is.'

'Argh, really? How long have you got?'

'Um, 'bout an hour.'

Mel tried hard to conceal her disappointment, but her cheeks drooped, and she lost her smile temporarily. Robert sensed it and cut in to avoid any embarrassment.

'Besides, I come here quite a bit with the family, and never have time to grab a brew at the end of our walk. It'd be nice to actually see the inside of that café for once.'

The family? Mel took a sneaky peek at Robert's left hand, and unless she was mistaken there seemed to be no sign of a wedding band. That's something she would have to seek clarity about. She regained her zest promptly. 'No problem. C'mon then, let's grab a hot cuppa. Aww, it's so good to see you!'

Mel forced her arm under his to link them as they walked towards the café. She began babbling away about her journey down from Farnborough, and as much as Robert wanted to ignore the waffle her enthusiasm was infectious. He learnt how Derek had gained his HGV licence and secured employment back in his homelands in Scotland, and how Lewis had decided to settle in Antigua irrespective of any possible worsening of his condition. As she spoke at a rate of knots that was off the scale, he looked her up and down inconspicuously, and had to admit to himself she looked good. He had the awareness about him not to lower his guard to give off mixed messages, or to get drawn into nostalgic conversations that could touch raw nerves. He was on edge and waiting for the curve ball to come, which inevitably it did once the small talk was up.

'So, come on, did it take much convincing for you to come and see me?'

'Actually, yes it did,' was the immediate thought that went through Robert's mind, but to be so defensive literally minutes after greeting her felt a bit too harsh. He refrained and took a more tactful approach, skirting round Mel's probing.

'It's nice to see you looking well, Mel. I'm glad you're ok. But you do know this ain't going to be a regular thing, this... meeting up, don't you?'

'I never said it would be, but why not? Aren't you happy that we've hooked back up?'

'The fact that I'm in a happy relationship with my missus

ought to be an obvious enough reason.'

'Doesn't she know you're here? You bad boy.'

'She – Hannah – wouldn't have stopped me if I said I was meeting you, but I'm not sure she'd have understood the reasons for poking around with the past.'

'Why are you making such a big deal about it?' she asked with more than a smidgen of irony.

Robert looked her up and down and huffed.

'Me?'

'Isn't it natural to come full circle over time? I mean, meeting the same people who you shared your fun times and memories with. People that knew you the way we were before… our lives moved on.'

'That's a feckin' great big circle then, how many years are we talking about?'

'Thirteen or so, I think, unless you take that time when we bumped into each other randomly. That was awkward.'

Robert ignored the last comment.

'The thing is, we're not those people anymore though, are we?'

'Aren't we?'

Robert looked at her, eyes squinting, while gently blowing the hot coffee in his cup.

'Mel, this is crazy, there's no turning back the clock. You're acting like it was yesterday.'

'I wish it was.'

He immediately closed her down.

'I certainly don't. *That* was just an adolescent episode back then and you know it. Seeing you today… to me you're like a storm moving in and then blowing over. End of.'

'You're right, my life has been pretty stormy. But that's not the way today feels like for me. It's been more like a nice slice of blue sky,' she replied smugly.

Robert sat back in his seat, sipping at his drink to temporarily avoid further confrontation. Mel was struggling to collect her thoughts with the adrenalin kicking around inside and beginning to overpower any control she had on her emotions. Given that Robert would forever believe that she was the cause of their falling apart, telling him how she felt would be nothing but trivial, and yet it didn't stop her from blurting it out.

'I've thought about us, you know. I've missed you and me.'

Robert let out a dismissive sigh and shook his head, offering Mel nothing other than a look of disappointment. 'Look at you Mel; you could have any one you want.'

'You reckon? That counts for nothing when none of them are what you want.' It had been a nice compliment all the same.

'Have you actually given any guys a chance?'

'Been engaged, but wedding bell clappers have never swung for me. To be honest, my love life is like my wardrobe half the time, always looking for something new without using what I've already got. Ha, I think someone has said that about me before.'

'You've got to get busy building a life that could be – and stop playing out old fantasies.'

'Did you even have an open mind about how you might feel seeing me today?'

'No way. Not at all. You can't just muscle in because it suits you, Mel. Hannah is the best mate I've ever had. She's my life. What makes you think for a moment that I'm vaguely interested in fucking that up for you – or anyone else for that matter?'

'I'm sorry,' Mel conceded. 'I find it difficult to get any sense out from here to here.' Mel jabbed the side of her head and lips. 'I think since being back in touch with you I've been trying to get my head around the void in time that I know nothing about.'

'Why on earth would you think that you should have a right to know anything about what's happened to me over these years? You went your way, I went mine. That's life, it's normal.'

Mel knew there was no point in being concerned with Robert's life. She was left behind before either of their lives had really taken off. From that point, every chapter thereafter excluded her so it made no sense to feel she could be part of it.

'Ok, well at least please help me to release myself from you, Rob.'

That offended Robert, he had no intention of holding on to her, so he delivered a cruel blow.

'Do you know how fuckin' immature and stupid that sounds? There is no 'me and you' and to be perfectly honest I'm not sure there ever should have been. It was a bit of a car crash that ended up a write off. Go and get a life and stop trying to hijack another person's happiness.'

Mel's hard exterior was caving into the onslaught of this reality check from Robert, and tears rolled down both cheeks.

'I don't believe you regret *everything*.'

'Regret? That's a dangerous thing to live your life by. No, I don't regret anything I've done. But I have always learnt from the mistakes I've made.'

Being a 'mistake' was no less harsh to hear than being a 'regret' for Mel.

'I'm sorry, seeing you… it's like letting out the genie.'

'Well, I'm not the solution, I'm not what you need to get sorted out. In fact, it was never particularly me that you wanted if you think about it, Mel, and it isn't now. You just wanted someone to fill a gap, a hole where there was no affection. You wanted someone that bowed to everything you wanted, with your selfishness masquerading as affectionate. Sounds like you're still very needy.'

Mel bit her lip and looked away; she didn't have the mental energy to fight that comment. Perhaps it was because Robert had hit the absolute truth of it.

'I thought I was getting my shit together up until I saw you at that millennium festival a few years later, me with my new bloke and you with Hannah. Of all the places to have bumped into you, and I couldn't think of anything sensible to say at the time. The thing is it completely threw me backwards again.'

'But we were finished Mel, it was over long before then. I knew it was going to kill you Mel, but I had to do it, and I honestly hoped you would pull through, dust yourself down, and find someone else who'd treat you the way you deserve to be. It just couldn't be me. But now? I can see no reason why you would go on punishing yourself for no reason, over something that only exists as a memory in your own imagination. We're not ever going back there, and meeting like this is not going to help you move on if it's bringing up these feelings. That's why I'm saying I don't want to do this again.'

'That works fine for you doesn't it, Rob. Take the past, fit it neatly into a box, and store it away somewhere that it won't confront you again. I'm not sure you're any better than me at dealing with your memories.'

Robert thrust his hand against his forehead with such frustration that it caused it to slap. He got up from his seat with a disgruntled frown plastered across his face.

'I can't do this anymore.'

'Don't leave. I've not asked you anything about your family. What about the rest of your coffee?'

'It didn't taste as nice as it looked. Besides, it's definitely time I was gone.'

The chair scraped on the tiled floor as Robert put it back under the table, and within a minute he was gone and out of sight. Sitting alone in the café, surrounded by the hum of excited kids with their families, put into perspective everything that was wrong about Mel's world. There was very little order in her life, and no special person she could rely on or share with. The pain for Mel wasn't unfamiliar; it was the type which felt like there was a cord attached between stomach pit and throat, pulling down tight like a bungee rope and briefly slacking off. In between each yank, it rattled the tear duct buckets causing salty droplets to spill over and slide along her lashes. She would usually be dismissive of such outpouring, and not allow herself to wallow in self-pity. But Robert's words were difficult to deal with and she endured the effects of the bungee cord for some time before she had the energy to escape the scene of the harsh lesson she'd been given.

31

Hannah Florey was not a lady to jump to conclusions or be judgemental where her Robert was concerned. They had been together for too many years to have any suspicions that either one of them might stray from their relationship. Besides, he was often quick to point out to people that his family was his world, so why would he entertain something that would make it come crashing down? The desktop was there for everyone in the household to access, be it school, work, or socially. Sitting at the computer that evening, Hannah thought nothing of the ping of an email arriving to tell Robert he had a message. It was the second one in quick succession that prompted her to see who it was from out of interest. Hannah noticed the emails were alerts to his social media account, and that they were both from 'Melanie B'. It didn't take too much thinking for her to work out who that might be.

Hannah sat looking out of the window at the setting sun, jabbing her index finger against her temple. She knew that she ought to trust Robert, and that this was nothing to worry about. But something inside told her this wasn't quite right. If her suspicions about the identity of the sender of those messages were correct, then she would be upset that Robert hadn't even mentioned he was in touch with her. Being friends with females was one thing but having an attachment to an ex was something else.

As much as she wanted to read the content, Hannah decided to refrain from logging into Robert's account. Instead, she calmly invited him to tell her about it when he arrived back from the gym. He told her everything, feeling some sense of relief for letting her know, but mostly stupidity forever hiding it from her in the first place.

Together they opened the messages that had caused this stir. The first one was incredibly vague, saying:

Just wanted to say a quick hello and thank you for meeting up. M x

And the second read:

What you said – it was all spot on. M x

Hannah knew that Robert had been telling the truth even without the messages, because he was useless at lying and would never have been able to carry the burden of a guilty secret. But reading Mel's words was confirmation for her that she was being a pest, and he had tried to be a good friend to her and nothing else. Hannah and Robert both agreed that the communication with Mel needed to stop. The intention was to defriend her, but not before Hannah had written a reply with Robert's blessing.

Hi Mel, this is Hannah – Robert's partner. If he hadn't made it clear enough for you the other day that he's not interested in rekindling any of the torment that he went through with you, then I'm delighted to make it even clearer for you myself. It's never going to happen. The only person cheating at the moment is YOU – on yourself with your desperate attempts to lure another woman's bloke. Robert wishes you all the best for the future, which given the circumstances is beyond gracious. I get the sense that as a person you're not the simpleton that your actions suggest, so I hope you'll not be so foolish as to do anything other than move on with your life and leave us to get on with ours.

Not for the first time, Robert cut Mel adrift. It was easier doing it via the internet, unlike their undoing in person many years beforehand. He was aghast at some of the things she said to him in Eastleigh, and at the frame of mind she seemed to be in regarding their past lives. Of course, he cared – it was in his nature to do so. But he couldn't empathise with someone that continued to believe that splitting up all those years ago was the wrong decision. How Mel remembered it was the antithesis of Robert's recollection.

When the two of them left Winchester for the East Midlands in the Autumn of 1997, it was not just the leaves on the trees that were beginning to change and wilt. Robert had shared some of his nagging doubts about their plans with his mum, while keeping deeper thoughts to himself. He wrestled with the knowledge that some months before this he could've turned to any one of two female friends with how he was feeling, and now he was unable to talk to either.

Settling into his apprenticeship went smoothly enough, and the challenge to learn new skills was a welcome mental diversion. The novelty of living independently with likeminded lads wore off steadily once the mundane necessities of shopping and cleaning hit them, and even this was overshadowed by the brewing storm that fridge items were being half inched. Finger pointing was commonplace, and accusations got thrown around, but the matter began to pass when it became obvious that there had been more than one culprit. Consequently, shelf space got divided, names were written in capital letters on wrappers to avoid confusion, and the first rook in the house was narrowly avoided as egos collided. An intake of a few beers on a group night out, and all had been forgiven.

Robert's bank balance at the end of each month made everything worthwhile, which was just as well as his car enjoyed soaking up the pennies in running costs and repairs. To begin with, both he and Mel looked forward to being together at the weekends, when Robert would make the short journeys over to

Nottingham in his pride and joy – a racing green coloured mini. Having expected there to be some kind of an eruption of emotional chaos, it surprised Robert that everything seemed to be plodding along normally. He felt guilty for doubting Mel's ability to chameleonize herself into university life and wondered whether it was possible for this plug to remain in place for any length of time. Even if it did, it rankled him how it was possible to be in a relationship where he was constantly doubting the ability of it staying on a positive course and not even feeling able to discuss it. Pessimism was hardly likely to be the flimsy pillars on which their love for one another could develop, and yet he resolutely cared for her well-being. Though Mel continued to bottle up her true feelings, the lasting effect of Poppy's death would always be their common ground.

By February the following year, the forecasted strain began to emerge. Robert found the constant ferrying over to Nottingham at the weekends meant he missed out on visiting his mum or a social life with his workmates. It was a difficult balancing act to explain to Mel that he would prefer to be with her, yet at the same time convince her that it was essential he went out on the town with people he merely worked with. A backfill of phone calls in the evenings were reassuring enough for Mel to be able to bypass his occasional absence, but even when he did visit, the mood began to feel weary. Robert found himself at a tangent to the lairy cliental in the student union, and never quite in tune with the same humour or interests. However unconvincing his efforts were, he tried to associate with Mel's friends to the point where he was wrongly accused of flirting by her after being so nice to her dorm mates. Student life wasn't his bag, and as if to compound the contrast, Mel was in her element. The frivolity of the social scene was absolutely her forum.

On the night when it all kicked off, Mel had reluctantly agreed to leave her own pastures to journey across to Derby. The apprentices were celebrating a milestone – the completion of six months training and core units towards their qualification. Mel couldn't see what all the fuss was about. It was hardly as if there was any awards ceremony, and it didn't seem an apt replacement for the 'Austin Powers' fancy dress house party that she would be passing up on. As a result, a belligerent undergraduate was intent on necking an excessive amount of liquor and bragging about it, before openly flirting to piss Robert off and to test his resilience. With nothing other than a meek appeal, Robert tried to distinguish the onslaught of ridicule being exhibited.

'I'll give you one thing, Mel, you're on form. Can we just enjoy the evening without giving away all of my dignity?'

But with her exuberance fuelled by shots, Mel also planted the seeds of a cunning little plan with some of the lads who lived in a rented pad in a neighbouring street. Flickering her long lashes unashamedly and whispering with a side glance she recruited the members for the plot.

'Who's up for a bit of fun with me later then, boys?'

Robert went to bed hastily, mostly to get away from Mel's mockery, and quickly nodded off. There was quite a delay before arriving in the bedroom herself. She had convinced her willing recruits to physically move Robert's mini down the road several hundred metres, beyond the sightline of where it had been originally parked up. How funny it would be to watch Robert's face when he woke up to find his car had magically disappeared, she thought.

Before it was Robert's pride and joy, there had been four previous owners of the mini, and while it's recent respray gave it a look of being newer than it was, the paint couldn't mask the fact that it wasn't kitted out with modern technological advancements. It had neither an alarm nor immobiliser. The five burly blokes found lifting the rear end easy enough, and as the road was fairly flat and straight, the escapade was easy to execute.

The dead of night in a leafy suburb ensured that the risk of there being any traffic was minimal. The only obstacle they faced were a trio of vehicles parked on the same side. To manoeuvre around them, the boys lifted the front end while Mel pushed the struts to one side so that the car could be moved sideward. Then, when it had been pushed carefully out into the middle to avoid a collision with the parked cars, the front end was lifted for the wheels to be straightened again. It was trickier to get around the small bend further down the street, and by then a combination of giggling and exhaustion led to the car's abandonment.

The whole household was awoken early the next morning by the thudding of Robert running up and down stairs and knocking on everyone's bedroom doors. The conversations were muffled, but Mel could hear raised voices and irate tones. Before she could crawl out of the bed, Robert had already burst back into the room, and looked like he was hyperventilating. When Mel saw the panic in his eyes the practical joke didn't seem so funny anymore, and she was immediately immersed in guilt and regret.

'My car's gone Mel, some bastard has made off in it.'

'Rob…'

'I've got to phone the police.'

'Robert…'

'How am I going to get across to Nottingham every week, or down to Cheltenham to see my mum?'

'There's something…'

'She's going to go mental, she told me not to buy a car until I'd saved up for one with proper security. The insurance is going to go off the scale!'

'It's not gone! Stop panicking for a second, will you? I know where it is.'

Robert paced around the room relentlessly, occasionally tugging at his hair, otherwise with his hands resting on the back of his neck as he listened painfully to the explanation of Mel's mischievous drunken stunt. She didn't withhold the truth but justified her actions by insinuating Robert was at fault.

'You're just so uptight these days, Rob. Ever since you started work up here you've turned into a square and lost your sense of humour.'

Robert sat down on the edge of the unmade bed, with Mel perched on the other side, just visible out of the corner of his right eye. He looked up to the bay window with the sun seeping through the small gap where the curtains had been opened in his panic to see where his car was, and calmly delivered his verdict.

'Yeah, I've changed for sure. But you're wrong – I've lost nothing. I've started to grow up and face up to my responsibilities. Doesn't that sound quite normal to you for anyone who wants to succeed?'

'Oh, my life, here we go – let's all listen to Pastor Robert telling us our sins.'

'D'ya know what Mel, you used to have a great group of mates around you, people that were willing to understand your problems and had your back when things went wrong. People that knew you, that knew what was really eating you up inside. But you haven't got any true friends anymore. If you had, they'd have told you by now what an arsehole you've become and to stop conning yourself that everything is going to be ok all of a sudden.'

'This is friggin' character assassination.'

'No, more like therapy, I'd say.'

'Oh yeah, well what the hell do you know about it? You're not me! You think that what you've been through in your life qualifies you to lecture me about how to be?'

'No. But I reckon your mum would want you to surround yourself with people that genuinely love you, not those being false who you amuse with your antics.'

'Don't you dare try pretending you know what she wanted for

me.'

'Look, you've got to stop pushing away everyone that wants to give you their love and support. You've pushed a selfish wedge between us so that you only ever take what you want, and never what you need. I know who you've been isn't who you really are, and I don't want to give up caring for you. But I can't see a way that I'm ever gonna get through to you. This is where it ends for us, and where it has to start again for me without you. Maybe you'll do better in finding your own way through it.'

Some deep furrows appeared across Mel's face as she frowned.

'You're being serious, aren't you? Are you seeing someone else Rob, is that what's going on here?'

'No, absolutely not.'

'Absolutely not, what? That there isn't anyone else, or there is but that's not what this is about?'

Robert didn't like being stumped.

'That's not what this is about, and you know it.'

'Oh my God, there is someone!'

'No, well not really.'

His answer may have been nervously vague, but Robert could recall meeting Hannah for the first time as clearly as a Mediterranean sky in high summer.

32

Robert never set out to meet another girl, even if it was becoming increasingly difficult to be devoted to someone as volatile as Mel. He'd driven to Loughborough University for the start of a three-day study block in December, feeling nervous about setting foot inside an academic institution again. Navigating his way around the sprawling site wasn't helped by the map he had been sent by the course leader, neither was it aided by the piss-taking being dished out by his passengers who were otherwise meant to be his work mates.

The car park was already rammed by the time they arrived at just after nine o'clock, but with several pairs of eyes on the lookout for a space they identified one on the far side by the exit. Robert drove round, ready to reverse into the tight gap. The lads in the back seat got out before he moved, to avoid an impossible task of squeezing out between their door and the vehicles next to them. Before Robert had time to manoeuvre, a car sped through a 'no-entry' access and stopped bumper-to-bumper with his mini. A girl jumped out of the heap she was driving, ran around to the driver side, and opened the door to knobble Robert. She began speaking to him faster than she'd driven in.

'Hi. Now you look like a guy I'd like to talk to more if I had the time, which I haven't, so I'll keep this short. I need that space honey, otherwise I'm going to be late for one of my engineering finals, and that will be a burden for me, and I'll feel guilty that you'll be feeling guilty for reducing my chances of doing well, and I can't let you carry that weight around with you for the rest of your life – which of course you will. Did you follow all of that?'

Robert heard every word but was perplexed with how to respond, while a gigantic swoosh rolled in his stomach. From the briefest of looks at her face, he could see that she was breathtakingly pretty. Robert's diffidence always came to the fore when he saw a gorgeous looking, confident girl. He couldn't cope with looking at her for more than a few seconds at a time, before looking away and blushing. It was a huge giveaway sign to Hannah that he liked her. Strands of her long, wavy hair blew round the front of her face catching Robert's cheek, as she was leaning in so close to him. She used her index finger to casually brush it behind her ear. Her cheeks formed dainty dumplings from her cute smile, and she smelt so sweet Robert could almost taste it at the back of his throat. He could usually muster up something witty to show off his likeability, but this time he was flummoxed when he looked at her mesmerising eyes. Hannah was out of his league.

'Erm, yeah.'

'C'mon, keep up babe. I need you to pull forward, so I can park up.'

The banter being inflicted on him was off-putting enough to cause him to stall the car, and for them to howl with laughter. It wasn't lost on Hannah either, who smiled to herself at how Robert was flapping. Hannah parked up, locked up, and was ready to make her way into the university building opposite. With his mates staring in appreciation of her gorgeousness, she walked back up to Robert in the mini that had come to a halt randomly a few yards away.

'Can't thank you enough, handsome. Least you deserve is a birthday kiss.'

'It's not my birthday.'

'Well, it will be at some point, so here's an advance.'

Hannah put her head down through the mini, planted a smacker on his lips, and was out of sight before Robert had time to react. He sat there trying to get his head free from the avalanche of confusion that had swept its way into his life in those few minutes. It would not be overstating the obvious to say that he was immediately smitten with Hannah.

Egged on by much whooping from the car share posse, he wrote a quick note on some paper from his college file asking for the kiss-queen's name, leaving his own name and number. Then carefully slipped it underneath one of the wiper blades. Upon leaving their studies later that afternoon, the mysterious girl had reciprocated by leaving a business card for a pub in Loughborough in the window seal of Robert's mini. On the reverse of the card she had written in lipstick 'Hannah x'. This group of apprentice engineers were no detectives, but they worked out that it was an invite to her place of work and duly paid a visit a couple of evenings later. They were greeted with the sweetest smile, which was the encouraging start Robert had hoped for.

'Out for birthday drinks are we, lads?' she joked and winked at Robert.

Hannah Florey's family were originally from Liverpool, and the tinge of scouse in her accent only made Robert like her more. She was more than two years older than him, but he didn't want to concede this as a reason for there not to be a connection, a friendship, or more than that. He wasn't to know at that stage that she thought he was cute, so he was working overtime to find some common ground that would prolong her interest in him. Both of them being aspiring engineers was a good start.

He couldn't believe his luck when she said that her hometown was Derby, which opened all kinds of opportunities for them if she was to stay in the area after graduating. But the topic that struck real mutual understanding was that of growing up in a broken home. Hannah explained that her mum had moved from Liverpool to escape an abusive relationship when she was two, and she had never seen her dad since. They both knew what the other was thinking and how they were hurting from something so torturous, and yet that was the foundation from which their feelings would grow from.

Knowing that it would crucify Mel, Robert chose to be conservative with the details of his affection for someone else. Thankfully, he managed to make it outside by the time he started to cry because he didn't want to give any mixed messages to her. He gasped for air.

It didn't feel difficult ending it because he had known for some time that this was the right thing to do. He just didn't enjoy walking out of the life of someone who was still on a meltdown and alienating herself from anything that presented itself as caring. She needed someone's affection, but he wasn't the solution. Mel had made one impetuous decision too many, and the fear was that she would continue to ruin anything before it had time to unravel its potential.

Robert had been so calm that Mel was shocked into submission, and she hadn't grasped the sheer gravity of what it all meant. Robert had just dumped her, was seeing another girl, and yet all she could focus on was his diagnosis that she wasn't stable in the head. Mel thought it was outrageous that he was making such a suggestion and using it against her as a way out of their relationship. She dashed to the window in the hope of catching his attention, but he was already pacing down the road in the direction of his car. She would refuse to be victimised in this way and was determined to show Robert and anyone else for that matter that she had broad shoulders and could stand on her own two feet.

As if to demonstrate her determination to prove him wrong, Mel swiftly exited the premises before Robert returned, not realising how much time she had to do so. Once it had been checked over for any damage and grubby marks, he had sat in his car for some time, mulling over what he would do should Mel start an altercation when he got back. But their paths were not to cross again that day, nor were there plans made to do so in the future. Mel was sent into free fall with no way of knowing how to stop. Her parting shot to him was a message written in lipstick on his window, saying:

You're WRONG

33

Following her graduation in 2002, Mel hadn't really taken stock of what her professional goals were. Having completed a year in employment as part of her sandwich degree, the only pursuit was of high status and big bucks. Getting those professional accounting qualifications in the city was certainly high octane, but the intensity of long working hours wasn't a joy and screamed 'burn-out'. A change of job and a move to Farnborough followed in 2007.

After nine years in her most recent role, Mel's career had become stagnant for sure, content to drift and become complacent about her job security. But the role of Finance Director at Central South Federation of Colleges had been well paid with a generous leave entitlement. Coordinating an operation across five colleges in two counties still presented plenty of professional challenges, but the experience that had been gained by being in post for so long meant it was largely stress free. She chose to base herself in her two-up two-down near the central office in Farnborough too. There was rarely the need to travel to the other sites in Hampshire or Berkshire. Anything warranting a visit out of Farnborough was addressed by a junior staff member in the first instance, and usually that was all it required. Finance had been a well-oiled machine that ensured budgetary responsibility was adhered to by all.

It was somewhat of a surprise to the staff at CSFC when a proposed round of redundancies was announced, especially hard to take as it was on the lead up to Christmas of all times. There had been no inkling from union representatives that conversations of that nature were being held or that the operation was struggling financially. Mel knew of course, but in her position as Finance Director, discretion and confidentiality on such matters was paramount. Some recurring issues had been highlighted on several occasions with senior management and waved aside. Mel had been clear in her own evaluations that falling student numbers across the federation would have a major impact and that it would be better to streamline the type of courses being offered at some of the colleges to become specialist institutions. There were simply too many academic staff being paid huge sums in salaries, for undesirable and undersubscribed courses that required large budgets.

The rumours of who was losing their job were finally laid to rest when an email to all staff was circulated by the Federation Executive Director in February 2016. It didn't matter to Mel. She already knew back in December that she would be leaving. Just like her father many years beforehand, Mel had chosen not to undergo the indignity of reapplying and being interviewed for a role that she already carried out effectively, perhaps only to be told that someone else was the preferred candidate. Instead she wanted to see out her three-month's notice and leave as soon as possible. The time to move on had come, and the only decision to make was to jump before being pushed. Superstitious or not, Friday 13th May was the date when that leap had to be taken.

Since leaving for university in 1997, Mel had only set foot back in Winchester a handful of times. That was a quite deliberate decision to avoid revisiting chapters of matters still too raw to comprehend. Her last visit was to oversee the clearing out of her belongings, some of which went into storage, before Derek put the house up for sale when he left for Scotland. There were no longer any permanent ties to the place.

Driving into the outskirts of Winchester for the first time in years felt strange. Things were instantly recognisable, but Mel felt like a visitor, a tourist even. She could only pinch a quick glimpse through the trees and buildings of the magnificent cathedral that continued to stand majestically as the landmark in the heart of the historic city. It made her smile; Poppy loved spending time lolling around the cathedral green, soaking up the atmosphere and staring in awe at the detail of the stone carvings which seemed so magical to her. It was reassuring to see the statue of King Alfred standing proud like the guardian of the town centre, and though progress and modernity had no doubt grabbed at the city's fabric, Mel noticed very little difference other than a splattering of new buildings and trendy bars where once a different trade was plied.

It was in one of those trendy bars where Mel joined a small gathering of former work colleagues. Loyal to the cause she may have been, but Mel wasn't held in such high regard in the popularity stakes amongst junior staff members. Nonetheless, some other long serving employees from across the federation chose to show some solidarity with their fellow redundancy casualty. The prosecco was not as free flowing as the disparaging remarks about CSFC for Mel's liking, so she sloped off at various intervals to discretely neck a cocktail or two. The alcohol intake was more than enough compensation for listening to the pointless moans and groans of people with gripes about their former employer. Now lubricated plentifully, Mel began perusing confidently through the clientele at the popular bar, stretching dog-legged round to the rear of the premises. At the far end stood a woman of a similar age standing by herself, one arm wrapped round her waist at the front, the other holding a glass of red wine which looked as if it was permanently perched on her bottom lip. Mel did a double take. Unless it was the liquor impairing her vision, the lady's face was instantly recognisable and though it had been the best part of twenty years, Ali's posture hadn't altered one bit.

Mel stood on her tiptoes and wobbled her head from side to side, attempting to catch Ali's attention. It didn't work, and she began swaying. If it weren't for a pillar next to her that she grabbed onto, Mel would have been sprawled across the floor.

Resorting to a more direct approach, Mel jostled her way through the crowded room and crept up behind Ali's shoulder.

'Jilted again?' Ali calmly turned around, and then rolled her eyes. 'Sorry, that wasn't meant to be nasty.'

'Well that's a first for you Mel, eh?'

It wasn't the friendliest of starts, and hardly surprising. These were the reverberations of the most tempestuous of run-ins the last time they saw each other in 1998, when the final nail in the abandonment in their friendship had been pummelled into the coffin once and for all.

'I'm out with a group at the other end of the bar. I spotted you straight away. You haven't changed.'

'Thanks,' replied Ali dryly.

'I didn't know whether to come and say something or leave it alone. I just thought it'd be a bit rude not to.'

'Are you living in Winchester again then?'

'Nope. I'm just here for a night out. A leaving bash actually, got made redundant recently. Drowning my sorrows with a crowd of old colleagues.'

Intrigued at that information, Ali strained her neck to peer down to the other end of the bar, trying to pick out the crowd of well-wishers. Her eyes squinted back at Mel.

'Perhaps a crowd is blagging it a bit.'

It was a smart response that broke Mel out in a smile. It was clear that Ali was no closer to being in a forgiving mood than she was all those years ago.

'Fair comment. I don't think I was ever very popular to be honest. Would it surprise you if I said I'd burnt some bridges over the years?'

'No, I'd be more surprised if you didn't say it, but it's sad that you are. Leopards and spots, I suppose.'

Ali's scorn stung Mel more than if it had come from anyone else.

'You ever hear from Rob?'

Ali closed that line of enquiry down with a definitive 'no' before Mel had even finished the name of the boy that had been the cause of so much animosity. It was an enormous hint to leave that topic well alone.

'There's been a lot of self-loathing, you know?'

'Yeah, right. Just a lot of loathing generally from what I can remember.'

'Wouldn't help if I said I'd accepted my indifference to everyone's criticism and got professional help for my state of mind, then?'

It wasn't meant to be condescending, but Ali's wide eyes and a congratulatory smile, as if to say, 'I told you so' caused Mel to blush.

'It was never a criticism you prat. Look, *this* is *not* going to be a let's-make-up session, ok? I'm not here to say farewell and good luck like your work chums, or to dig up the past. But back then, people said those harsh things to snap you out of it because they loved and cared for you. They didn't know what to do to stop you from surrendering to misery. Everyone felt helpless with trying to... get you through that pain.'

Mel breathed in nervously.

'I know. Well, obviously I don't know everything, but I've thought about stuff that I did, things that happened. That's what counselling helped me to do – figure out the context. Should've taken the help available a long time ago, but it was difficult to listen...' Mel stalled. 'You're right, we shouldn't be talking about it. But I'm not going to be hypocritical about the past, I hate people that say, 'never look back' – how do you know how far you've come if you don't?'

That struck a chord, causing the pained expression on Ali's face to finally disappear.

'I actually totally agree with you. Depends on what you're trying to measure though, I guess.'

To avoid the chat becoming any more cryptic, Ali changed the subject.

'I'm sorry about your job. Have you got something else lined up?'

Mel shook her head.

'Not yet. How about you? What's your line of work?'

'I work with teenagers, helping out with any kind of crisis they might find themselves in.'

Mel smiled. 'You went and did what you wanted to do then. Good on you, Ali. So, are you living in the town?'

'I wish. Way too expensive. My folks still live in the same place though.'

Ali started looking around as if expecting someone.

'Sorry, are you waiting for someone?'

'He's already here. Gone outside to take a *quick* call, he said.'

Though inquisitive to know more about who 'he' was, Mel knew that was her subtle cue to leave.

'You're probably the last person I expected to see tonight, Ali, but I'm glad I did.'

'Yeah, quite surreal.'

'Don't suppose there's any point leaving my mobile phone number with you?'

It felt too awkward to say no, and Ali really didn't want to. But she was also keen to rid herself of this unexpected company before Jamal returned, because then there would be a round of false pleasantries while introductions were made. Followed by an inquisition from Jamal on who, what, where, when, and why. So, despite the stains left behind from an eventful period of their youth, Ali thumbed each digit of Mel's number into her device as she read it out loud. Then Ali reciprocated. She was right – there was no point, and Ali had no intention whatsoever of making contact. Ever.

Until that was, some months later, on New Year's Eve when Ali inadvertently sent out a text to more people than she had intended.

> Wishing you all the very best for 2017!

Initially Ali's message came through to Mel showing a number that she didn't recognise and was not listed in her own contacts. She wanted to know who it was.

> Hi, thanks, who is this please?

> It's me – Ali! Soz, I've sent that message out to everyone in my contacts by mistake.

In the gloom of the bar area on the evening of her leaving drinks, Mel must have carelessly pressed an extra number on her touch pad, as Ali's number contained twelve digits making it invalid. It would explain the 'could not send' messages Mel received whenever she had tried to text her but not why Ali hadn't been in touch herself.

> No probs. So nice to hear from you. Drop me a line to let me know how you are.
> Happy new year to you too! x

That was the last communication between the pair until the last week in May the following year, when not for the first time Mel composed a desperate plea for help.

34

On the day she was dumped by Robert, Mel made it back to her university campus in Nottingham by mid-afternoon. By this time, her display of stubbornness from the morning had been transformed into an almighty sulk. The next calamitous instalment in her quest to self-destruct began.

It was eerily quiet along the corridors, where usually there would be the hum of conversation between some of her dorm mates, which in the circumstances suited her fine. She shuffled to her door and unlocked it. A dragging noise could be heard as it swung inwards, the sound being made by a sealed envelope caught on the bottom with 'Mel' written on the front. As Mel picked it up there was no prior indication that she was about to learn how her behaviour defined what others thought about her.

Hi Mel, it's Hayley here. I'm writing this 'cos I've got the neatest writing! Hope you had a nice time with Roberto. Anyway, there's a few things that you need to know have happened while you were away. We got the low down from student services on Friday afternoon about a pad to rent for next year, and the five of us went to see it. It's on Reardon Street, close enough to town as well as uni, and the rent price is reasonable. Problem was it had five rooms, a couple of 'em a bit pokey but we'll sort that I guess, and we had to decide that afternoon 'cos the landlord needed an answer and a deposit, so we all agreed that it was the right place. The geezer who owned it wouldn't let any of the rooms be made into a double. Sorry Mel, you're not in. We talked about it as a group, and some stuff has come out 'bout what people think. Some said you'd maybe wanna get a place by yourself, so your bloke can visit.

We ain't judging you Mel, but you getting off with a few lads and not telling Rob really shocked us, we don't like lying when he visits. And also, I don't think many of the girls were keen on living in a house with you – I think you're a bit lively for 'em. They're worried about you taking over and getting your own way. I will help you find a place if you like and come and look at them with you. There are some other girls in the other block that might have found a place with a spare room too, but it's with 'fish face Faye' and them lot upstairs, so don't know if you'd be interested. Anyway, speak to you when you've had a chance to read this – didn't know how else to tell you.

Hayls x

The grammar was far from perfect, but its purpose hit home as intended. There was no easy way of telling Mel that amongst the other five girls in her dorm, there had been some secretive chatting and bitching. The fact of the matter was Mel wasn't liked. Right there and then, it felt like being dragged underwater, desperately gasping for breath. Robert's words that morning had felt like punishment, but at least he knew her well enough to make those remarks. Mel had left Derby with every intention of deflecting the sting of what had happened there, and to carry on regardless. She felt lonely and trapped in a hall of mirrors, with each reflection pointing a finger of blame directly at her.

The public phone for the halls was in a basement area near the main entrance, at the bottom of a short but narrow staircase. There was a wooden shelf next to the payphone, on which various writing utensils were usually left. Some even worked. There was also a plastic chair to sit on in the cramped confines underneath the stairs. It certainly wasn't the easiest place to hold a private conversation, and many an eavesdrop had taken place outside the glazed door at ground level. It was there that Hayley overheard Mel's desperate tones in the early evening. The intention wasn't to be so nosey, but 'Hayls' guessed their note had been the root cause of the upset she was listening to. No one could have known that Mel's world was being turned upside down that day, or why she was pleading so insistently.

'Please come down, I'm begging you – you're the only one that'd understand. You're the only one that understands *me*. I'm absolutely lost without you.'

Having kept a very low profile the following week, a visit from Mel's dad and an outing at a renowned restaurant to celebrate her birthday was a welcome respite. Self-inflicted or not, being cooped up was an extreme measure and only served to direct greater attention upon her from whispering corners for the fact that she was doing something so out of character. The life and soul of the party had temporarily become lame and limp, and that's how it rolled in the short term. The tongue waggers observed no sign of Robert for regular weekend jaunts, and Mel simply became invisible to the social scene. Plenty of people had attempted to be courteous, but all were given the cold shoulder or a frosty glance.

One soggy Thursday morning before the end of the Easter term, the warden (ironically known as 'Happy Harry' amongst student banter) answered the intercom to a visitor asking for Mel. Upon seeing the figure dwarfed by their bulging rucksack and dripping wet from the relentless rain showers, he belied his folklore status and kindly let them into the accommodation block to take shelter. Perhaps it was the pleasant surprise of talking to a youngster who was polite and had manners instead of offering cheek and a grunt, but the old fella from Yorkshire was satisfied enough to escort them down to the communal kitchen area by Mel's room.

'You come down for a special occasion have you, my friend?'

'Hmm, not really. I think my mate's having a bit of a difficult time right now, so maybe it's a shoulder to cry on she's after.'

'Oh, I see. Well at least her tears can't make you any more wet than you are, could they, eh?' Harry chortled. 'Make yourself a brew while you're waiting if you like; kettle's over there. They're probably in lectures or something I would think – it's too early for the union bar to be open.'

Harry wheezed as he laughed again. He was on top form.

'Thanks a lot, you've been ever so helpful. I'm sure she'll be back soon enough.'

Before long, the thumping of fire doors opening and closing could be heard as students returned from, or headed off to, their lectures. The polished, rubbery floors soaked up the sound of some footsteps, but anyone wearing trainers with soles like Mel's literally squeaked as they walked, announcing their arrival to everyone else along the corridor. The rhythm of her strides sounded like a person in a hurry, not pausing for a minute as she darted through the kitchen area, oblivious to her damp guest. As Mel juggled with the room keys, she was startled by the voice of someone who had sneaked up on her.

'I brought wine.'

'Ali! You came. Bloody hell you scared me to death, I thought you were… doesn't matter. You look like a drowned rat! Come in, let me help you with that bag.'

Mel resorted to dragging the rucksack along the floor as it was so heavy, while Ali recounted her meeting with the 'nice old warden' who had let her in. Feeling flustered and overwhelmed, Mel froze to the spot. Standing statuesque, her chin fell onto her chest as she broke down in tears. Ali guided her friend to a seat and watched as a huge release of sobbing continued. It was one of those outpourings where almost as much snot contributed to the flow of emotion running down her face and chin. Regardless of how much she sniffed, and no matter how many tissue wipes there were, it was impossible to stem the flow. Judging by the phone call Ali had received some weeks prior to this visit, Mel's reaction wasn't to be unexpected.

'Crikey Ali,' she sniffled, 'how have you carried that on your back? And all to come and see me in this state. I can't believe you came. You're really here.'

'And a good job too I'd say. I'm sorry it's taken me so long, I did say that I needed to get through some coursework, and...' Ali paused. 'I wasn't sure how I felt about coming down here to talk to you about breaking up with Robert. This isn't easy for me either, Mel.'

Mel wasn't expecting that to get raked up so quickly, and conveniently changed the subject.

'Ooh, thank you for this – is it too early to crack it open?' Ali was too slow to react. She was going to suggest that it'd be good to leave until later, but the screw cap had already landed on the table next to her. 'You don't mind drinking from a mug, do you? Haven't got any glasses – don't do posh around here.'

Dutch courage – it's what Mel had become accustomed to. Whether it be to put her on a high for an evening out where she wanted to impress the liars and hangers-on, or to help her through awkward and 'feeling at rock bottom' moments. Either way, some plonk would help to relieve any tension for this unexpected gathering of two people that hadn't shared any words of camaraderie for some significant time. Though the time had barely crept into the afternoon, Mel went at it hard, with bourbon to follow. Ali sipped away at her mug, not in the least bit tempted to keep up. Being lubricated by different types of booze helped to stall conversations of a dire nature so that they could swap stories of student life generally. Predictably, Mel was curious to know about Ali's love-life, though it seemed to be littered with mishaps and not much else.

There was only so much small talk in the tank to be able to avoid their attention turning to the carnage that had enveloped Mel's life. She had gone passed being tipsy at that point anyway and was waiting to pounce on her opportunity to off-load. As painful as it was for Mel to explain the circumstances of her split from Robert, it didn't feel any less so for Ali having to listen to it all – and to curtail any thoughts about what could have been. Nonetheless, there was plenty of sympathy for Mel having to endure what sounded like an unpleasant experience – according to her explanation. Ali had a nagging doubt about whether she was getting an altogether objective version of events. Mel had made it sound as if Robert was wholly to blame, that he was the catalyst for all that went wrong. Ali couldn't help but think if that was the case, she would be better off without him and couldn't help herself from having a little dig.

'He's done you a big favour, Mel.'

'Why would you say that?'

'Because it sounds to me like you've had a lucky escape. Think about it – better that you found out now and are able to adjust your life while it's still early days at uni, than find out in a couple of years that you weren't suited and look back with regrets about what you might have done differently if you had your chance again as a single girl.'

It wasn't exactly the words of support that Mel was looking for. She wanted an opportunity to lambast the bastard in unity. The problem was that Ali had already seen straight through her story. Given what had happened previously, the last person on the planet that Ali thought she might ever feel sorry for was Robert, but on hearing Mel babbling she had heard enough to know that there was more to it: his car being moved to deliberately annoy him, antagonism about going across to Nottingham every week, accusations of no real friends, speaking out of turn about her mum, meeting a new girl. It seemed Robert had got to the point where he could stay silent no more and needed to get away.

'Why don't you show me this nasty letter your dorm mates sent you?'

Mel hesitated to hand it over, wary of how Ali might react to the inflammatory remarks it contained. But there was no getting away from the truth. Harsh though the method might have been, Hayley had simply depicted the reality of Mel's behaviour. Some of it resembled exactly the girl Ali knew from their Winchester days, but other aspects were a further distressing capitulation, corresponding with Robert's assessment before dumping her. Ali wasn't surprised at the reluctance of other undergraduates to live with someone who had the tendency to be a loose cannon. That aside, it was a complete shock to read the allegations that she had done the dirty on Robert.

'Is any of this true, Mel?'

'No! And I'm offended that you should need to ask.'

'So, you didn't two-time Robert behind his back?'

Mel looked at Ali with a telling look on her face, her mouth wide open without being able to find the words to defend her actions.

'How could... why would you do that? More than once! You can't use the excuse that it was a mistake.'

'Don't you go judging me Ali, you weren't there, it just... happened.'

'Oh my God, Mel. Have you not stopped to pick apart what everyone is actually saying about you?'

'You're supposed to be supporting me, not dragging out the same old shit as everyone else.'

'I am. There's a saying that goes something like, a real friend is someone who won't hide from pointing out your mistakes.'

'Fuck off, Ali. You sound like Robert.'

'Mel, listen to me. You need help, love; you need to speak to someone about losing your mum. Trust me, she'd want...'

'Why does everyone seem to think they're the expert on what

my mum thought or wanted?'

'Look, this needs to be said in one go, unrehearsed, raw and honest. She'd want you to break down this barrier that's blocking everything from coming out, otherwise you'll keep behaving like someone we don't really know – or like – anymore.'

'No! You stop! You don't know, how could you? Well here's something for you, Miss Psychologist. I'll tell you some of the shit that smacks me in the face every day, shall I? A little snippet about this bullshit barrier you reckon I've built. It's wrapped itself around me and it's suffocating. I didn't want to be in this situation by choice. At the funeral, everyone kept talking about it being a 'fitting tribute' – how she would have been proud about how the service went. Fitting tribute? What a load of bollocks. She didn't want a frigging tribute, she wanted to be alive for fuck's sake!'

In her fit of rage, Mel threw a mug at the wall. Fragments flew everywhere as it shattered, and the plaster had been gashed. Mel's screaming had already alerted students in other rooms that there was something going on, but they knew better than to get involved in one of Mel's tantrums. The smash of a missile the other side of her wall scared Hayley enough to take a tentative peep out in the corridor. At the same time, Ali had opened the door concerned about the noise being generated from Mel's violent episode. Though the two girls had never met before, Hayley offered Ali a room for the night if she felt unable to cope with any further outbursts from Mel.

After a period of calm, Ali judged it to be a better moment to speak.

'I know Poppy wants you to be happy and to learn from your mistakes because I found this.' It was Ali's turn to pull out a note from her bag.

'What is it?'

'Remember when you gave me a photo frame for Christmas? Well, it was last summer before I got around to putting a picture in it, and when I did this dropped out of the back. I didn't know what it was, and it had no name on the front. It wasn't sealed, so I read it. I cried my eyes out and didn't know what to do because it had gone all weird between us, and I thought this might upset you more than you already were.'

She passed the note to Mel and let her have some privacy.

'I'll be next door in Hayley's room for a bit if you need me.'

Mel unfolded the paper, and instantly recognised the writing as her mum's. It looked very similar to the message written inside her eighteenth birthday card, and the note that had dropped on the floor at Ali's house when she had taken round her Christmas present. Once again, she took a deep breath and whispered the words as she read.

Achievement. Now there's a word that the world is getting obsessed with and muddled about. Where is the fairness if one person's achievement is gauged as a failure to another? I would much rather tell you to measure your success on how happy you are, so live your life the way you want it to be, not how others signpost it for you. Don't be afraid to be who you want to be. You can lead or be led, so it's up to you whether you follow the herds that go to graze on mundane in the field of conventional, or not. We are, and will always be, proud of you no matter what. But go get your certificates if they're what you need to build the bridges between your dreams. And if you're going to make something of yourself be sure to be respected and judged on what's between your head, not what's between your legs. Feel the hurt from the knocks and blows of disappointment like any person but do it as a strong and determined woman and don't ever let any man put you down for that. Remember that all experiences are useful, especially the bad ones, and someone who is willing to learn from their mistakes is canny, no matter how young they be. You don't have to be old to be wise – just look in the mirror and you will realise that.

Love, Mamma x

Mel buried the pillow around her face to isolate the bawling. This was the compassion she needed, but the timing was extraordinarily bad. The effects of consuming alcohol were compromising her ability to think rationally. Her immediate reaction was to despise the idea that the letter had been withheld from her, and that it took a break-up with her fella to be able to retrieve it. It was anger and spite that was running through her veins, not gratitude. If there was an instance that Mel regretted most from her youth she would be spoilt for choice. But the one that hung most like a noose was when Ali reappeared. Her spitefulness was unparalleled.

'This changes nothing,' screamed Mel, quite ironically as it would end up changing an enormous amount. 'You think you're smart trying to interpret messages from the grave. You know it used to make me want to vomit seeing you and my mum, giggling away with each other like toddlers. Well, lady with all the answers, how is it that you and Robert never got together then, eh?'

'That's not fair Mel, it's got nothing to do with this.'

'Oh yeah, that's right. You seemed so certain it'd happen that you wrote him a little love letter. Only, he never got to see it. Doesn't know it ever existed – thinks you weren't interested in him. But don't worry, I read the pile of shit for him. There, now we're even on being honest about letters. How does that feel shoved up your arse?'

Ali clasped her hands together in front of her face, eyes

beginning to stream.

'You bitch. You fucking bitch. Then you took full advantage, didn't you?' She broke off and paused, fully intending to maintain her dignity. 'All I can say is, poor bloke. Yep, good one – you got me. Didn't see that coming, wouldn't have believed it if it hadn't come straight from you. Pff, if only you knew how damaging it was, but no matter now. It's done. I suggest you cherish your mum's words every day, she loved you so much. But I'm not so sure she'd be proud of you for this. Good luck, Mel.'

With that, Ali grabbed her belongings and disappeared from the room – and from Mel's life for good. There was never any further contact between the two of them.

Mel went on to flunk her first year at University. It was only by using a counsellor as a mediator that she was granted the opportunity to re-start the course on medical grounds and extraordinary personal circumstances. Before that matter had been fully resolved, she had attempted to contact Robert, in the hope that their relationship might be resurrected if he could see that she was finally accepting professional help and support for the demons in her head. He was right. Despite the constant revolving of time's digits, Mel still hadn't removed the shackles that chained her to the grief and despair of losing her mum. It was still holding her back, and anything else that she had any emotional attachment to when it had happened was frozen in that frame too. Robert didn't reply to the letters or return the phone calls.

Once it was obvious that he had rejected her plea to meet one last time, she took herself off to Antigua to spend time with her brother in her mum's homeland. There, she was able to chew over the meaning of Poppy's messages on life. This helped Mel to realise two things. Firstly, she finally accepted that her failure to deal with her mum's passing was the catalyst for the depression that she had been diagnosed with – and was ready to concede she had been suffering with it for some time. Secondly, she knew there was an awful lot to learn about the challenges of growing up. Miss Burchell hadn't quite mastered an ability to heed the lessons from her mistakes – and wouldn't, it transpired, for some time to come.

35

It had already been a restless night for Mel. Tossing and turning wasn't the half of it. The pillows had taken the brunt of the punishment, either being punched into a shape for comfort or thrown off the bed completely. It was the kind of sleep where she felt like she was watching herself dozing, which in theory meant she wasn't sleeping at all. It was yet another night where her head was swimming with thoughts and ideas, and she couldn't find an off switch to park them. After assuming a position that a contortionist would struggle to occupy, sprawled across the width of the bed, Mel could feel herself drifting into a proper slumber, in probably the most awkward looking posture she had been in all night.

At first it seemed as if the irritating noises in the background were part of her dream, too distant to be anything other than her imagination. But as her senses came to the fore and stirred up consciousness, it became clear that the resonant sound of the telephone was causing the disturbance. She bolted upright and took a glance at the clock before picking the handset up. All in a split second she was asking herself who the hell was calling at three in the morning, and then panicking that something might have happened to her dad or brother. Coming straight out of sleep mode it was difficult to get her mouth muscles operational, so the greeting to the caller was gruff and laboured rather like she was wearing a gum shield.

'Allo?'

A similarly slurred voice spoke back.

'Can I sh-peak to Laa-Larry; is that you Lar-ry?'

Her heavy eyes squinted as she considered the question. As far as she could remember in her comatose state, there had never been a Larry associated in her life in any capacity previously.

'Eh? No, it's not Larry. I think you've got the wrong number. Do you actually know what time it is?'

It went quiet briefly on the other end of the phone before the caller concluded the call, saying:

'Oh, just fuck off.'

The phone line went dead but Mel kept the unit to her ear, paralysed by the abuse and the incredulity that the bloke who just called had the audacity to dish out such grief having phoned so inconsiderately late at night. Partly from embarrassment at being hung up on, and partly angry at how she had been spoken to, Mel began to feel the heat rising at the back of her neck. Without considering the potential repercussions, she dialled '1-4-7-1' to retrieve the number of the rude caller, and then pressed '3' to return the call. It wasn't a code that she was immediately familiar with, and certainly wasn't a Farnborough number. It rang out a number of times before cutting to an answerphone. Mel recognised the laboured tones of the guy's greeting, before leaving him a gift of her own.

'Hello shit for brains, this is the person who you called a few minutes ago which turned out to be the wrong number, before telling me to f-off. I don't enjoy being woken in the middle of the night by a complete knobhead, so the next time you decide to make a call perhaps you want to check you've got the right number first? If your monkey knuckles are incapable of tapping in the right digits, then it's time to admit you shouldn't be allowed to use a phone. Prat!'

She slammed the receiver down, and snuggled back under the duvet, nodding off almost instantly. It felt good to off load some aggression, albeit not in the way she was accustomed to. Her usual routine for relieving tension used to be a full-on gym circuit followed by a swim and sauna, until she had to accept that the club membership was too much of a financial luxury to justify. Nowadays she had taken up jogging to help channel her thoughts more positively about the redundancy, to see this as a period of reflection to think about what she really wanted to do with her life and to take time to explore what opportunities were out there.

Having been so used to being in full-time employment, there was a temptation to take the first credible thing that came along to get out of the unemployment pit. Mel despised the thought of claiming benefits. She could just imagine her mum baulking at resorting to taking hand-outs however much she was entitled to them, so for now that would remain as a last resort. But the redundancy pay that Mel received would only hold off the mortgage repayments for so long, and the thought of losing her home hung heavy in her mind. The problem was that nothing was coming along on the job front that resembled 'professional' status.

Although she was close to her wits end after farming her CV out to more organisations and companies than she could remember, Mel was desperate to avoid attaching herself to agencies and all the false starts and pestering that went with it. There was also an element of keeping her pride intact, and of being able to get out of the mess through her own endeavours. The reality was that she needed to overcome this arrogant attitude and accept professional help. The employment market that produced a rich harvest of options upon graduating at the start of the new millennium was an altogether more competitive one now. It was partly for this reason that she eventually surrendered to the temptation that 'any job will do'.

Delivering parcels was undoubtedly meant to be a stopgap, just to tide her over and keep the red bills at bay. Being paid per item delivered didn't exactly give her a luxurious lifestyle. But it was flexible hours, and meant she got out meeting a lot of people. Having a self-employed status felt like she was taking control of the situation and putting herself in the driver's seat in more ways than one.

From the moment she lay in bed, Mel found it impossible to relax with all the ideas she raked over. The world seemed to be a far less colourful place because of a mithering menace implanting negativity and self-doubt in her mind, hijacking the plans she was attempting to devise for her next steps. How things might have been different if she were able to reach out to her mum. Poppy would have helped her to unlock the box of untold secrets of how to turn hopelessness into happiness.

Her frame of mind certainly didn't benefit from nuisance calls in the dead of the night. She hadn't given her recent rant a second thought until some weeks later when she was out on a delivery in the depths of Hampshire. It was mid-afternoon on an unusually warm and sunny Thursday in early May. The air conditioning in her car had masked the true temperature outside, so Mel was met with a blast of heat as she clambered out of her door. To keep herself cool, she quickly put her thick wavy hair up using the scrunchie she wore temporarily on her wrist.

Having made the majority of her drops for the day, the floor space in the boot of Mel's hatchback was visible again. She carefully clasped her hands on the small square box addressed for Filbert Crescent. It disgusted her to see how some delivery drivers man-handled their items at the depot when they were in a hurry, whereas she'd always taken care of the packages the way she hoped others would for hers. Mel turned around to the row of terraced houses, hoping that number eighty-seven was not the one with the music blaring out like a nightclub. 'Bugger' she mumbled to herself, realising she was heading straight for the din.

Mel was never someone to be prejudiced without good reason and knowledge, and this role had already taught her that class had very little correlation with manners and attitude. But there was something about the look of the house that just wasn't appealing. Downstairs windows were wide open with net curtains wrapping themselves around the frames and snagging after being trapped in the hinges, and motorbike spares cluttered the front 'lawn' like a scrapyard. It was not an abode of someone who was overly house proud. Undeterred, she made her way through a gateway with no gate on the hinges, and up the dusty bare patches where presumably there was once some paving slabs leading to the doors. Mel struggled to restrain the stereotypical images filling her mind of the inhabitants, thoughts that were trying to contaminate her sound judgement. But even she considered how fortunate it was that she wasn't the postie who'd regularly have to visit the gaff, undoubtedly with court orders or letters demanding money for overdue payments.

As Mel reached the front door, she could see no doorbell or knocker with which to alert the folks inside. The white PVC door, complete with grey dirty streaks, did not have a window, which must have added to the dinginess of the place inside. Mel gave the door a few raps with her knuckles, which produced a bang more than loud enough to compete with music output at a civilised level. There was no answer. The small, horizontal letter box was positioned so low to the floor that Mel had to get down on her knees to attempt to use the flap as a knocker. 'This is going to be fun,' she muttered sarcastically to herself. Pushing the flap in the hope that it would spring back heavily enough to cause a loud bang was useless, so instead she pushed the flap open as far as she could so that she could peer inside. She put her mouth as close to the opening as she dared without touching it and called out.

'Hello! Delivery!'

The force of her breath caused dust and grit to splatter her nostrils and lips, which caused her to splutter before wiping the grime away. Mel got up off the floor and brushed the dust off her knees. She tried banging the door again, this time quite forcibly using the palm of her hands to generate as much noise as possible. She started considering alternative options. There was no way of being able to get around the back, and to leave it with a neighbour assumed there would be someone willing to take it in for those in the noisy adjacent dwelling. Mel doubted whether this was the type of neighbourhood where people did favours for nothing. She looked at the delivery details on the box and could see that there was a contact number on the address label.

As she looked over the digits Mel's eyes widened with the realisation that she recognised the number. She could recall the area code and distinctly remembered the end sequence of her recent night-time nuisance call as being 666. It had registered in her mind at the time how ironic it was that the number of the beast should be aligned with such monstrous manners of her caller. Now she *had* to see who lived there. Driven on by a smidgen of anger, her last resort was to pull the flapping net curtains to one side at the downstairs window and peered into a gloomy looking living room where the walls were vibrating from the power of the super-sized speakers attached to them. Someone stirred on the couch, it looked like a teenage lad with his hoody on, but once they were sitting up Mel could see that it was a girl. She went across to the dock and relieved the unit of its volume noticeably.

'Hiya, sorry to disturb you from your kip. I've been knocking on your door but there's been no answer.'

'Oh, sorry. No one would've heard you with the music on.'

'You're not wrong. Is it actually possible to sleep through that banging noise?'

The girl with the ashen appearance didn't respond, and remained poker faced.

'What is it you want anyway? I don't think they'll buy anything from you. They usually let the dogs out the front if someone tries to flog something at the door that they haven't asked for.'

'Nah, I've got a parcel for… Mr Wall-en-vert.'

Mel read it out as three syllables, as much as anything to know who the irritant could be. There was no time for any verification. Right on cue, a guy appeared. Mel took an instant dislike to his attitude with the girl.

'Eve, have you turned that bloody music down? Who's this you're talking to?'

'I've got a delivery for you Guvnor – I did try the door, but I don't think my knocking could compete with your sick beats.'

The guy barely acknowledged Mel, before turning back to the girl to tug her arm to lead her to the doorway out of the room. With the music turned down Mel was able to hear the conversation, and the guy was hardly trying to be subtle. He started wagging his finger at the youngster.

'What've I told you about getting me if someone's at the door, yeah?'

'She wasn't at the door though, was she?'

'Whatever – and don't get smart. Think next time, she could've been anyone. Get out of here idiot.'

Eve's shoulder was shoved harshly as she sloped off causing her to stumble, and then the guy walked over to the window where Mel was perched. He sniffed and wiped his nostrils with his index finger. Mel couldn't believe what she had just seen and heard. The cruelty and injustice of it made her blood boil so much that inside her own mouth she was gritting her teeth.

'That for me?' he asked antagonistically, using the same snotty finger to point at the package.

Mel didn't bite and was biding her time until she had worked out who was who, and what was going on.

'Well that depends if you're Mr Ian Wall-en-vert?'

He looked suspiciously around the package that Mel was holding.

'Ah, no. He's not here right now, but I'm his bro, Larry. I can take it in for him if you want?'

It was Mel's turn to look suspiciously at him, she didn't believe this explanation. There was a sarcastic tone to his voice that suggested he was lying about who he was. She was sure this was the toe rag that had made the call to her, and that would indeed make him Ian Wallenvert. Mel noticed how he didn't stay still once, he was always swaying or twitching his toes or fingers. He was wearing no socks, jeans that were sagging round his arse and in need of a belt, and a black t-shirt that had food stains down the front with a collar that had seen better days. The black tattooed writing on the insides of his forearm was indistinguishable, and she guessed he would have no idea whether it said what he had requested the tattoo artist to do, or not. His hair was shaven to military length, and he had a short goatee without a moustache, as well as ridiculously long sideburns that looked completely out of place and fake. Quite frankly, she thought his loutish appearance went perfectly well with his previous conduct on the phone, if this were who she thought him to be. As he made the gesture to take the parcel from Mel, someone else could be heard speaking outside the room in a strained tone that was presumably a yawn.

'Who you talkin' to, Digger?'

Digger? Mel wondered whether that was a reference to the shockingly untrendy, spade-shaped facial hair on each side of his face. The chap that owned the yawny voice came into the sitting room stretching his arms in a pair of designer boxer shorts, and nothing else other than a pot belly. It was difficult to know who was more startled when their eyes met.

'You must be Ian Wallenvert then?'

'Are you a copper?'

'Do I look like a copper?'

'You're acting like a copper. Bollocks – plain clothed crew, yeah?'

The language wasn't pretty, but intimidated wasn't something she was going to allow herself to be. Mel knew she could be more than a match for them, however dangerous her sharp tongue might have been.

'When you've stopped shitting yourself, I need you to sign for this parcel.'

The two men looked at each other.

'Well, I'm not Ian Wallenvert, am I? That's him.'

He nodded to the other bloke who Mel had already concluded as being the scumbag.

'For fuck's sake Larry, shut up.'

'Ha ha, has Digger been giving you some old bull about who he is, love?'

'Yeah, he has, *love*,' she answered with venomous sarcasm. 'Digger here thinks for some reason he's you, Larry.'

'Pff, I think I'll leave you both to sort out your tiff. Put the music back up when you're done, Digger.'

The real Larry disappeared to leave a stony-faced Ian being stared at by Mel.

'Funny that, how you thought you weren't in, Ian. Takes a bit of a div to not know whether they are in the house or not – or someone off their face. Seems you've got something to hide.'

'Just give me the box and piss off.'

'You're a bit of a grumpy fucker aren't you, Ian?'

'And you're getting out of order, you know nothing about me. Who do you think you are spouting dirt about people? I should report you to the delivery place you work for.'

'Do it! Go ahead. But before you do, let me tell you this. You have no idea who I am, do you? I bet you were so high the other week that you can't remember being a complete prick on the phone to me, and so I called you back to let you know what I thought about ya.'

Ian looked dumbfounded.

'That arsehole was you? Sounded like a bloke to me,' he sniggered. 'Have you stalked me because of that – what's your problem?'

'You reckon I'd waste my time to do that on an arrogant loser like you? This is just a complete coincidence, buddy.' Mel gestured for Ian to take the package from her, which he did. 'I'd despise any piece of dirt prepared to dish out an insult for no reason, like you did.'

'Where do I sign?'

Mel thrust the clipboard within millimetres of his face, which Wallenvert fended away. He scrawled his name in the relevant box.

'Frisky little bitch, aren't you? All those threatening words. Sounds like fighting talk, my kinda game. You should watch your lip.'

'Or what? I heard you talk to that girl like shite, I'll have social services round here before you could drag on a joint if you even think about trying to be a big man with me or that kid again, do you hear me loud and clear, dumbass?'

'You stand there shouting the odds and know absolutely nothing. I'll tell you about caring for that 'kid' shall I? For your information, she's nothing to me – my cousin's ex actually, and right now it's taking me all my efforts to stop her getting into taking shit. She's the one that comes around here without her folks knowing, pestering us for a joint, or a tab or whatever. She's the one we're giving lectures to about her screwing her life up, but she's adamant on wanting to experiment. And if it weren't with us, she'd find some other den around here with arseholes less bothered about looking out for her. So, you know naff all. And if I can find your number, I'll dial it again and keep doin' it to annoy the shit out of you.'

'Hmm, but I know where you live now though don't I, tough man. Think on. Enjoy your mail – I hope it's legal.' She took several strides away from the door before shouting back, 'Laters.'

Mel thought she may have overstepped the mark and couldn't

get away quickly enough. Her heart was pounding. The scenario of what just happened kept playing out in her head, and she knew she had lost control. Although it was difficult to believe that she was so forthright, Mel was glad she had tried to put Ian in his place. She just hoped the repercussions of his obvious irritation didn't lend themselves to upsetting the teenage girl Mel had seen initially. She was just glad she'd gotten away with nothing more than a mini-slanging match.

For Mel, driving time was thinking time. The journeys on the roads and lanes of Hampshire allowed her space from the pressures she was under in her life, and the more parcels she was prepared to deliver the more time there was for escapism. Her imagination ran wild with entrepreneurial ideas about how she might earn enough money to be comfortable, but how to execute those ideas required some gumption she was yet to find.

The things that had been most damaging in Mel's life were never too distant from her thinking, but it was the images of the girl in that house in Lodden that haunted Mel for days, wondering whether that teenager would lock herself away in her own world of disorder, unable to find a way to get out without the assistance of illegal substances. The keepsake box in which the notes from her mum were safely stored had seen the light of day regularly in the days following her sobering experience with Wallenvert. If ever she reached a low point, those soothing and comforting words would be picked over as a remedy for dealing with the harshness of life.

36

Working at weekends was not something that Mel ever envisaged being an aspect of her career plan. As much as she embraced technology and modern life, she remained old fashioned in her view that the weekends were for resting and partying. Unfortunately for her, people needed their deliveries equally as urgent on a Saturday and Sunday as they did during the week. In her current predicament, she was in no position to refuse the work that came her way – especially if that meant a bonus rate per package over the weekend. What was unequivocal in her mind was that this role of hers was just deputising for the next corporate post that she would lay claim to. Her grumbles about the job aside, delivering items to all and sundry people she had never met before continued to illuminate dull days with humour, and the odd scrape with humans and pets alike. Either way, she was fairly streetwise and mostly took these things in her stride.

The journey to Meonstoke through the Meon Valley was so pleasant, with rolling hills and fields of pasture flanking the country roads. This was English countryside at its most beautiful, and at a price if there was a desire to live there. Mel arrived at leafy Ludlow Grove. Next to the access road leading up to the houses she saw the sign indicating that it was a 'private road'. She drove up the tree lined road to a cul-de-sac consisting of seven large, detached homes. If Mel didn't already realise that she was in an exclusive development, she soon did when she started looking for house numbers only to realise that in this road the houses had names. She double checked her dispatch notes to confirm there was one item for drop-off at the home called 'Carreg Cennen' for a Miss Florey.

The electric gates to the driveway were already ajar, so Mel drove through them carefully onto the gravel laid out to the front of the impressive double fronted building. The oversized front door stood proud beneath an arched porchway, with three steps leading up to it. Mel pressed the intercom buzzer on the side of the porch and waited for a reply. She cocked her left ear against the unit, facing back towards her vehicle. From her experience, intercoms tended to sound muffled unless she got up close to it, leaving her to guess what the homeowner was saying. There was a prompt reply from one of the occupants, and it sounded far clearer than she expected it to.

'Can I help you?' came the question from a man. Mel puckered her mouth to answer.

'Hi, I've got a delivery for a Miss Florence.'

It went quiet for a few moments before the next response.

'Florence? Do you mean Florey?'

'Ah, yes that's right, my mistake.' By this point she had started speaking louder. Her own voice was all she could hear. 'I'll just need to get a signature from you or her.'

'That's fine, perhaps you'd like to turn around and pass it to me then?'

Mel hadn't heard the front door opening, having been so intent on stooping down to chest height to deal with the potential challenge of a temperamental intercom. It was one of those moments where Mel knew she should act cool and carry on as if there was no drama. But the embarrassment of knowing there was a guy behind her staring and talking to her butt instinctively caused her to move in slow motion. Instead of disguising her distress, she magnified it, turning around still semi-hunched over like she was carrying a heavy weight, and hoping that it was a nice-looking guy rather than an old pervert relishing the view. Any feelings of humiliation vaporised instantly when the two of them caught sight of one another.

'Oh, for God's sake Mel. Not again!' came the familiar voice of Robert. 'Can't you remember what the old bill told you would happen last time if you broke your caution?'

How could Mel ever forget that time? It was meant to be the last, she had fully intended it to be. There was no way she would ever want to replay the agony she went through that day. Hannah's blunt email to Mel back in 2011 was intended to close whatever chapter had reopened from meeting Robert. No reply was received or expected. All electronic footprints in respect of Mel had been deleted – and that was it as far as the Floreys were concerned.

Then, at dawn on a chilly morning in October, nature's array of Autumnal colours had some competition. Blue lights danced across the bay windows of the houses on both sides of a quiet residential street in Romsey, the glass reflecting the emergency beacons like mirror balls and causing it to flash frantically. The car that had been intercepted was sandwiched between the two police vehicles, and the driver taken into one of them for questioning.

On the back seat, Mel didn't resist or deny, and merely told the officer the truth – that she had got carried away trying to find out about an old friend who had shunned her. Though it was a genuine admission, it masked the fact that Mel had been lurking in the shadows of the street where Robert lived on numerous occasions from what she thought was a discrete distance, hoping to find out more about his life. It went from being a quick drive-by to parking up along the road at different times of the morning and evening.

Her behaviour was bound to draw attention in a neighbourhood watch area made up predominantly of senior folk who were more than happy to twitch their curtains and blinds at the prospect of doing their duty for their fellow street dwellers. The registration plate had been noted and passed to the police by more than one household. But it was the call from Robert that led to the blue lights coming out, highly suspicious about who it was spying on them. The police officer informed Mel that she had given Mr Spitley – worried for the safety of himself and his family – no other option than to call the police, as her visits to the street were an invasion of privacy and verging on stalking, for which a sentence could be passed in a court of law. It was only her clean record and previous good character working in public service that prevented anything worse being passed down by the judge than a caution, and an order not to breach a two-mile exclusion zone of Robert and his family. This was an indignity Mel never thought possible, and she'd been in enough scrapes and messes to know that being arrested and charged was scratching at the surface of rock bottom.

Because the caution and order were such a stain on her work personnel file, it was glaringly obvious that her actions would not be overlooked when the college made their decisions on which staff to make redundant in 2016. It would have been more of a surprise to find Mel's name omitted from the list. Afterall, she was hardly likely to be considered as a role model for the young adults that populated the venues for which she held senior accountability for. It was those decisions that had in some peculiar coincidence led to Mel standing on the doorstep at Robert's house.

'Don't go jumping to conclusions Rob, it's not what you think. I've honestly got a parcel for you.'

Robert frowned, looking sternly at her. 'A delivery driver, you? How long did it take you to cook this one up with that warped imagination of yours, eh?'

'Why the hell would I get myself into trouble by tracking you down, and how could I have found out where you live anyway? Last I knew, you were in Romsey.'

Mel's heart rate accelerated as she began to panic, and almost breathlessly thrust the package in Robert's direction.

'It's not even been two years. It's really shallow that you've turned up here like a bad smell.'

Mel stood transfixed by Robert's words; the exasperation on her face would have made it clear to him that she knew nothing of what he mentioned. In the circumstances it would have been churlish to seek clarity.

'I, I... I'll honestly disappear again as quickly as possible, but I do... need... can you... sign please?'

Robert accepted the package, addressed to his daughter. He didn't look up as he gestured to Mel for her to pass the electronic pad for his signature. He passed the small unit back to her.

'Florey?' she asked tentatively.

'Dragged my feet a bit admittedly after our little one came along unexpectedly, but we eventually got married five years ago. Not long after all that stalking malarkey. I took her name. Great opportunity to finally release me from any further association to phlegm – and to disappear from any unwanted acquaintances.'

There hadn't been any mention of their wedding plans when they had met in Eastleigh, and he didn't sprinkle the slightest amount of humour in his explanation for dropping his previous surname. Her cautious response was by gently nodding. Mel's visit to the Florey household had been short and unwelcoming, the disturbing of an old flame regrettable and shocking. She needed to remove herself from the scene as quickly as possible; but rather than make an attempt to slam the door in her face Robert unexpectedly struck up further conversation.

'I wouldn't blame you for feeling angry with me. That tirade wasn't deserved, I'm sorry.'

'I can't stand here and say I don't deserve it Rob, my track record hasn't been great.'

'No, it hasn't, but I shouldn't be accusing you of... hang on a minute.' Robert juggled the package. He broke off and turned to place it on the floor inside the house. Taking a step backwards he peered round the door and shouted up the stairs. 'Have you been using my credit card again without asking?'

'No,' came the answer from a female voice.

'Well, that's strange because I can't remember ordering anything from a boutique and yet a large package has arrived here that's addressed to you.'

There was a brief pause, and then some footsteps hurriedly coming down the stairs. A conversation ensued between Robert and the girl hidden behind the tall door.

'Oh, yeah, forgot to tell you about that one. Sorry.'

'Can you make sure you don't forget please? And can I assume that's the last one for now?'

'If I'm online and I see something I like, what am I supposed to do?'

'Write it down – leave me a note, or give me a shout?'

'Dad, c'mon. I don't think so. I don't like disturbing you if you go upstairs and close your door. Anyway, if it's in the sale it'll have gone by the time that I've waited for you to make your mind up. I never buy things full price – you should be happy.'

'Go on, you'd better try it on – whatever it is.'

'New tops.'

'More than one? You little rascal.'

Mel heard some rustling, which she assumed was the girl opening the package. Sure enough, she removed the items from inside to show her dad to get his seal of approval. Robert nodded and smiled back at her, a clear fondness for the person in front of him. It was only when the phone went from inside the house that Mel got a glimpse of who it was that he was talking to.

'I'll get it,' was her insistent reply, as she dashed across the hallway to a room in the opposite direction.

It was enough for Mel to recognise exactly who the girl was. She knew it was Eve, even before Robert told her so in the conversation that followed. Eve looked towards the entrance way, and though she never caught sight of Mel properly, she saw enough to give a double take as if something was familiar about the delivery lady. It wasn't enough to alter her stride as she disappeared out of view and took the phone call. The link between Eve and Robert disturbed Mel, her concern immediately centred around the welfare of a former friend's daughter having seen her at the drugs den she had visited recently. Whatever previous baggage existed that disunited Mel and Robert, she still cared for him – reciprocated or not. Her brief acquaintance with Ian Wallenvert was one which she had no intention of reconvening, but she would trample all over the scum bag if it meant that Robert's daughter fell into no bother.

'That little madam is my daughter, Eve.'

'Yeah I know.'

No sooner had Mel said it than she realised her brain hadn't been engaged. This wasn't the time or place to land on Robert where she had first discovered Eve. She was sure that if Robert had the slightest whiff that Wallenvert was somehow associated with his daughter he would have no hesitation of paying him an ugly visit. A quick recovery was required, with no fluffed lines.

'Well, I assumed that's who it was from the parcel you gave her addressed to Miss Florey.'

'I suppose you're thinking I'm a bit overbearing on her?'

'Not really, but I doubt you're looking for any advice on it from me, Rob.'

How else was she meant to respond to that? With no time for analysis, Robert offered something altogether more dismal.

'Well, anyway, I'm sorry to shove this down your throat, but her mum – my wife, Hannah – I'm sure you remember her, right? She was killed a couple of years ago. It's me and Eve against the world, so I'm unashamedly protective of her.'

Mel cupped her hands around her nose and mouth in utter shock at what Robert had revealed 'I can't believe it. You must be heartbroken.' That's what he was referring to some minutes beforehand; she was hurt by his presupposition that she would have used the death to attempt contacting him again. 'What about her family?'

'They try their best to understand but…'

'I just don't have the words Rob, I'm so sorry.'

'Nothing you can say. It's so unimaginably difficult.'

Mel bowed her head. 'I can imagine. I know how that hurt pierces.'

Robert winced. He didn't mean his remark to be a challenge to the scale of her own loss.

'Have you got a minute to step inside? There's something I need to get for you. Look, a little bit of honesty first. Whatever I said to you when we met up in Eastleigh, it's impossible to forget everything about you, Mel. And your mum – she lives on forever in my mind. There's something I wanted to tell you about so many times.'

This was clearly spontaneous.

'About my mum?'

'Yes. I didn't think you'd cope with it, and then… it was impossible to think of a time when this could ever happen. Just wait here.'

'Okay then.'

Robert disappeared into his study leaving Mel anxiously waiting in the hallway. Amongst a collection of beautifully decorated photo frames stood a psychedelically coloured wooden piece, out of place with the other wooden, chrome and brass models around it. He gently pulled it out from the group and turned it over. A couple of extra hinges had been fitted retrospectively to ensure the backing stayed firmly in place. They were difficult to manoeuvre having been screwed in so tightly, but with a bit of force Robert displaced the rear section from which he pulled out a small envelope.

He had been tinged with guilt for withholding this from Mel. The photo that it housed may have changed but the very fact the frame remained visual amongst a collection of other memories meant that Robert chose never to forget Poppy's letter existed. He just didn't know how or when he could get it to the intended destination. This was as good an opportunity as he was ever going to get, reappearing hurriedly in the hallway clutching the item he knew Mel would find precious. He watched her gazing up at the open hallway and balcony staircase.

'You checking out how to break in?' he joked.

'Blimey Rob, how the hell have you ended up living in a pad like this?'

'Worked hard. Engineering has been good to me and was to Han before she passed. And her grandparents owned land which they sold and passed down as inheritance.'

'What, you married a shit kicker?'

'Erm no. She transformed from city kid to country kid, but wasn't a farmer's daughter, thank you. Anyway, it's my turn to play postman. I'm just going to come out and say it – this is a note from your mum. It was in…'

'The back of a photo frame?'

Robert was astonished. 'Yeah, in the back of the photo frame you gave me for Christmas years ago when we were going out together. How did you know that?'

That was a question with a difficult, painful answer, its origins going right back to the day that Robert broke up with her in 1998 and the subsequent events that unfolded with Ali shortly afterwards. It required an explanation in a capacity entirely separate from that which they had found themselves in that moment. Mel chose to play it down completely.

'Doesn't matter. How did you know it was from my mum?'

'This is very awkward for me. I just didn't know what to do. It was in an unsealed envelope, so I read it.'

'You could've given it to me, Rob! It was meant for me, not you.'

'I thought – no, I knew – it would make things more difficult for you, at a time when you were melting down in front of my eyes. I thought I was helping. I had it with me in Derby and dropped it on the floor when we met at Eastleigh, but I didn't think the timing was right then either. And her words – it's like she knew how you'd be, and what advice you would need if she were with you now. Totally bizarre.'

'I've not come here to piss on your parade Rob, but it feels like you've stolen some of that privacy, and you've deprived me of something that was supposed to help me grieve. So why give it to me, why now?'

'Don't think bad of me, Mel. It feels like *this* is the right time to pass this to you. One thing Hannah's death has taught me is that time is most definitely not on our side. You never know what's around the corner, so grab your happiness while you can.'

'And is that what you are, Rob – happy?'

'Let's not start this up again.'

'I'm not, I promise. Only, I see a miserable looking guy in front of me…'

They both lowered their tone, and then cut the conversation dead as Eve came back into the hallway, and across to where Robert was standing with Mel, just inside the front door.

'Dad, I'm going out for a bit.'

'Where are you going?'

'Just out – going to catch a bus into Lodden. That ok with you?'

'Hang on, I'll give you a lift.'

'No, it's ok. I like getting there by myself.'

'I'll pick you up later instead then?'

'Stop fussing dad! I'll call you when I'm getting the bus back, but I might stay over.'

'Where? At Martin's? What about food?'

'His family will be there, dad. I've just checked with him on the phone. They'll look after me.'

Mel bit her lip and looked down at the floor, holding her

breath. She dared not exhale for fear of not being able to keep shtum about what she already knew about *that* family. It riled Mel to hear that Eve was going to be looked after in their world of narcotic abuse.

'Can you at least let me know when you're there please?'

'Ok, ok. Please get used to the fact that I'm not a little girl anymore.'

'Fine. But what about revising for your exams? They're only a few weeks away – you know how much it'd mean to…' Robert faded; he couldn't bring himself to mention Hannah. Eve knew though. She rolled her eyeballs.

'I'll pick it up again tomorrow. I can't stay cooped up in my room revising hour after hour with no downtime.'

She was right, but it didn't prevent Robert from wearing an overprotective look of worry. She slipped on her bomber jacket and pecked her dad on the cheek as she glided out of the door, barely acknowledging Mel. Robert watched as his daughter's footsteps crunched the gravel as she walked out of the driveway. He continued his conversation with Mel, not once taking his eye off Eve until she was out of sight.

'Miserable guy you reckon? Yeah, I'm struggling and at least I'm strong enough to admit it. You'd never believe that there are people out there who can't face up to the fact they're not pulling through very well. Know what I mean?'

Mel swerved the obvious dig intended for her.

'But with Eve growing up so fast, I'm having to come good for her. I'm worried sick about her when she goes out.'

'And what about Eve – is she coping ok?'

Robert turned towards Mel abruptly.

'That's where you and I are going to draw a line in the sand, Mel. Look, giving this letter to you is long overdue I admit, but it's most definitely a trade-off, ok? This should be very precious to you. Please let me get on with my life, and you go out and find yours while there's time.'

'You know nothing about my life now to pass judgement, Rob.'

'And I don't want to know, Mel, I'm not sorry about that.'

Mel had been in some surreal moments, but this was right up there with the worst of them. She didn't know what she was meant to do next: read her letter on the doorstep, shout at him for not letting her have the letter when he first discovered it, remonstrate with Robert about his state of mind, put up a fight to keep the one fella in her life she genuinely regretted letting down? She didn't react quickly enough, as the confident clunk of the door shutting made it feel like Robert meant this goodbye to be unequivocal.

The dilemma was simple. Should she respect his wishes and slip away like rainwater down a drain, or be a responsible adult and help the kid inside the house who was suffering without her mum? It may have taken a couple of decades on her part to realise, but Mel knew that she had never recovered from that gap in her life. And as for pushing everything and everyone away that attempted to zone in on her pain – it seemed as if Eve was also intent on blocking it all out by taking drugs. She was at a serious risk of being on the receiving end of abuse of one sort or another. Mel wasn't prepared to pull away and turn a blind eye to that prospect without trying to speak to Eve about it first.

37

Even as she completed her round of parcel drop-offs, Mel knew she shouldn't be contemplating going back into Meonstoke. A connection had already been felt with the place though, because that was where her Mamma's letter had been in storage for a good while, under the safe keeping of the Florey household. It's where she wanted to unfold the paper and read it for the first time.

Whether to return to the quaint village or not should have been an irrelevance, as Mel's intention was to read the letter immediately after driving away from Robert's house, and then move on. But there had been an unavoidable distraction. She had pulled into the gateway to a farmer's field, looking for some seclusion to do Poppy's words justice. It was no more than a mile from Carreg Cennen just off the main route into the village. The entry she had pulled into was a steep, narrow, concrete track that stretched a good five metres in from the road. The field was bordered by fencing and hedges, which also flanked the entrance. It was a perfectly chosen concealed spot.

Before the neatly folded letter had even been unravelled, she caught a glimpse of Eve in her rear-view mirror walking along the path to the bus stop on the other side of the road, and a few yards further on from where Mel had parked up. The angle of the slope where her car rested meant that only the bottom half of the person was visible as they passed by, but Mel recalled the same blue jeans and dark trainers that Eve was wearing as she left the house and walked out across the gravel driveway. To be sure it was her, Mel got out of the car and took a peep to where the girl had walked by, and although only her back could be seen, the long blonde hair was enough to confirm that it was Robert's daughter.

The bus stop had a wooden shelter and bench. Mel watched Eve sit down elegantly like a proper lady, knees together and legs to one side. Her hands were stuffed in her jacket pocket, where she was fiddling with her music. Her earphones dangled down the sides of her cheeks and disappeared into the front of her clothing somewhere. Her head was nodding slightly as she listened to her favourite tunes, her face pointing back up the road from where she had walked anticipating the arrival of her bus. It was the image of a regular teenager, nothing untoward. Mel simply couldn't imagine this girl becoming rowdy or making poor life choices and giving into temptation through the goading of others less able to resist.

Eve was the only person in the vicinity. Other than Mel, of course, who seized the opportunity and strode away from the car to go and speak to her. She didn't want to startle Eve, so Mel staggered sideways across the road so that she was in her line of vision. Eve glanced to her right at the strange lady giving her a jazz-hands wave and a cheesy smile. It wasn't the coolest of entrances from a lady who should have known better having spent many years working in the proximity of post-sixteen students, and thoroughly warranted the filthy look of disdain afforded her from the teenager minding her own business. Eve took her earphones out.

'Do you need directions or something?'

'Directions?'

'You're the delivery woman, aren't you? Are you lost?'

'Ah, no it's ok, I've got a satnav.'

'So, is there something else you want then? My bus will be here in a minute, and you're acting a bit random if you don't mind me saying.'

'Eve, a couple of weeks ago I went to Lodden with a delivery – it was me who you spoke to when I came to that pit of a place where that Wallenvert bloke lives. That's where you're off to now, isn't it?'

'Yeah, I remember now. Don't want to seem rude, 'cos I've been brought up well, but what the actual fuck has it got to do with you where I'm going?'

'Knowing your old man, I'd be more surprised if your parents hadn't taught you some decent manners. You were polite to me when I met you on my delivery. I'm not sure he'd be too impressed with your colourful language though.'

'You know my dad?'

'Used to, really well, a long time ago.'

'Is that why you were hanging around for so long at our house earlier?'

'Sort of. It's been a while since we've been in touch, and I think we were a bit surprised to see each other. Here's the thing, your dad hasn't a clue about where you go to in Lodden does he? But I've sussed what's going on from what I heard and saw with my own eyes, and I know he'd go mental if he knew what… goes on in that hovel.'

'Well I haven't asked for the opinion of a good Samaritan, so you can jog on. I can look after myself, I'm not a kid.'

'Yeah, you are! That's what I'm bothered about. I'd still be having this chat if you were older but you're what, fifteen? Sixteen? That rings all kinds of alarm bells for me.'

'I'm having a bit of a laugh with a few friends before my exams, before all the serious stuff comes along like going onto college or something.'

'If your life is so sorted, what the hell are you doing knocking about with that toe rag for?'

Eve didn't answer the question but looked out thoughtfully onto the fields opposite.

'You gonna say anything to my dad?'

'Depends.'

'On what?'

'On what you decide to do next.'

'I don't get it.'

'Give up that rabble in the next town, and your dad will be none the wiser.'

'That's blackmail! You can't stop me seeing my mates.'

'Mates? Is that *really* what you think they are? You think they'd seriously be there for you if things go tits up? Bet they were nowhere to be seen when your mum died?'

'They were actually.'

'Oh, I bet they were, for a pick-me-up.'

'What's that supposed to mean?'

'Let's cut to the chase. I doubt you go round to that house for their warm welcome and take-away pizza.'

Eve fidgeted awkwardly on the bench; her cover exposed by a snitch she didn't even know. She would get a lifetime curfew from her dad if this woman was to say anything to him. The problem was, Eve was drawn to that household to escape – she couldn't see any other way around dealing with her issues.

'Well at least they're no grassers. They understand me.'

'Why? Because you walk out of there in a different state to when you walked in? Do me a favour. That's the problem being off your face, it doesn't last, and you get sucked back in and become a slave to the grip it'll have on you. You think you're dealing with it, but the problems are only just beginning and start mounting up before you know it.'

'And what would you know about it?'

Mel dodged having to make any admissions of her own, but floored Eve all the same with her openness about her past.

'I lost my mum when I was seventeen.'

'Then I don't need to say anything to you that you haven't already heard from other people. I'm sorry, I don't even know your name.'

'I'm Mel.'

'Well Mel, it's no consolation for me or you, but I know what that stabbing pain feels like.'

'Yeah, I've got an idea what you must have been going

through, but everyone's different. For me, that stabbing feeling has never left. I've tried, but it just won't go. You're younger than I was though, and it must be doubly difficult with your exams coming up.'

'You just have to get on otherwise you stand still. It's not just that though... the losing her... there's a reason I've started to take drugs, but I've never told anyone why.'

Though Mel could relate to how Eve felt, there was a limit to how well she could deal with someone disclosing something confidential. She felt a little bit out of her depth. When Mel had worked at CSFC, there was a set procedure to adhere to in such instances, which would usually require a referral to a specialist youth worker. Mel had no time to think about what to say next. Her suggested understanding of the situation promised more than the hurried response that followed, and it wasn't as reassuring as Eve had hoped to hear.

'I'll try to help if you want me to Eve. But if you tell me something that makes me think you or someone else is at risk of any harm then I can't keep it a secret. You know that, right?'

'I'm hardly bloody likely to tell you anything if you're gonna sound all official, am I?'

As quickly as she had Eve, she lost her again.

'I want to make sure that you're ok – but I might not be able to do it by myself.'

'So, what the fuck are you going to do to help me, eh? What magical remedy did you discover for your torment that you think will work on me? I'm getting bored of this already. Are you married?'

'No.'

'Divorced?'

'No.'

'Gay?'

'NO! Why would it matter if I were? What is this?'

'It isn't nice people poking their unwanted noses in and

making assumptions, is it? You were screwed up then, and you're still screwed up, because you can't deal with the fact that you blame yourself for your mum dying. I'm right, aren't I?'

'Is that what it is – you blame yourself?'

'You haven't got a clue, so stop trying to pretend you understand me. You don't get me, and you have no right to interfere. You're naff all to do with me so just leave me alone.'

Mel was riled, she was the one that had been psycho analysed.

'Ok you little rat, you can piss off down there to put shit inside your body if you like, it's your life. But just think for a minute about your dad and what it'd do to him if he knew what you were doing. He'd implode like my own dad did.'

Not another word was spoken as the bus slowly made its way down the country road. Mel stood and watched the angry youth board the bus and sit down, deliberately choosing to stare out of the opposite window. As the bus pulled away, the acceleration caused Mel to choke in the diesel cloud from its exhaust. 'Shit!' she yelled, stamping the floor, and gritting her teeth, knowing what she needed to do next. It wasn't something she was looking forward to, and patently not a decision out of choice.

38

There were some obvious reasons why Mel raced ahead of the bus to get to Lodden before Eve did, not least because of whose daughter it was. Not making that journey would have left the least favoured alternative, which would be to tell Robert everything she knew. The risk with that option was that it might not solve a single thing, and Mel's concerns were that it might escalate the nature of Eve's behaviour, making her more erratic and unpredictable. That would be a devastating scenario for Robert to deal with. She couldn't do that to him.

It was because Eve had struck a nerve deep inside that resigned Mel to speed down the country roads. It couldn't have been the innocence of youth, more the being on the receiving end of a similar trauma as a teenager, that meant Eve had absolutely nailed the reason why Mel found it so difficult to escape that day in July 1996. She had been told countless times by family and experts that it was in no way her fault that her mum passed away. Nonetheless, Mel couldn't banish the lingering idea that if she had been home earlier from school that day she would have been there for her mum – if not to save her then to at least ensure that she wouldn't have died alone. Eve got it.

The familiar grey, concrete facades of the council estate greeted Mel as she arrived on Filbert Crescent. The strip of communal grass did its best to brighten up the weariness of the place, but even that was a yellowish tinge of gloom. Mel felt the butterflies in her stomach trying to burst free. At number eighty-seven, a man sat on the doorstep smoking a cigarette and surveying the comings and goings on the crescent. Mel could hear the sound of her blood pumping in her ears as she walked up to the terraced property. It felt dreamlike, almost having to force each stride forwards. This time there were no windows open wide and no blaring music. The whole road was eerily quiet.

The sideburns on the side of the face of the guy taking a drag were unmistakably owned by Ian Wallenvert. On the drive across, Mel was rehearsing what she was going to say, because there would be limited time before Eve arrived at the house as well. Now that she was walking through the gateway with no gate, her head had become a vacuum and she no longer had any idea how this was going to play out.

'Hello again, Ian.'

'You've got some nerve. What the fuck are you doing showing your face round here again?' Digger got up and circled around Mel. 'Nope, doesn't look like you've got a parcel for me. Hmm, I know – you fancy some grams yourself don't ya, is that what it is?'

Mel was expressionless, but she was struggling to contain her quick breathing and racing heart. Whatever she said next needed to sound calm and confident, not confrontational.

'Didn't expect to be making a social call myself, Digger.'

'Digger? That's a name used by people that know who I am and what I'm about, if you know what I mean? It's not my name to you, snotty bitch.'

'Fair enough then, Ian. Best if I tell why I'm here, then we can all get on. You can think what you want about me, I don't give a shit. Turns out though, Eve is the daughter of a dear pal of mine, and he has no idea that she spends time round here. I think he'd be more than a little bit upset if he were to find out what she gets up to. He's pretty well connected himself by all accounts, if you know what I mean?'

'Sounds like a threat that does. You know how easy it'd be to pay someone in grams to make you disappear you interfering little cow?'

'This is your turf Ian, but there's no need to look at me like you're smelling shit. I'm here because that kid has got a chance to sort herself out. She's got exams coming up over the next few weeks, and if her grades are decent, she could go on and do something positive with her life. I doubt even you'd want her to mix with low-life scum.'

The force of Wallenvert grabbing Mel's arm would leave her with a bruise for her trouble.

'Are you for real? You think you can get away with calling me scum? I'd like to slap you myself but you definitely ain't worth getting arrested for.'

'You've not got to do anything, just don't let her come round here anymore.'

'Why should I be bothered what she does?'

'Because if I squeal to her old man, at best the place will be crawling with blue lights, at worst he'll take matters into his own hands. You know the bloke has lost his missus? He'll not think twice about twatting someone if he thinks they've done something wrong by his daughter.'

Wallenvert released Mel's arm and shoved her towards the end of the path.

'Time for you to run along, you've outstayed your welcome.'

For once, they agreed on something.

Mel didn't hang around on the estate long enough to see Eve arrive. She had grabbed some sandwiches at a petrol station and made her way back to Meonstoke by early evening, having completed a couple of final deliveries in the south of the county. The quiet lane where she eventually parked was adjacent to the village square, and next to a low-level wall marking the boundary of the church grounds. The church sat on the top of a hill, overlooking the main road through the village, its clock tower chiming precisely on the hour. Mel slowly chomped through the food, mulling over the necessary brush with unwanted bother. Her appetite had waned to the extent that she couldn't eat the crusts, which were tossed out of the car window in the direction of the church grounds. It was a welcome luxury for the birds that swooped in from the surrounding roof tops. Mel looked on at the squabbling and squawking over the pieces of bread, and it temporarily broke her thoughts about Eve's whereabouts.

It was the second time the clock tower chimed before Mel remembered the letter from her mum in her jacket pocket. She took it out and held it against her cheek with eyes closed, imagining that Poppy was giving her a cuddle. She convinced herself that it still had the scent of their house in Winchester. Mel kissed the paper as if it were her mum's cheek and felt a shiver shoot through her spine as it was unfolded, using the steering wheel to rest it against.

You can be as rich as you want to be without a bank balance. Money, jewels, possessions? You can keep them, they not what I want. I've seen people that suffer silent and lonely trauma from personal greed and gain. Their eyes empty of colour, darkened by the guilt of selfish deeds, and for foolishly thinking they be better than any other soul because of their wealth. Me? I tell you, I'm happy to have nothing, because I already know that I have everything. My children are the most precious gift imaginable, riches that grow in value every day and yet can't be counted. But daughter, to find your soulmate is priceless, a beautiful bond that no money can buy. It might be the toughest journey you will go on in your life to get it right, the hardest thing for a person to discover. But don't give up on your search for this hidden treasure, because if ever your world collides with another, look out for the explosion of love and drench yourself in its colourful rainbow. The sun, the

*moon and the stars will shine brighter than you have
ever noticed them, and the light that shines between you
and that special person never dims.*
Love, Mamma x

As with the previous notes that she had stored in her
collection, reading through the handwritten words caused a huge
surge of emotion. Such was the depth of Poppy's love being
nailed to Mel's heart that it caused tears to collide as they fell
down her face and underneath her chin, before dropping onto her
top and soaking into the cotton. Mel rubbed her finger over the
dry ink where her mum's hand had carefully scribed her heartfelt
insight on life, and sat staring into nothing, gnawing at her
knuckles while her thoughts ran riot.

The notes were meant to have been read together as she turned
eighteen years old, a loose guide map about how life could be
for a young woman about to embark on her adult journey. This
one felt like it was a sign, the one Mel had always needed, the
intervention that would change the course of her outlook on
where her love life was heading. Naturally, thoughts turned to
how Robert might have been affected by the words in the note,
and whether it influenced his own commitment to his wife. He'd
read it, and possibly many times over, so already knew how it
was going to make her feel. But rather than hope that he would
be the one to help dust her down, a pursuit to win over Robert
would not be reignited. He wasn't 'the one'. A re-energised Mel
would instead commit to finding her own soulmate who she
knew existed 'out there'. Of that she was sure because her
Mamma told her so.

39

The setting sun behind the hillside on which the charming church stood proudly was causing the headstones in the churchyard to cast long shadows, stretched so long that it was impossible to see where one finished and another started. They merged into one big dark mass. Mel had overstayed her welcome in the village. One final glance up at the clock tower confirmed it was nearly eight o'clock, and time to make a move. Out of the corner of her eye, Mel noticed some movement over in the far corner of the churchyard. She squinted, as it was a fair distance from the car, but she wasn't imagining a restless individual charging and kicking at a headstone.

'You little toe rag,' mumbled Mel at the apparent vandalism playing out. A reluctant witness to what was happening she may have been, but it wasn't something to which a blind eye could be turned. The thought that this might have been her own mum's resting place infuriated Mel. That anger motivated her to act.

Previous efforts to operate covertly in an adventure in her younger life had ended messily, and strangely that played heavily on Mel's mind as she crept up and around the perimeter wall to the churchyard. Throwing caution to the wind, she bunked up and over the wall and promptly challenged the perpetrator who sat amongst chunks of a broken headstone.

'Oi! What the hell do you think you're doing?'

Mel continued to march towards the person crumpled alongside the carnage they had created and could hear them sobbing. Worse still was the realisation it was someone she recognised.

'Eve! What the…'

Eve barely moved; her head remained bowed.

'Leave me alone,' she remonstrated.

But Mel would do no such thing, instead collapsing next to the hysterical teenager and wrapping her arm around Eve's shoulder. Through the sniffling and shuddering, an explanation for this predicament became clearer. Her attempts to take advantage of the Wallenvert's generosity to offer out class A substances, and become one of the smack heads, were rebuffed. Digger had delivered a familiar crude and tactless offering to let Eve know that she should not return.

'You're a liability. If it ain't the pigs putting their snouts in where they're not wanted, it'll be your old man. You're a problem we don't want. We ain't your bail out and we ain't your family or friends. Take your troubles elsewhere and don't take the piss out of us no more.'

As distasteful as it sounded, and as much of a low-life thug Mel believed him to be, she was thankful and relieved to know that Digger had taken her threats seriously.

Unbeknown to the pair, during the time that Eve had been consoled, the disruption in the churchyard had attracted the attention of some worried elderly locals. Even in the dimming light, it was impossible not to realise that a place of rest had been decimated and, just as Mel did, the logical conclusion to draw was that it was mindless vandalism. The flashing blue lights of the two police cars could be seen flickering through the trees well before they pulled up by the church. Mel instinctively knew that they were coming because of the damage caused to the headstone, and without thinking twice ordered Eve to get away.

'Run! Get home as quick as you can and say nothing to your dad.'

Eve had made it to the war memorial in the village square before stopping to watch the police enter the churchyard, the torch beams giving away their position as they scanned the grounds for the person responsible for the ugly misdemeanour. She couldn't stand back and do nothing, nor race off as instructed by Mel. Instead she made her way gingerly back up the path towards the church. That was when a constable approached and stopped her. Initially it seemed the decision to see what was happening was poor judgement. Fortunately for Eve, the long arm of the law considered her a nosey bystander and did nothing more than to tell her to stand back while his colleagues apprehended an offender.

The sight of Mel cuffed and being led into a patrol car churned the teenager's stomach, and her lip quivered as their eyes met. Mel winked at Eve to try and reassure her, but it only served to pile immense guilt upon the youngster's shoulders. This was a lady that had shown interest and taken time to understand her situation even if it had seemed a bit intrusive at first. This was a lady that had shown kindness in her recent breakdown and bout of upset. She was the one who had gone out of her way, literally, to put an end to her access to drugs. This was the lady who had taken the hit for something she had played no part in.

The next morning Eve woke in a panic, still distressed at the events of the previous evening. Other than the usual lecture about her lateness and lack of communication, she had managed to avoid any long drawn out conversations with her dad about her whereabouts before escaping to bed. But the sound of several voices downstairs so early on a Sunday led her to believe that it must be linked to what had happened. She was petrified to go down in case the truth had been realised and she was going to be in deep doo-doo. She kept asking herself the same question on her way down the flight of stairs. Mel wouldn't have grassed her up – would she?

The noisy voices were coming from the kitchen area, and alarmingly she could hear her dad sounding incredibly irate. She interrupted his flow as she opened the door.

'She's not meant to be anywhere near my family. There's no way my daughter… oh, morning love. You startled me – why are you creeping about?'

'There's no way what, dad?'

'These two police officers have called round to tell us something pretty awful, Eve. Come and sit on one of the stools.'

'I don't want to sit down dad, just tell me.'

'Last night someone vandalised your mum's grave, completely destroyed the head stone, smashed it into pieces. The police arrested the person – it was the lady you saw here yesterday delivering your parcel. What possessed that lunatic to do it... probably goes back to when I knew her years ago. You don't need to get involved with that; it isn't important for you to know. Anyway, the police need to ask you a couple of things about what she's done. Is that ok?'

'Me?' she tried to answer innocently.

'Morning Miss Florey, I'm WPC Tanner and this is PC Bilkington. Like your dad said, we're just making some enquiries based on what the lady we arrested has said in her own testimony. Don't worry that we may take notes while we ask you some questions, it's quite ordinary that we do that, so we don't forget what you tell us, and you don't have to keep repeating yourself. Now, we understand that you were out and about in that area last night, is that correct?'

'Yes.'

'Did you see what happened at the churchyard?'

'No.'

'Are you sure? Only, that's not what the accused claims, and a witness said there was a younger girl matching your description with the woman at the time. But when our colleagues arrived there was only the accused at the scene. The witness claims to have recognised you walking past the memorial at the time of the woman's arrest.'

'Yeah that's right, I got back from Lodden on the bus and was walking home, then saw something going off by the church. I could see the blue lights. I walked up to the side road, but a copper told me I couldn't go any further.'

'So, you aren't acquainted with a Miss Burchell then?'

'Not really.'

'Could you be more specific?'

'She talked to me earlier in the day at the bus stop before I went off to Lodden.'

'She did what?' interrupted Robert. 'What was that all about, Eve?'

'Nothing, she was just asking me if I was alright, and was sorry to hear about my mum. Something about her mum had died when she was young too. What's going on dad?'

Robert delivered his verdict to the police officers.

'There you go! What did I tell you? That woman is still harassing us.'

'She said that *you* had approached *her* in the graveyard, and she told you to leave. Is that not the case Eve?'

Eve shrugged. 'No, don't think so.'

WPC Tanner gave a sceptical glance towards her colleague.

'Ok Eve, that's all for now. Thank you for your time, we might need to speak to you again at some point, but perhaps you could leave us to have a quiet word with your dad?'

'No problem.'

Eve didn't need a second invitation to get out of the firing line and closed the kitchen door behind her purposefully. She thought better of perching her head against the door to listen for fear of being caught. That would require further explanation, and as anxiety was already running riot throughout her body, she couldn't cope with a second grilling.

In the kitchen, WPC Tanner shared her concerns with Robert.

'Hard as this may sound, sir, we get the sense that Miss Burchell may actually be covering for your daughter.'

'Doesn't her previous misconduct speak for itself? She's broken a court order! I've told you about her turning up unexpectedly with a parcel, and that's obviously stirred things up again in her head. The sick bitch has then gone and danced on my wife's grave for fuck's sake! Look, you do what you have to do with your enquiries but keep that woman away from my family. I can assure you I will be instructing my lawyer to press charges and I want to see her locked up for this.'

40

Eve was desperate to speak to Mel. The police would undoubtedly be returning to speak with the Floreys again at some point, sooner rather than later probably. Eve would continue to mither until she was able to find out whether she had dropped Mel in it with the vague recollection she gave to Officer Tanner, or if Mel had framed herself. To have an opportunity to corroborate their stories would be mutually beneficial.

There was much more to it than that though. Eve would voluntarily confess to the crime, unconcerned about taking the flak for something she was guilty of doing and already resigned to being prosecuted for the rampage anyway. The events of that day had begun to form a bond between the two females. Eve was in awe of Mel for taking the decision to protect her from serious trouble with the police, and potential danger in Lodden. The care that Mel had shown towards the messed-up kid inevitably enticed Eve to put her trust in Mel. This was someone who could help her to confront the emotional torment haunting her daily, and to deal with the demons trying to drag her down. She could be the one to stop her from spiralling out of control and into a cess pit of little hope and no escape. This adult was the one Eve felt could calm the storm that was causing her to go berserk with fear and guilt. She just needed an opportunity to be able to open up and let out what was going on in her head. Eve wasn't to know, but it was a big ask of someone not yet altogether in control of her own struggles – not to mention the major issue of a court order preventing Mel from having any contact with the family whatsoever.

Eve rummaged through the rubbish bin in her room, looking for the packaging that her tops had arrived in on Saturday. Tissues, used post-it notes for revision, a barely used but 'not-as-good-as-this-new-one' mascara, more tissues, and enough hair from her brush to use as insulation, all piled up and around the plastic mailing bag. Exactly as she had hoped for, the delivery label on the front conveniently contained the contact number of the delivery person. The first couple of attempts at dialling the number only succeeded in being taken to a generic answerphone message. Calls were being vetted; unknown numbers were being ignored. Eve didn't want to leave a message, she needed to be sure it was still Mel's phone for a start and secondly, she didn't know what to say without sounding frantic. As a last resort, she sent a bland text instead.

Hi, it's Eve. How are you?

The reply was instant, and to the point.

Text back 'ok' ONLY if you are alone and no one can hear our conversation and your phone is on silent mode.

Eve looked out of her window but couldn't tell if the police car was still there from the angle she looked down from, so having crept onto the landing to listen for voices it confirmed that her dad was still in discussion with the police officers. A text was returned as instructed, and then Eve waited in her room. The phone vibrated when the call finally came through a few minutes later. It was a hushed tone that greeted Mel on the other end. Eve feared that the adults in the kitchen on the back of the house might be able to hear the conversation upstairs, along the corridor, through the oak door to the bedroom on the front of the house, and underneath the duvet where Eve had camped. She was taking no chances.

'Eve, you shouldn't be contacting me. We could both get

into… well I was going to say trouble, but significantly worse trouble, let's put it that way.'

'I'm sorry, I panicked a bit. The cops are here, downstairs, they came to speak to me and dad. I didn't know what to say.'

'What did you tell 'em?'

'They asked if I knew you, I said we spoke at the bus stop. They wanted to know if I had spoken to you at the churchyard and I said I hadn't.'

'Shit! That's not good. I'd told them you were there, and that I told you to piss off and mind your own business.'

'I didn't want to stitch you up, did I? So, what've you said happened?'

'There's a bit of history between me and your dad, so I've made out it was a jealousy thing.'

'You're joking? And they believe that?'

'Actually, I don't think they do. My brief said he thinks they might be considering a charge of perverting the course of justice, worst case scenario a four to six month stretch, best outcome maybe community service.'

'Prison? Why would you invent such a crap story? I wouldn't believe it. Anyway, I don't care if they find out the truth Mel, you can't take the punishment for me. I'll confess if they keep asking, I'm rubbish at lying.'

'Shh! Keep your voice down. No, that's definitely not what's going to happen. You'll have some serious explaining to do if you confess to criminal damage. You'll end up having to tell them about the Wallenverts. Your dad will go nuts.'

'Well maybe that's what I want, to be able to speak about stuff.'

'Do that anyway then, but don't add to your troubles by owning up to this.'

The conversation stalled, and the call went quiet for a short time before Eve responded.

'I find it difficult speaking about it, but I'd tell you. You're

303

the only person I think would understand me.'

Mel silently clenched her fist victoriously and screwed her eyes up in delight. The breakthrough meant Eve had every chance of removing whatever burden it was on her shoulders if she could communicate the bother in her troubled mind to someone else. But while the willingness to share her angst with this new-found friend wasn't unexpected, it didn't mean that Mel wanted to be that person whom Eve ought to have been confiding in. Mel hadn't dealt with her own situation anywhere near effectively enough to know what would work best, so what made her qualified to help this kid? She couldn't cope with listening to pain reminiscent of her own. It would need some sensitive handling to get around Eve's delicate situation without the teenager bolting into her shell again.

'Eve, I am gonna help you, but you've got to trust me. I know someone who is the loveliest, most caring person and amazing at helping young people with difficulties. If anyone would be able to make sure you are ok, it would be Alistair. He'd be more than happy to get involved; I know he would. So, what do you think to me getting in touch with him?'

Alistair Cliverice was a former colleague. Rotund and balding he may have been, but he had a reputation amongst the College Federation as a fabulous youth counsellor. Camp though he was, he spoke with a low, captivating, and reassuring tone. He maintained a simple and compelling declaration for any of the clients he worked with.

'I want us to make decisions for the betterment of kids who are hard to reach, so that they can grow up knowing society does care, they are *never* unwanted, and they really can have a similar set of choices to everyone else.'

It was no wonder that every student held a lot of affection for him.

How unfortunate it was then that Mel sent a text thinking it was to Alistair, only for it to end up arriving in Ali Crofts' inbox. Somehow in her enthusiasm to store Ali's number following her new year's message, she had drunkenly overwritten the original contact listed as 'Ali C' on her phone. Alistair Cliverice had mistakenly and unintentionally become Alison Crofts.

Quite coincidentally, one advocate of youth had been replaced with another. Unaware of the blunder she had made, the wording of Mel's message was carefully crafted with a different recipient in mind to the one that received it, exacerbating the oversight further.

Hi Ali, hope you are well. Sorry for the urgent tone of this text – I need your help. I have come across a teenage girl who needs support from a professional. I wouldn't ask but I remember how passionate you were about getting kids sorted out, and know you are damn good at what you do. You also know a network of other people that can be called on to support this kid too. I've tried to help a little bit, but I'm not really the best person to deal with her issues. If you are happy to help, could you please let me know so I can give you her name to check on your database?

Thanks, Mel x

41

It sent shivers through Ali Crofts whenever she recalled the first time that she recognised the possible signs of child abuse during her training to become a youth support worker. She was on a home visit with a lead practitioner to see a teenager who'd been charged with actual bodily harm, with the prospect of a trial in a youth court looming. Ali was invited along to get an insight into the family life of the accused and to learn the basics of the youth justice system. The youngster lacked confidence, couldn't maintain eye contact, and was clearly remorseful for his wrong doings. The best hope for a more favourable, leaner sentence was if he could work with his youth offending officer to prove he had a plan of action regarding his future; that he was intent on a positive, law-abiding lifestyle.

The lad's mother was busily attempting to feed some lunch to her young daughter, no more than three years old. The toddler seemed intent on fidgeting in her highchair and throwing the plastic utensils from her tray, much to the annoyance of the mum. It immediately struck Ali how strange it was that a child was refusing the offer of fromage frais, and how increasingly agitated she was becoming. The woman reached down to pick the spoon up off the floor, and went to return it to the girl, causing the toddler to flinch. Her reaction exploded the alarm bells in Ali's head; it was the response of someone expecting to have been hit around the head and face. It was probably the regular outcome of her tantrums and was probably a surprise for the youngster that she was given temporary respite from a slap on that occasion. Disclosing such an unpleasant experience to social services was part and parcel of her job, as she always knew it would be. It meant she was rarely phased by the next big challenge a client might present.

Ali wasn't quite sure how she felt about the over-familiar text from Mel. It had come as a massive surprise to receive it, and quite how Mel had made the assumption about her undoubted talents as a practitioner was a mystery to her. But patently in Mel's eyes there was a kid in trouble which had mithered her to the extent of making contact, and after all, working through problems with kids was her skill. Now that Ali had been entrusted to help turn this youngster's situation around, there was some uninvited pressure to prove herself.

Eve Florey was on the common database shared by different agencies. That was nothing unusual because every child in the county was logged on there. She wasn't based in Ali's locality of work, but that wouldn't stop her from helping the kid even if it meant having to travel into the south of the region. She would just have to be slightly more creative about adding Eve onto her caseload. There was nothing untoward on her record, no alerts highlighting specific risks. The only additional note was posted under her family record which highlighted the death of her mum in November 2015. It wasn't difficult to see the connection Mel had with this girl, and the similarities were further evident in Mel's subsequent text.

She's been dabbling with drugs, but I haven't asked to what extent. There's a connection between her mum's death and her drug use. She hasn't told me what it is, but I know it's eating away at her. Has exams coming up, wants to go to college. She's an only child, lives with her dad who has no idea about any of this, and that's the way Eve wants it to stay. I'll text her to say you're going to be in touch, and then I'll send you her number. Can you let me know how things are going, and perhaps we could meet for a catch up at some point? Mel x

A teenager struggling to deal with the death of a parent, and consequently behaving erratically – Mel was better placed than anyone to recognise the need for peremptory action for Eve.

Ali wasted little time in texting the number that Mel sent through but did so with a few assumptions. The message was sent at a time in the late afternoon when she hoped Eve would be at home, away from friends and before her dad got home from work. It was half-term for schools in the area, so there was an outside chance that her new client could be away. However, given that exams were due to begin in the following week, Ali hoped that the kid's attention was being given to some last-minute revision.

Eve replied cautiously, tying to gauge what this Ali bloke was all about. Whoever he was, he was making a good first impression on her. Eve was due to be at school in Waterlooville the next day for some revision classes in history and science, and that seemed like a good sign to Ali that the girl was taking her studies seriously.

How about meeting when you get back from your classes tomorrow, maybe grab a chat before your dad gets back from work? A.

Ok, can you meet me where the bus stops at the junction of Chapel Road and High Street, by the post office? It'll be about two o'clock.
Eve.

That's fine. I'll wait for any other kids to walk away before coming across to speak to you, so no one asks you any questions about who I am. A.

42

The next day, Ali perused the houses for sale in the estate agent window across the road from the bus stop where Eve was due to disembark. The glass in the large bay at the front acted as a mirror so that she could see the girl standing alone, and not chatting with anyone else. She watched her looking about nervously up and down the road before taking something out of her pocket and putting it to her mouth. Ali couldn't make out what it was and suspecting it may be a cigarette she hastily walked around the side of the building to send a discrete text.

> Eve, its Ali. I'm across the road sitting on a bench at the entrance to the small park, meet me there in a minute? A.

Ali knew it was Eve that wandered into the park as it was the same girl lingering by the bus stop. The teenager walked over hesitantly, and then seemed to overlook Ali sitting on the bench. When she began looking around and behind her Ali began to feel invisible, and the behaviour suggested that she might have been using something of an illegal nature. It prompted Ali to get up from where she was sitting to initiate a greeting.

'Hi Eve, I didn't know if you could see me sitting over there. Are you ok?'

Eve looked gone out.

'You're Ali?'

'Yeah, that's me.'

'Oh, are you sure? I thought…'

'You look totally confused, is this too much for you?'

'No, I'm fine. It's just… doesn't matter, you're just not what I expected from what Mel said.'

'Oh great! That makes me feel a bit nervous,' Ali joked.

Eve had handled the situation remarkably calmly, but it was little wonder that she still looked slightly startled. She was chatting to a thirty-something, pale-faced, bobbed-hair lady; she was sure that Mel had described the person entrusted to work with her as being a late-forties, bald, and slightly chubby bloke. The similarities were non-existent, so it took a bit of convincing that Ali was who she said she was, and that an embarrassing and unlikely mistake wasn't being made. Above all, Eve hoped that she wasn't suddenly talking to a complete and random stranger that just happened to hit on her need for support.

She needn't have worried; within minutes of chatting, Ali made her feel at ease. Talking was natural and unforced with Ali. Not once did the youth worker bring anything up about her personal challenges or the issues that Mel had outlined. Ali was so in tune with the young lady she had just met. Her philosophy had always been that the greatest gift you could give to a kid was time – and if you gave them time, they would know you were genuine; it would earn you their respect, but most of all their trust would be secured.

'S'pose Mel told you all about me then – the drugs and stuff?'

'Not really Eve, that's not how it works you know – gossiping about what goes on in young people's lives. Yeah, she was concerned, so I'm here to help you if there are things going off that you'd like to get sorted out. I'm not on commission, and you're not going to be given a time limit. The only thing that matters is that you're ok.'

This was a verbal comfort blanket for Eve. She wasn't obliged to say or do anything, but she had an outlet to be able to do so if she wanted to. It gave her back some control over her feelings that someone was prepared to listen and not judge, to treat her at face value and not scoff at her thoughts however warped they might sound. She no longer had the feeling of being surrounded by so many people yet still managing to be lonely. The care and protection pulling round her shoulders encouraged her to begin talking openly.

'I didn't like taking drugs, I've stopped now anyway apart from a drag on a spliff at a mate's house the other night. I don't even like that.'

'What were you into before then?'

'Well, the people at the house where I used to hang out did loads of stuff. I never did coke or heroin and that stuff. I asked but they said no. I tried speed a few times, but that's about it.'

'How did it make you feel?'

'Great – and crap. I just wanted to forget about things, and for a bit it helped. But then it made me feel down. I felt sick. And guilty too.'

'Why guilty?'

'My dad. He'd be mad and disappointed. And my mum...' Eve stopped and looked sorrowful. It wasn't Ali's role to push a youngster into opening up about the things that were troubling them.

'Are you tempted to try taking something again?'

'Honestly? I'm not sure. I know I'm not hooked 'cos I didn't enjoy the idea of doing it. It's the reason why I started taking them that's the problem really. Can I tell you another time? It doesn't feel right here.'

'Yeah, of course. If you want to – whatever feels comfortable. Just take your time with it. If it's ok with you, I'm going to let your school know that I'm supporting you.'

'Oh, shit. No way – they'll go telling my dad. Please don't.'

'Not if we stress the need for it to remain confidential.'

'Can we do that?'

'Yes.'

'Why do they even need to know?'

'Because they know you better than most, and they see you more often than I could. They'll see you at times that I won't, and might be able to work out if you're not your normal self –

like, I don't know, what if you have a bad moment during your exams? If something like that happens, they can let me know so that I can get to speak with you.'

Eve pondered the reasoning, and accepted it was a sensible suggestion.

'Alright then – I trust you.'

It was the best she had felt for some time, and optimism around the upcoming exams began to surface. The trust in Ali wasn't misplaced, and that proved to be a well calculated judgement soon after their first meeting.

The school's pastoral manager Mrs Shelia Gardner was relieved to learn of Ali's intervention with Eve and wished her more success with her input than the school had accomplished. Having witnessed the teenager wobbling in her commitment to her studies following Hannah's fatal accident, various attempts were made to encourage her to see a counsellor. For Ali there was something worryingly familiar about that scenario having watched Mel suffer the same way.

It was a frantic Mrs Gardner who telephoned Ali's mobile phone number to explain that Eve hadn't shown up for her pre-exam history revision tutorial. None of her friends had seen her, and there was no answer on any contact numbers that the school held on file. The exam secretary and assistant headteacher were both flapping. Ali wondered why the exam secretary and assistant headteacher hadn't made the call themselves, because all she could hear was them both in the background wittering about how there was just over an hour before the paper commenced, and the exam board wouldn't accept late arrivals without a valid reason.

Ali thought nothing of dropping her own admin tasks piling up beside the desktop to rescue the situation for Eve. With the home address scribbled onto her notepad, she hurried out to her car to tap the details into her sat nav. Even if she got hold of Miss

Florey on the way, to instruct her to be ready by the time her lift turned up, the journey to Waterlooville via Meonstoke from Andover was still likely to be a good hour.

The persistent hammering on the large wooden front doors failed to alert anyone inside and ate away valuable minutes in the quest to get Eve to the exam hall on time. A couple of well-aimed handfuls of gravel lobbed at an upstairs window where the curtains were closed did the trick. The curtains parted slightly, and then widely, revealing a bleary-eyed teenage girl looking confused at the sight of her support worker gesticulating energetically. With the window opened, Ali calmly relayed her message.

'You've got five minutes to get changed and into this car if you want to make your exam.'

The gravity of the situation wasn't lost on Eve, but she remained cool, got dressed, and grabbed some make-up necessities before throwing herself into the car seat. At first, she was too breathless to even acknowledge Ali. The first thing she did before putting her seatbelt round her was to take out an inhaler and take a large puff from it. That made a lot of sense to Ali, it curbed the curiosity she held when she saw Eve at the bus stop before their first meeting, and realised it was the inhaler she had taken from her pocket and put to her mouth in that instance also. She was relieved it hadn't been a cigarette.

'Sorry, needed to do that. Hay fever brings on my asthma a bit.'

Ali threw a banana at her passenger. 'Eat this while I phone Mrs Gardner to tell her we're on the way.'

Ali made the call to the school, urging them to also leave a follow-up message for Eve's dad to eradicate any alarm he might experience upon learning his daughter hadn't arrived at school. Then she waited patiently for Eve to devour the banana and apply her mascara and lipstick, trying not to pre-empt the explanation for this gaffe.

'Here, have a mint.'

'No thanks – I don't like mints much.'

'Your breath reeks.'

'I didn't have time to brush my teeth, did I?'

Eve fumbled with the packet, trying to extract one of the circular sweets. She ripped the paper, and a couple rolled out. She was taking no chances with the state of her personal hygiene and put them both in her mouth for a double dose of freshening.

'Thank you for not giving up on me the first time something goes pear-shaped. Not sure what else I can say.'

'Don't worry about that now. Disaster has been averted so the only thinking you need to focus on is smashing that paper.'

'Bet you think I was deliberately going to miss it?'

'No, definitely not, that's why I've raced to get here. I know you've been revising – Mel told me. But I can't say I wasn't worried.'

'Bet you're thinking I've been back on the crap again, don't you?'

Ali didn't flinch, even though she could feel the weight of Eve's stare to the side of her.

'I think you already know I'm not a person who'll judge you like that.'

Then the car share started to giggle.

'On my own life, this is the truth, ok? My dad went away on business yesterday afternoon for one night. He wanted to ask a family friend to stop over to make sure I was ok, but I just wanted to get on with my work without someone else bugging me in my own home, so I told him to stop fussing. I revised all day until my eyeballs ached and I felt completely knackered. But when I went to bed, I just couldn't get to sleep with all these friggin' facts rattling around my head. I ended up watching a movie until late. When you threw those stones at the window, I didn't know what was going on. My clock was off, and my bedside lamp wouldn't switch on. Obviously, I just thought there'd been a power cut in my area so that would've screwed my alarm up, and I've slept through cos I'm so tired. But when I looked out the window to see you, I noticed our neighbour trimming his hedges, so his power was working. My dad has told me to check our electrics box in the cupboard under the stairs if all the lights and plug sockets don't work, and guess what? I looked on the way out – the main trip switch was off. A bulb must've blown or something. I always keep some lamps on at night if I'm on my own. It was probably one of them. Oh, and my mobile was on silent as well, so that my mates didn't distract me when I was studying. I'm sorry Ali, it's just one of those things.'

It was a perfectly viable explanation, and a reassuring one at that. Ali had braced herself to be in receipt of a far more reckless tale. Eve was still in a vulnerable frame of mind and gifted with a house free of parental control to take advantage of. The fact that she decided to refrain from any temptation and put her revision first was a positive indication that she had already responded to the efforts of positive role models in Mel and Ali.

'Do you need me to hang around to take you home again?'

'No, it's ok. I'll either get the bus, or my dad has said he'd be over in Southampton from midday, so he could pick me up on his way home. Mind you, I've got the urge to speak about things that have bothered me for ages. When will we be able to meet again?'

'The thing is, if you start thinking about the things that bother you now, it'll be at the front of your mind. Don't you think it might be good to try and park it, and let all that knowledge from your revision flood your thoughts instead? I mean, just for now.'

'Sounds like the right thing to do. I've done almost half of the exams now anyway, so I'll be finished in another week.'

'There you go then. I've got no problems seeing you whenever you want, but if I don't hear from you beforehand why don't you text me after your last exam? Assuming you don't intend to make everyone a nervous wreck by making today's glitch a habit.'

43

The sudden referral that Mel made to Ali ensured that the most unimaginable connection existed between the two women. While one was oblivious to the absurdity of the situation, for the other – blissfully unaware of the entanglement herself – it remained slightly awkward. Ali chose not to pepper Mel with a string of texts updating her about every interaction she had with Eve. Nonetheless, a courteous and carefully worded few lines was meant to ensure that Mel had no cause for concern about the girl's progress. The desired outcome was to keep their dealings professional, and to a minimum. However, the communication between the pair over the following weeks was far from one-sided, and Mel's attempts to help were occasionally obscure.

Hi Ali! Hope you don't mind me asking you a personal question, but I think we know each other well enough! Here goes – when did you realise that you were gay? I might be barking up the wrong tree, but do you think that Eve's sexuality has got anything to do with how she is feeling – struggling to come out maybe? Would be good to know when you get to the bottom of what's causing her so much grief – maybe we can meet for that coffee? Speak soon, Mel x

Ali had no issue with the care and interest that Mel was investing in Eve's progress, but she couldn't help but wonder whether the unsubtle humour was another jibe at her previous, hopeless, loveless life in order to get around to asking a perfectly legitimate reference point regarding the client. If the insinuation that Ali was gay was an attempt to knock her off her stride somehow, it lacked potency – and Ali had form when it came to that. Nothing would ever compare to the time in her life when Ali knew she was struggling to get Robert out of her system.

Right from the start of her first year at university, she'd developed a mistrust for lads that showed even the remotest interest in her, an insecurity that had the potential to damage any prospect of a long-term relationship. That first disaster with Will didn't help. She had somehow got herself involved with the female rugby team at the Freshers' Fair, and then enjoyed the training sessions even though it invited attention from the male squad members. They would huddle together like they were in a scrum watching the girls train and were hardly subtle in the conversations that were being had. When they could be heard to be talking about 'talent' it wasn't the ladies' ball handling or line out technique that they were admiring.

The chances of picking up the wrong training hoody was quite remote given that the name of the team member was printed on the back, and naturally they were all different shapes and sizes – and different states of cleanliness. But at the end of one gruelling session at the end of November, there was a stampede to exit the training field and into the club house as a deluge of hail suddenly swept through the grounds. It was only when she returned to her dorm that Ali realised, she had picked up Lydia Booth's top by mistake, and it was anyone's guess who would be in possession of her own. She would just swap it back at training the following week.

That simple mistake was to cause confusion at the student union bar, where some of the rugger lads had made it their intention to make a move on the girls that they had been eyeing up at the training sessions. As the female team openly paraded themselves with their training tops around campus as well as at training, it was an easy ice breaker for the lads to know the name of the one they were going to chat up. Rumours spread like wildfire throughout the bar area that this was their plan, much to the amusement of the lasses who realised the obvious flaw in the objective after the mix-up with tops.

It was mid-week, so some players had chosen to pass up on a bevvy that night in order to catch up with their studies, and consequently Chinese whispers began to spread. By the time they had reached Ali the next day, she couldn't believe her luck when she was told that the star fly half of the first team, the rather fit William Krimtide, had been looking for her whereabouts; the apparent rumour being he had the hots for her. His appearance at her room in the halls of residence suggested there was some substance to the story.

'I'm looking for Alison Crofts?'

'Yeah, ok.'

'Well, can you tell me where she is or when she'll be back?'

'Are you pissed?'

'No, why? Are you always this rude?'

'Well, seeing as Alison Crofts is standing in front of you, I'd say you've had a few too many knocks on the head in your scrummages. Do you wear head protection to protect your delicate bonce?'

'Funny. Hang on, has one of my mates set me up?'

'I don't know any of your mates – and I'm not sure if I want to know you particularly, Willy.'

'It's William; and don't worry there's no danger of me getting to know you Miss Arrogant. But Alison, well that's a different matter. Are you a mate of hers?'

'I'm Alison Crofts.'

'Yeah right, and I'm Jonny Wilkinson. Look, no disrespect, you seem a nice girl, but I saw Alison walk into the club house the other day; I saw her, she was well fit. It definitely wasn't you – no offense.'

'None taken, you'd need to punch above your weight to land me anyway. Looks like there'd be a fair bit of weight to punch above too.'

'Good one, you got me; we're even.'

'Just tell me something – how did you know that girl was Alison Crofts then?'

'Duh! She had her training top on, with her name on the back.'

'Hang on a minute.' Ali grabbed the top which she had inherited and brought it to the door to show Will. 'This is a long shot, but I wonder if it's Lydia you might be trying to find?'

After helping Will to understand the muddle, the mystery was solved, leaving two embarrassed undergraduates, and Alison out of luck and second best to Lydia. She did make a friend through it though – her and Will became good buddies and shared many laughs and some tears together throughout their student days. If ever he seemed to be getting one up on her, she would bring him back down to earth with the story about the hoody.

It was at a party in February of their first year when Will realised there was something amiss with Ali. It was being held in the basement of an off-campus student dorm, on a weekend when coincidently the warden was away, and unable to police the social exuberance of the residents. It was soon after Ali had returned from the unpleasantness that overshadowed the genuine intentions of her visit to see Mel in Nottingham. She'd answered the call of someone in distress, and instead came away reeling herself.

Will had noticed one of his rugger pals checking her out and encouraged him to try talking to his new friend. Aman, himself a shy chap, took his chance and went across to where she was sitting. The second Ali turned to see him smiling at her she moved to the other side of the room. Undeterred, and thinking perhaps it was unconnected with his approach, Aman followed her across some moments later with the intention of chatting her up. Each time she moved, Aman seemed to follow to the very place she went to, making her feel uncomfortable. But she completely misread the signals; here was a lad who genuinely liked her, albeit struggling to show it apart from an awkward, nervous smile, and she mistook it for a wind-up – suspecting the lads were playing a joke at her expense. Losing her temper was not something she was prone to often, but her misinterpretation that he was somehow stalking her led to some shrieking.

'You're fucking creeping me out!'

Will leapt to Aman's defence, before taking Ali outside to deflect the derogatory comments being flung in her direction.

'What's going on, Ali?'

'That knobby knobhead kept following me around!'

'So?'

'Either that weirdo was put up to it by your mates, or he was off his face.'

'Or maybe the lad actually just likes you, Ali?'

Will's precisely posed question was telling; she just didn't have a clue about how to deal with that kind of situation because she didn't want to. It was the one and only time she remotely opened up to anyone about the situation running through her head and soul. Will bowed his head and listened without interrupting as she explained the extent of her dreadful trip to see Mel. Ali was so confused from not knowing whether the things that were said were just a spiteful reaction, or if it was true that Robert had never received her letter to him. If that were really the case, he had no idea how Ali had really felt, and she had been going through a silent anguish that should never have been.

The giggles and banter she shared with Will reminded her a little bit of the early days with Robert, so it seemed somehow comforting that it should be him who would be able to help convince her to start believing in herself again, and to put past traumas behind her. She moved on, she had to; but the faith Will put in her was slightly misplaced. What he was asking her to do regarding Robert felt impossible. She couldn't completely forget him.

The calamity of the undelivered letter produced far reaching consequences over the course of time. It was still a difficult memory to deal with, and a challenge to keep her mind distant from it. But the sands kept shifting, and a corner was turned; Ali had been dating Jamal for over a year, an eternity in comparison to any of her previous flings. She was happy and content, feelings that she couldn't recall being aroused in her previous relationships. The high-flying accountant doted on her, and a proposal seemed inevitable.

The only thing Ali could do in response to Mel's text was to cautiously update her with the plain truth about Eve, and in her mind at least to tactfully address the slanderous suggestion that she wasn't straight.

44

Mel, cheers for your message. I don't think that's the issue but can't rule anything out I suppose. Fact is she still hasn't said anything to me. Didn't get round to telling you I've been seeing a really nice guy for over twelve months. Yes, I'm open to a cuppa at some point, perhaps when there's a development with Eve. Best wishes, Ali.

That coming together began to look increasingly probable once Eve had returned from a fortnight in the sun with her dad, recuperating from her exertions in her finals. Ali could sense that the teenager was preoccupied the first time they met again, partly through over-thinking her pending results, some of it from over-analysing her lack of friendships, but mostly out of missing her mum. It was nice to spend some proper time with her dad, however annoying and embarrassing he could be in public with his fashion sense, and the need to sing out loud which only he found humorous. But holidaying without her mum felt empty. It was a time when they would giggle, bond and connect. She missed their fashion chats each night as they got ready to go out, and chilling with each other at the poolside sharing books and their music. Eve would do anything to take one more silly selfie with the lady that left her with so many regrets.

They agreed to meet at Abbey Gardens in Winchester. Eve sometimes liked to go shopping there in the school holidays for a change of scenery, so her dad wouldn't have suspected anything out of the ordinary about who she might have been meeting. It was a glorious mid-August morning. The air was still, the sun sparkled, and barely a cloud had the audacity to interrupt an otherwise perfect blue sky. Eve had walked down through the high street from the train station and was sitting on a bench in the shade sipping some orange juice she had bought on the way when Ali arrived. She looked older than her years with her hair straightened, cropped top and shades on, and only when she gestured with a little wave did Ali realise it was her.

'You've chosen a damn nice day for a catch up, Eve. And not a bad venue either.'

'My dad said he used to like it in Winchester when he was younger, but he's gone off the place now. He's a bit of a grumpy git.'

'He must be, what's not to like about this?' Ali emphasised the point by wafting her hand in the direction of the perfectly manicured grounds, and the cathedral peeping over the top of the far end. They both sat there sucking up the view. 'I keep meaning to say something to you from when I picked you up back in June. What an amazing house you live in!'

'Thanks. It's a bit big for two.'

'What's your dad do?' Eve stared, not quite grasping the nature of the question. 'For a job?' Ali qualified herself.

'Oh. Some kind of engineer – don't really know to be honest. My mum did something like that too.'

'Blimey, he must be good at what he does living in a mansion like yours!'

The wit was lost on the youngster. Eve was quite a serious soul that morning. The walls of the dam of secrets were beginning to show cracks, through which a leak would appear, followed by a gush.

'Ali, how well do you know Mel?'

One moment they were have having pleasant small talk, the next she was grabbed by a question out of nowhere, completely throwing her. Ali tried to keep her composure to think straight, and to give Eve no inclination of the sourness in her former relationship.

'She was a new kid in town, but I got to know her and the family pretty well. If you've spoken with Mel, then I guess you already know her mum died when she was a teenager, a lot like you?'

'Yeah, she had told me.'

'It's one of the reasons she was so keen to make sure that you are ok – she gets it.'

Eve sat thoughtfully, perched forward with her chin resting on the palms of her hands, and elbows on knees.

'But the difference is she said she wishes she could've opened up more about it. I don't want to live my life like a locked safe the same way as her, Ali. It's all I think about some days. It's killing me already and it hasn't even been two years since she's gone. God knows how Mel did it for so long.'

'You're a smart kid Eve. If you realise something is eating away at you and making a pit full of misery, then talking to someone about it is a good bet for helping to deal with it.'

Eve delivered a shocking prelude to her sorrowful tale.

'How do I deal with the fact that it's my fault my mum died?'

'Do you want to talk about it now – here?'

Eve barely nodded. She didn't need a second invitation and couldn't get the words stuffed in her head out quickly enough.

'The night my mum had the car crash, we'd been arguing. I wasn't being allowed to go out to see my boyfriend in Lodden. My parents weren't keen on me seeing a lad a couple of years older than me. We rowed about it a lot. I kept asking them why they didn't trust me, like they thought I was gonna get up the duff or something. It still annoys me that does, there's no way I would've done that.'

Eve was very animated, flailing her arms and hands to emphasise her points. The pitch in her voice had risen noticeably, to the extent that a lady on the next bench glanced over in their direction. It caused Eve to stop and look up and turn herself inwards towards Ali to make sure no one else nearby could hear the rest of the narrative.

'Anyway, I know it was stupid, but I messaged Martin – my boyfriend – and asked him to meet me. When I knew mum and dad weren't listening, I crept out the house and hopped on Martin's moped and went up to Lodden with him.'

'Did your parents know you'd done that?'

'No. My dad doesn't get angry very often, but he'd have gone absolutely mental if he'd seen me. The thing is my mum came into my room not long after and obviously I wasn't there. She got worried cos she knew I'd done a bunk. She texted me to ask where I was...' There was a spontaneous outburst of sobbing, lines of tears trickled like mini streams from under her shades. 'I didn't reply, so she tried to call but I sent it straight to answerphone. Mum being mum, she left a message.'

Eve laboured to take her phone from the back pocket of her jeans. With a pained expression and her bottom lip downturned she flicked through her menu to find her saved messages, one of them being the one she had just described to Ali. She pressed play and thrust the handset towards her support worker to listen to. Most reluctantly, Ali took the phone and put it to her ear. What could be heard was an anxious parent, her voice trembling on the verge of crying, clearly panicking for the welfare of her baby but showing just enough strength to keep it together.

'Hi Eve, it's mum. I've just sent you a text, but hey, listen, I'm guessing you've gone to Martin's. I've not told your dad so don't worry, he doesn't know so you're not going to get into trouble, ok? I'm not going to nag you either, but I'm coming up to bring your inhaler. Please be there to take it from me in case you need it darling. You can stay a couple of hours, and then, I tell you what, I'll come back over to pick you up and grab a take-away on the way back. I'm on my way... can you let me know you've got this message? Love you.'

Ali bit her top lip; it was all she could do to avoid breaking down herself. She was in a battle with herself, her heart strings hadn't been pulled like this before professionally. Despite her experience, this was unchartered territory even for her.

'Would it be too upsetting to ask what happened?'

'It was on the way to Lodden, down one of the country lanes, she swerved to miss a huge branch that had fallen down in the wind and rain. The car skidded, overturned, and hit a tree. They say the impact... she wouldn't have had time to react. Her head injury was so bad, the medics said she died instantly.'

In stark contrast to the numbness that had struck Ali and Eve, little children's laughter echoed off the sides of the buildings next to the gardens. Along with the sound of trickling water in the river that flowed close by, and the vibrant colours of the flowers in the beds next to where they sat, the joy of the playtime being enjoyed by the little ones was a sure paradox of life going on as normal irrespective of the sadness that it can also deliver. The key question was beginning to nag away in Ali's head, and unless she put it to Eve it would be difficult to work out how best to get the girl through this awful experience. With one hand gently placed on Eve's shoulder, she started to speak in a hushed tone.

'This has been one of the hardest things I've ever had to listen to in my life, an utterly tragic event for any family to have experienced. But how on earth is this your fault?'

'If I'd not been so feisty and gone against their wishes by sodding off with Martin, or even if I'd only remembered my inhaler, she'd never have got into her car and wouldn't have made that journey, down that particular road, at that time.'

'She'd have come for you anyway Eve, whether you had your inhaler or not. She was being a mum.'

'The 'what ifs?' are all I can think about most of the time. Don't you reckon that even in the smallest way I'm to blame?'

Eve began shaking her head in utter despondency, obsessed

with a flawed rationale for her mum's untimely death. Ali dug deep into her repertoire of guidance techniques to find the right words of wisdom for her tortured client.

'Honestly? You're confusing coincidences for what was a horrifically unfortunate accident. But it doesn't matter what I think, does it? If what someone says to you is different to the story playing out in your head, all you'll hear are words – and not the ones you've already told yourself, so you're not going to like them.'

'I don't understand.'

'You've told yourself so many times that it's your fault, too many times for your head to deal with. You've convinced yourself of a false truth. All that analysing has forced your brain to see it how you want it to, turned the fuzzy images created by your own anxiety into a crystal-clear picture that you have painted as the truth. And now you totally believe that's what really happened.'

'Do you think that's what happened to Mel?'

'Maybe that's something you should ask her. She's never told me that in so many words, but I can only suspect that's pretty close to what went on with her as well.'

Eve got up from her bench and walked across to the railings that bordered the cathedral green. As usual, it was a magnet to tourists and locals, groups, and singles. The youngster lost herself in thinking about the lives of all of those she could see in front of her, and what kinds of troubles might have stared them in the face, and how they were getting through it. She didn't want the feeling of being defeated any more. She shuffled back over to the bench where Ali had been collecting her own thoughts.

'I know it wasn't a sensible thing to do but I started experimenting with drugs to forget everything, to get rid of everything in my head that was hassling me. I wanted to take stronger stuff as insurance it would work – so I wouldn't be disappointed and could escape for as long as possible.'

'It's beyond scary to think where you'd be if you had followed through with that plan. One thing's for sure, the future would've been dangling by mist if you had. Your best chance of getting through this is by speaking to someone to help you see things differently, to reverse that bleak version that has taken hold in your mind. Mel realised counselling was the right way to go, it just took her quite a while to figure it out.'

To have become entangled with the need to take drugs was evidence enough that Eve was enduring a bumpy journey. Her brief flirtation with self-destruction began to falter now that a platform for rebuilding had been provided by the timely intervention of Mel and Ali, giving Eve some renewed self-belief and the courage to speak about her pain. She took the next difficult step – and started her first session of bereavement counselling the following week.

One thing Eve quickly learnt was that talking to the right person, however daunting it seemed, helped to calm the storm blowing in her mind. The pain of losing her mum would ebb and flow, she was already mature enough to have grasped that would always be the way. But she learned that the torture she was putting herself through could be tamed and put into proper perspective. Eve began to realise that there was no blame attached to her mum's death. She even invented a fighting slogan to help cope with the reality of the situation:

'The more shit life throws out, the bigger the bog roll I'll use.'

Whether that was oversimplifying it or not, it helped her to break down her challenges into smaller chunks and to realise that she could overcome them. She knew that there would always be a difficult past to deal with, but there would always a brighter future to grasp hold of too.

45

Ali began considering closing Eve's case, since the youngster had thrived on the support that had been put her way. The rewards in her line of work were never going to be financial, and that's the last reason why Ali had pursued that career anyway. But to be able to watch someone she had worked with beginning to flourish independently having previously scraped the lowest emotional pit made the efforts of her advocacy more than worthwhile. At the end of August, there was simply no better feeling than watching the joy on Eve's face as she realised her own potential, gleefully relaying her exam results. It also produced a much more exuberant return of texts between Mel and Ali at the good news and heralded an agreement to finally meet face-to-face in early September.

Until May, there had been no desire to plan a future of any sort, and every closing date for applications for courses or apprenticeships had long since vanished. So rejuvenated was her outlook on her life that Eve chose to take A Levels, already with half an eye on a career in social care and helping others. The offer of a place in the sixth form was testament to Eve's academic efforts, and this it seemed was the final piece in the jigsaw. The school was delighted that she had chosen to stay on, and assured Ali that they would continue to offer their support in any way they could – academically or otherwise. Eve went along to enrol with her proud dad for support, and a new and exciting chapter beckoned.

It was particularly cruel that it should be on induction day, the first day of term, that everything came crashing down. However discrete the intention was, uniformed officers walking into school premises inevitably drew the attention of sharp-eyed students. The speculation was rife and overflowing when a parent was spotted arriving soon afterwards, with plenty of effort being exerted by kids that were intent on playing detectives themselves. The head of sixth form's personal assistant calling into a classroom was another giveaway that something had happened involving one of the lower-sixth students. Eve's self-confidence was no longer as fragile as it had been, but the whispered message in her ear to follow the PA down to the sixth form office under the gaze of her peers was demoralising.

After being asked to sit outside for fifteen minutes, listening to muffled conversations on the other side of the wall, Eve was invited into the room too. Mr Jondar's office already looked like a courtroom with so many people inside. Her dad got up from his seat in the corner to greet her with a hug.

'What's going on, dad – have I done something wrong?'

'It's not great, Eve. The officers are going to explain everything properly. You're being charged with criminal damage to your mum's headstone and perverting the course of justice for allowing another person to take the blame for the crime.'

Ali was already fully aware of the unfolding situation having received a call from Lilly Seijayeff, announcing herself as Eve's youth offending officer. Having utilised the multi-agency database, Mrs Seijayeff was privy to the range of work Ali had undertaken with Eve and deemed it necessary to involve her going forward in the process of her pending prosecution. Ali knew how the system worked. It wasn't a problem in supporting a colleague from another agency, particularly if the common goal was to ensure the case notes for Eve illustrated a person so far removed from the crime they were accused of that the judge must take that into account in sentencing.

What baffled Ali was how Eve had conveniently overlooked mentioning the small issue of being questioned by the police whenever they met to discuss her welfare. She paced the office floor with the handset glued to her ear, listening intently to Lilly citing the case details of the incident at the churchyard in Meonstoke. When it emerged that an adult had also been involved, that was the bit she struggled to assimilate. Only when Eve had provided some explanation could the confused practitioner rest easy from the multitude of worrying questions in her head. She just hoped that the involvement of an adult had nothing to do with drugs.

The worry over why Eve had hidden something from their conversations was prevalent in her thoughts on the journey from Andover. Ali imagined Eve caving in and feeling alone given that her dad was unaware of all that had been uncovered over the previous weeks. The mobile phone bleeped in her handbag on the passenger seat just as she was driving through the gates of the school. A car had just reversed from a space, leaving a saloon shaped dry patch where the vehicle had shielded the ground from the drizzle. Ali had no idea that it had been Robert who was parked there, now leaving to get to work since the meeting at school had finished. It was so nearly a bittersweet collision, creating levels of shame she wouldn't have been able to handle.

The text had been a desperate plea from Eve.

Need to speak to you urgently. Shit hit the fan. Don't know what to do.

No sooner had Ali read it than she was walking into Mr Jondar's meeting room, where Mrs Gardner was speaking with Lilly Seijayeff. Eve was nowhere to be seen.

'Hi both. I'm sorry I couldn't get to the meeting, I raced as quickly as I could from Andover. Any chance you could fill me in?'

Lilly was enthusiastically complimentary over the thoroughness of the work Ali had undertaken with Eve, before explaining that an adult had falsely admitted to the charge of criminal damage. The youth court process was initiated because of the charge of perverting the course of justice. Ali was shocked; though the facts were being laid out in front of her, it didn't make any sense. Their agreed priority was to compose a glowing witness testimony in Eve's defence, in time for the initial hearing which had been set for ten days from then.

'Where is Eve anyway?'

'She's gone home for the rest of the day. She was so upset that Mr Jondar asked whether Mr Florey could drop her off. You must've practically passed each other.'

Ali walked with Lilly back out to the car park, where small talk produced the next bombshell just before they went their separate ways.

'I'll get straight onto it and send my draft testimony across to you by first thing tomorrow, Lilly. Strange circumstances or what?'

'You're not wrong. Isn't it baffling why this Burchell woman should want to take the blame for Eve? Oh well, that's something for the other courts to deal with, not us.'

Up to that point there had been no mention of the identity of the adult. It simply wasn't the priority. The name-dropping paralysed Ali. She didn't want to jump to conclusions, but then it would be far too coincidental for it to be anyone else other than Mel. Though Mrs Seijayeff bid her farewell, the words didn't filter through. Ali was dumbstruck by the question this posed. If the adult in the criminal activity was Mel, what kind of involvement did she have with Eve to risk a criminal prosecution? Time for some straight talking was evidently required.

46

Some miles away from the school, neither father nor daughter knew what to say to one another on the twenty-minute journey back to Meonstoke. For Eve, it was purely about avoidance of further shame. For Robert, he was mulling over the prospect of having to eat his words. It annoyed the hell out of him that Mel had interfered in his family matters. But if she had genuinely put herself in the firing line, prepared to take the flak for his daughter, then he had misjudged her to the extent that it warranted an apology. That aside, Robert also had to deal with the allegation that his daughter had lied and had in fact set out to destroy her own mum's gravestone. His heart sank. Had he not been attentive enough to how she was feeling, and let her down by being a shit dad? That was the last thing he ever wanted to be to the child he cherished. It would hurt him beyond belief if he had failed her, putting him in the same category as his own father.

'I'm going up to my room,' Eve announced, only to be overruled by her dad.

'No, you're not. Let's have a cuppa together love.'

Reluctantly, the teenager sat on a bar stool in the kitchen, not once daring to catch her dad's eye for fear it would instigate a conversation. She hadn't bargained on her dad's diplomacy skills.

'I'm not angry, ashamed or disappointed. I love you and will help you through all of this. The only thing I need to know is why did you do it, Eve?'

She could feel the blood rushing to her cheeks, and the heat of the embarrassment.

'I love you too dad, but you wouldn't understand.'

'Try me. Please.'

The pinging of Eve's phone was untimely. She scooped her hand around the screen, so her dad couldn't see, and saw that there was a new message from Ali. Robert was not amused by the interruption and his daughter's insistence on checking her phone, and though it wasn't done deliberately, he held a disagreeable expression that she had seen far too often.

'You'll do your usual and start lecturing me before you've had the chance to really hear me out, closing off my sentences, and then shouting when I try to interrupt when you're not right. Then you'll end up laying down the law. And I've had enough of that dad, it pisses me off.'

He was quite used to Eve giving back a little bit of cheek, but this was different. It was feisty and edgy. It was a mature reaction, not a tantrum. This was a side to his girl that he needed to get in tune with if he had any hope that she would confide in him.

'Fair enough. Sounds like I need to get my game together, right? I guess that because I'm the adult, trying to deal with the challenge and responsibility of being both your mum and dad, I automatically think I'm always right. And clearly, I'm not. And if I admit that I am definitely a right moody bastard sometimes, I bet that won't surprise you. I should know better.' Robert paused. 'It's not an excuse, because I'm sure you can throw exactly the same thing back at me, but some days I can't get the thought of your mum out of my head. I see her lovely face smiling at me, and for the rest of the day it cripples me so much that I can't do anything to make it real and not just a memory. I've probably taken that out on people around me, and I'm sorry that you've been the punch bag sometimes too.'

Eve felt strangely comforted that her dad was being so open about his feelings and misgivings. It was an opportunity begging for a response, and it spurred her on to offer up some honesty.

'I like it when you talk with me like that dad. It makes me want to hug you because I can hear you being so genuine. You think I don't know how cut up you are about mum. You think you hide it from me, and by doing that it makes it okay. But you're crap at hiding it, and it doesn't make it better. I want to know that you're in pain so that I can tell you I feel the same and we can sort it out together. I think I reached my newest low point smashing the grave up. I don't think you'll like what I've got to say dad, I think if I'm honest you will think badly of me.'

'No way. I won't. I absolutely promise that I will listen to you and not scoff.'

'Ok, well there are things you don't know about the night mum died. You know I ran off to Martin's because that's where you came for me. But mum was coming across with my inhaler because like an idiot I forgot it. She was worried I'd have an attack, she told me on her message. Here, listen to this. It's something you've never heard before.'

Eve played back her mum's final message, just like she had done with Ali. It scared her to see the look in her dad's eyes, and as he began to crumble it was unbearable to watch. Robert stared at the mobile before passing it back to Eve. He moved across to the sink where he poured a glass of water to hydrate the dryness at the back of his throat, and to help hold back the tears. If he started crying it wouldn't stop, and he didn't want to break down like that in front of Eve.

'See, I told you it'd make you want to puke. If mum didn't have to come out to me in Lodden she would never have crashed the car. I've been playing that over and over in my mind since she died, always ending up deciding that it was my fault.'

'All this time that's what you've thought?' Robert was frantically shaking his head. 'There's something I need to tell you. How would you feel if I said that I also felt responsible for her death, and that's been tearing me apart ever since too?'

Now Eve shook her head.

'How?'

Robert began laughing but with no sound, which scared Eve.

His expression turned to a strain and grimace, before taking a large intake of breath and wailing. His daughter jumped off her stool and cradled him while he shuddered, letting out his heartache like that of a broken man too proud to admit to his pain. That he was rescued at that moment by his only child was fitting, the realisation that they needed to look out for each other the way Hannah would have expected them to. It was the beginning of a bond that would flourish thereafter. Once the intermittent sobs ceased and he became more composed, Robert told his daughter about his own feelings of guilt.

'I remember her going out, Eve. She said you needed some ingredients for your food technology class that we didn't have in the cupboard. I thought it was bizarre at the time cos she was never so disorganised to need to nip out to the village store for something. She went to stack the dishwasher with the dirty plates, then realised it hadn't been emptied from the previous cycle. I was working on my laptop here, at this breakfast bar. I glanced up, and I could tell she went to ask if I would do the clearing up – and then stopped herself. She must've felt guilty – about disturbing me, and because she knew she was keeping it from me that she was about to dash across to see you in Lodden. She could've just left the mess; it wouldn't have mattered. Instead she took all the clean stuff out in a hurry and then piled in all the dirty crocks. That chore took her the best part of fifteen minutes, and had she been those minutes earlier on her journey, that branch wouldn't have already been broken off from what other drivers have said. I am forever riddled with the guilt of not offering to do that clearing up, or just asking her to leave it. It just feels so shit.'

'Dad, please don't think like that. When I feel ready, I'll tell you everything, but I now realise that no one is to blame. Mum would be mad at us for living our lives like this, she'd tell us off for being so paranoid. It's a weight I've started removing from my back, and I'm going to help you do the same.'

Robert stepped back and rested his forehead on Eve's, whispering 'thank you' as he did so. 'When did that scruffy little tom-boy start turning into a beautiful lady, and an authority on life's challenges? Your mum adored you, and if I haven't made it very clear, I love you to bits.'

'Love you too, dad.'

The frenetic pace of events that had defined the morning were replaced with some much-needed calm washing through the Florey household by lunchtime. Their heart-to-heart that day had been a timely revelation for them both, and neither father nor daughter felt they were moving forward singularly any longer. Rather than being at logger heads with her dad over the embarrassment of a court appearance, Eve now knew he would be a rock of support to help her get through it. It didn't completely remove the trepidation of what was to come, but the thing that was fuelling her anxiety the most wasn't her own situation, but what must have been going on with Mel. Eve wasn't the only one who had been thinking about Ms Burchell either.

'Eve, how come Mel ended up in the graveyard with you that night? I don't get it.'

'I honestly have no idea why she was there at the same time as me, dad. It's true that I'd seen her earlier on in the day, and she said she used to know you. Is that true?' Robert nodded. 'But the thing is… she just wanted to help, and she really, really has dad.'

'What do you mean? How?'

'I don't want to explain everything right now, please just trust me?'

That request set the benchmark for testing their newly formed bond. Robert passed with flying colours.

'Okay, yeah, I trust you. Doesn't mean I'm not concerned though. Should I be worried?'

'No! Not now,' she answered cryptically. 'I think you'll understand eventually.' Eve was desperate to take the focus off her. 'Why does it seem like there's something going on that I don't know about?'

'You're not daft, are you? It's a bit complicated Eve, and I don't know how I feel about telling you about her.'

'Was she your girlfriend or something?'

Robert gave it away by blushing.

'Yeah, that's about right, but to be honest she was a bullet I dodged.'

Eve squealed. 'She definitely didn't tell me that. Do you have photos of you and her back then?'

'Somewhere maybe, not many. It wasn't like it is now with your camera phones and social media. Anyway, the past is the past – everyone has one, you will too one day. You have to move on from stuff way back. I won't lie to you – I'm going to be frustrated at not knowing what's going on between you two, but it does seem like she was trying to protect you, so I guess I'll be patient for the explanation. I'll probably need to tell her that I'm grateful. Whenever you're ready to spill the beans I'll be ready to listen, okay? Just don't leave it too long.'

'I won't, but until then please don't worry.'

'If you say so. Listen, are you going to be okay if I go into work for a couple of hours this afternoon? I won't go if you don't want me to.'

'No, I'm good. I've got some sixth form stuff to read through anyway.'

For the first time in a long time, she didn't really want her dad to go out. At least it meant she would have some time to contact Ali about the quandary she was in. Her only surprise was that Ali hadn't already tried to contact her. But what she didn't realise was that her support worker was on her way to Meonstoke with a loaded agenda of her own.

47

'Am I glad to see you. Didn't you get my text this morning?'

'Nice to see you too, Eve,' replied Ali sarcastically.

'Sorry, it's been a dismal morning and there's so much to tell you.'

'Can I come in, or do you want to chat while I'm camped out here?'

Eve tentatively showed her guest into the hallway, but Ali sensed the reluctance.

'Is your dad here or something Eve? You seem a bit edgy.'

'No, you've literally just missed him.'

'Hmm, it's becoming a habit. That's the second time I've done that today. You left the school just as I arrived apparently. Never mind.'

'How come you went to the school?'

Ali took time to explain to Eve about her contact with Lilly Seijayeff, and how together they were going to try to help with her defence.

'I'm scared, Ali.'

'I'm not surprised, going to a youth court isn't something you'd choose to do. You're not going to be a person who gets into trouble often Eve, so it's bound to be upsetting. Look, this doesn't need to interfere with your new goals. In fact, getting your head down and stuck into your studies is exactly the message we want to convey to the judge. I just don't want you to have any thoughts about getting into old habits.'

'No way! That's not going to happen.'

'Good, I'm pleased to hear you say that. Dare I ask how your dad has been about it all?'

'He's been amazing! I can't believe it Ali, me and him cleared the air when we got back – talked properly for the first time about mum's accident. I opened up and told him about blaming myself.' Ali looked astonished. 'I know, right? But that's not all. He told me that he has been blaming himself, so we ended up talking about that too.'

'Blimey Eve, that's incredible. I'm so proud of you. What a huge leap forward. The counsellor will feel her work with you is done. But you do seem uptight about something – anything I can help with?'

'Maybe. What about Mel?'

Now, *there* was a question. She had stolen her thunder by asking it first. Ali was not usually so direct with the kids she worked with, but then nothing usually phased her in the way that this incident had.

'I'm not sure Eve – maybe it'd help if you told me what the heck she was doing taking the rap for vandalising your mum's grave?'

'Not you as well? That's exactly what my dad was trying to quiz me about. What's the big deal?'

'It's a bit strange that she should be there in the first place. Was it a coincidence that she should be randomly in the same place as you?' Eve couldn't find the words to speak, standing instead like a freeze frame with her mouth half open. 'Did you not think to mention to me before that you and she were linked by an allegation of vandalism?'

Eve's reaction was petulant, frustrated as if she were being accused of something not set up by her.

'Well I don't have all the answers, do I? You know her, so why don't you ask her yourself? Why didn't *she* tell you that something had kicked off, eh? Don't you think that's weird too?'

It was a good point. Mel could have easily sent a text message to explain the misadventure. Eve's pertinent questions were avoided in the quest to gain more clarification about what happened.

'Did you actually do it then Eve, you know, smash the

headstone?'

'Yes. I'd been up to Lodden earlier to get some gear, but the people there wouldn't allow me in the house let alone give me anything. So, I came back and slumped down by the grave. It was as close to my mum as I could get. I chatted away, and I knew she was listening. But I just got mad thinking about what had happened, and then...'

'It's okay. I'm sorry to have asked. It was obviously a bad moment for you.'

'Mel had been to our house earlier on to deliver a parcel, so she was in the area anyway I guess.'

'Parcels?' Ali had no idea that Mel was working as a courier, another update that failed to be forthcoming.

'Maybe it was a good thing Mel was there, cos after that happened, she got in touch with you.'

At that point, the conversation was broken when the doorbell rang, causing them both to jump. Eve could see through the peep hole on the door that it was Gillian, one of her friends from school. Not wanting her mate to see Ali, she hastily showed her support worker into the study and pulled the door shut. Ali could hear the enthusiastic conversation the pair were having in the hallway. Gillian had been concerned about the rumours spreading round the sixth form common room and wanted to make sure that Eve was alright. She played it down, and smartly moved the subject matter onto what work she had missed over the rest of the day.

The study had two windows, one overlooking the drive at the front and the other to the side of the house. Despite the gloomy skies outside, the room was well lit. Ali's feet were tired from standing and talking with Eve, so she quietly sat down at the corner desk. To the side there was a cabinet, on top of which a collection of seven or eight picture frames were perched and arranged quite haphazardly as if someone had been manhandling them. Some of them were unmistakably family snaps, and while Ali didn't want to pry, she was curious to know what Eve's mum looked like. But as she got out of the seat and walked up to the cabinet, it was not a photograph that caught her attention. In the middle of the assortment of frames one in particular stood out. It was wooden and brightly coloured, almost fluorescent. It was an unusual design but very familiar; Ali knew instantly that she had exactly the same frame at home.

The heat rush through her body felt immediately uncomfortable, and her heart began to race. These were not mass manufactured frames, they were man-made one offs, the possessions of three youths from a Christmas many years ago. To get confirmation of the identity of the owner, Ali needed to peruse through the photographs for evidence, but her eyes were reluctant to take their gaze from the colourful frame for fear of what might be revealed. Many expletives were whispered to herself as she recognised the male figure smiling and staring back at her; it was unmistakably Robert. Ali felt giddy and held onto the corner of the furniture, struggling to think rationally, and gasping for air. All this time she had been working tirelessly for his daughter without knowing the family connection. She collapsed back into the office chair, and instantly started rocking with her clenched fists to her forehead. It was an image of insanity.

The clunk of the heavy front door was followed by a swoosh as the study door glided over the carpet. Ali was sitting cross legged and alert, and completely duped Eve into believing that all was well.

'Finally got rid of her, she's a nice girl but she can't shut her trap once she gets going.'

'Don't worry, it was quite nice to take the weight off my feet in this lovely room.'

'You look well chilled out in that seat.'

'Actually Eve, is there any chance I could have a glass of

water please?'

While the girl set off for the kitchen, Ali continued her torment by looking once more over the photographs of the guy she once knew, but in images of circumstances completely alien to her. Without a thought for what would happen if Eve walked back in, Ali quickly whipped the colourful frame out from the collection and fiddled with the backing. It was a struggle to loosen a couple of hinges but eventually they budged. The backboard came away, revealing nothing other than the reverse side of the photograph it housed. It was difficult to feel disappointed without knowing whether there was ever a letter hidden inside, but she had a hunch that it may have done so at some point.

Having replaced the frame, Ali wandered into the kitchen. After taking a few long sips from a glass of water to quench her thirst, her mind was focussed on delicately gaining answers from Eve that would confirm her father was Robert Spitley.

'Thanks, I needed that,' she began. 'Hope you don't mind but I took a peek at some of your photographs in that room. Your mum was beautiful.'

'Yeah, she was – inside and out.'

'You must get your looks from her then. What's your dad's name?'

'Robert.'

It had to be the same person, but it was peculiar that the family's surname was 'Florey'. She dared not ask anything further about that, as Eve was sure to pick up a vibe about why Ali wanted to know all of that information.

'Where's he from?'

'Winchester. That's why I said to you the other week he's gone off the place.'

'Yes, I remember now. Such a beautiful place, I can't imagine why anyone could go off it. Any ideas?'

'Nope, never said. You could ask Mel, she used to be his

girlfriend apparently.' Eve mimed throwing up with fingers down her throat. 'But you must've known that, right?'

Ali responded to the inference but dodged the question. 'Good idea, I might just do that.'

'I think she was a bit of a mistake though from what he was saying. Don't know if she said anything about it to you but something happened with them recently. I reckon she still fancied him.'

Mel wouldn't have said anything about that in a million years.

'Why? Did she say something about it?'

Eve chuckled. 'No, but maybe that's why she was so keen to help me?'

Eve couldn't have realised how much that light-hearted suggestion stirred some long-forgotten negativity in Ali.

'Perhaps the best thing to do is for me to contact Mel, to find out what's happened with this business with the police. I doubt Lilly Seijayeff would be too happy to find out that you'd thought about contacting her, seeing as she's the accessory to your crime. And besides, Mel might have been instructed not to make contact with you.'

With Eve's concerns pacified, Ali left in a hurry to avoid any awkwardness that would be inevitable if Robert returned home while she was still there. In any case, there was an urgent message she needed to compose. It wasn't just unusual, more unheard of in fact, for Ali to phone in sick at work. But with her head completely scrambled from what she had discovered about Eve, it was futile to expect that she would be able to get anything meaningful done in the rest of the afternoon. She genuinely felt ill.

The drive back to Andover was doing nothing to help the nausea, so a pit stop was made in Winchester. Once there, she avoided going to her parents. An inquisition was the last thing required. Instead the car was parked at the bottom end of town, where Ali got out for some fresh air. She took the steep walk up Aethelred Hill, and to the bench by the pigeon trees. It was always familiar and comforting to sit there, and yet there was a tinge of remorse on that occasion, overlooking the town where the feelings she was churning had originally begun. It gave her the bit between her teeth to message her old adversary.

Mel, I think we need to bring forward our meeting, it's urgent. It seems you forgot to tell me about yours and Eve's trouble with the police? And also got more than a small shock to discover who her dad is. Let me know when is convenient please – Ali.

Ali, hi! Thanks for messaging; how about Saturday morning – Winchester's fairly central for us both, ok to meet there? Coffee shop in the arcade off Parchment Street @ 10:00. Should've said about the arrest, sorry. I'm in some hot water with that. Bit puzzled why you're bothered about Eve's dad? Tell me over a brew – look forward to seeing you. Mel x

She damn well knew why, thought Ali. She knew from past experiences that there would be nothing other than a nonchalant response, nonetheless it still grated on her nerves.

The onset of early Autumn wouldn't leave the hillside alone. The pigeon tress stood proud and looked like they were wearing festive garlands with the changing colours of the leaves on some of the branches. Some deliberately deep breaths filled Ali's lungs with the light breeze blowing through the woody backdrop, before making her way back down the steps to her car. She hoped it wouldn't be too long before she was able to return to her 'go-to' place.

48

In comparison to the drama in the middle of the week, the back end was surprisingly quiet for Ali, with no further messages from either Eve or Mel. Then, Saturday morning was greeted with a purply sunrise and a largely traffic free drive into the old town again.

The music on the radio had largely been ignored on the journey having been put on as a background distraction in preference to the coarse sound of rubber tyres on tarmac. Ali Crofts' love of music went deeper than just a good melody and a sing-along. She liked to get to know the song in the way someone would buy an item of clothing – trying it on for size, feel and comfort. For Ali, to understand why someone liked a song would be to understand how the person ticks.

Many a boozy evening in her undergraduate years were spent agonising over the lyrics and the meaning of tunes with likeminded students. Often opinions would be divisive with arguments aplenty, where a classic for one student would be condemned as 'pretentious shite' by another. The heartfelt words in a favourite tune were the inspiration for the stories that played out in her own mind as she listened, and she held her own theory about a person's emotional connection with music. She thought that anyone who stopped listening to lyrics or working out what they meant were people in some kind of denial, afraid to relate to the story of the song as it would be an admission to themselves. It perhaps said more about her own frame of mind than anything else, and an indication that she was never far from being overwhelmed by her imagination and memory tank.

Ali had a list of songs that were unbearably difficult to listen to. That morning it just happened to be Don Henley's 'Boys of Summer' that caused her to lurch forward to turn off the song before it got to *that* lyric – the one that strummed and rattled her heart strings when she heard it; the one that reminded her she was still grappling with the past; the one that exacerbated the ache she sometimes felt throughout her body as she heard those poisonous words: 'I thought I knew what love was, what did I know? Those days are gone forever, I should just let 'em go'. She was in such a frantic rush to turn the radio off that she missed the button and merely proceeded to turn the volume up instead. She'd asked herself that question in the song more than a few times, sometimes calculating that maybe she was losing her mind to think that as a teenager she had a clue about the answer. But when she judged it against the lingering bruise around her heart, it seemed she knew exactly how powerful the effects of love could be.

Ali would always go off into a deep mood after listening to one of the 'forbidden songs' fighting herself with contrasting thoughts about a relationship that nearly was. On the one hand she would feel like a useless piece of shit for letting the lyrics reduce her to such a mess. But there was also a stubborn argument against that put down, a logical interpretation that it was about how she really felt – and there was nothing wrong with that. It was real, not something that had been made up in a fantasy. And at least this was an improvement. Ali had recollections of a time when every song was 'him' and eventually realised that the stories within the songs were purely circumstantial, and that other people were suffering in the same way she was.

Driving around the streets of her former hometown there were no more answers than when she was there last, just the same unanswerable questions. She had grown stronger over the years and learning to have a thicker skin meant she rarely felt emotionally vulnerable and insecure anymore. Besides, with an intense meeting awaiting her, melancholy was the last thing Ali was going to be affording Mel.

The arcade was slightly dated, but charming, with a large café spread over two storeys that was popular with the locals throughout the week. Ali arrived by half-past-nine, just as the arcade shutters were opening. There was no sign of Mel. She decided to wait outside the main entrance rather than stand inside or find a table in the café, just in case her positioning was obscured by people on other tables, making it difficult for Mel to spot her. It was no surprise to receive a text at ten o'clock from Mel to say she was running a few minutes late. Ali killed the time people watching, and generally trying to imagine how their conversation was going to unfold.

There were plenty of people milling around, mainly tourists, by the time Mel was dashing up Silver Hill. She looked purposeful with her head bowed, oblivious to anyone else on the pavement in the direction she was heading. She was within feet of the entrance where Ali was standing before she looked up and was startled to see the familiar face looking at her.

'Oh, my goodness! Hi Ali. Well this is a coincidence, I'm just about to go into the arcade to see an old colleague of mine. Don't suppose you've seen a chubby, bald bloke wearing a waistcoat go in have you?'

Ali froze. She could do nothing but play along with this obscure introduction.

'Err, no,' she answered blandly.

'What're you doing here? Seeing your mum and dad or something I expect?'

'Yeah, I'm meeting them in town, so I'd better go.'

'And me – I'm already late. I hope he hasn't given up on me. Anyway, nice to bump into you again. I've still got your number.'

'Maybe see you again then. Bye.'

The two women walked off in opposite directions, one banking on her colleague waiting for her in the café, the other wandering aimlessly without a plan. Both on a collision course

349

to disbelief. It was the most perplexing situation Ali had ever found herself in. The confusion had her questioning whether it was another attempt by Mel to ridicule her. She had walked through to the cathedral green by the time she took her phone out and dialled Mel's number. She answered instantly.

'Hi Ali, where are you? I'm waiting in the café.'

'I know, I've just seen you.'

'Have you? Where?'

'You damn well know, even you're not that lame.'

'Alison Crofts – is that you?'

'Stop taking the piss, Mel.'

The line went deathly silent of conversation temporarily, but Ali could hear the chinking of crockery in the background. Mel was frantically trying to work out what was going on.

'Ali Crofts – really?' she asked panicky.

'You know it is!' responded Ali, beyond agitated.

'What the hell are you doing on Alistair's phone?'

'Alistair? What are you on about? This isn't Alistair's phone and never has been. This is my phone and you bloody well know it is from the messages we've been sending each other these last few months.'

The heavy breathing that followed was broken by a forlorn sounding Mel.

'Oh jeez, there's been a massive miscommunication balls-up. I thought you were an old work pal of mine, Ali Cliverice. I have always had this as his number in my phone. But turns out it's been you?'

'Hang on, all this time that we've been messaging about Eve, you didn't know it was me?'

'Not a clue.'

Ali hung up. She had already been making her way back through Butter Cross and was entering the arcade when she abruptly finished the conversation.

49

Ali found Mel sitting in the far corner on the ground floor at a table for two, head in hands, and flushed with embarrassment. She looked up to see a stern looking Ali taking the seat opposite, her face expectant of some answers.

'This is a bit awkward. All that stuff about me asking you if you were gay?'

'You've got form, Mel. I wouldn't have known whether you were taking the piss or not.'

'Well I wasn't. I didn't know it was you, so how could I? No disrespect, but I would never have been messaging if I knew it was *you*. I wanted Alistair's help, I thought he'd have been perfect to help Eve.'

'Thanks.' Ali's reply had a sharp edge to it.

'I didn't mean it like that. You weren't someone I'd have thought would help me. You hadn't stayed in touch, so I just didn't think we had a place for one another in our lives. But seems I got that wrong.'

'Let me be clear to you; we're not leaving this gaff until I have got all the answers I want and need. Is that understood?'

It was the most bolshie and candid that she had ever been with Mel, and with good reason.

'Fine by me. Fire away.'

'How did you know Eve was Robert's kid?'

'Long story. I worked it out from the job I've been doing. I'm delivering parcels until something else comes along.'

'So I gather; unemployable elsewhere perhaps?'

Mel let that go.

'I recognised his kid from a delivery I'd made to a different place to where she lives. Let's just say I realised she was in a lot of trouble when I found out that drugs were involved. Not really something I'm well placed to help with.'

'Bullshit! You were the best person to understand what she had gone through in losing her mum. Why did you need Alistair to help Eve, when you were doing a good job by yourself?'

It was Ali's intention to make Mel squirm, but they were interrupted by a waitress bringing a pot of tea to the table.

'I'd already ordered when I was waiting. Hope you like tea?'

'Quit the niceties and the crap and start talking.'

'Crikey Ali, calm down.'

'TALK!' she responded through gritted teeth.

'Alright, alright. A few years ago, I was at a low point, which was no excuse, and looking back I'm still mortified.'

'What about?'

'I got back in touch with Rob and got carried away, became a pest. Seeing him again... I guess it got me thinking of the past, and my regrets. I'd not seen him since we split up. He and Hannah got hacked off with it and called the police. I was given a court order to stay away from where they lived.'

Ali clapped sarcastically drawing some strange looks from other customers inside the café.

'You just don't learn, do you? You just keep pushing until it breaks. That serves you right.'

'That was a turning point for me, Ali.'

'Funny – another one.'

'There wasn't a lot else I could mess up, other than losing my job.'

'Hang on a minute, you got a criminal record for stalking the family, and because of that you *did* lose your job. And yet, despite all the warnings from the court you still turned up at their house *again*. It beggars belief.'

'Up until Rob opened that door, I didn't know he lived there. His surname had changed to Florey for a start which I knew nothing about. He told me he took Hannah's name when they got married rather than keep his own.'

That information about the surname cleared up one of the issues buzzing around in Ali's head.

'Bet he was delighted to see you again – not.'

'No, he definitely wasn't. But once I'd realised who Eve was it was something that I couldn't risk fucking up – his daughter is his world. Bottom line? I didn't handle my own mum's death anywhere near well enough to be able to get someone else through the same ordeal. If I had anything to do with it, I was bound to screw it up, so it was better putting it in the hands of someone else that could be trusted.'

'And I bet you want everyone to kiss your arse for that?'

'Look, Eve was in trouble emotionally, and I don't think Rob could've coped with his daughter being arrested, so I took one for the team and tried to convince the police that I'd vandalised the grave.'

'Oh, good lord – get you. You're unbelievable. What no one seems to know is what the hell you were doing in the area, *coincidently*, just at the time Eve was in the graveyard.'

'I'll tell you then, shall I? And then you can believe what you want, but it *was* a complete fluke. I was delivering parcels around that area anyway. I knew Eve was getting the bus up to the druggie's house in Lodden, so I drove up there before she arrived. I threatened to grass them up if they carried on supplying her with gear, and nearly got a slap. When I dropped off the package at their house earlier, Rob gave me a letter from my mum that he'd found in the back of his picture frame. Sound familiar? I was reading that in Meonstoke at the same time Eve got to the cemetery. The rest you know.'

There was a break in proceedings while Ali poured them both some tea. She had been right to guess that a letter was once stowed in the picture frame at Eve's house, just like one had been in her own. She wondered what the letter said. The explanations Mel had given were diluted versions, but it all stacked up. From the outside, two young ladies sipping tea together was a scene of serenity. The frown lines were the giveaway sign that frustration still grabbed hold of Ali's mood though.

'So, what's going to happen now then, Mel?'

'Regarding what?'

'Eve's situation.'

'I'm not sure. What's happening about her and the police?'

'Don't you know? She's got a hearing at the youth court next Friday, charged with vandalism and perverting the course of justice.'

'No? He didn't say.'

'Who?'

'Rob. He phoned and left a message for me. Didn't mention anything about the court case.'

Robert hadn't waited for an explanation from Eve about Mel's involvement. He concluded that whatever water had passed under the bridge she had put her neck on the line for the most precious thing in his life. That couldn't be ignored. He struggled to think how to get hold of her number, and then remembered that Eve had itemised billing for her phone. As he was the account holder for paying the bills, it gave him access to the information he required. Then he had to work out which of those numbers was Mel's. Intuitively, he wondered whether the two of them had chatted on the day that the police first called round to speak to Eve following the vandalism in the cemetery. Sure enough, there was a string of texts and calls to the same number at the very time the police were at the house, and he surmised that was Mel's number. This was confirmed when his call went to the answerphone.

'What did he say?'

'Why don't you listen for yourself?'

Mel passed the mobile across the small bistro table, into a trembling hand the other side. Ali was about to listen to a voice she had always hoped to hear again but hadn't for twenty years.

'Hi Mel, it's Robert here. I just wanted to say that I owe you an apology. I know you've risked a lot by getting yourself into trouble for Eve, and it also seems your support has helped turn her life around. I don't know where to start with telling you how grateful I am, but maybe a hug when we meet up would be a good start? I'll call you again and hope we can chat properly. Cheers.'

It was a complete anti-climax, and Ali wished she hadn't listened to it.

'He's thanking you for fuck's sake. He thinks you've been the one helping his daughter.'

'Shh! Keep your voice down. Everyone's looking over at us.'

'Just like old times, eh? You'd trample over me to gain his affection. Have you rung him back to put him in the picture?'

'No, I haven't. Not yet. Do you really think it'd be a good idea to add to Rob's turmoil by telling him that both me *and* you had been helping his daughter behind his back? Besides, why should it even matter to you? Didn't you say that you were seeing someone – or is that not true?'

'That's not the point.'

'Why shouldn't I show an interest in him?'

'Because it's taking advantage.'

'Bloody hell Ali, it feels like we're going back to square one again.'

'No, we're not – we haven't even got a square to go back to.'

It was a realistic verdict. Mel shook her head.

'Are you going to stay bitter and twisted for the rest of your life about what's happened?'

'Are you ever going to apologise *and* face up to the fact that you were always second best to him?'

'Am I sorry for what happened between me and you, Ali, and the upset that it caused? Yes. But I can't be sorry for going out with someone I adored and ended up being the first lad I slept with. That'll always be special no matter what.'

'Well that just about sums it up, the shallowness of it all. I bet you thought you were his first too?' Getting one-up on somebody wasn't something Ali was used to doing, but this was unique. The smirk on her face wasn't befitting of her character. 'Only, I wouldn't be so sure about that if I were you.'

Mel gulped from her teacup to disguise her anguish. She knew immediately that Ali was telling the truth. Her revelation ought not to have mattered since so much time had separated events between then and now, but this genuinely hurt. A solitary tear squeezed itself from the corner of her right eye.

'You know what, I don't cry any more. I emptied out when mum died, and I thought I had nothing more to give anyone. That must make us quits.'

Mel would have to block this revelation out. It was gone, nothing could be done about it. Ali knew better than to rub salt into wounds. She knew what it felt like being on the receiving end of that, and to have something cherished taken away for good. The bitterness between them needed to be parked to finish their conversation. It was Ali who resumed it in a very matter of fact manner.

'Mel, have you even stopped to consider there's every chance that Eve might say something to Robert? That it's been me who's been guiding her.'

'Why don't we cross that bridge if we ever get there? I doubt she'd say anything.'

'By that you mean you'll have a quiet word with her?'

Mel didn't respond to the inference.

'I'll go along to the youth court on Friday, and will obviously let you know the outcome,' Mel announced. 'If Eve feels she needs your support, she can always contact you. What you have done with her is unbelievable, but it doesn't come as any surprise to me. If she's the only link that we are ever likely to have between us, then at least something positive has come out of it. I'm sorry for any hurt and confusion, but I'm not sorry for getting on with my life – whoever that may be with.'

Ali slipped her arms into her coat from off the back of the chair. It seemed an appropriate time to go but she intended to have the last say.

'Eve is still on my caseload. You and your situation will be the last thing I'll take account of if she needs my support – wherever and whenever that might be. The tea is on me.'

Ali slipped a ten-pound note onto the table and left the premises without saying another word.

50

Eve knew Ali wouldn't be at court the following Friday. Many messages had been exchanged between them throughout the week though, and the youngster was suitably reassured once Lilly Seijayeff had visited to help her prepare for what would happen on the day. Taking everything into account, the teenager could see that much had been done to ensure the experience was going to be as far from unpleasant as possible.

That didn't stop the dry throat and the nerves from jangling that morning; she was petrified. Seeing other youths in the waiting areas with their briefs didn't help ease her own concerns. It was the realisation that she was no better than anyone else there for committing an offence. The courtroom was stiflingly warm and had the disinfectant smell that was always present in old, run down, public buildings. It was not a place or a situation that Eve ever wanted to find herself in again, but firstly she needed to get through the challenge of this hearing.

The judge was not what Eve had expected. Middle aged, good hearing, and female eliminated the stereotypical image that she had held before the session commenced. The judge shuffled reference papers in front of her as the charges were outlined, and then she spoke directly to Eve to ask what she was currently doing and what her plans were. The girl explained that she had started sixth form and was hoping to go onto university. Eve didn't know what job she wanted to do, but she hoped it would involve helping others. Most of all she just wanted to make her mum and dad proud of her. Her nervous words did no harm to her case, to which the judge demonstrated a very clear understanding of in her sentencing.

'Young lady, I hope you've found that being in a courtroom with charges hanging over your head is off-putting?'

Eve nodded.

'Being in here will do nothing for your plans for the future. These are serious charges, Miss Florey, and I must take that into consideration. Your behaviour was indeed reckless.'

The teenager glanced over worriedly to her dad and looked suitably shame faced.

'However, I am prepared to drop the charge of criminal damage because of the circumstances relating directly to your mother. I think you have all suffered enough through her loss, but I hope that you will take time to look after her place of rest in the future. Perverting the course of justice is an altogether more serious matter.'

Once again, the judge took time to read her case notes.

'I have received a detailed supporting letter from your support worker, which is a glowing report about you and the challenges you have had to overcome. If I am to be lenient on this matter, you will have her to thank for being so heavily involved with your progress. I doubt very much that you had any knowledge of the illegality of what the co-accused told you to do. Taking everything into account, any thought about a custodial sentence would be self-defeating. I am going to issue you with a caution, but in addition there will be forty hours of community service to be served. I'd like you to see that as an opportunity to help others, as you have already suggested you would like to pursue something along those lines as a career.'

Robert couldn't thank Lilly enough for coordinating the pre-hearing support given to his daughter. According to her, it was the best outcome that the family could have hoped for. The effects of a worst-case scenario were unimaginable. The fresh air wafting on her face outside was like medicine for Eve, who felt completely numb and drained from the experience. Mrs Gardner from the school had attended the hearing to support their student, and she was standing at the bottom of the steps talking to a familiar face who hadn't been seen for a while. While Robert was speaking to Lilly, Eve wandered down to join the two other ladies.

It felt a bit hollow giving Mel a hug since her own court case was still a few weeks away, but both adults were delighted that the dark cloud hanging over Eve had been removed, and she could set about enjoying being a teenager again. Robert eventually joined the group, and then hung back with Mel while Mrs Gardner and Eve stood by their cars to go home. The teenager looked on in astonishment as her dad embraced the lady that he'd suggested he loathed. It made for an interesting topic of conversation on the journey home.

'I didn't think Mel was your type, dad?'

'What do you mean?'

'You were all over her at the end there.'

'I certainly was not. I was thanking her for everything she has done for you – and us. Why, don't you think I should've made the effort?'

'No, she's been great. It's just a bit strange seeing you hug another woman, especially as you said Mel had been a bit of a nuisance.'

'I see. Well, to be fair I wasn't very nice to her the last time we spoke. I needed to correct myself.'

'Oh right, I daren't ask what that was about, though I can guess. What else were you talking about then? I saw you both looking at your phones.'

'I said I'd take her out for a catch-up meal, as a proper thank you.' That was unexpected and had Eve's eyes bulging in disbelief. 'You could always come as well if you like?'

'To be the third wheel? Err, no thanks.'

Eve couldn't get her head around how adults think. One minute a person is the enemy, the next they're hugging and making up. It was very odd.

'Who are you texting?'

'My support worker. That's who you should be really thanking.'

Robert looked confused.

'I thought Mel was your support worker?'

'I did promise I would tell you more when I was ready, dad. This seems like a good time. Mel started off looking out for me, but after getting arrested at the cemetery she put me in touch with this amazing person, who I thought was going to be a bloke, but ended up being a woman.'

Robert was doing his best to avoid being muddled up.

'So, it wasn't Mel who did all these things for you?'

'Not everything, it was mostly Ali.'

'Ali? As in Alison?'

'Yeah, Alison Crofts. She's the most caring person; really listened to me. I felt so comfortable with her dad, I don't know what I would have done without her. There're still some things you don't know yet, but she is the person that has made me want to look forward and enjoy life again. Now, she seems much more your type I'd say, dad!'

Eve giggled childishly, but Robert couldn't respond. His hands were sweaty, and he was struggling to focus on driving the car carefully. He turned the air conditioning on to its lowest setting, causing Eve to remark how cold it was becoming. But Robert needed to feel the sharpness of cold air blowing on his face to release him from the tension making him so uneasy. He knew it had to be Ali from long ago – his Ali. It would be pure chance for it to be another lady with the same name, working in the same area and doing a job that she'd she always wanted to do. Just the very description of what she was like and what had been done for his daughter smacked of the girl he once knew.

However difficult it was to comprehend he was beyond thrilled but at the same time completely taken back by this twist of fate. It was unsettling to think that Ali and Mel were in touch with one another, let alone on such good terms that they would come together to coordinate support for Eve. But from what Eve had said, his daughter didn't realise that there was a connection between him and Ali.

It was disbelief and anger that mostly filled his head though. Looking out for Eve in the way that Mel had done was beyond unselfish, and had Robert thinking that he was wrong to have judged her so harshly. Perhaps her re-introduction into his life had been a positive sign after all. It prompted him to plan an evening out to wine and dine her as a sign of his gratitude. But this news – Eve's admission – had put a completely different slant on his thoughts about her. Naturally, Mel had happily accepted the invitation for a date on the back of a heap of praise, knowing full well that she hadn't been as instrumental as Robert proclaimed. The lack of a denial, and not highlighting the input of the real hero told Robert everything he needed to know; when it came down to the nuts and bolts, Mel hadn't changed.

51

The calendar was just about to nudge October before their night out. Winchester's skyline in the fading Autumn sun had never looked so beautiful on Mel's route into the town centre from Farnborough. She couldn't remember the last time she had looked forward to an evening out so much, but then the company that she would be keeping held a special place in her life – as did his daughter. Not that she was getting carried away with thoughts and expectations of this being a romantic new beginning. This was a pleasant catch up and nothing more. Robert would be the first to scoff, no doubt, that she had learned from her faults. Fingers being burned, and the harsh consequences of too many mistakes were episodes that had run their course. The bottom line was she missed his company. Robert was a genuine guy who understood how she ticked, and that wasn't a label she could pin to any other of her friendships. Mel was able to take his criticism because he was generally always right. She remembered exactly what he had once told her – that a true friend was the one who would always be honest, however unsympathetic it might sound.

Robert didn't think the evening boded well. Earlier in the day he had established that it was twenty years ago to the day that they had left Winchester for their next adventure in the East Midlands. There was something uncomfortable about returning to the place on such an anniversary, though he was quick to remember that out of those difficult days came Hannah. It crossed his mind on numerous occasions to cancel the arrangements, but ultimately, he was curious to see how far Mel would go down the line of adulation and wanted to be able to confront her directly about it. By that point Eve had opened up to her dad about everything – apart from the identity of the people pushing drugs for fear that it would result in another appearance in a court room if Robert got hold of them. It meant he had a clear idea about who had done what for Eve.

The evening had barely reached pre-dinner drinks before the topic of conversation landed on Eve and their criminal connection. Robert found it difficult to contain himself, but he couldn't shut Mel up long enough to challenge her. She had already launched into her own misfortune of having to attend court in early November and, depending on the outcome, how that might affect her chances of securing employment. Mel's brief even suggested asking Robert whether he would be prepared to write a witness testimony in support of the extreme actions she took to prevent his daughter from becoming entangled in a criminal offence. Then there was much waffling about her intentions to set up a book-keeping business to utilise her skills and experience. It was during her next round of the verbal marathon that Mel noticed the look on Robert's face.

'Blimey, I'm sorry. Have I been gabbling too much? You've not said anything. And you've gone very quiet, with that look on your face when something's bothering you.'

'Well, I'm still waiting and hoping, but probably in vain.'

'You've lost me, Rob.'

'There's not been one mention yet of the most important component in Eve's escape from her desperate situation.'

'Are you serious? What am I missing?'

'Ali.'

Mel looked shattered. She hadn't been expecting that. The cat was out the bag.

'If this is going to be a rant, why on earth did you come out for a nice meal to do it, when you could've just picked up the phone and saved yourself a whole load of time, money and effort?'

'Because I wanted to see you fidget while I grilled you over the fact that you did fuck all compared to what Ali did, and yet you've been quite happy to take all the accolades for Eve's revival!'

'I have *never* claimed to be the person most pivotal in it all.'

'You *never* denied it either.'

'Have you spoken to her?'

'No.'

'Then aren't you forgetting something major? If it weren't for me, Eve would never have been introduced to Ali, and we can only guess what would have happened.'

'And was it ok for the two of you to work with my kid behind my back, without stopping to consider what I might think about it?'

'Shitting hell, Rob! For a start we were too busy rescuing her. And besides, Eve didn't want you to know she was having problems. There's probably a good reason for that – she didn't come looking for the help from you did she, so what does that say, man-with-all-the-answers? And anyway, Ali had absolutely no idea that she was your kid – you'll have to ask her about that.'

There was a brief reprieve while Robert was mulling this over.

'Oh yeah, that's right. Eve reckons you said it was a man that you were going to speak to about helping her. But Ali Crofts turns up. I don't know what it is, but something didn't go to plan there did it? You hadn't expected it to be Ali either so that was some fluke.'

When it came to fight or flight, Mel was never one to be a shrinking violet. Her genes were laced with the headstrong qualities of Poppy, so if she was going to be backed into a corner there would always be a forceful response.

'There are things that you and Eve have no idea about, Rob, and neither does Ali properly.'

'Save your breath darling, Eve has told me *everything*.'

'Then you'll know whether I'm telling you the truth, or not. Your daughter was being given drugs Rob, and I put a stop to that. Nobody knows this, because I've never spoken about it, but

I was so scared about going to that house. I went to tell them, not ask them, to flick Eve off. I threatened to snitch on them. Can you imagine that, me calling the shots to dealers with no scruples? And if I hadn't made that journey on the afternoon when Eve smashed up Hannah's grave, I can't imagine what would've become of your baby. So, I'm not looking to bask in any glory, but I made some decisions that I hope helped that lovely girl of yours. And without doing that, Ali might not have been able to pick up the baton.'

Robert grimaced.

'You were always good at ducking the issue. You were going to take credit for it all, and in doing so lap up my affection for everything that had been done, when in fact I am indebted to Ali.'

'There was a time, for a long time, that I would've done something as callous as that. You know that Rob. But I honestly don't feel that way about you now. I'd like you to be in my life sometimes as someone who I could sound out as a friend, but I swear that I don't want you Rob. I love and care for you, and Eve, but I'm not in love with you. Can't we be civilized for one evening, and tomorrow I will prove to you that I'm not talking bullshit.'

'I've got so used to you letting people down Mel, so no, I'm not going to spend a moment longer in your company than I need to. I've had a gut full of you and lost my appetite.'

The evening ended abruptly and prematurely. Mel sat in the bar area of the restaurant for a considerable amount of time, watching the comings and goings of people on their night out. Being abandoned in a social setting was becoming habitual. Though she felt empty of any self-worth – Robert had seen to that – she wouldn't be discouraged from her promise to prove to him that any of her attempts to help Eve were not about gaining his affection. He was right, she should have come clean about Ali, but she had only recently come to realise herself the identity of Eve's support worker. It was a sombre drive back home, and the opportunity to put things right the next morning couldn't come around quickly enough.

The doorbell ringing was followed immediately by the repetitive rapping on the door. It didn't amuse Robert that this wake-up call was at seven o'clock on a dark, wet Sunday morning. He raced down the gallery landing and stairs, and turned the burglar alarm off. Throughout the process of undoing the bolts at the top and bottom of the oversized doors, the banging continued. Robert was ready to have an altercation with the person responsible and opened the door aggressively. Standing in front of him, looking dishevelled, was the last person he wanted to see. Mel had barely slept a wink, and any pride in her personal appearance had deserted her that morning.

'On my mum's memory, I'm not here to make you any more annoyed than you already are with me. I made you a promise – I'm begging you. Please let me give something to you that could change your life, and then I'll be gone.'

Robert didn't know what choice he had other than to show Mel through to the kitchen. She looked consumed by the need to complete a mission.

'You look bloody awful,' Robert observed. 'Let's get you a hot drink.'

'You don't have to go to any trouble.'

'Mel, you've just got me out of bed early on the one day I get to have a snooze. I was already in a foul and stinking mood from last night, and then the cause of said mood rocks up trying to kick my door down. And I so hate impatient people. But I'm gonna give you the benefit of the doubt that there's a good reason for it.'

'Thanks. I'll have a tea then, please.'

Crouching on the bottom step of the staircase out of view from the kitchen was Eve, also woken by the incessant banging. She wanted to see Mel but thought better of interrupting the adults on hearing her dad's words. Whatever had happened sounded troubling. She pulled her dressing gown round her to keep warm and waited to see what materialised before making her entry.

Mel read her cue to speak as soon as the teaspoon stopped clinking against the side of the cup.

'You always used to look for the good in people, Rob. You'd try to steer away from confrontation. But last night I saw the complete opposite of those two things in you.'

'That's pure comedy gold coming from you. If I needed a reality check, you'd be the last person I would sound out. With all the crap that has followed you around I really don't think you're very well placed to make judgments about other people's characteristics.'

'Oh, it'd be ever so convenient to blame me for it all wouldn't it? You're right, I haven't exactly covered myself in glory over the years. But I'm not an altogether bad person. I've struggled to get there, but I am finally free from the shackles that held me back from when my mum died. So, the one thing I'm damn well sure about is what it's like to be lost.'

'Are you insinuating that's me? This is what I've let you into my house to tell me?'

'Hang on a minute, this isn't coming out right. Bugger. My mum always knew which words to choose. She said she was happy to have nothing Rob, because her treasure chest was full of love from people closest to her. Eve is doing her best to be your jewel, but your chest is pretty empty.'

Her words made Robert displace his antagonism. Mel walked over to stand next to him.

'Maybe it's just me, but you're missing something – or someone.'

At this point, Robert was worriedly looking her up and down. He was already dubious about Mel's motives for being there, and now it seemed she was making a move on him.

'What the hell are you doing Mel?'

'This…'

Mel toyed with Robert by being suggestive with her fingertips on his cheek, and then reached into the back pocket of her jeans. She smiled at him as she took out two items. One was a tatty looking envelope; the other was a yellow notelet with an address scribbled on it in green ink. She held the latter up in front of her face.

'I know I have a shitty job and people baulk at it. But you know what, it throws up little gems from time to time. Just ask Eve – she'll vouch for that.' Mel winked at him. 'The address on this note is a house I took a parcel to some time ago. Funnily enough it's the address that's the most important thing when you deliver a package, but the name becomes the crucial part if it needs signing for. This bloke was surprisingly pleasant and chatty, and his name hit me between the eyes. I didn't know if I'd be interfering or messing with your head. But I kept wondering whether you ought to take a look for yourself, cos I doubt there'd be too many other Andrew Spitleys in the Hampshire area of his age?'

A chill shivered down Robert's spine as he took the paper off Mel. He stared at the writing, breathing heavily through his nostrils. He was silent.

'Rob, for all the shit that I've ever caused you I don't know if I can ever make up for it. I'm going to give you something in my hand which is probably my biggest sin.'

Robert looked up from the post-it note he was holding with a frightened expression.

'Hate me all you like, but I'm owning up to a poor decision I made long ago. I'm giving it to you as a nudge to go and get the girl you were supposed to have been with.'

She slid the envelope face down onto the breakfast bar where he stood motionless and gave him a peck on the cheek.

'Don't read it until I'm gone. Thanks for the tea.'

On her way out, Mel was startled by Eve on the stairs. The teenager shot up and threw her arms around Mel.

'Hello you. That's a nice cuddle! Everything ok?'

'Yeah, I'm good. What's going on Mel?'

'Life balancing itself out I guess, but maybe it's best if I leave that for your dad to explain. Look after him – he'll need you more than ever today.'

'Please don't go.'

'I've got to. It's the only way, sweetheart.'

Eve watched the front door close behind Mel, then hurried into the kitchen where she found her dad with his head in his hands and tears streaming down his face. She raced forward to hug him tightly.

'Everything's gonna be ok dad.'

52

Robert hadn't been up to the top of Aethelred Hill for years. He misjudged how long it took to get up by the pigeon trees via the steep steps and arrived at ten-past-eleven. Other than him, the only other movement on the hillside were the leaves being blown, the brittle remnants rustling noisily as they swept past and over the brow of the hillside. There was no expectation to be as pleasantly surprised as he was to see the view across to the water meadows and the old town again. It made him feel sad for neglecting those memories.

The bitterly cold morning was the kind that nips at exposed fingertips, and where every breath produces a mini cloud. Robert hadn't brought his gloves so packed his hands deep into the pockets of his coat. The shivering was as much a sign of apprehension as it was of the icy breeze blowing from behind the pigeon trees. His body was tense. It would have to be a fool or a desperate soul that would be venturing out to this elevated and exposed point in this temperature, he thought. It was open to question which one of those he was.

He started to doubt his intuition about the meeting place and for being so sure that this would be it. The text that he had sent was short and to the point, but not something that could be misunderstood.

Hi, it's Robert. I know this is unexpected but please don't ignore me. I really need to see you. Any chance of meeting for a chat?

The reply, however, took several days to arrive, and when it did it was enigmatic and bereft of information.

Fine. 11:00 this Saturday morning? You know where to find me, but if you don't, it wasn't meant to happen.

Aethelred Hill was the only place that seemed immediately obvious, but even if it was right, turning up late looked like costing him his opportunity to reconcile the misunderstanding. As he contemplated leaving the hillside to itself, a fur-lined hood bobbed up and down some distance away along the path and slowly headed towards him. Robert could see that it was pulled up around the woman's face, hiding her identity. But even when she was many metres away, he already recognised the lips and knew the smile on her pretty face so well, even after twenty years. Ali stopped in front of Robert, and the pair stood and stared at one another for several seconds, both owning the warmest of smiles.

'I didn't think you were going to be here Ali. I nearly left.'

'I nearly didn't come.'

'Really? I'm so glad you did though.'

On the morning of the meeting, it seemed that things had conspired against Ali getting there, as she explained to Robert when she eventually arrived on the hill.

'Transport issues. Huge screw sticking out of my tyre, and no time to swap the spare. Had to catch a train in the end. It's a pretty long walk from the top end of town to here, you know.'

'I remember. I'd have picked you up if I'd known.'

'Hmm, that might have been a bit strange.'

'What am I saying? Ignore me. I'm sorry if it shocked you, getting in touch out of the blue.'

'It wasn't completely unexpected to be honest. I'm guessing Eve must have said something then?'

Robert nodded.

'She did, and that's how I got hold of your number. I hope you don't mind. Eve said hello and she sends big hugs.'

Ali sucked in the words of Eve's message, smiling

affectionately. She missed her.

'What about you then?' Robert continued. 'All those ambitions when you were younger – and you went and did it.'

'I've hardly reached professional heights, Robert. I'm just a youth support worker. It's not exactly rocket science.'

'Looking after kids with problems, helping them with whatever issues they have? That's harder than rocket science, and far more important. Need to be a special kind of person to do that. Eve is a changed girl, loving sixth form. It's because of you that she's got her future to look forward to.'

Ali hated compliments and shuffled awkwardly.

'Anyway, I'm impressed that you worked out to come up to the hill to meet – and by the pigeon trees too. I could have sent you on a wild goose chase.'

'Nah, we spent a bit of time together up here, didn't we? It was a special place for us.'

'Yep. I remember.'

'Didn't we used to say that you and me time is my favourite time…'

'Anytime, and always.' Ali interjected and finished his sentence, and they grinned. Then she put on the facade of someone immune to sentimentality.

'Enough of that gushy stuff, you said you needed to chat. So, what's up?'

Robert stalled.

'Now I'm standing here, I don't know if it's going to be stupid. To be honest, I never thought I'd ever see you again, so this doesn't feel quite real us, here, chatting like we've never been apart all this time.'

'It must've made you feel nervous sending that message to me. I know it would've felt that way for me. I jumped up and out of my chair when it came through. So, whatever made you want to send it couldn't have been that stupid. C'mon, try me.'

'Mel popped by unannounced and uninvited recently.'

Ali smirked.

'I gather that's been a bit of a habit of hers?'

'You could put it that way, I guess. But for once in her life she seems to have done something admirable out of something unforgivable.'

He brought out a faded, off-white envelope. Ali instantly recognised the writing and gasped, putting one hand to her mouth.

'I just need you to know that I had absolutely no idea that this ever existed until she left it with me the other day.'

'Have you read it?'

Robert looked up to the sky.

'I did. So lovely. It's difficult to know what else to say.'

Ali cut him off, gently taking his grip off the letter and held it herself.

'Don't worry, I knew you didn't ever receive it, she told me years ago how spiteful she'd been.'

'I didn't know that. When did she tell you? I thought you two weren't keeping in touch.'

'It was around the time you pair split up – story for another time.'

'What – you knew we broke up? Why didn't you contact me when you found out about me not getting it?'

'I should've done, but what was the point? By then you'd started seeing someone else. There's no way you'd have left Mel unless you really liked the girl you started going out with. And you obviously did – she became your wife, Eve's mum. I'm not stupid, I knew throughout this time you would be someone else's, and never be mine. I just couldn't take any more hurt. I only knew how far I'd fallen for you by how difficult it was to stay away and not contact you. I missed you – my friend. It's so sad that all this time you're the best mate I never had, Robert.'

Ali's honesty was beginning to hang heavier than the freezing November air.

'Blimey. Probably best to look on it as just another mark on the tally for loved and lost.'

'*Really*? Well to me it felt more like I was mugged.'

'At the time you went about your business like it didn't matter.'

Ali mistook his frivolity and snapped back.

'You went about your business by getting off with Mel. I was soon forgotten.'

Robert was gobsmacked as he had a strong recollection of Ali calling the shots.

'Who was it that decided we weren't going to see each other ever again? It wasn't something I ever agreed to.'

'And yet I still bothered to find out if you'd got your grades and gone to Derby.'

'How did you find out?'

'From your mum. She was sad that we weren't keeping in touch but gave me her word that nothing would be said of our phone call. Looks like she stuck to it too. So, did I mean that little to you that you didn't come searching for me, or find out where I was at any point?'

'No! It's because you meant so much to me that I didn't. I respected your wishes and realised that you needed to get on with building your life, without me being in it to complicate it or make it difficult.'

'It killed me to say that to you then, and it's hurt somewhere inside of me ever since. Telling you I didn't want you in my life – there could be nothing further from the truth. How could that have been the best and worst decision at the same time? I spent that year trying to fall out of love with you, because I didn't just love you, I was *totally* in love with you. That's why it hurt so bad and left the scar that it has. It was amongst the hardest things I've ever had to do.'

'Look Ali, I understand, but if we start living off regrets of what could've or should've been then what kind of mockery does it make of the lives that we've created for ourselves since?'

'Is that it? Is that all you've got? Well, I can't un-pour the emotion I've just spilt. You won't even be bothered about what I went through in those days and weeks after that party, years even. I don't blame you for getting on with your life Robert, but don't stand there and tell me you understand – how could you possibly?'

Despite being in an open space to themselves, Ali made a deal of squeezing past Robert and without saying anything she moved back to where the pigeon trees loomed tall. They were mostly looking in a sorry state with next to nothing other than dark, course bark. As she approached, the fluttering of wings began as birds dispersed from their favourite perch, disturbed by the noisy humans below. Robert shuffled after Ali like a little lad scolded by his mother, and watched her face staring up at the branches.

'I tried to forget you Robert, but I couldn't. I kept forgetting to forget. We can have a dig about Mel for not sorting herself out when she was younger, but I don't think I've coped any better than her. Sometimes it feels like I'm stuck, but how can I explain it when I don't understand myself? I've done the getting drunk thing to heighten the pleasure of the pain, but never drank to forget 'cos I didn't want to. I wanted to *feel* the pain, to know it was real. I've done sleeping for hours to block it all out in the hope the rest will make me feel better. But my head was far too foggy with despair half the time to be able to get on with a positive attitude.'

'Seems to me like you were beating yourself up for no reason, Ali. No good is going to come from explaining to me how you felt back then.'

'Maybe not – if it had stopped back then. I have no idea how I've managed to conceal how I feel. Not a single person has ever worked out that I'm still shattered inside.'

'*Still?* That can't be right.' Robert frowned. 'Everyone has memories – good and bad. But this? It's a fantasy played out in your head. You can't possibly still feel like it was twenty years ago.'

'Oh, believe me, you *can* easily find the same pain again from back then. It was the first time I realised that it's possible to be grabbed lower than the pit of your stomach. At first when it all happened, I'd deliberately play the right songs to get to the right level of hurt, and only listened to them to confirm the bruises were real. Because I've thought about it so often there's a lot that's still clear in my head, and however much resistance I put up to remembering it, it still pokes me in the ribs. You've got to realise that I thought you'd been given the letter, so what hurt the most was not knowing whether you were deliberately blocking me out or fighting against your feelings.'

'This is all just nostalgic clap trap. You're clinging onto the past when you need to move on.'

'You're right, I have clung on.' Ali took a step back and pointed above Robert's head. 'Just like the last leaf on that branch up there. I didn't want to let go and end up falling onto the ground and for that to be it, to wilt and be forgotten. There's more strength than shame in that.'

'How the hell do other people manage to get over their break-ups, and not you? There was nothing extraordinary about us.'

'I guess it's easier if it's not meant to be.'

'Bloody hell Ali, this is a stranglehold over you that I have never agreed to.'

Feeling that Robert's comments were dismissive of her honesty, and insensitive to her feelings, Ali stormed off leaving the man alone once more on the hilltop. No sooner had Croftsy been there in his life than she'd gone again, leaving him to rue how it had come to this. He hadn't realised anything had been said that was particularly offensive, but her actions suggested otherwise.

53

Robert wasn't to know it, but Ali's journey to Aethelred Hill on that Saturday morning very nearly didn't happen. It had been a problem that Ali always hoped to be presented with, but when the contact came from Robert it required a lot of soul searching to know whether to meet him or not. The thought of having a conversation with her boyfriend, Jamal, about whether he would be cool about her meeting with an ex from two decades ago would sound ludicrous, if not insensitive, tasteless and inappropriate. None of her best friends lived locally, and even if they had done it was unlikely that she might confide in them about this. Instead her decisions were reached after talking to the unlikeliest of sources. Her mum unsurprisingly took the moral high ground and was scathing at the idea.

'You're going to risk having to walk away from the security of someone who dotes on you, a successful accountant no less, for the slightest chance that you *might* get back with someone you once knew a bit, with all his baggage?'

'Fine, so how do you go about fighting for something that you know will always be second best then, mum?'

While she was no better placed than anyone else to know exactly how Ali had felt about Robert over the years, Helen Crofts had seen the unhappiness sketched on her daughter's face caused by the hold 'this boy' seemed to have had.

'Alison, do you honestly think you could be happier with someone else, not Jamal?'

'I think so. I'm sure to everyone it looks like a perfect, loving, and stable relationship. So why do I still feel so lonely? That's not right is it?'

Helen just wanted to see her daughter happy, and if Robert were to be the source of that, she would embrace it unreservedly.

'Then you mustn't play games with yours or other people's emotions.'

An unthinkable situation had developed which felt like torture. There was the opportunity to take hold of what she had been dreaming of, often pining for, only for it to feel impossible to do so because she was in a relationship with someone else. Jamal had done nothing wrong; he just wasn't Robert. Why would she risk losing a guy that was doing all he could to become her rock? But how could she let Robert slip through her hands like grains of sand? Ali was in a conundrum that nothing could have prepared her for. Though riddled with guilt about the plan that had been made behind her boyfriend's back, she always intended to go through with it come what may.

With the risks she had taken to get to Winchester that morning, Ali was already uptight and anxious. The last thing she wanted to be presented with was Robert on a different wavelength as she confessed to the torment of her heart and soul. She had gone off in the opposite direction to the path that Robert took back to his car. The descent down the steep, windy track was interrupted by his phone ringing. The call was almost sent to voicemail, until he realised it was Eve.

'Hi dad, did you meet Ali on the mountain?' she chuckled.

'Coming back down the ruddy thing again now.'

'That wasn't long. Did it go alright?'

Robert didn't respond immediately, which was itself a giveaway sign that the morning was not as successful as hoped.

'She's walked off.'

'Oh, you muppet, what did you say to her?'

'Nothing.'

'What, you never even spoke to her?'

'No, I mean I didn't say anything to make her go off in a huff.'

'Well you must've done; that doesn't sound like Ali. Where has she gone?'

'I've no idea, she's disappeared. I've tried phoning, but it went straight to her answerphone. She doesn't want to speak to me.'

'You need to go and find her, dad. Speak to her. Actually – don't just speak. Listen to her. You'll regret it if you don't get to her in time.'

Robert choked. 'I don't know what to do, Eve. I'm out of my depth.'

'DAD! Mum's gone, but this lady hasn't. Please, go and open up to her about the letter. Don't let the chance go by.'

It would have been easier to have walked through the town at midday on a Saturday. The traffic was heavy, but eventually Robert crawled up High Street in his car, and round to the station. He was fortunate to be able to dump his car in a short stay space and run onto the platform. The next train was due, with people spread along its entire length waiting for its arrival, eager to claim a seat to avoid standing on their journey.

Robert weaved in and out as politely as he could looking for Ali, but she was nowhere to be seen. He stood on a bench at the far end of the platform, looking back down to where he had walked up. He smiled apologetically to the station manager, and then winced at the sound of the engine's brakes squealing as it came to a halt. The doors swung open and people disembarked before the mad scramble for a seat in the carriages began. It was hopeless, he couldn't see her. The train pulled away with him still standing on the bench, looking resigned to the outcome with hands on hips. Other than getting onto the train himself, there was nothing else he could've done.

Robert watched the rear of the train disappearing down the long stretch of straight track, trying desperately to block out the tannoy blurting out the next arrival on the opposite platform. His unconscious listening caught the names of stations that the other train was calling at on the announcement. He was looking in the wrong place; the train to Andover was due on the other side. He looked over, and locked eyes onto the woman staring back at him over the tracks just before a line of carriages blurred the line of vision. She may have been there looking out of one of the windows, but the light reflecting on the glass made it impossible to see through and meant he didn't have a chance to see Ali one more time.

54

Robert drove off the main road into a bleak looking area that was the start of the estate. It was a sea of grey concrete, and only the lightly coloured curb stones distinguished where the tarmac of the road ended, and the accommodation started off the narrow paths. There was a distinct lack of greenery, bar the weeds that protruded from between the slabs on the pavement. Robert grimaced. He had been in plenty of council estates where it looked colourful, and neighbours talked to each other from across their yards. But here it seemed to be devoid of life, cold, and the grimness portending. This part of Aldershot was not what he had expected it to be.

'What a shit heap,' he muttered to himself as he drove in low gear, one hand on the steering wheel while crouched forward and peering out of the windscreen and side window. The approaching of a car engine caused a lone youth standing in the shadows of an alleyway to turn their head sharply to inspect the driver. Robert could barely differentiate the figure that appeared in dark, bland clothing from the colourless walls of the housing. It was after passing the shadowy silhouette that he realised he must have looked suspicious, which partly accounted for the prolonged stare afforded to him. In this neighbourhood, it was easy to look at out of place if you weren't recognised.

He loyally followed the spoken instructions on his satnav, which directed him into a dead end lined with garages on one side and a turning area at the end. As he looked around, he couldn't understand why there would be the need to have lockups in this area. Most of the garage doors were twisted and bent where they had either been misused or broken into.

As the car came to a standstill, he was struck by the juxtaposition of a Porsche parked in the middle of this run-down area – and yet it was receiving no attention from the locals whatsoever. There were alleyways to the left, right and straight ahead like rat runs. He looked at the piece of paper with the address scribbled on and read the address out loud.

'Nine, Holly Walk. Fat chance of there being any holly bushes around here.'

Robert started contemplating turning around and going home, looking for some reasoning as to why he was there at all. His own experiences had shown him how life can meander through highs and lows, not always taking its true course because of emotional storms where things get flooded with negativity. Looking at the dwellings that penned him in, Robert felt some vindication for his visit to someone who clearly hadn't made much of their own life. There was a part of him that felt sorry for the situation that they had ended up in, because to them this was normality – this was their way of life, and there didn't seem to be many other choices around here.

He got out of his car and looked up and down the road, feeling self-conscious as if he was being spied upon in different directions by people out of sight. There was some signage on the wall that indicated the direction of the properties in numerical order. Numbers one to seventeen were through the alleyway ahead of him. Hesitantly, he locked his car and walked tentatively towards the alleyway looking down it to ensure it was not populated with anyone that may have taken a fancy to his set of wheels. He looked back at his car one more time before turning right and concluded that it looked safe sitting next to the other premium brand motor.

One or two of the households had made an effort to prettify the front of their yards with plant pots, some of which were empty, and others contained the remnants of something that once grew there but had not been nurtured. At another frontage, various colourful mobiles dangled from the edges of the fascia, the chimes from which sang in the breeze – a pleasant distraction from how tense he was feeling scurrying through Holly Walk. At number nine, he paused. The front gate had a latch in perfect working order, with white paint that wasn't flaking. The yard had a square, wooden, raised bed in the centre, in which plants grew alongside some vibrantly coloured flowers of a fuchsia, even at the early part of winter. The slabs that led up to the front door were clean, and there was no sign of litter or dirt anywhere. There was a mat at the front door, and a doorbell that worked. For a lad that had emerged from a modest upbringing himself, he felt such a snob for being pleasantly surprised – although it was not in keeping with other properties in the row.

When the door opened, Robert hadn't anticipated that he would be greeted so politely with the words 'Can I help?' Beneath the wrinkles on his face, the man instantly looked familiar. Rather than be taken back by the moment or the image of the person frowning in front of him, Robert seized the opportunity as he had envisaged.

'Mr Spitley?'

'That's right.'

'I thought we could do a bit of catching up if that's ok with you, dad?'

Andrew Spitley seemed unusually calm at this unannounced appearance of his son, particularly given that it had been more than thirty years. There was so little emotion in his face that Robert wondered whether the grey-haired man may have been confused. Perhaps he had mental health problems, and completely mistook who it was in front of him. Regardless, Robert followed his dad into the living room, nervously wondering how this was going to play out. When Andrew stood in the middle of the room gesturing with an open palm at another person sitting on the couch, it took him a couple of seconds to register who it was.

'This bloke thinks that you two might already know each other, am I right?'

'Jesus Christ, what are you doing here?'

Sitting cross legged with a cup of coffee in his hands was Oli Gemmell. Robert immediately went across to shake hands with his former school pal. His dad didn't seem at all surprised by any of this, and calmly offered to make his son a brew.

'I know we've got a lot to talk about Robert, son. But that can wait a bit. Oli here has turned up specially because you were coming to visit.'

It seemed Robert had been expected.

'Can someone please tell me what's going on?'

Oli spoke up.

'Hey Andy, why don't you get Robert that brew while I have a natter with him, eh?'

The older man gave a 'thumbs up' and left the other two to their business. Oli was a picture so far removed from the days when he was bullied. He was tanned and looked muscular. The most noticeable thing about him was his impeccable attire. He was dressed in a dark navy suit, set off casually with no tie on his patterned purple shirt.

'You look fantastic Oli!'

'Thanks Rob, you look pretty good too fella. The years haven't been too bad to us, have they? I feel like I've stolen your thunder a little bit by being here, and him already knowing you were going to drop by. I'll get to that. He's had some days to get used to the idea that he'd be seeing his son again, so it wasn't such a shock when you knocked the door.'

'Thirty odd years. I don't even know what to say to the guy.'

'Well, I'm sure there's stuff that you need to get off your chest with him mate, but that's not my business.'

'How on earth do you know him?'

'I've known him a good couple of years, didn't take long to realise he was your old man. He looks like you, and he's a cheeky chap like you were. Andy does voluntary work at the soup kitchen in the town centre here, they really struggle to get enough food supplies to deal with the number of down and outs – and I know only too well how shit it must be to not grab one hot meal a day.'

'Do you help them out as well then?'

'Not like Andy. I'm happy to lend a hand every now and then, but what I like to do is make sure I get them some supplies as often as I can.' Robert looked puzzled. 'You see, since I last saw you, I've not done too badly for myself. I trained as a chef, worked my way up in some top kitchens here and abroad, and now I'm a restaurateur myself. So, I like to put something back into the community. And most times I take the food stuff up to the homeless shelter, it'll be Andy waiting for me at the hatch. He's always good for a bit of banter, keeps me grounded.'

'Bloody hell Oli, that's incredible. Hey, is that your Porsche parked up round by the garages?'

'You think it's a bit flashy?'

Robert shook his head in amazement.

'Let's just say I'm not sure I'd have had the balls to park it out there though! How did my dad know about this today?'

'The last few times I've been, I saw someone else there that I was sure I recognised. Your dad said he knew her too; from some parcels she'd delivered to him in the past. It was Mel Burchell. They'd apparently chatted on his doorstep about where she was from and putting the world to right. When she realised Andy used to live in Winchester the penny dropped that he might be your dad. She didn't say anything to him though. But then she turned up at the soup kitchen at the start of her community service, and those pair hit it off again. She said it was thanks to you for writing to the court that prevented it being any worse. Anyway, the other night we went out and she was quiet and withdrawn…'

'Whoa, whoa! Hang on a minute. You're dating Mel?'

'Yeah, well I think that's what you'd call it. It's early days though mate. Your old man put in a good word actually. I always fancied her but would never have had a chance when we were kids – well, not while she was going out with you anyway. Still punching above my weight, I reckon, but couldn't let the opportunity pass this time without having a go. Can't believe she said yes. You don't mind, do you?'

'God, no! I mean, not at all. We finished years ago. I've told her that she needed to get herself a good bloke. And to be frank, the girl has gone and done that alright.'

'Cheers mate, I appreciate that. I like her a lot. When she went all upset on me the other night, I thought it was me and was half expecting to be dumped. But she said it was about a message she'd had from your kid, Eve.'

'Really – what was that about? Are you sure that was recently?'

'Yeah, it was definitely a couple of Saturdays ago. Eve said that you had fluffed your lines with Ali Crofts, and was pleading with Mel to help sort it out for you both. Mel didn't know what to do because you two have had a bit of bad history recently – or something like that? I haven't asked too many questions about that Rob, but she was desperate to help Eve out – and you – somehow.'

'Well that makes me nervous. I am literally hyperventilating listening to this. What's she gone and done – is it going to piss me off?'

'She's done nothing mate – it's me you need to blame if anyone. Basically, I have always felt indebted to you and Croftsy for everything you did to help me, you'll never know how much that turned my life around.'

'You already know you owe us nothing, Oli. We were in the right place at the right time, and I would do it all again at the drop of a hat.'

Oli tilted his head and smiled.

'The least I could do was to try and do something for you pair. Eve said you'd be calling in to see your dad today which is why I'm here. Mel spoke to Andy about it a week or so back and explained that she knew you; he cried when he realised that we knew his son and that he'd be seeing you. He needed to know because I needed to ask him if it would be ok for me to be here as there was something else that we needed to clear up. He was only too pleased to help.'

'Is every man and his dog in on this except me?'

'No, it's not like that. I'm not conceited Rob. We just wanted to do what we could. And anyway, it might've been a bit too much for him to take if you'd turned up out of the blue.'

'Fair comment. So, are you going to play relationship counsellor or something as well then Oli, because I'm pretty sure it's already dead in the water between me and Ali?'

'In fact, I've already spoken to Ali and it's far from finished. Listen, I've just renovated a gorgeous rural restaurant between Winchester and Salisbury, and you two have a reservation on me next Wednesday to try and work things out.'

'What? She wants to go out – with me?'

'You do know next Wednesday, the twenty-second of November is her birthday, right?' Robert shrugged. 'Well it is, and you're taking her to my plush place. She's expecting you at seven o'clock, your table is at eight; that's where she lives.' Oli handed him a note with an address on to add to his recent collection.

'The food and ambience will be beyond your expectations, hopefully – the rest is down to you pal. I haven't got a clue what obstacles are standing in your way. But I do know from experience that incredible things happen when you pair work together. I'm sure there's nothing that can't be sorted out. It must mean a lot to your daughter too if she's made the effort to ask us for help.'

'This can't be happening. I don't know if I can do this.'

'I'm no stranger to agony, Rob, and I think that's exactly what you're heading towards if you let this go. I thought about escaping from the area to be accepted, and to be free from the 'bin-dipper' jibes I still got after leaving school. But it's not me who has the problem, and running away doesn't change who I am. I'll see you next week geezer.'

Oli gave a reassuring pat on his old friend's back and said his goodbyes. Robert paced the room for a few moments lost for words before a mug of tea made its way into his hand, and his dad set himself down onto his favourite chair. He was perched forward with elbows on his knees in anticipation.

'He's a nice lad, that Oli.'

'He is.'

'I'm over the moon that you chose to come and see this old, daft bugger. Never believed you'd want to know me. But I thought it was best to put that to one side while you and Oli dealt with things that need mending.'

'It wasn't the easiest decision to come around here. I'm not sure it was the right thing to do.'

Andy rubbed his chin.

'Yes, I can imagine. Luckily, I've had a few days to get used to the idea that you'd be popping round and wondering what you might ask me. You're going to be disappointed with me, and angry no doubt.'

'Damn right.'

'I'm willing to fix some of the broken pieces back together if you'd like to try, son?'

'Are you?'

'Yes, if you'll let me. I promise to answer all those questions that are nagging away at you, and I'd understand you wanting to get up and walk away.'

'Like you did? I don't know if it's worth fixing. I reckon its irreparable. But I'm here now, so maybe you can start by telling me what kind of toe rag of a father would ever think of abandoning his post.'

And so those difficult conversations began, an opportunity taken that seemed beyond possible, to confront the resentment and sadness that lingered like a foul smell.

55

Spurred on by the surprising outcome of reconciliation with his dad at the weekend, and the joy on Eve's face at finding out about the plans made by Oli, Robert made the early evening drive to the north of the county in a positive frame of mind. That was until his recollection of the last time he visited Andover, when he and Hannah took Eve to a wildlife sanctuary for a family day out. It ended in tears for the three-year-old toddler – twice. Firstly, an over enthusiastic donkey took a nibble at more than just the carrot in Eve's hand as she attempted to feed it. Cue the first outpouring. Ice cream was the obvious remedy for curing the sore fingertip and hurt pride, but to their dismay the large scoop delicately balanced on the cornet fell stone-like to the ground as the little girl tottered to a bench and tried to climb up by herself. Cue round two. Being out of pocket for two trips to the ice cream van was more than worth it to relieve fellow visitors of the squealing from the distraught nipper. A repeat of such upset would be equally undesirable for the sequel with Ali.

He didn't need to say a thing; Ali could already see how remorseful Robert was. The puppy eyes he used to pull whenever he was in the wrong at school, usually deflecting any serious grief, were still being put to good use. He had made a huge effort with a birthday bouquet and looked far more handsome in his designer jeans and sport jacket than he had done in a beany hat on a frosty hillside. That wouldn't stop her from giving him a hard time to begin with though.

'It'd taken me close to twenty years to get somewhere close to being over you, and then you trampled on my delicate recovery.'

'I'm already in Eve's bad books for upsetting you, so I

promise to think before I speak. Besides, it's your special night and you look completely stunning.'

That compliment helped quell her opening tirade. Ali couldn't help but think that it was kind of cute that Robert had confided in his daughter about what had happened on Aethelred Hill and guessed that Eve must have read 'the letter' as well to have been quite so opinionated on his actions.

'If I'm going to get in the car then you have to appreciate that I might want to talk about things that have been bottled up all this time. I've been asking myself whether it's worth churning it over the way I do, but all I want to do is let you know. And don't worry, Robert, nobody else knows any of this stuff, I am the quintessential silent sufferer.'

There were no objections. Ali looked deep in thought at the start of the journey to the restaurant, perhaps finding it difficult to find the right words to explain to him, and in a way that didn't sound so obsessive. It was Robert who chose to strike up a conversation, sensing some rising tension.

'Eve wanted to come along tonight you know. She's claiming to be the peace maker and wants her reward.'

'Aww. She's obviously strong willed. I think we can all learn a thing or two from her.'

'So, you know Mel and Oli are seeing each other?'

'Yeah, I know, isn't that sweet? I don't want to have bad blood with her. I want it to work out for them.'

'Me too. Can I say something to you Croftsy?'

That wasn't a nickname she'd heard for decades, and it made her smile.

'Sure.'

'I honestly thought, hoped, assumed, that you'd be happily married – with kids of your own. I thought you'd be a wonderful mum. I know you've been telling me that I'm a fly in the ointment but why has it not happened?'

'Don't get too big-headed mister – I've not been unhappy, just not content. Please don't judge me – I'm not a nutter. But I've ballsed up relationships in the distant past on the whim that something might happen again between us. I was busy trying to lose you but failing. It's not that I haven't loved, it's just I've always known I loved you more and kept comparing.'

He didn't mean it to sound condescending, but a deep groan escaped from his throat, causing a sharp stare from Ali.

'I've been lucky enough to have grabbed onto an opportunity to be happy. If my head had been clouded like yours it would've passed me by. Think of all the chances that have come and gone for you, and you didn't even realise it.'

'I know it sounds ridiculous. It was completely irrational to think that a bloke holed up in a secure and loving relationship should ever consider a girl that once was.'

'Not knowing what had happened with the letter, I had to grow strong too, Ali. Then I met a woman who got me, which I didn't think would be possible after you. You can't let a gift like that slip through your fingers.'

'When you've been lucky enough to have someone like Eve come into your life, that makes absolute sense. I can see that.'

There was a lull in the cross-examination, and the silence took them both to another place. Ali was thinking things that even she thought would be crossing the line. Had he shared the same songs with his wife that were 'theirs' and what did he do now if he heard them? Did he look at Hannah the same way he looked at her, playfully into her eyes with their foreheads touching; and then all intensive when he gently caressed the contours of her face with the softness of his fingertips. It made Ali quiver.

Robert could see a reflection of his passenger in the windscreen. It hadn't escaped his attention that she was wearing a slinky, short evening dress – and she wore it very well. She caught his eye like no one else had done since Hannah. He felt like a hypocrite; old feelings were being stirred up inside him too, but he had been guarded with his words about that so far. He regained some composure when passing a sign showing the village of West Winterslow was five miles away.

'Do you keep anything that reminds you of me? Cards, cassette tapes, presents?' asked Ali.

'Souvenirs of the past? No, I don't think so, we've never hoarded things like that in our loft.'

'Have you ever thought about me on birthdays, or at Christmas?'

'I've got to admit, I wouldn't have remembered it was your birthday today unless Oli had reminded me. Sorry. But aside from those types of occasions, of course I've thought of you. Maybe just at random times. But you know what Ali, there's no right or wrong way to think back to then, we just do it in different ways.'

'I've looked out onto so many things thinking of you: moons, stars, seas, sunsets, storms. From cliff tops down into valleys, from bridges watching water tumbling. I've carried you in my thoughts to places you probably don't even know exist.'

'Right, that's enough.'

The look of astonishment on Ali's face was matched by one of panic as Robert pulled the car aggressively into a layby and skidded to a stop.

'Do you wish you'd never seen me again?' he demanded. 'Only, I'm wondering whether you think that would've been kinder.'

'No.'

'Well stop trying to turn this into a competition to find out who missed the other person more. You think that because I'm not the one breaking down that it meant nothing, that I just walked away and turned the corner, forgetting it all in an instant?'

Ali didn't have time to respond or catch her breath before a torrent of emotion gushed out of Robert.

'Not once have you asked me what I thought about the words in that letter. It's killed me, because at the time I was miserable, downright and utterly miserable, thinking I'd been spurned. I won't tell you about the songs *I* had to abandon listening to because they didn't help me being head fucked. But I figured you have to get out and start looking for good in the next situation, and not let the previous one show how broken you are to others around you. My feelings for you might be out of sight but they do run deep. You broke my heart too.'

Ali's mouth had dropped open. 'Where's this all come from? Everything I've told you... why haven't you said anything?'

'And you reckon you can remember what I was like. When did you ever know me to get embroiled in anything serious for too long before breaking out of it? All your mush I know is real for you – but it's all in the past, it's gone. I can't do anything about how it was for you, nobody can.'

'I still don't know whether to look back with a happy heart at all the good times we spent together, or with a heavy heart for all the time we have spent apart.'

'Ali, I don't deal with the past that well either, because it's where some of my worst nightmares linger too. The past is where my wife is, and I can't bare it. It's not so much about banishing it; I have strong, dazzling memories too. I miss telling her things – little, insignificant things; afterthoughts I suppose. And you know what? That's what love really is; being in tune with each other so intimately that you want to tell them everything – not over the top sentiments to impress. They're fake.'

Robert was blinking; he only used to do that when he was agitated. This confession session had been bubbling under the surface perpetually for Robert since the car crash. Until now, the right person had never been there to help him deal with it. Both of them had shifted in their seats so that they had turned to face the other. He wasn't finished.

'The truth is, seeing you again feels like being able to breathe again. I loved Hannah unconditionally, unlike anyone I have ever loved. But something has always nagged me in the back of my head somewhere, a little finger poke from time to time – like it is now. I've not been in your life but believe me you've never completely left mine. I'm sorry if I've given you the impression otherwise.'

'When I used to be with you it felt right – the warmth on a cold day. Everything that was bothering me in my mind poured away. There's been room in my heart for many people over time, but it has only ever beat a rhythm for one person, a sound that tells you how you make me feel. But at the moment things are complicated and I don't know what to do.'

'Are you still in love with me?'

Ali avoided the question. She rested her hand on Robert's neck, and pulled him to her. She kissed him softly on the lips.

'I'm used to living with the discomfort of not having you, not the pleasure of waking up and smiling next to you.'

'I'm afraid of trying to get on with my life. I'm scared of who I let into it too. But I'm not ashamed to tell you that you were, and always have been, my biggest weakness.'

'This can't go anywhere though, can it? I'm seeing someone else, and I love him. You broke my heart Robert, that's not something he's done. I don't think I could do the same to him.'

'But I didn't know that, and I'm here, aren't I? Sitting in front of you, telling you I'm willing to un-break it together. This is more than a spanner in the works for me too. You've rocked me to the core of my soul.'

'You weren't there when I needed you. Jamal is the one that's woken me from the years of sleepwalking.'

Robert didn't want to be misunderstood at such a critical moment, but it was difficult to put into words what was bouncing around in his head.

'I'm confused – everything you've said… I thought you were still keen?'

'I did too.'

'Then don't let me fall into the same sleepwalk that you did. What if I said you'll always be my someone if I ever feel there's no one? Think about your words in that letter.'

'Just stop! I don't want to be reminded anymore!' she yelled. Her forthright outburst delivered a phrase that Ali had never expected to be using. The hysteria and her confusion produced cold feet. 'We should go. It'd be a shame for a posh meal to go to waste.'

'But...'

'Please Robert, let's not spoil tonight any more than we already have.'

There was nothing more he could have said or done to have proven his love for Ali. It had been laid on the line for her. Thereafter, time wasn't going to be a friend to anyone that wanted to dwell on something that just wasn't meant be, and Robert knew he would have to accept that. It seemed Ali had choked when it was least expected.

56

December arrived and brought with it changes to embrace. The new headstone sat handsomely where Hannah was laid to rest. It was no chore to take time out amongst the festive arrangements to spend some time at her side. They missed her so much. A single crow squawked in the oak trees flanking the clock tower, breaking the silence that filled the cemetery. Robert knelt down to place some lilies onto the gently rising mound of earth and rubbed his finger along the shiny grey marble where her name was engraved, wiping away the raindrops that nestled in each of the golden letters and figures. His eyes became foggy with tears as he stared at the date of her passing, two years, and four weeks ago exactly. She loved Christmas Day; the pleasure of seeing Eve so excited, the opportunity to show off in the kitchen to produce a feast, and to invite as many people as their large dining table could accommodate. It was at that time of year particularly when Hannah liked to share her affection.

Only when he had been able to be close to her in the churchyard that day would Robert feel at ease with the developments in his own life. It wasn't about asking permission; it was more like he was admitting to himself that to move on meant letting go. His love for Hannah didn't die the day she left the people she was so devoted to, and her love would never cease to be around them. Robert would cherish her memory forever. He was just afraid to release her for someone else. But right there and then he could feel the warmth of Hannah's love and support, spurring him on to take that leap.

'Thank you; I'll love you always,' he whispered as he was joined by the others.

Mel bent down and handed him the posy that Eve had bought, and he put it next to the long stems of the lilies.

'You mucky pup, you're gonna have mud on your knees.'

'Ah, it was worth it,' he said, looking up to the sky and smiling. 'Anyway, they'll match with the muddy skies.'

'Aww, mum would love that you remembered her line.'

Something was distracting Robert, he seemed to be staring straight through Mel.

'It's not the only thing she said that will always stay with me. In that letter for you, the one I kept for years, she wrote something that were just words to me back then – but mean so much more to me now.'

'Really? Which bit?'

'She said she was happy to have nothing, because she already had everything that meant so much to her. Do you get what she meant?'

'Definitely. I'd happily give up and trade in everything to be able to keep my health.'

'Some things don't matter, do they? They only seem important if it's relative to monetary value. And we take so many things – people – for granted. In the blink of an eye those things can be snatched away when you least expect or deserve it. When you feel so empty and so low, you realise how absurd it all is. We've both been there, haven't we?'

Mel nodded.

'Mum just seemed to know how life ticks.'

'Well I want to live my life knowing exactly what I've got, not what I haven't, or letting fate intervene to tell me how lucky I was without realising it. Thanks to all the twists and turns in my life, this is what I've learned. There are plenty of things I could screw up or lose. But when you've found someone you can't live without, a person you adore, that's when I know that I'd be happy to have nothing else.'

It was as genuine and heartfelt as when Poppy had written it herself.

'Well I should think so. You've chosen to be with someone

absolutely perfect for you. It's a good job no one gave up on the tough journey to get here then. Who'd have thought even a few weeks ago that we'd be in this place together today? And with a girl you thought so remote from your life. My mum will be smiling down and saying love is big enough for all of us.'

'Hannah would too.'

It was a gift in itself to have someone as caring as Mel back in his life, back to the person he remembered her being when she was a young scally. And to finally know she was in the stable relationship she had long craved for filled him with as much contentment as it felt for her. She seemed to carry the same smile of peaceful happiness everywhere these days, and it was infectious. Robert stood up to give her a hug and pecked her on the cheek.

From across the path, a more perfect voice shouted across to him.

'Oi Greeny! I saw that. Anything for me to be concerned about?'

There, linking arms, was the sight of the two most precious people in his world. He was tempted to stay where he was in his beautiful daydream, hypnotised by how amazing they looked. But the urge to be beside them was too much. Instead, Eve giggled as Robert jogged across the yard bearlike to wrap his arms lovingly and reassuringly around her and Ali.

ACKNOWLEDGEMENTS

I am indebted to my wife and daughters for their constant and unconditional love, and unwavering belief. Words don't exist to be able to tell you how much you mean to me.

Thanks also to my lovely family and wonderful friends for their support on this journey.

I am particularly grateful to Catherine for her kindness and talent in producing this unique and captivating artwork, and to Eve for your expertise, patience and understanding.

Thank you to Brenda for being my go-to outside the inner circle, I cannot begin to tell you how priceless your enthusiastic feedback and encouragement has been.

To Yasmin and Amelia, I would be lost without your editorial advice and ideas. And to Nadia, my best friend, without you there would be no book.

To my mom, losing you inspired me above all to put my ideas into print. Love you always.

ABOUT THE AUTHOR

Stuart Hobrow worked for over eighteen years with young people. Much of this time was spent helping teenagers make decisions about their future, and with those facing issues or barriers to be able to move on, before spending several years as a secondary school teacher. *Happy to Have Nothing* is his first novel. He is married and has two children.

Printed in Great Britain
by Amazon